"And where did you go after you left the witch?"

"Only the marketplace, Master. For fruit." Lucius looked down at his empty hands.

"Not some temple? You weren't hanging around with lackwits planning some slave rebellion?"

"No, Master! Only the marketplace!"

"How did you come by a mark of Apollo?"

"I played my flute in the marketplace."

Master Gaius took a step backward, his head shaking from side to side.

"There was music, Master. You have not forbidden me music. I didn't disobey you, I swear it. I only stopped for a moment to play my flute with some children."

"The mark came then?"

"We played a hymn. It pleased the god, or so I thought. I never meant to disobey you."

"I imagine you didn't." Master Gaius sighed and handed the rag back to Sulia. "Too late to do anything about it now, I suppose," he said. "Maybe the mark will give you some protection from the witch. I had better send a bonus with you when you go tonight, and I'd better make plans to get you more training on that flute. I don't want the god angry with me."

"Master." A tension Lucius didn't know he was carrying eased from his shoulders.

"Perhaps you can be useful to me in different ways. I could hire you out to religous festvals. I'll talk to some priests. Go have some lunch, and then take a nap. The gods only know what the witch wants with you; you should probably rest up for it."

—from "The Curse Tablet" by Nina Kiriki Hoffman

Also Available from DAW Books:

MISSPELLED edited by Julie E. Czerneda
There is a right way and a wrong way to do practically anything. And when it comes to magic, skipping the directions, changing the ingredients, garbling up the words of a spell—all of these can lead to unusual, sometimes dire, sometimes comical consequences. Here seventeen authors—Kristen Britain, John Zakour, Doranna Drugin, Jim C. Hines, and others—accept the challenge of creating spell-driven situations that get out of control where: a cybermancer has her spell disk corrupted by unexpected input . . . two students out to brew up some spells completely outside the curriculum forgo a most important ingredient . . . a has-been golf pro finds an old family spell that *should* improve his game, but at what cost? . . . and a young woman orders a fairy-tale life, but she forgets to read the fine print and ends up with the worst parts of two fairy tales.

WE THINK, THEREFORE WE ARE, edited by Peter Crowther
Writers have been telling stories about sentient robots, computers, etc., since the Golden Age of science fiction began. Now fifteen masters of imagining have turned their talents to exploring the forms AIs may take in the not too distant future. Here are the descendants of Robby the Robot, the Terminator, and the Bicentennial Man, by authors such as Stephen Baxter, Brian Stableford, James Lovegrove, Tony Ballantyne, Robert Reed, Paul Di Filippo, Patrick O'Leary, Ian Watson, and others.

IMAGINARY FRIENDS edited by John Marco and Martin H. Greenberg
When you were a child, did you have an imaginary friend who kept you company when you were lonely or scared, or who had the most delightful adventures with you? For anyone who fondly remembers that unique companion no one else could see or hear, here is a chance to recapture that magical time of your life. Join thirteen top imaginers like Rick Hautala, Anne Bishop, Juliet McKenna, Kristine Kathryn Rusch, Kristen Britain, Bill Fawcett, Fiona Patton, and Jim C. Hines, as they introduce you to both special friends and special places in their spellbinding tales. From the adventurous doings of a dragon and a boy . . . to a young woman held captive in a tower, and the mysterious being who is her only companion though he can't enter her room . . . to a beggar, a bartender, and a stray dog in the heart of Nashville . . . and a woman who seems to have lost her creativity until a toy Canadian Mountie suddenly comes to life . . . you'll find an intriguing assortment of comrades to share some of your time with.

Ages
of Wonder

edited by

Julie E. Czerneda
and Rob St. Martin

DAW BOOKS, INC.
DONALD A. WOLLHEIM, FOUNDER
375 Hudson Street, New York, NY 10014

ELIZABETH R. WOLLHEIM
SHEILA E. GILBERT
PUBLISHERS
http://www.dawbooks.com

First Printing, March 2009
1 2 3 4 5 6 7 8 9

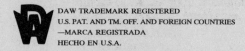

DAW TRADEMARK REGISTERED
U.S. PAT. AND TM. OFF. AND FOREIGN COUNTRIES
—MARCA REGISTRADA
HECHO EN U.S.A.

PRINTED IN THE U.S.A.

Acknowledgments

Introduction © 2009 by Julie E. Czerneda and Rob St. Martin
Section Introductions © 2009 by Rob St. Martin
The Curse Tablet © 2009 by Nina Kiriki Hoffman
To Play the Game of Men © 2009 by Caitlin Sweet
Mist Wraith © 2009 by Urania Fung
Written in Smoke © 2009 by Karina Sumner-Smith
Cloud Above Water © 2009 by Natalie Millman
Crossing the Waters © 2009 by Ika Vanderkoeck
Here There Be Monsters © 2009 by Brad Carson
A Swift Changing Course © 2009 by Jana Paniccia
Blood and Soil © 2009 by Ceri Young
Fletcher's Ghost © 2009 by Liz Holliday
Immigrant © 2009 by Sandra Tayler
A Small Sacrifice © 2009 by Kristen Bonn
Pony Up © 2009 by Linda A. B. Davis
Gold at the End of the Railroad © 2009 by Elizabeth Ann Scarborough
The Stone Orrery © 2009 by Jennifer Crow
Sphinx! © 2009 by Tony Pi
A Bird in the Hand © 2009 by Queenie Tirone
Mars Bound © 2009 by K. J. Gould
Angels and Moths © 2009 by Costi Gurgu

Table of Contents

The Colonial Age

The Age of Pioneers

The Pre-Modern Age

The Age Ahead

Introduction

When Rob and I started this anthology, we thought it would be simple. He's the historian. I have a love of unusual story settings. We both enjoy fantasy and had noticed that much of it was set in, to be honest, essentially the same place and time. While there's nothing wrong with castles, kings, and interesting peasantry—and nothing wrong with magic in a modern, western city of skyscrapers and cell phones—Rob brought up the notion of how much more there was in human history for writers to use. Every age offered myriad cultures, any of which could be mined for the basis of a wonderful fantasy setting.

Simple, right?

As the hard-working authors in this anthology will tell you (and the many whose otherwise excellent stories we had to turn down), it wasn't simple at all. We weren't after alternate history, however fascinating the premise. We wanted fantasy stories set in their own unique worlds, but those worlds had to be based on a lesser-used place, time, and culture of our own. A world drawn using the inks, as it were, of human history.

Such demanding editors. But we held true to our vision and, thanks to our authors, the result is in your hands. Enjoy the forgotten, the familiar, and the utterly fantastic settings of these delightful stories.

Welcome to the Ages of Wonder.

Julie E. Czerneda and Rob St. Martin

THE AGE OF ANTIQUITY

At the dawn of human civilization, small kingdoms grew into great empires that spanned vast areas of land. Though they worshipped different gods and spoke different languages, though they might go to war and slaughter one another, these empires were united in a common belief: that they shared the world with wonderful, fantastic creatures—mythic beings who strode the earth just as they themselves did, sometimes hidden, sometimes revealing their true nature to the mortals who worshipped, feared, and loved them.

The Curse Tablet

Nina Kiriki Hoffman

Lucius found the witch at one of the termopolia near Ostia Harbor. She sat on a stone bench near the sale counter of the sidewalk restaurant, a pottery bowl of puls porridge in her lap and a wedge of bread in her hand. The restaurant was doing brisk business— many people stopped by for their breakfasts; the man behind the counter was hard-pressed to keep up with requests for round loaves of bread. A child darted in and pulled a loaf from the bottom of a stack so skill-fully the shopkeeper never noticed it. Lucius remem-bered doing things like that before his mother sold him to Gaius Tullius Paulus.

The spring air was soft, damp, and almost warm, heavy with scents of smoke and sewage. A lot of good-natured shouting and joking filled the air. Toward the water, someone played a flute, but Lucius could not catch the melody, only a sense of the music, which was melancholy and carried a thin thread of power. Lucius had his own flute tucked into his waistband under a fold of tunic. It was a memento of his child-hood, when he had played for money and food in the marketplace with his mother, sister, and older brother. He rarely found time to play these days.

Most people ate as they walked toward their work, but some squatted on the sidewalk to eat, or sat on benches under the overhanging arches of the shops that lined the street. The donkey-driven mills in the center of the building were grinding grain, adding to the cacophony. The smell of baking bread made Lucius hungry; he had had his own breakfast at dawn, a couple hours earlier.

No one sat near the witch. She tossed crumbs into the street. Small birds landed to eat the crumbs, scattering every time someone came near.

Lucius approached the witch, his gaze on the muddy paving stones. He did not want to meet the witch's eyes. One of the other slaves in Master Gaius' household, a strapping man named Deodatus, had been bewitched only last week, falling into frequent fits, and afraid, now, of water. Since Deodatus' bewitching, Lucius had been pressed into accompanying their master to the public baths and then scraping the oil off his skin; Deodatus could no longer abide the sight of the pools.

"Have you a task for me?" the witch asked Lucius. Her voice was warm, low, and pleasant.

"Are you the one known as Cassia the Witch?" he asked. The cook had told him the witch had much shaggy red hair, and that she wore it loose instead of braided or dressed, and that the color of her tunic was usually blue, and that on cool mornings like this one, she wore an overrobe of paler blue. All of which she was and wore: he had seen as much, before he fixed his gaze on the ground.

"I am called Cassia," she said.

"My master wants to hire you."

"I won't work for someone who won't look at me," said Cassia. She tossed crumbs toward his feet, and he was standing so still that the birds landed, pecking near his sandals.

"Honored mistress, I don't want you to work for me," Lucius told the birds at his feet. "It is my master who needs your services."

"I won't accept his commission unless you look at me," she said.

He sighed and closed his hand around the bag of

denarii tied at his waist, enough to hire the witch for ten curse tablets, if the cook was to be believed. The cook had told the master's personal servant about the witch's powers. The personal servant had gossiped to the master, and the master had decided this was the route he wanted to go. The master's marketplace rival had stolen and imprisoned the master's mistress, and such a deed could not go unavenged.

Lucius touched the slave collar around his neck, with its inscription of ownership. Most of Master Gaius' slaves didn't wear collars, but Lucius had made one unwise attempt to run away when he was ten years old and new to the household, before he realized that life could be much worse. The collar was his penance; he had been wearing it for five years now. He had never done anything else to jeopardize his position in Master Gaius' household. He wasn't ready to start now.

He had been charged to find and hire this witch. He looked into her eyes.

They were as green as the glass tiles in a water mosaic. The witch did not blink. Lucius felt his will run out of him like sand.

"You're a pretty boy," she said. "Hold out your hand."

His arm lifted, though he did not direct it. The witch set her bread on top of her porridge bowl, reached into a wallet at her waist, pulled out a red string, and tied it around his wrist. He felt the magic in the knots as she laced the ends together. "There, now. You'll come when I call you, won't you, Lucius?"

He swallowed. His adam's apple bobbed against the collar, where his name was written for anyone who could read to see: "I am Lucius. Hold me so that I do not run away, and take me back to my master, the most illustrious man Gaius Tullius Paulus, who lives on the corner of Cardo Maximus and Via Di Diana."

"Yes, mistress," Lucius said to the witch.

"What does your master want?"

"A curse tablet." His voice was steady. Now that

the worst had happened and he had been bewitched, he was no longer afraid of her. Fear would come later, when she pulled the red thread and made him do her bidding.

"Do you know the text of it?"

"I've memorized the outline." He had scribed what his master wanted onto a wax tablet, smoothed it out, written it again twice more, each time erasing it, trusting his mind to hold it; he didn't want to carry a curse through the streets, where any citizen or freedman might claim authority over him and ask to see what he carried.

"Do you have money to pay me? I charge by the word. Does he want many words?"

"He does," said Lucius.

"Do you have any personal thing from the one he is cursing? Hair? Nail clippings? Lost teeth, or something the accursed has touched often?"

Lucius touched the other pouch at his waist. He had sneaked into Quintus Valerius Cato's house, with generous bribes to Master Quintus' slaves at a time when Master Quintus was in his shop and his wife and children had gone to visit relatives. The slaves, unhappy in their household and willing to take small risks, had let Lucius into Master Quintus' room, though they warned him Quintus was meticulous in burning any hair he brushed and any nails he clipped. They had also let him see Prisca, Master Gaius' mistress, chained to a bed in one of the slave rooms near the back of the house. She had cried and begged for his help. All he had been able to do for her was give Master Quintus' slaves money and hope they spent at least a fraction of it on food for her.

On a pillow of Master Quintus' sleeping couch, Lucius had found a single short and shining hair. He had pressed it into a ball of wax so he wouldn't lose it. "I have it," he told the witch.

"Come to my workshop." She handed him her food, the bread still stacked atop the bowl, tossed a coin to the baker—"I'll bring the bowl back tomorrow," she said, and he nodded to her—and strode down the street toward a block of sagging tenements. Lucius, who had lived in worse places, followed her up a rickety staircase to a hallway on the third floor, which was built of wood. The ceiling was blackened from lamp smoke; one window at the far end of the hall let in a little light.

The witch unlocked the third door to the right and let Lucius into a cramped apartment. A sturdy work table took up most of the room. Shelves to the left overflowed with filled glass and pottery jars and wooden boxes and some things that were dried and looked as though they had joints and bones. "Sit," said the witch, gesturing toward a square stool.

Lucius sat while the witch went to a shelf and fetched a rolled papyrus scroll with many darkened finger marks on it, a stack of prepared lead sheets, and a stylus. She also brought a wax tablet. "Tell me," she said, opening the hinged wood backing of the tablet to reveal the waxed surfaces inside.

"Since it is a matter of love, he thought the curse should be directed to Venus," Lucius said.

The witch shook her head. "Venus is cruel, but she doesn't traffic in the kinds of curses I write. This is a curse to harm another unless restitution is made, correct?"

"Yes."

"Was something stolen?"

"My master's mistress has been taken captive and imprisoned by his rival. She was a slave at the brothel down on the crossroads by the water, the House of the Three Gorgons. My master paid for her exclusive use, but his rival bought her from the proprietress and now has her imprisoned in his house."

The witch tapped her lower lip with the tip of the stylus. Her eyes narrowed. "Interesting. Not a situation I've encountered before. Usually I work with stolen objects, not people." She straightened. "Make the appeal to Mars or Mercurius. They'll get this sort of work done for you."

"All right," said Lucius. "You choose."

The witch's green eyes gleamed as she stared at him. She bent, unrolled the scroll, consulted it, and wrote on the wax.

Lucius watched the stylus trace elegant letters. He had learned to read and write along with Master Gaius' younger children, who were still being taught by a Greek slave at home. Master Gaius knew Lucius had a good mind, and hoped to make a secretary of him if he proved steady and reliable. Seven years in the slave collar, and then Lucius would be freed of it, with more trust to grow as he could earn it. The master also let him practice the flute and play for guests at dinner sometimes. Without the click of his sister's castanets and the strum of his brother's lyre, Lucius couldn't infuse the music with power, but he played songs he had learned from sailors and travelers and soldiers, anyone he had met as a child, and all those songs carried a power of memory from everyone who had sung them and passed them on. He wasn't sure he'd ever reclaim his music magic, which had died the day his brother died, killed by a drunken soldier for an imagined insult. Since that day he had played alone, for his mother sold him soon after, with his consent, so she would have enough money to protect his sister from becoming a slave until she was older. Maybe his price had given her enough of a dowry that she could marry. Lucius didn't know; his mother and sister had left Ostia, hoping Rome would be kinder to them.

"Most holy Mercurius," wrote the witch. "Your master's name?" she asked Lucius.

Even though he knew the master's name was an important part of the invocation, Lucius hesitated. A name was power, and she was a witch. "Gaius Tullius Paulus," he said. He touched his collar, a nervous habit he had been trying to lose. Of course his master's name was right there, the etched letters dents under his fingertips.

The witch wrote again. "Gaius Tullius Paulus salutes you, offers you the gift of this prayer, and begs you act on his behalf. In return for your help he will give half the worth of the woman, when recovered, to your temple." She looked to Lucius, her eyebrows lifted in question.

"We don't know what Master Quintus paid for her," he said.

"How much does your master want the woman's freedom?"

"I think he wishes he had thought to buy her himself," Lucius said, "but his wife would never have allowed him to have her in the house. I don't think he could have afforded her, either." Master Gaius had inherited money, but he was not the wisest trader, and had lately invested in several ventures that had failed.

"What did he tell you to offer the god?" She smoothed the wax, erasing the words.

"A hundred denarii."

"Cheapskate."

Lucius shrugged.

"What does he want in return for this gift?" she asked.

Lucius closed his eyes and recited the curse. "Let the thief, Quintus Valerius Cato, suffer in every part until he releases the stolen woman Prisca. Let him not eat nor drink nor sleep nor defecate until he has made restitution and freed her. Holy one, I give to you his heart and mind, his name, his reputation, his whole being to punish in the worst possible ways until he releases her. Bind him to justice or make him suffer. Blind his eyes and close up his ears. Dry up his speech and cripple his feet. Render him useless in bed. Make his hands feeble and his bones ache. For this aid I will give a gift of—" Lucius stopped, checked to see if she had written down everything he said.

"Go on, go on," she said, irritated.

"One hundred denarii to the temple of Venus," he said.

"Yes. I'll change that to Mercurius."

"My master said I was to ask you if all this were in the correct form."

"Close enough. I can craft it to fit. This is going to take a big tablet, though, and I charge a sestertius a word. Also, one denarius for the ritual components, which I will do in secret, and another for the curse doll. Give me the hair."

Lucius fetched the ball of wax from its pouch and set it before her, turning it so the hair showed on top.

"Good," said the witch. "For the placement of the tablet and the curse doll in the appropriate well or temple with the right words and objects—hmm, that's where I'll take my payment from you, my boy."

He gazed at her steadily. Light shimmered across her eyes from a source he could not see. She smiled.

"If my master refuses to pay the last part of the price?" Lucius asked.

"Tell him I won't take anything from you you can't spare." She leaned over her draft of the curse, added more words. He watched them flow in the trail of her stylus: a string of words in a language he did not understand, full of doubled vowels and strange combinations of consonants. She glanced up, saw him watching, and said, "I'll write the same thing at the top. It's an incantation to other forces, and will make the spell more binding still." She counted the words, counting the last words twice, then told him the total. "I want half of it now."

He turned his back on her and counted out coins. She was charging him more than the cook had predicted, but less than he had in his purse.

"Come back tonight. You can help me with the placement, and then I'll take the rest of my pay," she said.

On the way back to his master's house, Lucius went through the market to pick up some fruit for the cook. He saw a pair of young musicians playing in front of the fish stall, which had sold its catch earlier and had

closed its shutters for the day. The girl played the lyre
and the boy played a double flute. There was enough
similarity in their features and the pale gold of their
hair that he suspected they were siblings. Their instruments sounded pure and pitch-perfect, but when they
sang (Greek songs poorly translated into Latin), their
voices were rough. Few coins fell into the brass bowl
at their feet.

He leaned against a wall under a portico not far
from them and took out his flute. As they began a
new song, an old hymn to Apollo, Lucius lifted his
flute to his lips and played a counter melody.

For the first time since his brother's death the music
pulsed through him like his own heartbeat. Power
gathered as he played, lifted him on his own feet and
brought him to the other musicians until they stood
in a triangle, each facing the others, the music growing
without regard to anyone or anything around them, a
paean to Apollo, god of music and light. He felt the
song arrow up into the air, rising to greet the god and
surround him in golden light. He felt the blessing return, three golden arrows dropping from the sky,
which struck them with warmth, a brief flare of fire
on each of their foreheads, and a nimbus of light. For
an age the music held them, every breath an element
of the whole, all notes weaving together to sustain
them outside of time, in the center of prayer.

The slave collar tightened around Lucius' throat,
narrowing his access to air. The red thread burned his
wrist, and he lost the melody. The girl stilled her fingers on the strings. The boy, gasping, lowered the double flute. The three of them glittered with godlight a
moment longer, and then it faded.

"What—?" said the boy, his accent heavy.

"How—who are you?" the girl asked, her voice almost breathless.

Lucius blinked, woke from a dream where he was
back in the center of his family. He stood in the marketplace with strangers, surrounded by the noise of
bargaining, arguments, and shopkeepers calling their

wares, the shuffle of feet, the air alive with the smells
of meat grilling, sweaty people, baking bread, heavy
perfumes.

He tugged at his collar, but it no longer choked him;
it had loosened as soon as he stopped playing. "Thank
you," he said to the boy, the girl, and the god. He
turned and nearly tripped over the couple's brass offering bowl, now overflowing with brass and bronze
coins. A few passersby who had stopped near them
moved on. Lucius tucked his flute into his belt and
plunged into the crowd. He didn't stop for fruit, too
shaken by what had happened, but headed straight
home.

Master Gaius took him into the library as soon as
he returned and asked for an accounting, and Lucius
repeated back his conversation with the witch almost
word for word. He held out his wrist and showed Master Gaius the red thread, stood mute and waited to hear
what his master would say to the witch's demands.

"She won't take anything from you you can't spare,
eh?" said Master Gaius.

"So she said." Lucius stared at the mosaic on the
library floor. It showed a troupe of actors in costume
for a comedy. The scheming slave's face was stretched
into a grotesque smile. Perhaps he did not know that
he would embrace his downfall by the end of the play.

"Was she pretty?"

It hadn't occurred to Lucius to consider the witch's
looks in that light. Her wild hair, her glowing eyes,
their unnatural green; the power of her gaze, holding
him helpless. His own fear and then resignation. "She
was beautiful," he said.

Gaius clapped Lucius' shoulder. "Then I say, enjoy
your night with her. Time you had some seasoning,
anyway. I only hope you don't acquire a taste for it.
I have plans for you when the collar comes off. Say,
what's that smudge on your forehead?"

"Master?"

Gaius leaned closer, peered at Lucius' forehead.
Lucius smelled wine on his breath. "Odd," said Gaius.

"I thought it was soot, but there's something else there. Sulia!"

A flustered house slave arrived, a bucket of dirty water and wet rag in hand. She had been washing the floor in the atrium when Lucius returned.

"There's a good girl. Loan me your rag."

She held out the rag, and Gaius dipped it in the water, then pressed it to Lucius' forehead. When he lowered it, both he and Sulia stared at Lucius, speechless.

Finally, Master Gaius said, "And where did you go after you left the witch?"

"Only the marketplace, Master. For fruit." Lucius looked down at his empty hands.

"Not some temple? You weren't hanging around with lackwits planning some slave rebellion?"

"No, Master! Only the marketplace!"

"How did you come by a mark of Apollo?"

"I played my flute in the marketplace."

Master Gaius took a step backward, his head shaking from side to side.

"There was music, Master. You have not forbidden me music. I didn't disobey you, I swear it. I only stopped for a moment to play my flute with some children."

"The mark came then?"

"We played a hymn. It pleased the god, or so I thought. I never meant to disobey you."

"I imagine you didn't." Master Gaius sighed and handed the rag back to Sulia. "Too late to do anything about it now, I suppose," he said. "Maybe the mark will give you some protection from the witch. I had better send a bonus with you when you go tonight, and I'd better make plans to get you more training on that flute. I don't want the god angry with me."

"Master." A tension Lucius didn't know he was carrying eased from his shoulders.

"Perhaps you can be useful to me in different ways. I could hire you out to religious festivals. I'll talk to some priests. Go have some lunch, and then take a

nap. The gods only know what the witch wants with
you; you should probably rest up for it."

"Thank you, Master."

Carrying the rest of the witch's payment, Lucius left
the house just after dusk, one hand on his knife-
sheath. Under cover of night, different kinds of criminals operated, more dangerous ones, and the witch
didn't live in a good neighborhood.

He passed a large house where torches in the hold-
ers outside signified a party. The sounds of laughter,
talk, and music came through the vestibule, the scent
of grilled meat and spilled wine, and the flicker of
olive oil lamps. He walked through the orange light
on the street, then froze as the music caught him. The
mark on his forehead burned. His hand went to his
flute. With an act of will he forced it away again and
made himself walk past, as quickly as he could, to get
away from the siren sound. It wasn't even a song he
knew, he thought, and something else in him thought:
the song no longer matters. All of music is mine.

But my lord Apollo, not all of me is yours, Lucius
thought. He clasped one hand around the red thread
and ran through the streets from shadow to shadow,
as he had done as a child, speeding faster whenever
he heard any thread of music in the air.

The witch's apartment was full of incense smoke.
More burned in a small brazier in the center of her
table. He coughed at first, and then found the powerful scent intriguing, even pleasant. She ushered him in
and showed him the tablet and the doll on the table:
the doll was a rough wax figure as long as a man's
hand, dressed in a coarse linen tunic. Its head was
made of the wax ball he had left for her, crude facial
features picked out with some sharp implement. The
tablet, oxidized lead, gleamed with fresh silver letters
cut through its darkened surface. The text flowed,
drawing his gaze along the twists and turns of strange
words so that he almost repeated them aloud. She
clapped a hand over his mouth. "This is an address

to the chthonic gods," she said. "You don't want to draw their attention to you." Then she turned his head toward her and stared at his forehead. "What have you done?" she demanded, angry now.

His master's wife's dresser had let him use the master's wife's mirror see the mark on his forehead. It was faint, a gold tracery in the outline of a lyre. He had never seen another like it on anyone. He couldn't remember whether the other two musicians in the marketplace had been marked.

Lucius shrugged.

"Stupid boy," she grumbled, and then said, "God-marked or not, I need your help to complete the ritual. Are you satisfied that the tablet reads as it should?"

He read through the words. In her script, they took on an elegance that made them foreign and strange. He closed his eyes and compared what she had written to the curse he had in the tablets of his memory. A word changed here or there, but the meaning was the same, perhaps even clearer. He nodded.

"Give me your hand. I need three drops of your blood to seal the curse."

"My blood?"

"Someone's blood. Anyone's blood. It tells the gods we're serious about this. Your blood; I don't care to use mine."

"Is this the payment you wanted?"

"No. It's for your master, though, so you'll do it, won't you?"

He held out his hand. "Could you cut somewhere other than my fingers? I need them for my flute."

"A flute, is it? You fool." She searched his wrist and made a tiny nick with a short curved golden knife. Blood welled up. She directed it to the tablet, where it dripped and sizzled. Then she stood with her thumb pressed against the wound she had made. She said words that lifted the hair on the back of his neck. The tablet glowed with dull silvery light. His blood vanished from its surface.

"Sit," said the witch. "I need silence for the next part of this."

He sat on a stool at her table, with his hands resting on his thighs. She spoke more words over the tablet, crooning them, and gently rolled the soft metal into a scroll. She tied the doll to it with red thread, then pushed a nail through doll and scroll, chanting in some other language, her face fierce, her eyes mad. Finally she held her hands above the bundle of doll and scroll, spoke three words, and sagged back on her stool.

"It is done," she said. "Fetch me water." She waved toward a blue glass pitcher on a nearby shelf. A squat sardonyx cup sat beside the pitcher. He poured water for her, and she drank.

"Is this service my payment?" he asked.

"You know it isn't." She fetched a length of bronze silk from the shelf and wrapped the tablet and doll in it, carefully so that her skin never touched the tablet. "Take this and follow me."

She carried a lamp, but it did not light the way behind her. He followed at her heels, the tablet cradled in both hands. It was a cold hard lump in its silk shroud, and it did not warm in his hands; it weighed more than it seemed it should.

She led him along many streets, some so twisty he got lost. People sometimes approached them along the streets, but something about the witch made them turn and run away. He wondered if she wore a different face.

The witch stopped him in an alley. Finally he recognized where they were: near the northern end of the city, between rooming houses. A small temple to Mithras stood nearby, and the witch led him to the threshold.

"Only the priest will be there at this time, and he is at his dinner. I sent someone with food that contains a sleeping powder," whispered the witch. "In the first room as you enter, there is a well. A curse tablet works best when it is sunk into dark, deep water where the sun has never shone. It will send your ene-

my's spirit into the depths. Drop the curse into the
well and say, 'Mithras, I entreat you to aid this curse
in its execution in this life and the next.'"

Mithras was the god of soldiers. Lucius had feared
soldiers and their god since his brother's death.

"Go," said the witch. "No women are allowed inside. The priest may be sleepy, but he would smell
me."

Lucius stepped over the threshold into a dark room.
A chill struck through him. The witch held out the
lamp, and he reached back for it. The floor was covered with black and white tiles, diamonds and full
moons in white, the spaces in between black. The well
stood in the center of the room. He walked toward it.
Each step grew harder to take, as if the air were solidi-
fying around him, trapping him like an insect in
amber. He pushed against it, but it brought him to a
complete stop three steps away from the well. He
looked back toward the witch. He could not see her.
The air had darkened around him; only a small circle
of light remained around his lamp, enough to light his
forearm and hand and a circle of his tunic. "Mithras,"
he said, but his throat swallowed the word before it
came out. He pushed again. The air was like stone.
He could go neither forward nor back.

"Apollo," he whispered.

Play me there, murmured a voice.

Lucius set the lamp and the swaddled curse tablet
at his feet and took out his flute. He played the paean
he and the siblings had played that afternoon. He expected nothing now: it had always taken at least three
musicians to bring magic into the music. He played,
his breath steadying, the song growing from a limping
twitter to a strong string of melody, and then he felt
huge hands on his shoulders, steadying him. He
played, wondering if the priest would hear and come
to curse him for being in this holy place where he did
not belong.

I am here, murmured the voice. Do your deed, if
you must.

Strengthened by the hands on his shoulders, Lucius
lowered his flute. The air was soft again, no barrier.
He stooped and lifted the curse tablet, took the last
three steps to the well.

He paused.

Dropping the curse tablet into the well would set
the curse in motion. Was he ready to aid in such a
terrible undertaking? He remembered the words he
had memorized, all the afflictions to be set upon
Quintus Valerius Cato. How could he wish such ills
on another man?

Quintus had chained Prisca in a dark room. He did
not feed her enough, and he misused her, too, showing
his contempt for his rival by mistreating something
Master Gaius loved. Quintus' other slaves had had
plenty of complaints, and they were supposedly the
lucky ones.

Prisca was a slave, less than human, chattel. Her
legal owner had the right to decide what to do with
her.

Lucius was a slave, and he had been ordered to do
this duty.

He could say he had failed. Only Apollo and
Mithras would know the truth.

Lucius held the lamp out over the lip of the well
and looked down into darkness blacker than tar. No
gleam of light came back to him, only a deep chill and
a cascade of faint whispers.

He tossed the tablet in. "Mithras, I entreat you to
aid this curse in its execution in this life and the next."
He did not hear a splash, but he felt a shift in the air,
and spikes of frozen nails drove through his bones.
His blood on the tablet. His hand in its initiation. It
was part of him now, like all his other masters.

The warm hands on his shoulders pressed once
more against his knotted muscles, then vanished. Lucius turned and walked out of the temple. His stomach
curdled. Lines of cold lay along his bones.

The witch waited for him. She tucked her arm

through his and they walked back to her apartment building. He stopped at the entrance to the stairs, though, and touched the red thread around his wrist. It unknotted itself and dropped off, the red fading from it until it was pale brown.

"What? I haven't gotten my payment out of you yet," she said.

He untied the purse with her fee from his belt and handed it to her.

"That's not what I meant, and you know it."

"You may not have gotten the payment you want, but it was payment, just the same," he said. "I did a piece of your work for you, and it hurt me." He didn't recognize his own voice: cold had lodged in it.

She opened the pouch and looked inside, then up at him.

"This is more than I asked for," she said.

"The master thought my encounter with the god would make me less useful to you," he said. "He sent a bonus."

She made the pouch disappear under her heavy shawl and took the lamp from him. "A wise man, your master," she said. "I'd be pleased to work for him again. Have him send me someone else next time."

On the way home, Lucius stopped outside the house where the party had been. The lights were lower now, the talk quieted to murmurs, but somewhere a lyre strummed softly; someone blew across Pan pipes. He leaned against the wall and took out his flute, played a line of melody to match the one the hidden musicians played inside. At first he could not find the pitch nor the rhythm, but then heat kindled in the center of his forehead, and the music opened up to him again. His newest god had not rejected him, so he played himself inside a prayer and stayed there until the others stilled their instruments in sleep.

By the time he reached home, the household was dark. He went to his pallet and lay listening to others

breathing sleep around him. Deodatus cried out in his
sleep, but they were used to that now, and no one
else stirred.

In the space of one day, Lucius had acquired three
new masters and cast off one. The cold silver in his
bones told him he was bound to Mithras still, by calling down the god to work the curse; the mark on his
forehead, the new joy in his music, told him he was
still tied to Apollo; but the witch had lost her hold.
He touched the slave collar, the chafing sign of his
first master, sighed, and slept.

The curse took days to beat Quintus Valerius Cato
down. Master Gaius set Lucius to watch the house
and see what transpired. Lucius learned the outside of
the house very well, and watched a procession of visitors and slaves enter and leave. He noticed when new
graffiti was scratched into the bricks. He learned which
narrow slit of window led into Prisca's cell, and sometimes he lingered outside it and played quietly on the
flute. At those times, her soft sobs stopped.

He met with Quintus' slaves in the marketplace or
a tavern near the house and bought them food and
drink in exchange for news from inside the house. The
curse started slowly, but its effects grew, until Quintus
could hardly leave his bed without pain, and what
sleep he managed was haunted by nightmares, the
slaves said. A physician was called in three times, and
finally Quintus sent for a soothsayer.

In the long, increasingly warm and humid afternoons, Lucius had time to contemplate. The cold
Mithras needles in his bones pricked him sometimes;
that was when he knew the curse was working. Times
like that, he had no hunger for food; his stomach
soured.

Sometimes a thread of music called him from his
post, drew him toward the river or the market, and at
those times he gave himself up to the god, until his
collar choked him back to the uncomfortable present.

He was at his post, an alcove shaded by a potted
tree, when the curse finally bore fruit. Prisca, frail,

pale, and wrapped in a red robe, was led stumbling from the house by one of Quintus' German slaves, a big, light-haired man whose language Lucius did not know, though he had learned which drink the man liked best at the tavern. The German was half-carrying Prisca. Lucius followed them until they were beyond sight of the house's vestibule, then slipped up beside the German. The big man nodded, but continued on through the streets.

"Prisca?" Lucius said softly. Her eyes were red with weeping.

"Oh, Lucius!" she said. "Finally I am free of that place!"

"Will you come home with me?" he said. Master Gaius would surely want to see to her safety; he could arrange lodging for her.

"I cannot. Master Quintus sends me to the temple of Mercurius, so the soothsayer told him." She held out her chafed wrists. "Look, Lucius. I am free."

"Free," he echoed, and fell back a step.

"I am to be purified and released. He even gave me three denarii. I can go home to my mother and my sister now."

Lucius stood where he was and watched the German coax Prisca down the street toward the temple. Soon they were lost amid the afternoon traffic. The curse had been worded that way: Quintus could only break it by freeing the girl.

Already Lucius felt a faint warmth along his bones, though he still felt the pricking of a silvery needle in his neck. The god had looked toward him and might never turn entirely away.

He went home to his first master to report.

To Play the Game of Men

Caitlin Sweet

It's lonely, being the only horse in hell.

There are diversions, certainly. The Abyss is fairly dark, but the sounds are loud and often entertaining: the Toiler's grunts, the faster-faster rumble of his stone, and the gusty sigh he always heaves in the silence after its descent. The Yearner's infuriated shouts are so dramatic that my ears flick, and when the First Giants roll over in their sleep I actually wish for human ears and human hands to cover them with. At least the Giants have each other. At least the Toiler and the Yearner can shout back and forth through the gloom—even if all they ever do is whine about too much exercise and not enough food. But I'm alone. My own fault, but I'll complain anyway.

I still have my looks, which is something. As I've said, it's dark here, thanks to the smoke, and of course the three layers of night that hang over the bronze wall. But sometimes the night thins, or a gout of flame shoots up from the pit, and I catch a glimpse of my reflection in the wall. A handsome beast, even if my brown-black sides aren't quite as glossy as they used to be. The blaze on my forehead looks wonderfully white and unsullied. You can still see why I was so popular on the Peak.

It wasn't just that I was handsome, though—I was also dependable. From the moment I was given my first assignment among men, I performed precisely as my divine audience expected me to. "They'll love you," hissed my harpy mother, tangling her claws in my mane as she always did, when she tried to stroke it. "They'll name you and feed you and think you're theirs," whispered my wind father, his breath warm and sweet as flowers. Neither of them mentioned that these men would sit on me, their bodies sharp and lumpy and ungainly, or that they'd strap me to chariots so loaded down with bronze that even I grew tired of pulling. But I was eager to please. When the Father of all Gods cried, "Lead them to glory and ruin! Make us laugh and weep!" I tossed my head and pawed at the mountain earth.

I never expected to disobey—but then, I never expected the Boy.

"There's a boy," the Judge said. Everyone squinted at her. You could only ever really see her on rainy days; in sunlight she was far too sparkly, with all that armor and the spear. "Looks promising."

The Warrior grunted. "That's what you said about the one who ended up goring himself on a boar. My magical hounds wasted a lot of effort on that one."

"No," the Judge said slowly, "this one's different. He's a prince. Adores his mother, hates his father. Small, but already good with weapons. Great wrestler. Thinks deep thoughts." She turned to the Father in a blur of gold. "I say he's next."

"*I* say we choose a girl," the Huntress put in. Everyone laughed and shouted at her, and she ran down into the woods, her bow bouncing off her back. (She never could deal with criticism.)

"Very well, then," the Mother said, shifting on her throne so that the folds of her gown rippled. "We've already let them figure out fire, and mining, and smelting—all very entertaining. We've blown their ships off course and allowed them to discover new lands. And their music and writing—we've done well there. What will we have this one do?"

The Father set down his wine jug. He wiped the back of his hand over his mouth, trailing a new, glistening swath of purple through his beard. "New lands." Even when he spoke quietly, his words shuddered with thunder. "Been a long time. There's blood in that. Burning. Lots of ecstasy and anguish. Yes." He nodded. His brown eyes had already turned silver with tears.

"The kid's good with horses," the Strongman commented. (He was spending the summer with us, even though the Mother hated him.)

Everyone turned to me. I took one more nibble of grass, trying to seem nonchalant. It had been more than a thousand years since the last War, and I was young for an immortal: I was giddy with excitement, but too proud to let anyone see it.

"You," the Father said. (Men give us names; we have no need of them among ourselves.) "You've been idle, while your brothers have been busy below. Go"—the thunder rumbled, through wind and sunlight—"Go and make him yours, and you will be rewarded."

I went, and even when the high, thin mountain air gave way to the oppressive sky of men, I felt light with joy and purpose.

Innocence only turns into ignorance when it's too late to matter.

The Boy *was* small. He was twelve years old; at the same age, my former master, the Hero, had looked like a man. I wondered whether the Judge knew what she was doing with this one.

The Boy noticed me immediately. I was making quite a show of it, of course, bucking and rearing so that the men around me scattered like frightened birds. He tugged on his father's tunic and pointed at me.

"No," I heard the King say, as he regarded me with his good eye (his blind one was puckered shut). "No—and how dare you bring such an unruly beast onto my grounds?" The question he addressed to the horse trader who had brought me to the palace, along with several more docile (and mortal) creatures. The man stammered and flushed; the King's rages were legendary.

"I will ride him." The Boy's voice was as high and clear as water. The crowd was quiet, suddenly. I gave an especially piercing whinny and a snort that ruffled the hair on the nearest man's head.

"No." More growl than word, but the Boy's gray eyes remained fixed on the King.

"Yes, Father. I swear by the King of all Gods that I will ride him."

A wind from the east swirled around us all, raising dust from the riding ground. I knew the wind would carry the Boy's words and image to the Father, and that he would laugh with delight.

The King's hands were shaking. "You are a boy," he said through gritted teeth. Spittle shone in his dark beard. "Do you think you will succeed where your elders have failed?"

"I do." The Boy looked at me; a child with golden hair and a gaze like fire. Maybe it was too late for me, even then? (A sentimental thought. I have too many of these in the Abyss, but who can blame me?)

After the King and the trader had murmured to each other, the King swept his own gaze around the assembly and gave a broad, false smile. "He costs thirteen talents, Boy. If you are unable to make good on your intention, you'll have to pay for him yourself."

The Boy nodded solemnly. "I accept your terms," he said, "but only because I intend to succeed."

The gods are going to *love* this kid, I thought as I wrenched my bridle away from the man who held it. The laughter that had risen after the Boy's declaration turned to concerned muttering. He ignored everyone. He walked slowly toward me, his head high, shoulders back. I pawed sharp grooves into the dirt. I could have killed him with one blow; could have killed all of them. This knowledge had helped me endure many unpleasant interactions with men in the past.

He glanced at the ground, where my shadow shied and shivered, then back up at me. The Strongman had been right: the Boy knew horses—mortal ones, anyway, which were frequently startled by their own shadows. The Boy approached me, his face serious. "Hello, Ox-Head," he said—and so he named me, before he had even touched me. "Ox-Head," after the shape of the white blaze on my forehead. "You're the most beautiful horse I've ever seen—do you belong to the gods?" Before I could master my surprise, he had grasped the trailing bridle and turned me directly into the sun. "Now, then," he continued, "there's no more shadow; nothing to be afraid of. And as you can probably see, I'm very light. My father says my sister looks like more of a boy than I do." And he was up, somehow, mid-sentence; up, a slender shape in the air beside me; a slight but firm weight upon my back. "I'll be a man soon, though. Let's show him, Ox-Head."

I let him lead, though it wasn't hard: he was strong and sure, his knees and heels pressing just enough to direct me. (The Hero had kicked me twice the first time he rode me. He was lucky he survived it.) The Boy and I rode in a slow, wide circle before the palace. I pretended to be restive, at first, but soon I let him feel me calming. He leaned forward, said again, "Let's show him," and dug his heels into my sides.

I galloped. It's never the same off the Peak—my earthly body is heavy, as is the air—but this time felt surprisingly close. We nearly flew—away from the palace, into a stand of trees, and then in a curving arc back. The Boy's whoops rang in my ears. You have no idea, I thought, how happy you should be. I'm yours now, and you're already great.

The crowd cheered wildly as I reared to a stop (taking care not to unseat the Boy). The King walked over to us. There were tears trickling from his good eye, over his scar-seamed cheek. "Son," he said, as the Boy slid from my back, "we'll have to find a worthier kingdom. This one's going to be much too small for you." Man and child looked at each other and smiled, a moment I knew would play well on the Peak. Indeed, a wind from the north brought me the gods' voices just as the Boy was turning back to me.

"Bravo, Ox-Head!" the Father cried, obviously relishing my new name. "You've got him!" The Lover sighed and sniffed (her sighs and sniffs were unmistakable, even from a distance). I lowered my nose into the boy's cupped hand, warm with a happiness that seemed simple at the time.

My first human master had ignored me—my brother and I were just another wedding present from the gods. His son, the Hero, had reveled in my ability to make him look impressive (I wasn't even a little sorry when the Thinker decided to let him die). These two men, who knew I was immortal, had cared little for me—but the Boy, who did not know, loved me. From the moment he turned me away from my shadow and spoke my name, he loved me. I think I knew that then, though I can name it only now.

People think that immortal beings live lives of variety, richness and excitement. This is utterly untrue. Immortality can drag, when you're always happy and the rain is always warm and the flowers always taste like ambrosia. (Don't misunderstand me: I'd take this kind of boredom any day, over the dark, malodorous monotony I have to deal with now.) This is precisely why the gods were always at each other, always courting the kinds of jealousies, ecstasies and rages they so enjoyed watching men feel. It's why they needed me, the immortal who was able, effortlessly, to go down and live among humankind, without needing to turn into a shaft of sunlight or a bull that could tread water.

I loved pleasing the gods with my work. At first this was the only kind of satisfaction I was aware of. I'd wait for my kin the winds to bring me voices: the Father's boom, the Mother's regal whine, the Thinker's clear, ringing bronze. Even the Lover's sniffling was praise. I was lending the Boy my divine aura; I was affecting the courses of men and nations for my masters' diversion. It was a fine game, and I was proud of my part in it.

Things got complicated as the Boy grew into the Great King (everyone called him this, but to me he was always the Boy). There was no reason for it: the game was going so well, had all the elements the gods so desired. The political: the Boy was a natural, intelligent, often ruthless leader, from the time he assumed his assassinated father's throne at age eighteen until he was thirty-three and king of the known world. The intellectual: he was insatiably curious, sent plant specimens home to his old tutor, sketched the flora and fauna he encountered in the strange lands he conquered. The emotional too, of course: he continued to be obsessed with his mother, who was overbearing even when vast distances separated them. He loved a boyhood companion, tolerated the jealousies of his two wives. Drunken murders, the burning of cities and razing of temples: he did it all with the protection of my presence, and the gods wept and rejoiced, as he did.

But for me, it got complicated.

He talked to me. "A hard day, Ox-Head." The darkness of a palace stable, or a tent pitched in hissing sand. "He's angry at me; he's thinks I'm paying too much attention to the dancing boy . . ." I should have been happy about this latest fodder for the Peak-dwellers—but there was the Boy's head, heavy against my neck, and his hand wrapped in my mane. His fear and sadness dragged at me—and his joy, when the Companion called his name from the darkness outside, gave me joy.

Maybe if he had been a petulant fool like the Hero, nothing would have come of it, for me. But for every moment the Boy sulked, or declared himself a deity, or—gods forbid—called himself the Hero, there was a moment of selflessness or humor or compassion. He unsettled me so much that I forgot about the game.

"It's me again, old friend." Tired, smiling, brushing me until my own weariness fell away. (His long marches were exhausting, even for a supernatural

being like myself.) "My men want to go home. So
many of them hate what I've done, accepting the foreigners, adopting their dress, their ways. Marrying
them to my people, so that their children will inherit
my kingdom. Maybe they simply fear the strangeness
of it all, and only think they hate." More brush-
strokes, and a whistled tune. He always whistled under
his breath when he was worried. "They're not ready
for my vision. I'm forging one new world out of all
the old ones, Ox-Head, and all they want to do is shut
their eyes and run back to the memory of a place that
hasn't changed. But . . ." His head against my neck
again. "What if they're right? What if . . . I don't
know. And even though I offer prayers and sacrifices,
the gods give me no guidance."

Perhaps my doubts were born of his.

The order to let the Boy die came from the Warrior.

"You're just jealous," said the Huntress (her voice
was thin, carried to me on a southern breeze).

"Ha!" the Warrior scoffed. "Never! I might just as
well be jealous of *you*, wench"— which caused a scuf-
fle and a yelp, and the sound of footsteps retreating
into woods.

"You may be right." The Thinker now, speaking in
his careful, measured way. "He's winning too much.
He's faced no serious trials of late. There's no real
balance in his life."

I gave my head a violent shake, but the wind still
wrapped me in words.

"Ox-Head?" The Boy was with me. Of course, the
divine conversation had to happen when he was at my
side. The Companion was leaning against a tent pole,
staring intently at a map, clicking his tongue against
his teeth (this always made the Boy growl with false
annoyance). "What's troubling you, old man?"

I whickered to reassure him, but the words didn't
go away.

"Yes," the Father said, "it's getting tiresome. We've
seen it all before. May be time to move on."

I felt a rush of relief; after all, it had been twenty human years since I'd frolicked in the Peak's meadows. A rush of relief, and then a rush of dread.

"Tomorrow's battle. Do you hear me, servant? We'll give you further orders then."

No other night has ever seemed longer to me. Even now, after countless nights in hell, I can say this without exaggeration. I tried not to think, and when I did, I thought ridiculous things like, "The Reveler will get them all drunk and they'll forget." But they didn't forget, and neither did I.

The Boy came to get me before dawn. The river before us was nearly invisible; lightning-shot clouds roiled above it. "The gods' Father speaks," the Boy said, lifting his head to the thunder, and I wished he were wrong. He led his men and their mounts down the mud-slick bank and into the water, whose cold I hardly felt. Winds tore at my mane—the dry winds of this desert country, but others as well, which smelled of mountain spring. The Boy's legs and hands guided me firmly, as always. He sat upon me with coiled, expectant joy, as he had before so many other battles. This one was no different, to him—except for the elephants (his army had never even seen one of these before, let alone 200), and the seven-foot-tall king who sat astride the largest of the beasts. "Look, Ox-Head," I heard Alexander say, as the gale shrieked around us and the river rose up tall and white. "Look, but don't be afraid. Let's show them now, you and I."

He did show them. From the cover of an island, he determined that a direct approach would fail, for the horses were all petrified of the elephants. (I didn't blame them.) So he deployed a lesser force behind and around the opposing army's right flank. He ordered this calmly, addressing several soldiers by name, smiling at them, even as the distant elephants trumpeted and stamped their enormous feet. He waited for the surprise attack to have its effect; then, as daylight broke the storm apart, he cried out and drove his army back into the river.

"Let him fall." The Father's voice; thunder within thunder. "Leave him, now—return to us."

I could have obeyed my master and thrown the Boy, or pretended to stumble—something that would have left him unprotected, vulnerable to a spear or an arrow or the underside of an elephant's foot. (I had so often saved him from these sorts of disasters, simply by bearing him.) This might have been easier for both of us. I could have sped home to the Peak; he could have died quickly and gloriously, just as the Hero had, after my brother and I removed our divine protection from him during the War.

"The Father of all Gods commands you: *Leave him now!*"

I carried the Boy up the steep, muddy bank. I carried him through ranks of elephants and men, which parted before us and fell behind. The screams and clashing of metal were muffled, for although the skies of men had cleared, the storm still roared within me.

"You have one more chance to obey—one more chance, and if you do not take it, you will be punished. You cannot imagine the suffering . . . Look there, to your left. The Great King's enemies retreat or die, save that one—he has an arrow, and it will fly soon. Let it find its mark. *Let it find its mark.*"

I did.

I reared, higher than I'd ever allowed myself to before, among men. The Boy slid and clung but didn't fall. I held myself like this, too tall and still to be a mortal beast—held myself, until the arrow had sped past the place where his throat had been and found my own instead.

I had been injured in battle before: slashes, stabs, glancing blows. The gods' favor had kept me safe (though they did have me shed some blood and retain some scars for the sake of credibility). There was no such favor now. A maelstrom engulfed me: words and

winds, agonies of mind and body. I assume the Boy
cried out my name, or something of the sort, though
I wasn't sure: the gods allowed me no more time to
play the game of men.

I know what happened afterward. (The winds still
reach the Abyss, though their news is often out-of-
date.) The Boy won the battle and granted clemency
to the giant-king. The Boy mourned me, built a city
in my honor. His men mutinied. The Companion died.
The Boy went mad. He fell ill in a city of gardens and
then *he* died. His worlds fractured, and yet the one
that was born was still his. The stuff, all of it, of divine
desire. It must have frustrated the gods to no end that
there was no divine design involved.

I protested my innocence after the river battle. I
had to: I knew where I'd end up and I was terrified.
"I was sentimental," I stammered, hanging my head.
"I was confused. I made a bad decision." I didn't look
up at them, even when the silence stretched on.

"Down," the Father rumbled at last.

I fell, through layers of sky and then the hard, jagged flesh of the earth. Down, down, into night and
smoke and stink, until the stones of the pit broke
my fall.

And now here I stand, chewing on blackened straw
(though I suppose I should be grateful, listening to
the Yearner's racket, that I have anything to chew
on), remembering the dew-sweet grass of the Peak
and wondering, as I will for all eternity, what I was
thinking. Sometimes, when I catch one of those
glimpses of myself in the bronze wall, I imagine for a
moment that there's a rider on my back—a boy, a
youth, a man?—and that both of us are gilded with
sun. At such moments my foolishness almost makes
sense.

"The Great King rode to glory," men will say (of
this, at least, I have no doubt). "The Great King rode
into a new world."

Only the world's old winds will know the rest.

Mist Wraith

Urania Fung

Trinh hugged her knees as she sat on a beach, the
red scarf around her hair wafting in the sea breeze,
her rainbow belt contrasting with her black dress.
Alone, she watched her husband's skiff distance itself
from her and join the company of others. Van was an
excellent fisherman, and all the younger villagers
treated him like their leader. Trinh and her family
had thought she would do well with him, but now she
wondered how well she could do if Van never loved
her. She told herself to be patient as they were only
four months into their arranged marriage.

Fog rose over the sea, moving like a mass of wraiths
among the boats. Fearful of the blinding whiteness,
fishermen in cone-shaped straw hats and sandals hurried back to shore. Van arrived first, and Trinh helped
him pull his skiff onto the beach. Lying inside was a
drenched woman, pale with a mole beside her nose.
Her green silk gown and white trousers were so tat-
tered they exposed her battered limbs and threatened
to slide off her body.

"What happened to her?" Trinh asked, checking
the woman for breath.

Van shrugged and lifted the woman out, water from
her rags seeping into his gray shirt and rolled-up pants.

They returned to the village, which was much like
Trinh's old home. Laundry flapped from clotheslines

35

strung between thatched houses. Small altars offered cups of tea to ancestors and gods. But instead of her relatives, it was Van's mother and aunts cleaning the day's catch while gulls snatched the discarded guts. It was his sister and his cousins hanging fish from racks, placed in the shade of palms to keep the drying flesh from souring in the sun.

"Back already?" Van's sister asked, pulling twine through a slit in a cod tail. Her gaze fell on the stranger. "Where did she come from?"

"Saw her floating in the sea and rescued her," Van replied.

Scaling a catfish, his mother beamed from her shaded chair. "How good of you!"

"She can stay with me," his sister said.

"I don't want to burden you," Van replied, tightening his grip on the stranger. "I'm sure Trinh won't mind having her with us."

"How generous of you!" his mother gushed.

Trinh had prided herself in having the blackest hair and the largest eyes of everyone she knew, but next to the stranger's luscious breasts and hips, she felt too flat and boyish to be attractive.

She tugged at Van's sleeve. "It is a little awkward."

Van turned on her. "How can you be so heartless?"

Trinh wanted to say nothing was heartless about letting his sister care for the stranger, but Van's temper warned her against the temptation.

"It's laziness," Van's sister said, smirking at Trinh. "I knew any girl of Trinh's lowly family couldn't be bothered to help others, but this marriage was Grandfather's dying wish."

"And it was only his wish because he lost so much money playing dice," a cousin said, elbowing Van's sister.

Trinh wanted to argue that her family was equal to theirs and their grandfathers had been best friends, desirous of seeing a connection between their families, but she knew it would be futile.

"Your choice," she told Van.

As they headed home, Trinh imagined going beyond the village to the fields of yellow slipper flowers mixed with pink cuckoo flowers, and farther, to the three mountains smothered in fog and evergreens. The tallest was Suong Ma Mountain, whose majesty had inspired plenty of stories. Trinh loved the peace she felt when looking at it, a peace she longed for more than ever now that a stranger was about to complicate her life.

At home she discarded the woman's rags, bathed her in a wooden tub, bandaged her limbs, and wrapped her in a cotton robe. Their house was one of the largest with two bedrooms, Van's and hers. Trinh heaved the unconscious woman into her bed, fed her porridge, and slept on a mat that night.

The next day Van came home early, demanding to know how well Trinh had taken care of their guest. Then he shooed her out of her room. Trinh was scrubbing her anger out on chopsticks and clay bowls when she heard croaking. She stopped washing and pressed her ear against the wall.

The woman was speaking. She called herself Hong Yen and asked where she was and how she had come to be here. After Van explained, Hong Yen didn't thank him for saving her and refused to answer questions about her past. She only wanted to know how to reach Suong Ma Mountain.

"Why do you want to go there?" Van asked.

"On Suong Ma Mountain is Mist Wraith Pond," Hong Yen replied. "When I'm in sight of it, the pond's spirit, the Mist Wraith, will quench my longing and shape itself into my son."

"That legend is false. Even if it were true, you shouldn't spend your life with an inhuman thing. You're better off having another baby."

"Is Suong Ma Mountain one of those three over there?"

"It's nowhere in sight."

Trinh was stunned to hear Van lie. Why not let Hong Yen go to the mountain and see for herself?

Hong Yen cried, and Van stayed with her until morning. After that, Van spent all his nights with her and made Trinh sleep in his room instead. Loneliness lengthened Trinh's nights and made her sensitive to the songs of frogs and crickets blending in a harmony that surrounded but excluded her. It darkened her days, making her wish she could talk to someone, but none of the villagers would tolerate her complaints. Trinh put in more effort to pretty herself, padding her breasts and wearing jewelry. She tried to make meals more delicious and keep their house cleaner, but Van noticed none of it.

One day when Van was out fishing, Trinh took the chair next to her rival, who was sitting up in bed. Hollowness expanded in Trinh's chest as she faced the fact that her bed had become Van and Hong Yen's. Trinh had taught her rival to repair baskets the day before. They worked on a pile of them while Trinh tried to compose herself. She finished replacing a handle and admired her work.

"Hong Yen, don't you think these baskets are lucky? Here we are, restoring them, making them wanted."

"They are lucky since they can be restored. Many things cannot," Hong Yen said, looking from her basket to the window. "Do you really not know where Suong Ma Mountain is?"

Van had ordered Trinh not to tell, but after watching him spend night after night with Hong Yen, Trinh considered risking his wrath.

"If you can help me, perhaps I'll help you," Trinh said, setting down a basket and picking up another.

Hong Yen raised an eyebrow. "Really? What do you need help with?"

"I'm treated like a ghost here. Unseen. Unwanted. I've been Van's wife for nearly five months, yet I'm still a virgin. My husband spends his nights with you. Why?"

Hong Yen's face contorted into a snarl. "Why care

about a beast like him? You can give and give, but
he won't give back."

Trinh had assumed from Hong Yen's silk rags that
she had come from high society. Now she was sure
Hong Yen had been a prostitute, accustomed to manip-
ulating men. Trinh scooted away. She wanted to leave
the house but forced herself to complete her mission.

"Don't avoid my question."

Hong Yen groaned as though finally realizing how
stupid her hostess was. "Perhaps because I'm new.
Different. His fascination should wear off soon."

Months of helpless rage erupted. Trinh threw her
basket at the floor and stood up. "I've been new! I
was new to this village when I married him. He didn't
care for that. I had thought Van liked everyone else
better because he had known them longer. But you're
a newcomer. You're more of a newcomer than I am.
You don't tell anyone about your past, most likely
because it's dirty. Why doesn't Van care? Are you
that much more attractive?"

"I don't know," Hong Yen said, "but if you tell me
where Suong Ma Mountain is, I'll leave the village.
I'm sure that'll help."

Trinh clenched her fists. Hong Yen wouldn't spare
a thought for anyone or anything except a worthless
legend. "There's no such thing as a Mist Wraith."

"Yes, there is. When I find it, it'll look like my son
and know everything I know about him," Hong Yen
insisted, a wildness kindling in her eyes. "I'll have him
back. My dear son!"

Realizing she couldn't change Hong Yen's mind
about the Wraith's existence, Trinh tried another
angle. "I'm sure the spirit has its own shape to be
content with. Why not leave it alone?"

"Water doesn't have its own shape. Its nature is to
fill in gaps. Its spirit can be no different."

"How many Mist Wraiths do you think there are?"

Hong Yen frowned. "It's the spirit of a pond. Of
course there's only one."

"So, assuming it exists, what if it's already filling the gap in another mourner's life?"

"I'll kill that other mourner," Hong Yen said, her expression serious.

Chilled, Trinh stepped back from her.

"Tell me," Hong Yen said, pushing herself out of bed, her hair a tangled mass hanging down to her waist, her robes parting, revealing new bruises. She limped toward Trinh. "Where is it?"

Trinh's heartbeat quickened. What would Hong Yen do if she didn't answer? Where had the bruises come from? What had Van and Hong Yen been doing? Why shouldn't she tell Hong Yen where to go and be rid of her?

"Look out the window. See those three mountains? Suong Ma Mountain is the tallest one."

Hong Yen's wild eyes burned wilder. "That close?"

Trinh nodded.

Hong Yen rushed out barefoot, leaving the front doorway gaping in the morning sunlight. Trinh hurried outside and watched for trouble. Villagers stopped cleaning nets. Some of them asked Hong Yen where she thought she was going and that she should at least wear some shoes.

Carrying a basket of clams, Van's sister turned to Trinh. "Why the rush?"

"She had a dream about her son. She'll return when she realizes it was nothing but a dream," Trinh said hastily.

Van's sister shook her head. "You let her dream too much."

The villagers resumed their chores. Relieved, Trinh went inside and continued mending baskets as she thought about her future. Once Hong Yen discovered there was no Wraith, she would leave forever. Her departure would anger Van, but hopefully not for long. Trinh envisioned how she might comfort him and how he might come to love her.

The front door banged open. Van hung his hat on a hook and marched toward her.

"My sister says you let Hong Yen go. Why didn't you stop her?"

Trinh hesitated. "I couldn't. She would go or die."

"Where does she think her son is?"

"The tallest mountain," Trinh said, uncertain why. Perhaps it came from guilt.

"She'll search that mountain till she starves. I have to stop her," Van said, turning and leaving the house.

Trinh dropped her basket, ran outside, and caught Van's arm. "She's already gone mad. What's the use?"

Around them villagers paused, watching them.

"People don't have to stay mad," Van said. "They can recover. I can save her."

"How courageous of you!" his mother said, mending clothes in her shaded chair.

Seeing no way to dissuade Van at the moment, Trinh said, "Let me help you."

They searched the fields of slipper and cuckoo flowers and yelled for Hong Yen. As they neared Suong Ma Mountain, the flowers thinned and finally disappeared. The lush land sloped upward, the top half buried under fog. Trinh looked wistfully at a flock of geese flying in the opposite direction.

Van studied the mountain trail and found tracks, seemingly human. He ran. Trinh chased him. She stumbled over rocks. She breathed hard. But she would not lose him. Van slowed as the tracks faded and the fog thickened, hanging like layers of spider webs speared on the evergreens. The cold, pine-scented vapor was heavy in Trinh's every breath. Feet hurting, she glanced at the afternoon sun, a weak blur behind white veils.

They climbed higher. Pine trees leaned, their branches reaching sideways, the shape of their foliage cloud-like. Something nagged at Trinh. When she realized she had neither seen nor heard any animals in the past hour, the emptiness became terrifying.

The trail passed a small, stone house and forked. Van searched both paths for tracks, but fog overwhelmed him. He retreated to the house and knocked.

The door creaked open enough for a skinny man with matted, gray hair to peek out. "What do you want?"

"Have you seen anyone pass by here?" Van asked while Trinh looked over his shoulder.

"Oh!" the man said, his mouth melting into a huge grin. His teeth were rotting, and he smelled moldy. He opened the door wide. "Come in, friends."

Trinh stared at his strange outfit. A ripped purple vest. Yellow baggy pants tight at the waist and ankles. On his left foot, a green slipper that curled up at the toes. The right foot bare. Behind him were piles of rusting swords, pieces of armor, ratty clothes and shoes. Poor, rich, ancient, exotic. He had plenty of every style. Trinh wondered how someone so isolated could possess such a varied collection.

"I don't have time to waste," Van said. "Tell me if you've seen anyone pass by here."

"Plenty," the gray-haired man said.

"Today. What about today?"

"Today. Yesterday. What's the difference? Everyone at the pond. Everyone the same."

Van thought about that. "Where's the pond?"

"I can lead the way."

Van studied the man and wrinkled his nose. "No thank you. Give me directions."

Still grinning, the man pointed to the path on the left. "That way."

"Thank you."

As the man shut the door, Trinh thought she spotted a familiar cotton robe among the clothes, but she couldn't be sure. Van plunged into the fog.

"Stop!" Trinh cried, running after him.

The path took them higher and ended at a precipice. Nearby pines scattered before a pond. Evening sunrays bled through mist, glistening red on the water.

"Hong Yen!" Van yelled as he approached. Dirt softened into mud. He avoided weeds and kept to rocks. "Where are you?"

Trinh blocked his way. "Turn back. Haven't you

noticed how strange this place is? No animals any-where. Only that strange gray-haired man. Don't you have a bad feeling about this?"

"I'm waiting here until Hong Yen arrives. Go back on your own," Van said as mist coiled into brief shapes around him. A mass of tangled hair. A nose with a mole beside it. Hong Yen caressing him.

Horrified, Trinh didn't react in time when Van shoved her. Rocks scraped her hands. Mud grasped her skirts.

"Go on," Van said with a jerk of his head.

Trinh caught his ankle. "Please, Van, let Hong Yen go and return to the village."

"Oh, I know," Van said, his eyes narrowing at her. "You killed Hong Yen."

Trinh scrambled backward. "How can you think so?"

"You hid her body and told everyone she had left," Van said. In his eyes burned the wildness that had been in Hong Yen's.

"Everyone in the village saw her leave. Ask them," Trinh said, panic rising. She glanced side to side for an escape.

Van yanked a sharp, mossy rock out of the mud with both hands. "You've acted well. So patient. So helpful. But your show is over."

He advanced, raising the rock. Screaming, Trinh kicked his shin and rolled aside. Van fell, his rock hitting the ground, his head hitting the rock.

A crack. Silence.

Trinh watched for movement before finding the courage to near him. Van's eyes were open but no longer blinking. Trinh turned his head and smoothed away warm, bloodied hair. The side of his skull had been smashed.

Losing Van meant losing her honor. Trinh couldn't return to the village or to her parents.

She had to undo this damage. She had to repair his skull. She would do this, and he would recover. She would apologize for hurting him. He would under-

stand and be sorry for scaring her. They would go
home together. Ignoring the blood and its coppery
smell on her fingers, Trinh worked and worked, piec-
ing together her dream until she fell asleep beside him.

Night settled, waking her with chills. The moon slid
out from behind black clouds. The world appeared in
gray. Van was gone, leaving his shape in the moss and
mud. Fresh tracks, the left of a shoe and the right of
a bare foot, led back to the path. Trinh followed them
to the precipice. She leaned over. She couldn't see the
bottom through the fog, but she knew the gray-haired
man had dumped Van's body down there, stripped of
clothes and sandals like everyone else who had died
in their quest for the Wraith.

Mist rubbed against her legs. She stumbled to the
pond, half mad with the intention of making the
Wraith restore everything, half hopeful she was wrong
and Van had simply gone for a stroll. Her haggard
face looked back through floating pine needles and
jutting rocks. She sank to her knees, tears falling on
her bloodstained hands.

"Trinh, don't cry."

She was imagining her husband's voice. She knew
this. She was imagining his arm worming around her,
pulling her against his side.

"I'm sorry about Hong Yen. You won't leave me,
will you?"

She looked up. In his straw hat and rolled-up pants,
Van sat beside her, absorbing her tears as he brushed
his fingers across her cheeks. Trinh didn't want a
spirit, but she couldn't help clinging to it.

Smiling, the Mist Wraith solidified in her arms.

Written in Smoke

Karina Sumner-Smith

Coils of white rose slowly, smoke twisting into the air like rope unwinding. Blinking, Nasrah leaned over her makeshift incense burner and inhaled, drawing the haze deep into her lungs. She tried to focus on the smoke's sweet fragrance, its taste, its gentle movement through still air, as if such details could shield her from the sounds of her family dying outside the tent walls.

Before her bent knees small chips of resin smoldered in a clay cup, pale yellow flaring to red as they burned. They were so tiny, Nasrah thought. So few. She did not let the thought go further, only clenched her hand around the ruins of the golden pendant that had concealed the resin, long hidden beneath the layers of her dress. Her neck still stung from the bite of the cord on which it had hung, the silken necklace snapped in her haste.

Her other hand trembled against her gently rounded stomach, as if mere fingers could protect her unborn child.

Just outside, her aged father-in-law screamed curses at his attacker, his oiled blade hissing through the air. Nasrah closed her eyes as he gasped and choked wetly, and then came the thump of something large falling. There was a sound of steel entering flesh once, twice, and the crunch of heavy footsteps. Farther away, a child's cry rose shrill, and was silenced.

She had to bite her lip to keep from sobbing.

These tents had been her home, her safety. Here she had lived as A'isha, an identity birthed in empty sand from lips cracked and bloody, earned with humility and a willingness to work. Dark and quiet, A'isha had gained their trust, had been taken as wife by a man as strong as he was gentle, had been loved. Now the name seemed a curse, and the one who called herself "she who lives" breathed fragrant smoke as the people who had given her a home died for that shelter.

The slaughter felt endless, but at last the screaming stopped, the ring of blade on blade ceasing, the final pleas and whimpers of the dying whispering away to nothing. Then there was only the slow sound of footsteps across the stony ground—pausing, scuffing, kicking at unmoving bodies, and moving on.

On her knees, Nasrah stared ahead and watched through tears as breath and smoke mixed in the darkened confines of the tent. Then, the resin's fog steady and sweet all around her, she waited. They searched the largest tents first, as she'd known they would, the silent attackers speaking for the first time since they'd ridden up and greeted offers of spiced tea with drawn blades. Nasrah heard claims of ownership of the few treasures the tents held, though most of the attackers would leave empty-handed; her in-laws had not been rich in anything but laughter.

At last one approached the small tent at the camp's edge, its front closed and sides lowered despite the afternoon heat. A man brushed aside the heavy goat's-hair fabric, letting in a wave of fresh, dry air, and crouched to enter. He started when he saw Nasrah kneeling silently in a ring of worn cushions, and drew breath to cry out, hand reaching for his weapon.

Nasrah watched as he blinked in sudden confusion, his intent expression turning vague, mouth opened to cry words he had forgotten. He inhaled again, and his gaze slipped from Nasrah's face, slid down her body unseeing. At last his eyes settled on the clay cup and the last wisps of smoke rising above its lip. He sniffed.

"*Al-lubán*," he murmured. Frankincense.

He hadn't even struggled.

Cautiously, he stepped into the tent's shadowed interior, letting the flap fall closed behind him, trapping the rest of the precious smoke inside. Nasrah did not move as he began to search their few belongings, her husband's leather traveling bag and carved pipe, her sh'ela headdress beaded in blue; merely closed her eyes as A'isha's life was laid bare beneath the hands of this stranger.

He was soon joined by another, and this man's awareness of Nasrah's presence fled quicker, swept away in a breath of frankincense-scented air. Her skill, it seemed, had not faded in her years of hiding.

In silence she listened as they derided the threadbare clothes, the worn silver jewelry, as if they had believed they would find more. Why, she wanted to ask; why her family? But the frankincense smoke was too thin to coax answers from the strangers' distracted minds, too little to force them to talk. And in truth, what could they say that she didn't already know, hadn't learned in the first moment she'd seen the upraised blades: they had come for her. More than three years and uncounted stretches of desert sand lay between A'isha and her true identity as Nasrah bint Shahin, and never in that time had she revealed herself in the smoke or spoken the name of her lost people. And still they'd found her.

When they finally left the tent, they already spoke of the journey away. For a time she could hear them outside, one calling orders as others loaded the camels with stolen goods and water. She listened as they moved on, the camels' gait unhurried; listened as the sound of their small caravan faded; listened until she could hear nothing but sand.

And though she knew they were gone, Nasrah knelt in the center of the tent and shivered, suddenly more

afraid than even swords or the screams of the dying
had made her. For as the men passed but a hand's
length from her face, she'd smelled something on their
clothes that the tang of blood and sweat had hidden.
A scent both sharp and bitter, with a faint and lingering sweetness.

The scent of her people's enemy.

Myrrh.

The afternoon had begun to cool, light lengthening,
before Nasrah gained the courage to enter the smoke.
Much of the frankincense had escaped, gusting out the
opened tent's flap and seeping slowly through the
walls themselves. Still, she thought as she brought herself to the edge of trance, there would be enough. It
was not a tool, now; merely a door.

As she slipped into the smoke, the details of her
surroundings sharpened while the feel of her body receded. Her awareness drifted with the smoke, senses
swaying in eddies of air through the tent's shadowed
interior, easing through gaps in the fabric's weave and
expanding into the desert's heat. Rising to the farthest
edges of the incense she had burned, Nasrah leapt,
her awareness flying outward until it caught on another cloud of smoke, burning leagues distant: a small
temple on the edge of the desert, its stone altar at-
tended by a prone worshipper. Caught in the smoke
and all it touched, Nasrah knew she could influence
this man as she had the attackers, but left him to his
silent prayer.

Again she leapt, and again, again: to a small house
filled with young children, to a jewelry shop on the
southern coast, to an amir's harem. And with each
leap something of her stayed behind, as if she drew a
map of the world in her mind with the twisting passage
of frankincense clouds.

At last Nasrah slowed, not wanting to reach all the
way to Egypt or Parthia, though leaps of such distances were possible. Instead she peered at the whole,
seeking through smoke those who meant her harm.

Here and there she felt sharp sense of another mind of her blood, attuned to the smoke, but they were rare and scattered, the secret network of her people in disarray.

Perhaps, Nasrah thought, others hid from the smoke, as she had. A thin hope, and one she couldn't truly believe. Besides, she had been found even with her talent damped; she would not wait to be caught again unaware. Instead, she sought places where myrrh tainted the smoke, a shadow across the white, a sharp scent amidst the sweet.

Such flaws pulled—yet she found herself moving not towards the coast or foreign lands, but the desert's heart. With a cold shock, she recognized the place: the golden stone, the outline of a tumbled outer wall. The ruins of her true home. Irem's fallen pillars were before her, neither seen nor felt nor sensed, but something of all three. No frankincense burned here now, no people of the smoke waited: she found only silence and places unfilled. Yet the smoke lingered, years of its burning staining the city's very stones.

And here, even years distant, lay the evidence of a slaughter as terrible as the one outside her tent. The frankincense shuddered with the memory of fear and pain, as if the air itself still held the city's dying cries. And worse—

Nasrah jerked, eyes opening wide as if light could banish what the smoke held. But sight of the tent's dark walls couldn't hide what had been written in smoke for her to find. Through the lingering smoke burned a dark streak of myrrh, the Romans' funeral scent mocking the vast grave of her people, vivid against the frankincense like a bruise across flesh.

Smoke so new, so plentiful, could only be a sign. Even now, she realized, the enemy had a spy that stood in the ruins of her city and burned myrrh, plumes of incense rising skywards to remind her scattered people of their defeat and promise their deaths.

What did they want? Nasrah placed her head in her hands, her cheeks soaked with tears. Power hungry, her father had called the Romans, thieves and conquerors beneath the rule of a madman. A madman driven to rage by the thoughts of a talent he could not possess; driven to murder by knowledge of spies who could influence him, even kill him, through the very incense burned across his vast empire.

Who had whispered the secret of the Ad into the Roman emperor's ear, none had learned; not before the emperor had caused the fall of their great desert city. Was that not enough, she asked silently. Must he drive each survivor into the ground until all that was left of their blood was powder?

Even so distant, the scent of myrrh made her sick. Nasrah struggled to rise and cried out, cramped legs sending her sprawling across the cushions. Breath hissing through her teeth, she crawled out of the tent to the clean air beyond.

The air, and the dead.

Though little time had passed, the sun had already taken its toll on the fallen: blood dried to flakes on skin turned ashy, open eyes clouding as the dry air stole their tears. Beside the tent, her father-in-law lay curled, his bloodied sword beside him, caked in sand. Turning away, Nasrah struggled to her feet. She shut her eyes as she passed the main tent, unable to face what lay behind the women's shielding curtain where her sisters-in-law had hidden the smallest children.

She staggered onward. There, by the communal cookfire, lay her husband's aunt, face obscured by her favorite yellow scarf. There, the youngest of her husband's brothers, the flesh of his belly opened onto the ground. And there, just where she had last seen him, lay Talib, her husband. First to raise a hand in greeting, and first to fall. Nasrah approached with unsteady steps.

"Talib . . ." she whispered, dry voice cracking. If he hadn't been the first, the hateful thought came, she would have fought. She would have been beside him.

Her hand rose to clutch at her neck where her necklace had once hung, and she felt that she was choking on tears. "Talib, there wasn't enough for—" She couldn't say their names: his sisters, his baby nieces and nephews. Not enough smoke to fill the large tent, and not enough time to reach them safely. And the same hot afternoon breeze that tugged at her hair would have whisked the smoke away long before any could breathe it.

Yet she bowed her head, heavy with sorrow and guilt. "Talib," she whispered in confession. "I'm with child." A son who would never know his father.

And the one who had caused the slaughter of these people and her blood-kin alike hunted her, had writ his name clumsy and large in smoke that still trembled with cries of betrayal and death. She knew not what myrrh-puppet burned incense in the ruins of Irem, only that even a controlled mind could lead her closer to its true master. She would find the person responsible, be he the emperor himself; in body or smoke, he could not hide.

So she vowed, hands covering her hidden pregnancy. She would not falter.

And if she shuddered and collapsed, touched Talib's cooling body and his blood splattered across the gravel—if she threw back her head and wailed into the empty sky—it was only the last of the woman called A'isha, dying in her husband's arms.

When the sun set and she rose from the rocky ground, only Nasrah bint Shahin, last daughter of Irem, remained.

Nasrah left before dawn, whispering prayers of apology for leaving their bodies unburied. She had done what she could, but she was but one woman, and hunted. The attackers had stolen all but two thin, aged camels, and Nasrah took both: one to ride, and one to bear an extra burden of water. She left the familiar ground of the family's trading route, leaving the shadows of the coastal mountains for the empty desert. Her face and lashes turned white as she crossed the flats, her camels' feet churning up clouds of chalky powder. She navigated the dunes, hills of sand towering forty man-heights or more, and stumbled through rocky expanses that threatened even the camels' feet.

Even with all the water her camels could carry, she sought the wells she knew. Where they were guarded, she disguised her gender and paid, giving her bracelets, her red headscarf, Talib's pipe. At last she had to trade her second camel for enough food and water to finish her journey.

Soon, she guided her camel onto the old trading roads, wide trails pounded to rock firmness over centuries. Yet few traveled these routes now, choosing instead to forge more difficult paths to avoid fallen Irem, and she met no other travelers.

As she rode, Nasrah thought of the camp as she'd left it, the row of bloating bodies and their hideous wounds. She thought of her birth family, the people of her blood destroyed as the earth shook, screaming as the walls fell, vanishing below the sand.

Night and day she smelled myrrh, and her anger burned hotter than smoke.

Eight days passed before Nasrah was jarred from her furious remembrances by sight of a familiar ridge of limestone. Turning her camel, she hurried to the site, then fell to her knees and dug. Few had known of these places, fewer still among women, yet Shahin al-Adi had shown each of his daughters. Any who worked the smoke, he said, needed to know these places.

Nasrah trembled with fatigue before she uncovered one of the great stone vats, forgotten beneath the sand. The harvest had been stored here, frankincense of the finest quality hidden safely until it went to market. She forced aside the lid and filled her dress with chunks of the pale resin, and something inside her eased: if not the anger, then the fear that had laced it. She would not return to her city—or find the ones who hid in its ruins—unarmed.

Nasrah made a hasty camp, eating strips of dried fish before pitching a shelter of scarves and curling in their shade. Come nightfall, she would approach what was left of the city's walls, shrouded by darkness and sleep. She tried clear her mind of all but the tasks to come, yet memories of her home intruded. For the first time in years, she thought of the date groves planted at the city's heart by the Temple, kept green by water drawn from the great cavern below the city. There had been music and morning calls to market as the city's gates were opened to let traders enter. As a child, she'd lived immersed in Irem's riches: gold and cinnamon and cassia, silk and red Parthian pottery. Each day had smelled of frankincense, the resin's sweetness so constant that she only noticed its lack.

But for all those bright years, it was still the final days of Irem that remained vivid. Her father's last words seemed to echo around her.

Run, he'd screamed as he threw her over Irem's outer wall. *Hide!* Nasrah had hit the hard ground and rolled as the earth shook beneath her. She'd looked back, expecting to see her sisters following, her father and brother climbing the wall; yet saw only the great spire of the Temple shudder and slowly fall. Nasrah hid her face in her dress from the cloud of dust and rock, but mere cloth could not shield her from the sounds: a city screaming, earth and golden stone breaking as the City of Pillars tumbled into the ground.

Nasrah had hidden in the ruins of an outer tower as the few survivors pulled themselves from the ruins. But they were normal people, and Nasrah's calls into the smoke went unanswered. Many of the caravans camped beyond the city's walls fled after the earthquake, making signs against evil when the wounded begged for help or shelter. The very earth moved against the people of Ad, the traders said, their voices harsh; the lake in the vast cavern beneath the city had run dry in a day. Irem had been cursed and cast down; they would not bring that fate on their own.

In the tower's shadows, Nasrah had known that their words were true. Yet she alone smelled the evidence in the smoke, the scent that curled through the dust that choked the air and shadowed the sun: myrrh. Earth and water had turned against them, but only, she knew, at the hands of the Romans. Strange foreigners who wielded their smoke clumsily, the Romans were said to have other powers: mages who could control earth and water alike, gathered in their conquest of kingdoms and yoked to their empire's will with myrrh.

When at last she stumbled from the city, the sands around Irem were empty. With little food or water, she'd only managed a day's travel down the trade roads before collapsing. It was only chance that the young son of a trader saw her huddled form, and the grace of the divine that brought his family to care for her, treat her, until she returned to health.

Talib, she thought, and covered her growing belly with her hands.

Nasrah awoke to the sudden press of a hand across her face. She started upwards, thrashing and disoriented, but a man pushed down on her shoulders while his hand silenced her cries. Chewing, the camel watched dispassionately. She fought wildly, cursing herself for falling asleep, yet even against her nails and flailing arms the man stood unmoving. At last, Nasrah stilled, letting him haul her to her feet. At the sight of his weathered face, hope withered; she did not know him.

Yet it was the man who waited some steps distant that made Nasrah freeze like prey. Neither tall nor imposing, he stood like royalty, watching her. His head was covered with a pale cloth bound with a brown band, and the trailing edges had been drawn across his face, leaving only his eyes exposed. Yet even so disguised, the man could not hide his heritage. Burned and peeling, his skin was too pale for a man of the desert; the nose that shaped the fabric too sharp and aquiline. Most startling was the color of his eyes: a brown so pale it rivaled the desert, flecked with green.

Roman, she named him, and spat on the sand at his feet.

The desert man struck her face with a closed fist and she fell, ears roaring.

A trap, she thought, struggling to think through the furious sound, struggling to breathe. A trap, all of it—the murders a ploy designed to make her seek the power and protection of the smoke. This Roman would have seen her frankincense burn through the smoke as surely as she'd seen his plume of myrrh—he had been watching, waiting. And, armed only with incense and a knife, she had run straight to him.

He killed them, she thought, tasting bile. He had killed them all.

She looked up in time to see the Roman flick a dismissive hand, and speak. His words might have been unintelligible, but his meaning was not; she had a moment to steel herself before the other man's hands were upon her, dragging her upright and searching her clothes. Her face flushed hot, and she turned her head away from the men, jaw tight. He was efficient, finding the chunks of frankincense hidden inside the layered fabric of her dress and rolled into her sleeves, and tossing them into the Roman's outstretched hands.

Nasrah whimpered, reaching unbidden for the incense. The Roman snorted and turned, trusting the other man to bring her. Still reeling, Nasrah staggered behind as they traveled across the sand. The sun had all but vanished before they crested a last rise and Nasrah's ruined city lay before them.

There were no towers now to mark Irem's presence, only empty space where the spires and pillared buildings had once risen above the desert like a sultan's palace. The city's great wall was but a tumbled-down ring of yellow stones; and where the caravans had gathered, tents and camels spread out from the city like a sea, there was only sand.

Nasrah stumbled, staring at the hole where once stood her home. Though sand had covered most of the city's surviving walls, the empty space still gaped wide as the day she'd first seen it, as if having devoured all of Irem it struggled to swallow more. The Roman laughed at Nasrah's expression, and gestured widely towards the city as if towards strange riches. Still laughing, he led the way across ground pounded flat by untold centuries of tents, traders, and camels' feet, to a small camp hidden just inside the ruins of the great wall.

"Sit," the desert man commanded her, pushing her to the ground. Traitor, she named him in the depths of her mind. She could smell no myrrh on him, and yet he worked as the Roman's guide, had allowed this enemy to cross the sands where no foreign foot had before stepped. He knelt, and carefully lit a small fire, already set, to help stave off the desert's creeping cold.

Yet it was not only against the cold that the fire burned, Nasrah saw, watching as the Roman locked away her frankincense in a wooden box, and filled his hands with deep amber pieces of myrrh. He placed the largest piece in a stone dish lined with wood chips that he lit from the open flame. Smoke curled upwards and he quickly blew it across her face. As myrrh filled her lungs, the Roman attacked through the smoke.

Nasrah pulled back in surprise. She had heard of the crudeness of control gained with myrrh-smoke and the fumbling skill with which the Romans employed it, but never had she imagined anything so primitive. The pressure of the smoke against her mind had power, yes, but no smoothness, no subtlety. Mere noise where she'd expected song.

She looked up at this man, the creases of concentration between his pale eyes, the rawness of his sunburned skin. It took no blood-talent to wield myrrh, she remembered; only practice. And it seemed clear that this Roman had never been submitted to the daily tests she had endured, the constant smoke-borne struggle of wills between sisters to decide who would sweep the hearth and who would steep tea, which one of them would mend the clothing while another got first use of the washwater.

If he wanted her to submit, she thought, he would be better served to bind her with rope. Yet she let her eyes go wide and pushed back through the smoke, pitiful struggles, while in truth she held his invasion at bay. She fought briefly, in body and smoke, and then sagged in the traitor's arms. The Roman's smoke enveloped her, bitter myrrh in every breath.

"You stay," the Roman commanded in his halting attempt at her language. "You listen only to me. Only."

"Yes," Nasrah said, nodding weakly.

With this, the questioning began. Though the traitor was forced to translate, the Roman seemed to follow her responses, watching intently. Where she could, Nasrah told the truth or feigned ignorance of matters usually kept from women. She spoke of frankincense groves and trading routes, the resin's price at market. She spoke of the talent of smoke, the exercises and tests to hone the inborn skill—practiced by her father and brother, she said, but never herself. Never her sisters.

She grew confused when he spoke of spies, frightened when he pressed for details of the men of Ad, disguised as merchants and traders, scattered across his empire. He tested her truthfulness and the smoke's control, and Nasrah danced on blade's edge to hide her deception. The questions seemed endless, yet at last the Roman was satisfied. He sighed, then asked, "Do you have children?"

"No," she said.

"Are you with child?"

"No."

At this, the Roman muttered something and leaned back, shaking his head.

"She lies," the desert man said, once more a traitor. Nasrah flushed, suddenly remembering the feel of his hands searching her dress and her body beneath.

"A lie?" the Roman asked haltingly in her tongue, his accent mangling the words. A hint of a smile touched his face. "You fight the smoke. Your blood is strong. Powerful."

"I don't—" she began, but he brushed the words away.

"Frankincense. The empire needs this power." As he spoke, he placed another chip of myrrh in the dish.

Pretenses dropping, Nasrah's voice twisted with scorn. "You can't learn it, Roman, and you can't steal it from blood."

"No?" the Roman asked, and gestured to her midsection.

"No! Not my son—" Nasrah choked into silence as the Roman lit the resin and it burst into flame, smoke billowing into her face.

She pulled back, blinking, as the men's faces, Irem's crumbling walls, seemed suddenly to spin and sway around her. She did not fight but reached out, fingers grasping empty air.

"You are young," the Roman said, smiling as he wafted more smoke towards her. "Your first child, yes? You will have more."

Again, the Roman blew bitter myrrh in her face, drowning her senses, stinging her eyes and her throat. Nasrah coughed and inhaled. She could feel the Roman's sudden press upon her mind, his presence closer than the smoke that swirled between them. The sickening scent surrounded her, sharp and spicy, and her body began to shake as it filled her.

Eyes wide, Nasrah opened her mouth to scream, to cry—

But there was only myrrh.

It was full dark before the Roman at last settled down to sleep, gesturing for the desert man to keep watch. Nasrah listened as the traitor's steps receded, listened as the Roman's breathing slowed, listened to the fire popping in the silence of the desert night.

Then slowly, Nasrah pushed herself upright and

rolled her shoulders to loosen them of the tension from her feigned tremors. Only myrrh, she thought; and the Roman was not the only one to lay traps. She looked down at his naked face, then reached into her clothing, fingers seeking hidden seams while the fire before her crackled and burned.

"You know little of frankincense, Roman," Nasrah said at last, her voice quiet enough to be the play of wind across sand. "We of Irem, we were born of it: we inhale it in our first breath and our spirits ride its smoke after death. The first harvest of the resin—it comes as a shock. A blade from nowhere, a gash in smooth bark, sap dripping like tears."

With a flick of her wrist, she cast a handful of what seemed to be small stones towards the fire. They pattered to the desert sand like rain. "The second cut opens that old wound. The resin runs stronger, faster, more plentifully during the second harvest—but its quality is not the same."

She barely moved, and yet again there came a sound of something falling to the ground—larger pieces, this time, and more of them. "But the third . . . the tree's third harvest needs not cut long nor deep, and yet from that slice comes the finest resin. Smoke fit for the sultan, the smallest piece worth more than gold."

And again her hand flashed from the shadows of her sleeve, and tossed something into the stones ringing the fire. As she watched, it began to smoke. "You killed my family," Nasrah bint Shahin said. "You turned your mages against us, cast our city into the sand, then hunted the gift of our blood nearly to extinction."

She looked up and stared into the Roman's slumbering face, his features made harsh in the fire's light. "You killed my husband. You killed his family down to the smallest child, and they knew nothing of our war. You ruined what joy I'd found."

From all around the fire, tiny shapes that had seemed to be stone suddenly smoldered red, wisps of white rising from their pale surfaces.

"But now, Roman, you threaten my son." Nasrah shook her head slowly, one steady hand resting across her belly. "I will not let you take him."

With a flick of the wrist, she cast the last and largest piece of resin into the fire.

With the sound of the frankincense falling into the embers, the Roman started awake, his eyes going wide as he looked from her steady gaze to the fire. He reached blindly, though for sword or myrrh, she did not know—and he was too late. For the smoke had already surrounded him in slow wisps and eddies as he'd slept, and the plume of white that rose from the fire's core only gave her the strength to tighten her hold on his mind.

"When you wake," she told him, her will echoing through the smoke, "you will take us from here. You will leave off the search for my people—I am the last of Irem, the last of this blood, and you will know it to be true. I carry a son, and you will believe him be a product of this night. You will know and love and care for my child as your own, and will let me live to raise him."

His eyes were dark in the firelight, his whole body trembling in fear and rage as he struggled fruitlessly against her control. It did not matter if he could not understand her words; the smoke needed no language.

"You will think me harmless," she whispered savagely, even as she forced him to close his eyes and drove his struggling mind back down into sleep. "And each night you will burn frankincense to sweeten our home."

The Roman collapsed into his blankets as if cut down, his head striking the ground with a loud thump. Drawn at last by the noise and movement, the traitor hurried back to the fire and stared at the Roman's limp form. "What have you done to him?" he hissed, keeping his distance.

Nasrah bowed her head, and murmured, "He has . . . tired himself." A subtle wisp of smoke reinforced the misdirection of her words. The traitor shot her a look of disgust, then turned his back on them both, returning to his sentry.

At last, Nasrah lay back in her blankets, Irem's fallen wall at her back and both arms wrapped across her belly. Tears slipped down her cheeks as she stared at the coil of white still rising from the fire's heart. But for her child's presence, she felt empty.

"Is it enough?" she whispered at last. The smoke held no answers, only curled and twisted as it vanished into the dark.

THE AGE OF SAIL

By the end of the Middle Ages, when the Renaissance had sparked scientific inquiry and classical thought once more, great sailing vessels crisscrossed the seas, seeking faster routes, delivering the riches and wonders of far distant lands with greater and greater speed. Foreign treasure fueled exploration and wars, but these vessels were limited by one necessity: they relied upon the wind. The race was on to find the best way to harness nature's tempestuous resource, for to control the seas was to control the world.

Cloud Above Water

Natalie Millman

Cloud pulled at the skin on her arm. She scratched it, bit it, and pulled it again, trying to pull it off. It squeezed her, crushed her spirit. Trapped in its tight prison, she thought she'd go mad.

The darkness weighed on her too, and the awareness of being underground. Cloud was a creature of light and air, not of earth and stone. But far worse than being surrounded by mud and rock was being caged inside this skin. She tore at it until it bled. If she couldn't get out soon, she would go mad.

Sound cut the silence. Cloud froze. The man was coming, and he would be angry. Frantically she dabbed at the welling blood. When he had found her bleeding the first time he had stretched this body's arms far apart and chained them to the wall. The metal had burned, scorched like fire, though it left no mark. Iron, the man had called it, Cold Iron. He seemed to think it would mean something to her.

It did not. In fact she didn't understand most of what the man said to her, though he carried on at great length sometimes. Whether it was the shock of transition and would pass, or whether this was a place the People had not been before, she didn't know. But she did know the man was becoming more and more frustrated with her lack of response.

The door scraped open. Cloud caught a fleeting

glimpse of light beyond, and though it was only torch-
light, she yearned all the more for sun. Waiting while
his eyes grew accustomed to her dim cell, the man
spoke. "Areyougoingtocooperatetoday?"

Cloud strained to put meaning to the words. There
seemed a threat behind them. The body moved one
leg, and the tether attached to its ankle clanked. He
had wrapped a piece of soft leather tightly around that
leg before fastening the metal to it, a kindness he
could easily take back. "Botheringyouisit?" The man
fitted his torch into a bracket and pushed the door
shut with a dull thud. He crossed the little room in
three steps to loom over her. "Icanfixthat," he said.
"Icanremovethe Cold Iron andsetyou free."

Cold Iron. Free. Three words she understood. Three
words. But how to put them together? Free he had
shown her. On his last visit he had conjured a vision—
a bird flying—and had told her, *free*. Cold Iron he had
named when he fastened it onto this prison of a body.
Panic gripped her as the man leaned closer. "What's
this?" He had said that before too. Cloud tried to hide
the bloody arm, but he caught it in his big fist, looked
at it, and shook his head. "No!" he said. He rattled
one of the chains he had used earlier. "MustIusethisa-
gain?" His voice was so loud it hurt her. She flinched
and cowered as far away as she could with one ankle
held fast. Dropping the hated metal links, the man put
his finger to the ragged red furrows her nails had
carved in the smooth brown skin. "No!" he repeated,
and she learned another word.

So it went. With no sight of sun or moon, Cloud
had no way to tell how long she lay imprisoned underground or how often the man came. She began to
know this body she wore, to understand the difference
between the rolling of its gut and the pumping of
blood through arteries and veins, between the cramp-
ing of muscles held too long in one place and the
grinding of sinew and bone when she tried to move.
There were scores of such sensations. They were not
pain, but they were hideous.

"Food," said the man on one visit, and threw something to the floor beside her. She looked at it without comprehension, but the body responded with a lurch of its innards. "Food," said the man again, pointing. "Eat." The body told Cloud what to do. Arms reached of their own accord toward what the man had brought, bringing handfuls of it to the mouth. The mouth chewed and swallowed. Cloud was horrified, but understood. This body needed sustenance other than wind and sun. This body needed what the man brought, it needed *food*. Perhaps that was a good thing since there was no sun or wind in this dark, still, and soundless place.

The People didn't sleep, not exactly, but sometimes when the body was quiet Cloud dreamed. In her dreams she soared on the wind, riding the air currents clothed in nothing but sunlight. She breathed in the joyous perfumes of multicolored flowers and played among their petals. She drank sweet rainwater and sipped at nectar, though light and air were nourishment enough.

It was while dreaming that she first felt the presence of the other. High in the sky she flew, looking down on forests and mountains and gently rolling oceans, when suddenly she felt the scream. Not heard it, felt it, for the scream had no true voice, but the terror in it was plain. It shook Cloud out of her flight and she plunged back into the dark, unnatural world of the cell, into the tight confines of skin and the not-quite-pain of constantly pulsing organs. "Hello?" she thought into the silence when she got her bearings. "Who screamed?" It was a silly question, and she did not expect an answer. She was alone; she had known that from the beginning, completely, unbearably alone.

Yet answer someone did, softly, timidly. "Me. I screamed. You scared me with your flying."

"Who are you?" thought Cloud, then, "Where are you?"

There was a long pause, as if the owner of that small voice was wondering how to answer. But just as

Cloud decided it must have been only a part of her dream, the whisper returned, tiny and tentative. "I am Jata. Please, can I have my body back?"

"I don't understand," thought Cloud. "This is yours, this skin I am wearing?"

Fear radiated from somewhere deep inside, perhaps the place to which this Jata had been banished. "You are not the wizard?" asked the thought-voice in despair.

"I am Cloud Above Water," Cloud told the voice, "I am of the People. I do not know how I got here, or how I am kept here. If I could, I would leave."

"You cannot give my body back to me?" the voice asked softly.

"I am sorry," Cloud tried to cushion the thought with good will.

The voice considered this. "Then we are both lost," it said with infinite sadness.

Something in the resignation of that statement stirred Cloud's soul. "No," she thought firmly. "We are not lost. We will find a way."

After that the body began to feel less alien, more as if it belonged to her. At first that frightened Cloud more than when she'd first awakened to find herself entrapped, but Jata whispered to calm her. She helped Cloud learn to move the limbs to her will, and to use spoken language. The man gave commands: stand up, turn around, smile. When she obeyed he rewarded her with food, or with a torch left in the bracket on the wall until it burned out. When she refused, he punished her with Cold Iron.

Eventually he gave her a different command. "Summon wind." It could not be done, of course, not in a hollow under the earth, and in this way the wizard proved his ignorance. Speaking to wind or any other element required that she be in touch with sun and sky. In any case, wind or water, earth or fire, the things of nature, these were not to be ordered about. They would speak with her if they wished, would play with her if that was their mood, but they belonged to themselves, as she did. She told him so, using the body's voice for the first time. The man's eyes glittered with a triumph that puzzled her. She expected punishment. Instead, he simply left.

He returned after a shorter time than was usual, but he was not alone. He was talking to someone; his voice came to Cloud muffled by the thick wood of the cell's door. "The binding is firm this time, you will see." There were the familiar scraping sounds of the drop bar being lifted.

"The goods, Mugi, the goods. I did not pay you for promises." The new voice was cold. Cloud shrank into herself. She hated this place, she hated the man, but at least she knew what to expect of him.

"Indeed you did not, sir," said the man, and the door opened. The man, Mugi—he had a name now—stepped inside and placed his torch in the usual bracket, then reached behind him and produced a second torch. Holding it high, he made a sweeping gesture with his free arm, inviting the owner of the cold voice into Cloud's cell. "Come, Gitonga, and see what it is you did buy."

They crossed the floor and stood looking down at her. Cloud huddled against the wall, too conscious of the tethered ankle that held her to this spot.

Gitonga wrinkled his nose. "Doesn't look like much," he said.

"No," Mugi agreed. "But it's what's inside that counts. Your Elemental's in there, Gitonga, well bound and trained to obey." He turned to Cloud with a warning in his eye. "Stand up." She hesitated fractionally and the man reached toward a set of iron chains. Cloud leapt to her feet. "Turn around," he ordered, and she did.

Cold Voice nodded and they left her standing there while they discussed terms further. "What's my guarantee that this one will last? The others didn't."

"Ah," said Mugi triumphantly. "This one is different. It has gained full control of the body. It even speaks."

For the first time, Gitonga looked interested. He

raised an eyebrow. "Really?" Then with the same grim-
ace of distaste he had worn when he first approached,
he leaned down to inspect Cloud more closely. "And
just how did you manage that?" he asked.

Mugi shrugged. "Perhaps it was younger than the
others, more adaptable. I cannot say for sure, we don't
understand these things fully. But you came to the
right magician for your needs, sir. Not many can trap
these creatures, and I have had more success than any
other. I think you will find that you get your money's worth."

Gitonga turned his stony face to the man. "If not,
wizard, you'd better be far from here when I come
looking. Two failures I will forgive, a third . . ." He
let the threat hang. With a last snort of disgust in
Cloud's direction, he made for the door, adding,
"Very well. Clean her up, she stinks. Dress her appropriately and have her brought to my ship at dawn.
Make sure you send irons with her."

Mugi bowed, though Gitonga wasn't looking. "And
the final payment, sir?" he dared to ask.

Gitonga stopped in his tracks, appearing to consider, then spoke to the hallway rather than turn back
into the cell. "If your construct performs well and my
ship returns laden from a successful voyage, then you
will get your final payment." Without another word,
he was gone.

Mugi looked after the cold-voiced man for a full
minute, then turned to regard his captive. He took the
chains of Cold Iron and fastened them tightly about
her wrists. "To remind you what you are," he said.
Ignoring her cries, he bent to her ankle and pulled
the thin strip of leather free, allowing the metal to
touch her skin. It burned like fire. "You will perform
well for the merchant Gitonga, or suffer the consequences," he said. He was already halfway out the
door, when, as if remembering something, he turned
to Cloud again. "When the woman comes to make
you presentable, the Cold Iron will come off." And

though she had done nothing wrong, he took away the torch, leaving her in utter darkness.

Cloud was weeping when a woman entered. She placed a torch in the bracket beside the door and went back outside. Moments later she returned, carrying a basin and cloth; the basin looked heavy. Setting her burdens down, she removed the Irons, but for the cuff around Cloud's leg, muttering sympathies and clucking her tongue over the cruelties of men. Then, gently, she set about washing away the layers of filth.

To be outside again was exquisite pleasure. Despite the whimpering of the little voice inside her, Cloud lifted her face to the morning sun, drinking in its soul-restoring rays. She breathed deeply, savoring the scents of growing things, soil, and salt water. Beneath her feet the red earth was soft and warm, and she felt its murmuring life respond to her presence. *Welcome,* it said, *welcome among us.* There were trees nearby, narrow-leafed and gray-trunked. *Welcome, little one,* they told her. A bright yellow bird begged her, *fly with me,* flowers nodded her along, and best of all the wind caressed her, curling around the borrowed limbs, softly stroking the confining skin. *We will play together,* it promised.

Jata was terrified, afraid of the ship. But the idea of a sailing vessel was something Cloud simply could not understand, no matter that Jata had tried to explain it to her. The People did not have ships, they had no need of them. If the People wanted to travel on water, they simply did so, without the aid of wood or sail. Unable to comprehend Jata's fear, Cloud had no way to comfort her. Nor could she share her delight in being once more under sun and sky.

The wizard took no chances. He hired guards to help him take Cloud from his lair through the village of round, woven-twig huts to the ship, and he fastened a collar of Cold Iron about her neck. It was linked by a chain to the wrist of one guard, a piece of cloth kept

it from touching her skin. Jata wanted her body to
run away, but it was not possible. What good would
it do anyway, to run away in this body? Cloud went
as she was told and tried not to notice the links of
Cold Iron that from time to time brushed against her.

They came at last to the water's edge, and stopped.
The ocean greeted Cloud with quiet joy, reaching to
lap gently at her feet. *Come to me, sister,* it murmured.
She wiggled her toes in the mud, longing to be part
of the delightful dance of sun, wind, and water. But
Jata retreated, frightened into silence.

After a time Gitonga joined them, having already
supervised the loading of his cargo—ivory, precious
wood, and gold. Given luck, his vessel would return
with fine eastern cloth and spices that he could trade
along his own coast and up the Narrow Sea into Kush
and Kemet. "I'm surprised to see you here yourself,
Mugi," he told the wizard, then looked at the body
Cloud wore, scrubbed clean, hair meticulously braided
in dozens of thin black plaits and decorated with tiny
shells that made music when she walked. He nodded
his approval. "She cleaned up well," he said. "I'll have
to tell my captain to curb his men."

Mugi rubbed his chin thoughtfully. "It must not be
toyed with, sir, I cannot be held responsible for its
behavior if it is treated roughly. That is not a woman
there, but a tool to make you rich."

"And you, if the tool works well," Gitonga reminded him. "Is that not so? Isn't that why you came
today, to see your creation begin her work and rub
your hands in anticipation of the hefty payment to
come?"

Mugi inclined his head; it was true. He'd never had
wealth to spare, and his experiments with Elementals
had consumed nearly everything. This was his one
chance to live a comfortable old age. But his greater
motive was fame. He wanted his name to be whispered with awe in the spice lands on the other side of
this ocean, and all the way to the far north, where it

was said ice and snow lay unmelting on the ground
for half the year. He wanted his memory to live on
long after the earth claimed his body.

Cloud heard the talk with little understanding and
less interest. She was enraptured by ocean and air.
The wooden ship sitting offshore meant nothing to
her, and the outrigger now approaching to take her
to it was lost in the dazzle of sun on wave.

The merchant squinted, gauging the progress of the
little craft. "Does she understand her duties, wizard?"

"I have explained, but it will understand better once
it is aboard," Mugi said. "Tell the captain that if it
proves difficult, he need do no more than remove the
cloth from around its neck and let the Iron touch its
skin. It will mend its ways quickly enough then."

They watched in silence for some minutes as the
outrigger cut a swift path through the turquoise water,
then Mugi asked, "Why do you not simply use oars?
Why do you persist in this new way of moving boats
when so far it has not proven worthwhile?"

Gitonga gave him a twisted smile. "Why do you
persist in your experiments? Sail is the way of the
future, Mugi. In time, sail will rule all the oceans, and
the oceans will rule trade. If I can ensure fair winds
for my ships and those of my loyal friends, together
we will amass such riches . . . Wealth means power,
my friend wizard. It is not war that will conquer the
world, but trade."

A low swell helped the canoe draw smoothly up to
shore where it settled with a crunch, leaning lopsidedly
on its outrigging. The guard holding Cloud's chain
tugged her toward it. She took several steps, but a
scream began deep in the recesses of the body where
Jata now lived. It built, and built, until it blocked out
even the welcome song of the ocean, and Cloud herself wanted to scream. She found her feet rooted in
the mud.

"She looks afraid, Mugi," Gitonga commented.

"It can't be afraid; it is a creature of the elements.

It's simply balking at doing what it's told." The wizard splashed through the shallow water toward Cloud, his purpose plainly written on his face.

"Stop it, Jata!" Cloud thought at the screamer. "Stop it! There is no hope underground. On the sea with sky above and touching wind we will find a way. We will!" The screaming subsided and Cloud was able to go where she was led.

"You see?" said Mugi looking back at Gitonga from where he stood knee deep in seawater. "Even the threat is enough. Tell your captain it will perform well."

The wizard did not climb into the outrigger, but Gitonga the merchant did. The guard holding Cloud's chain got in, pushed her to the floor and crouched behind her, watchful. Mugi had paid him well. One of the paddlers pushed them free of the pebbly sand and jumped in, then he and his fellow put their backs to their task.

The ship seemed no more strange to Cloud than any other not-of-nature thing had seemed. It sat tall in the water, its wooden hull creaking with the movement of the swell, its single mast reaching for the sky. It smelled of pitch and sun-baked sailors, and after being borne upon the waves by the outrigger, Cloud had a better idea of what it was for.

The sailors reached down strong arms and hauled her up, deposited her like cargo on the deck. Then the guard drew himself over the side and landed next to her. Gitonga came up last, and with little more ceremony.

The men of the ship inspected Cloud with more than curiosity. One spoke, one whose skin was a lighter shade of brown and whose words were oddly accented. "This is your secret weapon, Gitonga? This little girl? She looks more like something for our amusement on long voyages. If so, you of the Zenj coast are thoughtful indeed."

"Watch your tongue, Kanja, or I will find myself another captain," the merchant snapped angrily. "I will not excuse impertinence simply because you are from the outside." Then he raised his voice so the whole crew could hear. "She is not what she seems and is not to be touched. Listen closely; I will explain only once."

Cloud did not listen, for the guard had dragged her to the mast and was busy with the chain. He looped it around the bottom of the sturdy pole, where it went through the deck and disappeared below. For the first time she noticed that the link at the end he'd been holding was open. Hooking that link through a closed one, he took a tool he'd brought with him, and hammered it shut. She was secured. He pulled mightily at the new join to be sure, then stepped away.

Finished with his instructions, Gitonga approached Cloud as she huddled at the foot of the mast. For the first time he addressed her directly. "Well, my little Elemental, now we'll find out if you are worth what I paid for you. Perform to my satisfaction, and you will be rewarded. Refuse your task and you will be punished." He made a motion as if to remove the cloth buffer between skin and Cold Iron. Cloud cringed and he backed off, his point made.

She had expected Gitonga to stay. Instead, after exchanging a few more words with the one he called Kanja, he went over the side to the waiting canoe. Shortly she saw him climb out to stand with the wizard on shore.

The ship erupted in activity. Above Cloud's head a huge triangle of heavy cloth was pulled up the mast from a crossbar—this was a sail. The wizard had told her about it, but she had been unable to understand until now. At last it came clear what they would ask of her.

Jata was keening deep inside the body where she lived, a steady soundless wail that spoke of fear so great it could not be adequately expressed. Cloud tried to comfort her to no avail; the girl was beyond knowing anything but that she was at sea, with no dry land to stand upon.

In air that was deathly still, the sail fluttered loosely.

Kanja scowled at the limp cloth, then at the sky. He walked the length of the deck in cool, determined strides, and shaded his eyes with his hand, scanning the ocean as if searching for something. "By Manat," he muttered, "this is a poor place for wind!" Cloud watched warily. Eventually he lowered his hand, turned, and came toward her.

He was big, this man. Bigger than the wizard Mugi, bigger than the merchant Gitonga. He towered over Cloud, staring down at her with open contempt. "So," he said, and nudged her with his foot. "I'm told you can work weather. Prove it. Make the wind blow. Make it fill our sail and send us across the sea to the land of silks and spices."

Cloud knew what the punishment would be should she not obey. She had also been promised reward if she did well. But how could they reward her? There was nothing of theirs she could possibly want, only her freedom. And that, no matter what she did, they would never give her. She must find a way to take it from them.

Kanja nudged her again and this time Cloud responded. She struggled to her feet, fighting the tether that dragged at her neck. The man did nothing to help her. On the shore, Mugi and Gitonga stood straighter to watch. Cloud lifted her arms and closed her eyes, feeling the sun against their lids. "I am Cloud Above Water," she sent her silent message into the sky. "Who will play with me?"

At first it was only the gentlest of caresses as the wind acknowledged her presence. *Little sister,* it murmured, tasting the skin that confined her, weaving itself around her borrowed arms, her legs, her body, wisping over her rounded cheeks and full, red lips. *Little sister, we will play.* The wind breathed out in a great sigh, the sail billowed from the mast and filled. Ropes strained, the wooden hull screeched in complaint, and waves splashed laughing over the bow as the ship began to move.

In a babble of excited voices, sailors ran barefoot

to their tasks. The captain stared in astonishment at
the burgeoning sail before sprinting to the stern and
his post at the great steering oar. On shore Mugi
grinned and rubbed his hands together, more de-
lighted with his achievement than with the payment
he could now expect, and already planning his next
capture. Gitonga nodded to himself cautiously. This
time perhaps the wizard's spell would work, but he
would not inventory his return cargo until it was un-
loaded and arrayed at his feet. The two men watched
as the ship headed toward the horizon at a speed that
could never be matched by oars alone. They watched
until the glare of sun on wave made them close their
eyes and turn away.

Well beyond sight of any land, the long swells of mid-
ocean produced an illusion of greater stability. Jata crept
out of her hiding place, the need to find out what was
happening finally greater than her fear. "Hello?" she
ventured tentatively. "Hello, are you here?"

Cloud didn't answer. She lay despondent on the
hard planks under the mast. Wind had abandoned her,
not understanding why she did not rise and soar.
Water lapped at the hull of the boat, but did not climb
over the bow to cool the body she wore. It no longer
called to her, *sister, sister*. Only sun stayed with her,
feeding her spirit, until now keeping a small hope
alive. But she had been unable to free herself from
the body, or the body from its Cold Iron leash, and
she could not imagine how it might be done.

A shadow fell across her. Kanja. He pushed her
with his foot. "What are you playing at?" he inquired
roughly. "Get up."

Cloud shook her head. "It will do no good," she
said softly.

"I will not sit here becalmed," the captain insisted,
and reaching down, he wrenched her to her feet. "Call
up the wind," he ordered. Anger radiated from him,
hot and violent.

"Wind does not answer to any command," she tried

to explain. "It chooses its own course. Now it has chosen to go elsewhere because I could not fly with it." She had tried to tell the wizard this could happen, but men like these seemed to recognize only obedience or disobedience. Kanja took her words for refusal. Cloud shrank against the mast, waiting for the punishment she knew must come. Quick as lightning he snatched away the cloth protecting her delicate skin from the Cold Iron collar. Fire! It burned! Cloud sank slowly to the deck and curled into a ball.

"Let's see how long your defiance lasts," said the captain, and walked away.

For the second time, Cloud wept. Before her entrapment, she had not known what weeping was.

"What is the matter?" Jata asked from somewhere not quite as deep as before. "Why are you crying?"

In her sorrow and pain Cloud had almost forgotten Jata, whose body she wore so bitterly. "I told you I would find a way to set us free, but it cannot be done. We are, as you have said, lost." Instead of retreating in panic, the girl reached out in love and comfort. It was like being enfolded by a warm and gentle breeze. Cloud let herself be lulled, even though the fire of Cold Iron coursed through her still.

"What do you need to be free?" Jata asked her.

"I need to leave this body," Cloud told her simply. "But I know of no way to do it. I thought that sun, wind, and water would help me, but they know no more than I. And they have no power over the Cold Iron that binds us to this ship."

Jata pondered. "If you were free of this body, then the Cold Iron would not hold you," she said.

"But there is no way to be free!" Cloud blurted in frustration.

"Except perhaps . . ." Jata began, and she did not need to finish.

Cloud grew still. This was something she had not considered. What would happen to her if Jata's body no longer existed? What would happen to Jata?

"There is no other way, Cloud Above Water." For

the first time Jata called Cloud by her name. "Neither of us can live any longer like this."

It was true. If Cloud was not released from this skin soon, she would surely go mad. "Are you not afraid?" she asked Jata, for the girl had been afraid always.

"Yes," said Jata. "But I am more afraid of having to stay like this forever. Are you afraid, Cloud?"

"Yes," said Cloud, "But I am more afraid of being trapped this way forever." She felt as if someone took her hand.

"Then we will speak to the wind together," Jata said.

With grim satisfaction Kanja watched the Elemental struggle to her feet again. He would withhold the cloth, he decided, until she had filled the sails. She lifted her arms to the sky and closed her eyes.

For a long time nothing happened, and the captain began to wonder if she was truly doing anything. Then a breeze ruffled his clothing, and the sail flapped loosely. He shouted orders to the men, and took the steering oar in hand. The sail billowed and filled, the ship took off across the water, waves leaping over its bow.

Kanja laughed to think that she had tried to thwart him, that little slip of a thing. But his laugh died in his throat as the wind built to a gale and the waves climbed higher. Then with a roar the blast changed direction. He fought to steer, but the oar snapped in his hands. Ropes tore loose as the wind shifted again. Men were shouting, crying out in dread, pointing. Kanja looked. A wall of water the size of a mountain bore down on his ship, and he suddenly understood. "Stop! Stop now!" he shouted, but his voice was drowned by the angry growl of the wave.

With a *crack* the mast shattered, sending splinters in all directions. Cloud and Jata held tight to each other as the deck ripped apart around them. Then for one brief moment, everything stood still, and the words whispered to Cloud by wind and water gave her hope.

Sister, little sister, we have come to play.

Crossing the Waters

by Ika Vanderkoeck

"So, you really think you can sail with the colonists' ship and land wherever you wish?" Tiqa asked her brother, trying to sound calm. She was sitting cross-legged on their veranda, weaving the last strands of dyed sago vines together for her floor mat.

Having returned from the colonists' camp, Aduka unlaced the strings of his slippers at the base of their house's steps. He knew he had upset her, saw her anger through the rough manner in which she knotted the leaves. Raised some meters above the ground, the veranda with its delicate, vine-riddled bamboo rails seemed to cage his sister's small frame.

"I don't see why I shouldn't," he said as he climbed up the steps. "The *Wayfarer* is larger, stronger than any *proas* we have ever built. No force known to man will be able to break this ship apart."

"Wonderful. They've made you arrogant too," she scoffed. Mention of the carrack made her glance towards the beach. Their late father's *proa,* the natives' small vessel, stood there, untouched ever since the outsiders came to their island. The torn sail needed to be patched; the paddles their father had lovingly, patiently carved were long due for a replacement. But her brother had ignored these tasks in pursuit of the outsiders' company.

He moved in a position that blocked her view of

the beach before she could remind him of his responsibilities. "And what's wrong with a little confidence? The outsiders are not going to hurt anyone. They just need someone to show them where the other islands are, for their maps! We'll be safe from danger, sister."

"The only danger I see is from *them*." Tiqa swiveled her gaze back to the mat's elaborate patterns and tugged the strands more viciously. "Their weapons frighten me, brother. We don't know what kind of damage those guns and cannons could wreak."

"Their weapons don't matter! I've seen their navigation tools, their gears, their equipment," Aduka said. "The outsiders are learned men, with knowledge that surpasses even our own!" When she gave no response, he nodded towards her handiwork. "You're going to tear that thing apart."

She tossed the mat aside and rose to her feet. Shafts of the hot tropical sun gilded her dark hair, revealed the elaborate patterns of her knee-length blouse. At sixteen and two years younger than he was, the young woman's persistence was often difficult to deflect. "That's not the point, brother. The islands the infidels—"

"Infidels?" Aduka repeated in surprise.

"Well, that's what they are, aren't they? They have *no* respect for our beliefs and culture, choosing instead to parade their religion as though ours is primitive, insignificant. The clans on the southern part of this archipelago have already been swayed by these outsiders' faith."

Aduka waved his hand as if he could brush the matter aside with a mere gesture. "But the outsiders have not done or said anything here—"

"Point is, the islands they want to reach are hallowed," she argued. "The spirits and guardians that protect the islands won't receive the heathens with open arms."

"That is why they need me with them," he said, more firmly this time.

"They're using you."

"Think of what they can offer in return! If we shun

them, the knowledge, the wisdom they have will remain beyond our reach while everything around us changes and evolves! Their technology will bring our people forward and keep us at pace with the changes around us."

Yet the ambitions of men knew no bounds—this he did *not* see. If these *Varamithians,* as they called themselves, could sail the world claiming other people's lands as their own, there was no telling if any mortal barriers existed to stop them. Their guns and cannons may have protected them, yet these technologies were also a danger to those they conquered.

"I know you're just trying to make things better for us." Tiqa strained to keep her frustration bridled. "But those islands remain unclaimed for a reason. The outsiders neither understand our laws nor our ties with the earth's magic. There are spirits out there, nameless forces that will stop the outsiders *and* you before you could even come close enough to smell the islands' soil."

Aduka refused to bend. "That's part of this journey's charm. We are moving into a new era, Tiqa. The time we spent hiding behind our fear for the unknown is ending. The magic we weave is no longer enough to help us keep up with the rest of the world."

"Mind your tone, brother," she said, and her nuance changed drastically this time, ripe with venom. "The magic you're insulting has aided our people for centuries."

"For the Maker's sake, woman! Will nothing I say convince you?"

"Aduka?" a third voice called out.

The intrusion made the siblings wince. For a moment, they stilled their argument to regard the inbound foreigner instead. His distinctive pale skin and bright-colored eyes were an oddity where brown skin and dark eyes prevailed. The polished breastplate, ill-suited for the hot conditions and weather, gleamed under the afternoon sun. He looked ridiculous under

his layers of clothing and was clearly suffering from
them.

More heads turned. Curious and suspicious neigh-
bors abandoned their gossiping to glance as the outsider strode past their houses. A crowd of noisy
children followed him, heedless of their mothers' shrill
protests until a harsh shout from one of the village
elders sent them scurrying back home.

Tiqa instinctively snatched her shawl from the floor
to cover her head. For the women here, such gesture
was necessary in the presence of a stranger to signify
propriety. "Ugh, I can smell him already," she
quipped. "Does he ever bathe, or were they all born
with that awful stench?"

"Stop exaggerating," Aduka hissed. To the outsider
just arrived at the base of their house, he grinned.
"Captain Lopo, welcome, my friend."

The foreign officer removed his polished helm and
wiped the sweat streaming down his forehead. "Did I
come at a bad time?" he asked in the native tongue.

Tiqa muttered something under her breath and slid
towards the door. Lopo tracked the girl's movements
until she disappeared into the house, the sign of dis-
comfort and regret clear behind his strange green eyes.

"She still hates me, yes?" he asked.

"She's just in a bad mood," Aduka spoke in the
foreigner's language, a skill he had picked up during
all those times he spent in their camp.

Lopo set his heavy satchel aside to untie his boots.
"On account of you leaving with us, I suppose?"

Aduka nodded.

"I don't blame her. You're the only family she has
left and this journey promises to be a long one." He
tugged the boots free, then rested his helm at the top
of the stairs. "There's nothing you can do now but let
her cool off on her own."

"I wish I could make her see . . ." Aduka shook
his head. "No, she won't understand. Few of the villagers will."

"Look, friend. People are wont to fear what they don't understand. Your willingness to help us will be repaid with knowledge and wisdom your people will thank you for. There will be many wonderful changes here because you have chosen to help us. Your sister will understand when she sees the rewards for herself, all right?"

"I guess so."

"You've *seen* what we can accomplish," Lopo said, green eyes locked straight to Aduka's brown in that strange, piercing way the outsiders seem to favor. "Soon those accomplishments will belong to your people as well. Have faith in what you're doing, my friend."

Aduka returned no response. Despite his eagerness to leave, a part of him, the part that grew with the magic here, writhed with a palpable sense of concern and doubt. *What if his sister was right? What if this was all a huge mistake?*

Aduka held his sister's hand tightly, trying his best to sound as calm as he appeared to be. "Look, I'll come back as soon as I can," he promised. "There's no reason for us to keep arguing."

"Ever since you learned their language and became part of their circle, you've lost your ties to our earth," Tiqa said. Worse, the hostility she threw at him yesterday had melted, replaced now with a concern that pained him even more. It was always easier to face her anger rather than her misery.

A lopsided smile turned one corner of his lips. He flicked his woven leaf sack over his shoulder. "Don't be silly. My gift can never be lost."

"Aduka, come on. We're late enough as it is!" Lopo called out to him. The outsider was already heading towards the beach. *Wayfarer*'s impressive sails and gilded dragon figurehead could be seen some short distance offshore, ready to leave with the tide.

"Everything will be fine, Tiqa. You'll see." With a

final reassuring squeeze, Aduka let go of her hand, then turned to take his leave.

He had taken barely two steps when a ringing sound raided the air around them. Warned by instinct, the man spun around seconds too late. A blast of white sand slammed onto his chest and knocked him several steps backwards.

"Tiqa!" He coughed and spat dirt from his mouth. The vortex of sand swirled around him, attuned to the graceful movements of his sister's supple hands as she summoned the elements to do her bidding.

"See? You *have* lost it." She let her hands drop. The sand fell as she stilled her movements. "What good are the *Varamithian* guns and technologies, when our lives are interlocked to magic?"

Aduka cursed, but in those final moments their gazes interlocked, his, wrapped in a mask of hope and optimism, and Tiqa's, mournful, fraught with the plea for him to stay here where it was safe. He turned his back, quelled the rest of his qualms with brute force, and jogged after his shipmate.

The carrack's bow sliced through water as glossy and dark as the deep abyss. The rolling sea seemed to groan under *Wayfarer*'s blundering passage. To Aduka, leaning over the rail, the ship was no longer the graceful instrument he thought her to be. In spite of all the wonders she had yielded before this, the novelty of her design was quick to leave him. His soul screamed with the sensation of being terribly out of place, of being confined. A yearning for the familiar, simple feel of his father's *proa* raided his thoughts unmercifully as he gazed into the briny sea. He did not belong here—that much he realized.

"Aduka? We need to talk." A familiar voice made him snap out of his musings.

Aduka turned to find his childhood friend Suria coming up to him. The night wind batted the man's face as he approached, forced him to squint. He

reached up to adjust his headwear before the breeze
could claim it.

Aduka lifted his hand to touch his own headwear,
forgetting he had worn it earlier to protect his head
against the sun. He gripped the knot that held it in
place to make certain it was secure, then trailed his
fingers to where a piece of the cloth was folded upwards to form a small pointed edge.

"I don't understand it, Suria. We've only been out
here four days, and I already feel like we've been out
here for an eternity." He sighed. "I sail on my father's
proa for days on end all the time. It never feels like
this."

"I think you have bigger things to worry about right
now," the other native said, and only then did Aduka
become aware of his friend's apprehension. Suria gave
one quick sweep of their surroundings and added,
"Have you been talking to any of the *Varamithians*
lately?"

"No. They're busy minding the ship. Captain Lopo
said we'll have more time to speak when we reach
the islands."

"Doesn't it strike you as odd that they have been
avoiding us ever since we left home?" Suria spoke in
a low tone, well aware that at least half of the sailhands on the carrack had picked up their language
during the few months they spent on their island.

Aduka frowned. "They can't be minding this ship
and talking to us at the same time."

But it was a poor defense. Even as he gathered the
words to salve his friend's concern, that part of him
which writhed uneasily at the thought of this journey
bothered him again.

Suria's expression was unreadable in this dim-lit atmosphere. "Come take a walk with me. You'll see
what I mean."

They made their way across the main deck towards
the aft end of the vessel. Made uncomfortable by the
confined spaces belowdecks, the natives kept to the

upper portions of the carrack. Most of the crewmembers had already retreated to the crew's quarters for some well-deserved sleep, but the few that stayed abovedecks that night did not fail to raise Aduka's hackles.

Their familiar faces counted for nothing, for in those brief moments when light from the swinging lanterns revealed their eyes, he glimpsed sentiments masked from him before. The sharp, intense glares they cast towards the natives were far from friendly. From the way their shoulders stiffened at the natives' approach, it was clear that they were disturbed by the villagers' presence.

"I don't remember seeing this much hostility back home," Aduka muttered.

"Exactly," Suria whispered. "I have a bad feeling about this, Aduka. I don't feel safe out here with them."

"Hey, you two!" someone shouted. Startled, the natives stopped dead in their tracks.

The Varamithian who challenged them stepped away from the shadows cast down by the towering mainmast, hands clasped firmly on his arquebus. His breastplate armor and their distinctive engravings reflected the light spilled from the lanterns. "It's late. What are you two still doing up here?" he demanded in the native tongue, his accent thick enough to make their language seem so primitive.

At least a head taller than the villagers, the outsider's height and build lent him the physical advantage. Suria acknowledged that fact with a muttered curse and backed a step.

Aduka tried a smile, but the gesture did naught to soften the outsider's stern carriage. "We prefer to stay where we can see the sky."

The foreigner sneered, turned his head, and spat. "Think you're better than us, is that it?"

"What? No, I didn't say—"

This time he shifted to his people's language. "I've spent weeks in that damned village of yours, listening to your people's insults, enduring their taunts and their damned snobbery. Since you think so highly of yourselves and your magic, why don't you show me what you can do?" The man took another step forward, tapped the muzzle of his arquebus on Aduka's shoulder. "Where is all that power your people claim to possess?"

Such rudeness would have caused his sister to bristle like a tigress. Understanding every word and no longer smiling, the villager clenched his fists until his knuckles turned white.

"Don't do it." Suria held him back. "Let's go back to the front part of the ship. We want no trouble here."

The outsider drew breath for a retort, but the words turned to a startled curse when something knocked the ship's side. *Wayfarer* swayed to the intrusion like a child's toy boat. Thrown off balance, the three men braced themselves against the mast as water splashed onto the deck.

"What's going on?" the outsider gasped.

No one dared to move, until they heard the patter of footsteps against the planks. Roused by that violent intrusion, Captain Lopo emerged from below—confused, anxious sailors at his heels.

"What happened?" Lopo asked as he rushed to the stern.

"Did we strike a rock?" asked another.

"Nonsense, we're in the middle of the ocean! That couldn't have been a rock."

"I don't see anything," one of the crew said.

The level-headed captain silenced them. Under his brisk instructions, the Varamithians dispersed to their stations and worked to steady the carrack against the waves.

Then, the air became torn by a deep, haunting cry.

It was a sound only the villagers could hear, one they both admired and dreaded.

"Are you hearing this? This is our doing!" Suria grabbed his friend's elbow. "We should never have

taken the foreigners out here. We have angered the
mythical beings. Now they will bring us down to the
bottom of the sea, and no one will find our bodies!"

Every fiber of Aduka's being shuddered at the cry
and the power that created it. To make matters worse,
wild waves continued to tear the sides of the carrack
like a demon thirsty for vengeance. Around him, frantic crewmembers hurried to draw the canvas, battling
the strong wind and the waves as they continued their
concerted efforts to bring the proud vessel down.

Barrels rolled along the deck. Splinters from some
part of the ship crashed down right next to him. Desperate to save their hides, Aduka reached for the
forces that brewed within him. A portion of his mind
drifted back home, to the tranquility and warmth of
familiar, safe surroundings. He thought about his sister, his people, and envisioned the pristine shoreline
and the plank houses with their clay tile roofs and
high stilts. *I don't belong out here with them!*

His mind surged forth into the sea. *"Mercy, great
guardians! We mean you no harm,"* he called out with
all his heart. *"A simple crossing on this ocean is all
we ask of you."*

The waves slowly stilled as though the sea had
heard him. For one brief moment, he thought the sea's
guardians would let them pass.

Then, the shadow of something *large* began to cloak
the deck. He felt his blood run cold, flinched when
the captain and his sailors screamed.

A massive creature had surfaced beside the ship, its
long neck arched, its head held high. Cloaked by the
darkness of the night, it was a creature conjured from
his people's greatest legends. Its only visible features
were the black-tipped spikes protruding out of its
scales and the eerie glow of its cat-slit eyes. Light
cast from lanterns still spared from the sea's thrashing
became reflected on the water that trickled down
scales blue, green, and black as the ocean.

None of the outsiders knew what it was. Men who
hadn't fled for the safety of the chambers belowdecks

headed for the cannons, propelled by fear. Among
that confusion the natives glimpsed the captain, but
failed to understand the instructions he threw at his
crewmembers.

"What is this? This vessel is not familiar to me."

The voice boomed inside his head. By the manner
in which Suria clasped his ears, Aduka guessed the
man had heard it too.

The creature curled its scaly lips. Lifting its head
with its crown of curved horns and spikes high above
the mainmast, it probed the carrack with the long
whiskers protruding from the sides of its mouth. The
movements of the sailors around them no longer made
sense, no longer mattered. If they fled for their lives,
if they froze in terror, or if they had gathered their
wits, Aduka no longer cared.

The natives fell to their knees and watched in awe
as the creature slowly, patiently, investigated the vessel. *"Wise Ailliach. Keeper of the ocean. Drake-
guardian of the sea. We are greatly humbled by your
presence,"* Aduka said.

The creature abandoned its interest on the sails to
look at them. The fins on its cheeks spread wide; it
let out a purr of delight. *"Your hearts beat with the
arcane forces of this land. You are children of the
Arasmor clan, are you not?"*

"Yes, wise one," Suria answered telepathically. His
voice shook. *"We live on the southwest shore of the
archipelago, near the bay with the strange rock
formations."*

The creature nodded. *"Weaver of elements, this vessel is too large for your needs. The trees you have
felled for it did not deserve their demise for your selfish
ambitions. Are the* proas *not serving their purpose?"*
The creature swiveled its head towards the outsiders,
eyes narrowed to angry slits. *"And these are not your
people. Why are you here with them?"*

Mesmerized by the depth of its eyes, Aduka was
oblivious to everything else on that ship. *"These men,*

these outsiders are friends of ours. They seek to explore the lands out here, for their maps."

An answer that failed to please, for *Ailliach* snorted incredulously. *"The islands out here belong to the other clans. Turn back, children of Arasmor. Leave the company of these outsiders."*

"Our passing through your territory will be brief. Please, let us all through."

The creature lowered its head until its snout was no more than a few inches away from his face. *"How much do you know of these friends of yours, impetuous one?"*

"They haven't done anything . . ."

"You have yet to answer my question. How much do you know of these outsiders?"

There was no easy answer for that. Despite all the time he had spent in their encampment, he knew far too little about them. Lopo never spoke of anything beyond the wonders of their advanced civilization.

"They've raised several forts in the northern part of the archipelago," said the creature. *"It will only be a matter of time before they claim the northern provinces as their own."*

"What?" Aduka and Suria gasped.

"This journey is a military expedition more than anything—to scout enemy territory for weaknesses. The way they hide behind their metal scales and carry their fire-spitters should have told you what their interests are. Soon they will take 'your' village and change your ways. Your people will be slaves to their technology, their beliefs, their arrogance."

Aduka flinched as disappointment coiled around his belly. *"Captain Lopo never told me."*

"Ah, you poor fool. You are not the first who was misled by these outsiders' lies. You will certainly not be the last."

Suria swallowed, then said, *"Tell us more, great drake."*

For what seemed hours, *Ailliach* spoke. The drake

unveiled the colonists' true nature, told the natives of the lands the outsiders have conquered, and the lies they had spun to gain the trust of the villagers. In the end, all the glories the Varamithians promised him lost their appeal. Tiqa was right all along. They *were* using him.

"Fire!"

That command jolted Aduka out of their telepathic conversation. The explosions that followed after came so loud they hammered the villagers' heightened senses and sent them reeling in confusion. Yet what they heard next would haunt them for many years to come. Rising above the echoes of the explosion was the creature's mournful, wretched wail.

The outsiders whooped with joy. Aduka and Suria ran to the side of the ship and cried out in dismay to see the creature falling into the water in a dead heap. Blood stained the water all around it. The natives could do no more than stare in dumbfounded shock while it sunk to the bottom of the ocean.

"Lopo, what have you done?" Face drained white, Aduka all but screamed. "You killed one of our sacred guardians!"

Lopo met that challenge unfazed. In one fluid move he spun on his heels, snatched a freshly loaded arquebus from his first mate, and lifted the weapon parallel to the native's head. "Stand back, *savage*. I can kill you now and send you down with the beast's corpse."

"Why are you doing this?" Aduka snarled, hurt by that betrayal. "I trusted you!"

"Your magic called the beast to us, for all we know. This victory is ours," the captain said smugly. To his sailors, he raised the weapon aloft. "Let that be a reminder of who we are and what we are capable of. Nothing in this world, magical or mythical, can stop us and the might of our guns!"

But the only response which came from his crew was absolute terror. All eyes were pinned not on their officer, but on the massive shadow that lurked behind him. He turned around to see what could have compelled his men to sudden silence. That moment, everyone, even Lopo, knew he was beyond salvation. His last vision of the world was of a beast's gaping maw, rows of jagged teeth, and the acrid stench of certain death.

Aduka looked away when the guardian took their captain's life. The sound of his bones breaking and his scream, cut short in death, was enough to spur the sailhands on deck to scatter like frightened rats. The few brave powder boys made a futile dash to the armory for dry gunpowder while the handful of men who stayed to mind the cannons fumbled to get the weapons reloaded.

Larger than the previous creature, this bristling guardian reared its horned head back and let out an indignant hiss. A sudden surge of power rattled the boards at Aduka's feet. He jerked his gaze towards Suria and watched as the villager gathered the water with his magic and threw it towards the Varamithians. Four men fell from that impact, their gunpowder soaked and rendered useless.

"Now is the time to act," Suria said. "You want to let them get away with this and use the cannons again?"

"They can't. It will take ages for them to find dry gunpowder and load the guns." Aduka lifted his hands high above his head; let his gift loose, then used water from the deck to freeze four horrified sailors in place before they could get to their weapons.

A clipped roar from the creature drew his gaze sideways. Aduka's heart nearly stopped when he realized that the beast's eyes were fixed upon him. It would be easy for the creature to tear the ship apart and claim vengeance for its lost kin. Regardless, as their gazes met, Aduka and the creature reached an unspoken agreement.

The final stroke lay in the villager's hands, for it was Aduka's impetuous decisions that led the

Varamithians out here. Only he could mend what he had inadvertently caused. Only then would he be able to redeem the ancestral trust he had violated.

The waves beneath the ship rose to a giant swell, lifting it terrifyingly high. *Wayfarer*'s remaining crew clung to whatever they could until the ship plummeted back down. Men were thrown overboard like ragged dolls, never to be seen again. The bowsprit shattered along with the dragon figurehead. Whatever was left of the shrouds and rigging were reduced to flotsam on the sea's surface, highlighted then by the first rays of the sun.

Balanced on the drake's spine, the villagers weaved the water and wind around them with the grace of dancers and the lethal precision of experienced warriors. Arms rising and falling in precise arches, they executed punches and strikes that turned the elements around them into deadly weapons. Aduka's anger lent power to his assaults. He flung cannonballs made of frozen water towards the ship, watched in grim satisfaction to see the damage he produced. Soon, the natives' paired efforts brought the mainmast down. The creature that bore them steered clear of danger, keeping them safe from the ocean's wrath.

Then, a wall of water, frozen to ice by Aduka's expert, quick handling of the winds, blocked the ship's path when it was thrust forward by the tide. *Wayfarer* slammed onto the thick block, smashed upon impact, and finally succumbed to the sea.

Both men fell against the drake's massive back, exhausted. Spent, no longer driven by adrenaline, they could do no more than cling to the guardian's scales when it turned to leave.

"What now?" Suria asked between fast breaths. "Where are we going?"

For long moments Aduka could not speak. The feeling of remorse that welled up in him was so great, he could barely contain it. Tears of frustration and deep anger stung his eyes. He grieved for the dead guardian, yearned to turn back to that crucial juncture when he was first swayed by Captain Lopo's lies.

"We go back, get the colonists to leave. I don't want them around anymore." Aduka placed the palm of his hand on the drake's scale. As it lifted its long neck from the sea to look at him, he sent a telepathic note of gratitude and gave an oath spurred by a new spark of determination. "No slinking outsider will ever soil our lands and sea again! I'll make certain of that."

Here There Be Monsters

Brad Carson

We are Afhasi. The Waterwise.
    Humans call us the Fin, the Meara or simply, Mer. My father is a Mer Man. My mother Mea, before succumbing to the lure of the Forbidden, was a Mer Wife.

I am Kya, a Mer Maid.

We are Afhasi.

Of the Sea.

The watersky that shrouds our hidden refuge grows warm again; another ship burns above us. The sea writhes with lost souls seeking guidance to the calm. I feel their pain, their fear, and their sin.

Our Eld Oncs tell us air is comprised of two parts obsession and one part disorder, while water is magic and calm. They say a storm is born when water meets air. They warn against contamination and order isolation.

But a heart has no ears.

My mother stole a man from the embrace of the sea and left us to follow her heart's command. Her rebellious spirit became a lesson of the Forbidden. My father retreated to the caves to overcome his anger and renew his calm. He abides there still.

Wreck falls on our white coral towers like droppings from a hungry fish. We gather our school of children, not to take them away from the horror, but to instruct them in the folly. The drifting dead are lessons to be learned.

Having no inner light of their own, Humans banish fear of the dark by burning the rendered flesh of the Wise Watchers. They think they own the sea. We left them the earth. Wasn't that enough?

They live to own things. Surface dwellers have fought for hundreds of years for the right to own other surface dwellers. They call them slaves. Even when we were air breathers, the word sounded soiled to our ears; now we are battered by great waves of sorrow, torment, and torture of each passing ship crammed to the breaking with sickness and misery. Our sand pillars tremble and shift with the cries of the forsaken.

We do not understand. How can you own another person's soul, when you don't even own your own?

But a heart is different. A heart can be owned.

It is Forbidden to seek the surface, Forbidden to know air breathers, Forbidden to interfere.

Too much is Forbidden.

I think the Eld Ones are wrong.

I am my mother's heir. The tide tugs at my heart from the watersky of our world as surely as it tugged at hers.

Tonight, I will follow.

Jonathon Diggs, bosun of the interceptor ship *Fortitude,* clung desperately to a narrow piece of powder-blasted deck. Blood still dripped from a gash in his forehead taken when a cannon shot had raked their barque from stem to stern, sending him and most of the forecastle into the water. His right leg throbbed but he didn't think it was broken.

He had watched impotently as the renegades boarded the *Fortitude,* the clash of swords washing over him like the cold waves that lapped at his spine. For a long time screams had sounded but as night descended and he had drifted farther from the sinking ship, the silence seemed eternal.

They had been lying off the coast of Africa waiting

to intercept the *Blackbird* on her return from the Americas laden with rum, firearms, and other trade goods preferred by the tribal leaders who provided the human cargo for work on sugar plantations. They were well hidden, yet somehow, Captain Edward Bane had slid out of a fogbank right across their bow in a classic maneuver called "Crossing the T." The sudden appearance of the bare-breasted, blue-haired mermaid that served as figurehead for the infamous slaver had preceded a heavy broadside that toppled their main mast and left them crippled, like an old man waiting to die. The same volley had blasted Jonathon into the sea.

He hated to see the end of the *Fortitude,* but even more, he hated to see the slaver win. Again. Maybe the scuttle that Bane had sold his soul was true after all.

It wasn't the first time the *'Bird* had avoided them, almost as if Bane knew where the navy ships lay. Maybe, as some of the old salts swore, the notorious master's good fortune was bound into the ship's figurehead. Word was Bane used to be a simple merchant trader before adopting the mermaid icon.

Jonathon well knew from his fifteen years before the mast that either tale could be true. The ocean was wide and full of mystery.

The wet cold dug deep into his bones, numbing him, luring him. He had heard that drowning was like falling into a lover's arms. Would that be so bad? The sea was his only love; it was only right she should claim him. Stars began to appear through gaps in the slowly spinning fog and he imagined a nice cup of hot grog in his warm hammock. He could almost hear the cabin boy's hushed soprano, drifting on the steady rhythm of the waves, lulling him.

His fingers slipped off the oakum-smeared planks. He spit salt and frantically kicked to regain purchase, but his leg screamed and he sank. He stroked upward with arms made powerful by years of hauling lines, but to little avail. The stars retreated. He dropped lower and lower.

A large fish brushed by him and an underwater swell like an errant current bobbed him to the surface. His buoyed spirits fell when he realized his planks had drifted away but to his surprise, they reversed direction and returned to his grasping hands as sure as if he'd hauled them in. Sputtering and gasping, he threw himself onto the decking as if he clutched a long-lost lover.

He barely noticed that the sea around him had calmed.

A burning ship as big as a Wise Watcher dangles halfway through our roof.

Debris and charred, broken bodies block the sparkle of stars. Fire stings my nose and makes me gag as if air went down the wrong way. Sharks roam, tidying.

Something snags me like the hooks that tear at my little brothers' mouths whenever they get too curious.

But this hook pulls at my heart.

I follow it downwind in time to see a dark-haired man slip into the sea. The barbs of the hook dig deeper and, against all reason, I flick him to the surface and retrieve his floating refuge.

Is this how my mother felt?

Later in the night, his strength fails again. I cannot let him die. I grasp his hands across the wooden boards and use my tail to support his body. I sing a Healing to close the cut in his forehead and mend the bone in his leg.

His bleary eyes find me. "Who are you?" he mumbles.

"I am Kya. I am Afhasi."

"Afa . . . Of the sea?" His head lolls, he drops further into the water, pulling me further out. "A vision," he murmurs. "A dream. The ocean is wide and full of mystery."

He drifts. Words begin to seep from his mouth. He tells me of his home, of his childhood.

I listen, I learn.

He rails against slavery. Justice fires his soul; he speaks revenge and regret with the same breath. He expresses his love of the sea. He gives me his name.

Jonathon.

I hold him. He holds me.

The night moves forward, the stars spin.

Wellness ebbs. I am too far out of the water. My mind tells me to let the Human go. It is Forbidden.

But a heart has no ears.

Our faces are near enough that I can smell the salt on his cheeks. He leans in and touches lips to my hair. "You're real," he says in surprise. "A real mermaid."

I tickle him with my tail and say, "The ocean is wide and full of mystery."

He laughs and grasps my hands more firmly, but oh so gently. My heart thrums like a deep ocean current.

"My leg? It's better."

"I sang a Healing."

"A mermaid." He speaks the term with grace. "I always hoped the stories were true. Tell me of your people."

"My ancestors long wandered the water, seeking a perfect harmonious home until they found Atland Dies. Shore of the Gods. Beautiful, bountiful, calm, our island nurtured us for hundreds of years. Then your race appeared."

"My race?"

"Humans. I suppose you had been appearing for millennia, but we were so busy celebrating convergence that we missed the unquenchable curiosity that changed Apes into Humans. Lost in accord, we fell to discord. Your race grew hungrier and tried to learn the secret of peace through acts of war."

"Great cost for a greater good," he says with disdain.

"Our Eld Ones went into the deep caves seeking enlightenment and returned with the Sundering song. My own fore-family sang it. Atland Dies, our island

paradise, sank. A great cost, for a greater good. We
became of the sea. Afhasi."

"Sad," he mumbles. "But beautiful. Like you."

He is what is missing from my ordered existence.

"You saved my life," he says.

"You gave me mine," I reply.

We hold each other.

The Eld Ones say the song of Sundering is still in
our blood. So is the lure of the Forbidden. I sing him
a Soothing.

He sleeps, restfully, deeply. A tide of weakness and
fatigue pull at me. I too must sleep.

But I know I will never let go.

Morning sun parches my skin through the thick fog. I
am stretched out. My upper body, bathed by the madness of air, thirsts for the calm of water.

Jonathon stares at me. "Kya. My mermaiden," he
whispers.

My heart crests, but the waves lap warning.

I hear the synchronized dip of oars before he does.
A low shadow bears down on us unerringly through
the haze. Jonathon tries to shake me loose. "Swim
away," he urges.

I cannot.

"Well, isn't this a pretty sight." A tall man wearing
a long coat stands in the boat, aiming a weapon at
me. "Avast, navy man," he says, "or your little friend
will suffer for it. And you bilge rats," he turns on his
oarsmen, "avert your eyes, or lose them." He leans
over, clothing in his hands. "If you would be so kind,
my dear, to remove your lower body from the water,
you will find that onboard, legs are more the fashion
than fins."

"You want to go through there?" Jonathon asked,
incredulously.

He stood in Captain Bane's well-appointed quarters
in the stern of the slave ship. A large ornate bookcase

was filled with books and charts. Odd but interesting seashells ornamented shelves and drawers. A chess set carved from coral was laid out below a wide window that ran the full beam of the ship, where Kya sat listening to dolphins chatter while rubbing at her legs.

The spacious quarters far outmatched the utilitarian cabins of a navy ship and contrasted even more fiercely with the pens in the tweendecks of the *Blackbird* where slaves were usually wedged together in low cells only three feet high, shut out from light or air. Those desolate spaces were barely big enough for twenty to sit with heads bowed to their knees, but Jonathon knew they could hold as many as two hundred pressed shoulder to shoulder, giving each an average of twenty inches, breathing in each other's stink and vomit for months on end.

Captain Bane pointed at a chart lying on a polished rosewood table, touching a section to the southeast of their current position. "Your navy gives me little choice. They nip at my heels like hounds at a stag."

"A stag is a noble beast," Jonathon said. "You are not."

Bane grunted, "Ah, bosun, a man of high morals. I once spoke as you do, but found that words did not fill my stomach."

"True, but they do not turn it, either."

Bane tapped the map. "My navigator says we can make it through."

"Then he is a fool."

The captain's light mood vanished like a squall rising on a calm sea. "Be careful what you call my navigator."

"To go where you propose is death for all. Here," Jonathon recited words on the map, "there be Monsters. No one goes there. The Kraken makes sure of that."

"Kraa'kken?" Kya asked, abandoning her view of the sea. Jonathon nodded and she shook her head slowly. "You must not disturb Kraa'kken."

A smug smile formed on his lips. "There. You see. Who would know more about the Kraken than Kya?"

"Indeed." Bane's own grin widened to show his teeth. "Kya is the reason I am going to succeed. She will calm the monster. After all, who would know more?"

Kya stumbled to an open porthole and put her face to the spray of the sea, breathing deeply. "Do you even know what you contain with the word 'monster'?"

"It's some kind of giant octopus or squid," Jonathon explained, watching her carefully.

"No, she said. "Kraa'kken is the last dragon. He fell into the sea and his wrath tore the ocean floor and shifted continents until—until he finally fell asleep."

Bane moved to her, wagging a headmaster's finger. "But you omitted something, my dear. He didn't just fall asleep, did he? The Afhasi calmed him, just like you will again, so we may pass in safety." He offered a slight bob of his head to Jonathon. "But, sadly, not your navy ships."

"You would wake this pitiful creature to use as a weapon?" Kya tottered away and almost fell, until Jonathon steadied her elbow. Her skin was cold and clammy. "You are disordered," she said to Bane. "I will not help you."

Bane drew his sword. "I think you will."

Jonathon charged, but the point of the sword forced him to stop.

Kya shivered, but replied. "Death is calm."

"Dear girl," Bane said, "You mistake my intent. I know Afhasi do not fear death. But I will kill the holder of your heart, carving him slowly like a fat whale, slice by slice, until he is barely alive. And if he manages to heal," Bane shrugged and smiled, "then I will begin anew."

Kya began to tremble, her mouth opened and closed, repeatedly.

Jonathon tried to ease her anxiety; he reached out overtop the sword. "He's bluffing," he said. The blade flicked a hot sting below his arm.

"There's the first one," Bain said as a sliver of flesh fell to the floor.

Jonathon reeled in shock and pain; Kya placed her hand on the bloody wound and began to sing.

"Ah, a Healing." Bane moved in close as if basking in the sound.

Jonathon's arm felt washed in cold water, the wound began to close, but then the song stopped abruptly.

"You didn't finish," Bane said regretfully.

Pain distorted Kya's face, her pale skin turned translucent and she fell.

Bane caught her, but after a glance, dropped her to the carpet.

Jonathon scooped her in his arms where she gasped like a fish out of water, her legs jerking and fluttering. "Kya! Kya!" His heart pounded in fear.

"Jonathon." Her hand trailed across his brow, then dropped and she lay still.

"No!" He pressed his face against hers, trying to warm her flesh with his breath. "Don't leave me!"

"How touching," Bane said.

"You bastard!" Jonathon shouted, then sputtered and spit as a jug of water splashed down on them.

Kya gasped, breathing again, but shallow.

"That will hold her for now," Bane said, "but you need to get her in the deep. It's the Afhasi source and they sicken when deprived of it. Fear not, they get over it, eventually."

The sea speaks.

Awake, daughter.

Mother?

Hush, my Kyamarantha. Let the water replenish.

Mother.

You must go back where you belong. You are Afhasi.

As are you.

Once. No longer. I have drifted away from the sea.

Where are you?

Near, but . . . far away. So far. Go home, child. Leave air to others.

And what of you?

I am other. I cannot go back.

Nor can I. My heart is my home. His name fills my soul.

Then I grieve for us both. I think you and I are the returning tide of the Eld One's decree of isolation. Prepare for pain and joy.

But that makes no sense. Joy is uplifting.

When heart rules over all, the price of joy is pain. I urge you to shut his name from your soul. He has too much power over you.

We have power over each other. The power of giving, of sharing. Of loving.

He will only hurt you. Go now, while the sea cradles you.

The water caresses my scales, calm, peaceful.

"Kya!" Jonathon's voice floods me. I pull away from the deep.

My daughter, you are lost.

She is gone; Jonathon is here.

I swim to him.

Jonathon stared over the side of the shallop, both hoping and fearing that Kya would swim away. It would mean his death, but should his love be the shackle that enslaved her to Bane's bidding? Was that love? Or was love setting free?

"Hail her again, bosun," Danby said from the seat behind. "The signal is hoisted."

"She needs more time." He glanced over at the mizzenmast where a green banner flapped in the lee breeze. "Bane will have to wait until she's healed."

The point of a dagger pricked his skin. "If the cap'n has to wait, we'll all need healing."

Jonathon instinctively pulled away, but then wondered if he had the courage to throw himself backwards. Before he could decide, long, pale fingers grasped the gunnels of the boat. He wanted to grab them and kiss them, or smash them and drive her away. Her blue-black hair appeared, shiny and lustrous again, followed by her aqua eyes, sparkling like light on the water. He reached to help her aboard but a flick of her powerful tail propelled her into his arms. He kissed her and then averted his eyes as her scales turned to flesh and her tail split into legs.

Bane's voice cut across the water. "I hate to interrupt your fun, but we needs be underway and smartly, too. Your navy is six leagues aft and coming on strong. You men," he pointed at the rigging, "into the ratlines with you. The rest of you, hand over hand and give us a tune."

Kya quickly dressed as the crew struck up a lively shanty, hauling the scallop toward the ship.

Jonathon stared up at the empty crow's-nest. "Even with the best glass no man can see six leagues away."

Kya tipped her head toward the northeast. "He's right. The waves whisper of three ships."

Jonathon nodded. "But how does *he* know?"

I am refreshed.

The slave captain stands on the forecastle waiting for us.

Jonathon immediately asks, "How do you know the interceptors approach? Do the waves whisper to you, too?"

"My navigator told me." Bane smiles, but not of happiness. "Helmsman!" he shouts, "south by southwest. Mr. Danby if you would." A noose drops over Jonathon's head and pulls tight, the other end tied to a rail above the deck. "Mr. Danby, the ship is yours. Keep a steady course, and make sure we're not disturbed."

"Aye, cap'n. Steady as she goes." Danby starts shouting orders as soon as he leaves.

"The rope is just a precaution, my dear," Bane says. "I wouldn't want the bosun getting heroic when he sees his colors flying. And sinking."

My Jonathon lunges at him but the tether drags him to his knees, with a gasp. Distress floods me and I charge at Bane with fists and nails. He tries to avoid me, tries to contain me, but I am fin-slippery and draw blood on his cheek. He curses and his pistol lashes out, catching me hard on side of the head.

Jonathon shouts, but his angry protest is overwhelmed by a wail that pours up from below deck. A cloaked figure bursts among us, shrieking, "You said she wouldn't be hurt." Short-bitten fingernails run through shorn blue-gray hair.

I jerk as if gaffed. "Mother?"

"Don't interfere, Mea," Bane commands.

She places gnarled fingers against my cut and begins to sing a Healing, but the notes are malformed. Uttering a despondent cry, she pulls back. "I told you to swim away," she says, "I told you." Her aqua eyes are cloudy; her face, lined and sallow, bears the ravages of soul sickness. She turns back to Bane; her hands tremble. "Please, Edward, let her go, for the sake of the love we once had."

I am stunned, rudderless.

His face changes from cold and hard to a soft warm smile. "Mea," he whispers, touching her hollow cheeks. "It's too late for that."

I spin her around. "Him?" I accuse. "You left us to go with him?"

She sobs, "He holds my heart!"

"How can your heart be so blind?"

"And yours isn't?" She points at my Jonathon. "What won't you do for him?"

Bane enwraps her. "I'm sorry I struck her, love. It was a craven act, done in haste. Once we lie on the other side of the monster, I will put about and she can stay with him or return to her home. The same decision you made ten years ago. Remember?"

"Oh, mother," I plead. "Leave this evil man."

Bane laughs. "And who do you think has aided me? Who warns me of your ships when my hold is crammed full of slaves?"

Horror fills me. "You are his navigator? How could you? Can not you feel those souls crying in agony?"

Bane grunts, "Slaves have no souls. They are little better than animals."

"At least they are *better* than animals," Jonathon says.

Mother pushes away from them. Tears streak her face. "Kya . . . my Kya. I feel them all the time. They diminish me. I hear their cries, their horrible, endless cries. But he has my heart," she wails, "and a heart has no ears!"

"Oh mother, the sea is so far from you."

"As it will be from you. Beware, child. Your magic will be your heart's undoing. It will change him."

I shake my head in denial as she speaks.

"One day, you calm the sea for favorable passage then, before you know it, you are reading it for ships in pursuit. You stir fog, raise waves, heal his wounds, anything to keep him safe." Tears roll down her hollow cheeks, her voice falters. "Anything."

Bane pats her shoulder. "Hush, love, hush. My poor sick Mea. You should go below and have another tot of grog. Let me run my ship."

"Edward, let me try to control Kraa'kken. I know the old songs. I might—"

"No, love, your power has almost faded. Kya is young, still of the sea. She will do it or her heart will die."

Jonathon pulls toward her. "More than I will die! You cannot—" He falls, his words cut off by a blow from Bane's pistol.

I drop to my knees and cradle his head. "Mother. Please! Help us!"

She shakes her head. "I can't. Don't ask. It's too late. Kya, please!" she howls, "Please, my child if you have any love left for me, just calm the beast!" She turns away from us, moving slowly along the deck, her hand outstretched to the spray.

I watch and whisper, "May you find calm, mother."

She touches her wet hand to her lips then wipes it on her cloak. "I no longer know how. You and I, we are alike. Afhasi no more." She staggers away without once looking back.

Bane's shoulders slump with her every stumble, but

once she is gone, he takes a deep breath, turns and lays his sword against the fleshy part of Jonathon's thigh. "Well?"

I hear cries of despair cresting on the surface of the sea. Those voices will be with me always, as they are with my mother, but even their constant torment cannot compare to the agony of losing my heart. Piece by piece.

Jonathon will live, the rest I will learn to live with.

Mother's accusation echoes in my mind, like the rumble of undersea quakes in the caverns of my distant home.

Afhasi no more.

Jonathon awoke to singing. Spray flew like white fire over the bulward rail, the foresails billowed, and sheets snapped in the favoring wind. To the stern, the interceptors were coming on strong, Bane leading them to their doom.

A high-pitched tune came from the direction of the bowsprit, one note flowing into another in endless waves, cresting and dropping, soothing . . . like a lullaby. He noticed a chain that wasn't a bobstay wrapping the capstan and peered toward the cutwater.

He recoiled at the sight of Kya bound face-forward to the ship's blue-haired figurehead, as if mother was whispering in daughter's ear. With each plunge of the hull, waves slammed her with a sound as dead as a falling sledgehammer. Her lower body had transformed, seawater sluiced off golden scales. He shouted above the thunder. "Kya! Nothing is worth the cost."

The high song stopped, her eyes found his. "Love is."

"What kind of love is paid with the lives of slaves?" He leaned over as far as he safely could, trying to touch her, trying to bring her back. Or was he trying to free her? A large wave pushed him away. He made to return but a sharp tug on the rope around his neck jerked him to his knees.

"The monster rises," Bane said, his sword pointing at Jonathon's chest.

*   *   *

Ancient power swells the sea.

Kraa'kken stirs. Rage flows. He burns.

I sing what little I know of the old song and merge it with a Soothing for children who awake in the night.

I feel his pain. I see into his soul, his memories. He burns with shame.

Born deformed. His wings are too small and though he tries mightily, he cannot fly. Cast out. His brothers and sisters beat him with their wings. Burned. His father's fire drives him from the nest. Abandoned. His mother turns her face away.

He cannot fly; he can only tumble into the sea where he cries his shame.

The last of his kind, he does not belong in this world. But do I?

He is only a tiny baby, lost, alone, searching for the mother who betrayed him. As am I.

Mother? Kraa'kken echoes the image. Curiosity peeks from under the rage. He sees me, I see him.

Poor wretched creature, his long undulating body, pale and transparent, burns from the inside. His dragon fire, developed underwater, could only rage inward. He consumes himself.

I gather all my strength, my power, and start to sing a Healing to his fiery pain. I sing to his strength, to the beauty of his marred soul, even as my own sinks in the suffering my love will unleash.

Shame swamps against me, pressing with a force greater than the weight of the sea. Kraa'kken's shame. Mine.

Jonathon's.

I feel him above me. Our fragile, forbidden love will not survive his honor. I see him. I hear him talking to the captain. I fear his words.

"You won't ever let Kya go," he says. "You're going keep the Kraken awake so you have a place to run from the hounds. She will never be free."

Bane shrugs. "Who of us is, bosun?"

He stares at the blade inches from his chest. "My

Kya will be," he whispers and lunges, impaling his heart on the steel point.

I scream. My heart is Sundered.

Healing redirects and wraps him in its embrace, holding, refusing to let him go. Love, dragon pain, power all flow through me. I scream again. Stays snap, sails shred, masts topple as soul magic powerful enough to sink an island is unleashed in fear and retribution. My chains shatter and I rise to the deck in a fist of water.

My mother charges through the quailing crew, distraught and fearful, shouting my name.

Jonathon's wound glows, blurs, and disappears. He gags on a breath he had never expected to feel again.

Relief pushes aside power.

Kraa'kken rises, wailing piteously, and tips the disabled ship beams-up. Bane windmills to keep his balance, but Jonathon jerks the tethering rope against his feet, toppling him into the angry sea where the dragon waits.

"Mea!" Bane shouts. "Calm the monster!"

She stares down at him, then at the baby burning with neglect. "We are all monsters," she murmurs. She looks at me, and smiles. "Use your power to heal this world," she says. "The Eld Ones are wrong. We should have always belonged." She dives over the side and surfaces singing, her scales gleam like diamonds.

I join her song, our voices pitched in a perfect, harmonious note of empathy and promise that sails the sea. The dragon's fire dims and he draws toward her. Our shared song ends and turns to tears in my mouth. "Mother is taking Kraa'kken far away," I say, "where they will die."

Bane paddles toward my shining mother. "My love," he cries, "save me from the monster."

"Of course, Edward," she says. She wraps him in her arms, presses her lips to his and drags him under.

I watch the bubbles swirl and wonder if I will someday have to do the same with my love.

Jonathon puts his arm around my shoulders. "We

will rename this ship the *Afhasi* and will honor your mother's memory through her figurehead. Let every slaver know, when they see her coming, that men will be free."

I return the embrace. It is enough.

We are Afhasi. Of the sea.

A Swift Changing Course

Jana Paniccia

From her position on the quarterdeck of the Shoteth great ship *Seadragon*, Kaimi Loraen could only watch as the wind shifted, sending wracking shivers through the ship's square-rigged canvas sails. A line of ominous clouds cut across the horizon, and her heartbeat grew faster as she watched their bulk spill upward, filling the sky with dark, deep-lined ridges.

"It'll be a bad one."

Kaimi jumped away from the deck rail, startled. Turning, she found Captain Aurus standing a foot away, his sun-darkened face calm despite his words. *Seadragon*'s captain carried a quiet confidence; the thigh-length black overcoat with its delicately engraved gold buttons done up to his neck only added to his authority. With the wind picking up, his gold-laced hat was tucked under one arm.

"Will it break our path?" she asked, giving him a slight bow, as she had seen some of his crew do. After three ten-days aboard, she was more relaxed with the captain and the crew than she had ever expected. While Captain Aurus had the gift of air, he was not a magis, and neither were most of the ship's company, though each had some affinity—mostly air, water, and fire. In the heat of the war with the Gida, crewing with anything less would be unconscionable. A spark of talent was enough to get a man impressed, and

113

most Shoteth ships didn't consider foreign citizenship a reason for freeing a man from service if he could make one of the cannons fire.

"It shouldn't," Captain Aurus said. "This is where having power-touched sailors comes in good stead. They aren't just for sinking enemy ships. Watch—" Without the slightest hesitancy, he motioned to a man standing by the wheel, First Lieutenant Makane. Kaimi recognized the officer's slim features and chestnut hair. While the lieutenant's uniform was not so different from the captain's, she imagined there were greater differences between the two men than just one having bone buttons instead of gold and white trousers instead of black. An even greater step separated the officers and the ordinary seamen, who wore little beyond canvas trousers and plain gray shirts.

"Get the captain of the maintop to ease the wind back to westward," the captain ordered, voice loud as the wind picked up.

Before Makane could move, a reedy dark-skinned boy ran out from beyond the great ship's wheel, offering up a speaking horn. *Amazing how so many people wait on his word.* Then again, four hundred men lived beneath *Seadragon*'s decks—far more than she would ever have imagined. *More than in all Lake Kelyar Academy.*

And all of them treated the captain with the same diffidence that people had once given her mother. The greatest air mage in a generation, Kailana Loraen had been called.

Kaimi grimaced. So many had expected her to take her mother's place, her mother who had given everything to save Shoteth from an airborne invasion.

If only they had sent me to a regular school. Instead she had been forced to endure life with those who did show great power; three turnings worth of ridicule, of pitying looks, and insults from those who had already attained magis status while she had shown no power at all. For five turnings she had been tested: earth, water, fire, air. She had shown an affinity toward none. *And everyone there made certain I knew it.*

"Wind back to west'ard," the lieutenant hollered, his voice echoing through the horn and breaking her reverie. Once he received acknowledgment from above, he handed the horn back to the boy, then said to the captain, "Wind back to west'ard ordered, sir."

Aurus nodded absently, eyes focused on the struggling sails.

Kaimi edged away, not wanting to intrude. Even though one was the captain and the other a lieutenant, there was a distinct ease between them. *They must know each other well living so close together, fighting together.* It wasn't a feeling she knew. At the academy she had always been an outcast. *The failed daughter.* Was this camaraderie what her mother had felt working from the tower of the senate building—what had pushed Kailana to give her life for Shoteth?

Up in the maintop, a man in a short oiled-cloth jacket moved to stand in the center of the slender platform, his balance steady despite the wind. Even at a distance, his bright red hair identified him as a native of Farshas Island, close enough to Traeis to make her wonder if *Seadragon* had made the extended journey before. *No doubt his would be an interesting story.*

Kaimi recognized his relaxed posture—the way his head bent toward his chest, eyes no doubt closed. A lump filled her throat as she recalled standing in that same position, hoping and praying for something to happen.

Everyone on deck turned to watch. Men scurried out onto the yards preparing to draw sail in tune with the shifting wind. She could imagine them reaching out to the wind, working to harness it into remembered patterns, ushering it back to support their course.

The wind grew stronger. A sudden chill coursed down her spine as she realized it wasn't the sailor's call the wind was following.

The captain noticed too. "Get Master Tywyn up here, immediately. We need his expertise." Master Tywyn was the ship's only first-level magis. She had heard from off-duty seamen that *Seadragon*'s master was strong with wind and water, a magis who had lived his entire life on the ocean fighting the Gida.

Kaimi had avoided the master as much as was possible on the two-decked great ship. She didn't want yet another set of condescending condolences like those of other high level magi she had encountered. She knew what they thought and it made her stomach churn. *At least Kailana Loraen didn't see her daughter fail.*

Kaimi wanted to get away before he could arrive, but the captain was standing between her and the hatchway. Instead, she inched farther along the rail, trying to skirt around the pair of officers without drawing attention. Before she could manage the maneuver, Master Tywyn, dressed in a loose black open-fitting shirt and the green woolen jacket worn by all Shoteth ship's masters, came on deck. The master's eyes widened as the rising wind threw him back a pace.

"Wind's act'n funny," he said, voice loud enough to be heard by most of the deck crew.

"Can you work it?" the captain requested.

Tywyn stepped to where he could see the compass-box and bent his head thoughtfully. From one moment to the next, he found the trance state. Kaimi felt a shudder run through the ship as the master gathered the wind to his hands and made to shift direction. Sweat puckered his brow, and his face gained lines of tension. "It's not want'n to move, Captain. It's as if someone's pressurin' it to stay its course."

"The Gida!" the lieutenant said. "Could they have learned of our orders?"

The captain's face went pale but his voice gave no hint of fear. "They cannot expect it, not from one ship traveling outside of a convoy."

What orders? They aren't just doing this for father?
Often the family of officials traveled by naval ship. *I
should have known there was more to it—I bet this
didn't cost him a thing. He'd have left me in Kanshet
otherwise. To be forgotten. Hidden.* No doubt the last
place he wanted her was anywhere she could draw
negative attention to him.

"Keep trying," the captain said to the master. Turning to Makane, he added. "Shorten sail, then hand out
rations. That storm will be on us in less than a bell."

As the lieutenant passed the orders, and the master
stooped to make a mark on the chart above the com-
pass, Kaimi focused on the approaching storm, her
attention drawn to the ocean running before the
clouds. No longer was it the gentle rolling that could
lull her with the ship's movement. Hints of white
showed on the waves now, and Kaimi leaned forward.
A fog rolled over her vision, catching a breath in her
throat. As the frothing sea burst toward the ship, she
twisted, tripping away.

A hand caught her elbow, helping her find footing:
the captain's, she realized, blinking her eyes clear.

"You need to go below," the captain said, his gaze
shifting back and forth between her and the water.
"It's safer for you there. This is no longer the place
for a young woman."

Kaimi picked her way to the captain's day room,
where she had been ensconced upon boarding. A scattering of books and papers littered the floor, and she
piled them haphazardly on the redwood desk. Most
were logbooks and letters of the ship's previous cap-
tains. Captain Aurus had offered the loan of them
when she had shown an interest.

Once she had the books in order, she tucked everything away into a packing trunk, then secured it tightly
so it wouldn't get opened when the sailors carried it
below. Which they would the moment the captain
called for battle quarters.

By the time she was finished, *Seadragon* was shifting more abruptly, each rise followed by a short, sharp drop.

Kaimi rubbed her eyes fiercely, missing the freedom of the deck, despite knowing she'd be a hindrance in the ship's preparations. She wondered what Captain Aurus was thinking. *What orders is he protecting?*

Despite her inexperience, the captain had welcomed her to spend as much time as she liked on the quarterdeck, and she had. "Bells and bells" as they told it in ship time, watching the seamen working the masts, from the topmost royals upon fore, main, and mizzen, to the thin triangular staysails stretched between. Other times she stared out at the endless expanse of ocean until her eyes watered, thinking the sea more alive than some places on land. Always moving. Always changing.

The captain had taken to speaking of the sea during the long afternoons, his spent pacing the length of the deck. She knew of his days on blockade in the bitter north as a fourth lieutenant, and of his first captaincy: a sloop which he worked amidst the islands ringing the equator. Through his words, she could almost hear the thrumming explosions as fire-trained seamen shot hot iron out of the ship's cannons. So different. So chaotic. Not like the daily ship drills at all.

From her time on *Seadragon,* she had seen days when water and air aligned to carry the ship in full glorious sail toward far off Traeis, and from the captain's stories, she imagined those where the wind was devilish calm, leaving the ship silent and becalmed.

Today it's a demon, she thought as the ship listed sharply to port. Before she could catch her balance, the cannon shutter burst open, sending a cascade of water into the cabin. She slipped and flew backward, cracking her head against the chest of books with a jarring thud that brought sharp daggers of pain.

Moments later, she sat up, head pounding along with the ebb and flow of the ship. A salty scent thick in her nose, she grimaced at the water soaking through the skirt of her dress. Cautiously, she took in the damage. Water blew in the open shutter, rain and seawater mixed. The sky beyond the opening was dark, leaving the cabin worse than a tomb.

Groping around, Kaimi found the desk and leveraged herself to her feet. She couldn't keep still—she wanted to move. A pressure built at the base of her spine, prompting her to sway forward to relieve it. Rocking with the movement of the boat, she found a balance. As her stomach grew tense, she could hear the pounding waves outside, beating in time with the rapid beats of her heart. Unnerved, she refused to stay in the cabin. *I can't stand this waiting—maybe the captain will know what's happening.* With that thought, she stumbled across the cabin and outside.

The moment Kaimi stepped into the storm, a wall of wind whipped a sheet of rain across her back, spiking across her neck and soaking all the way through the linen and lace of her dress. She gasped in enough air to whimper, a more full-throated scream locking in her chest. As a wave barreled against the side, she fell forward as if the storm swells pummeled her. She kept her feet by catching the safety line, the hairy rope cord crossing the deck. Desperately wanting to shut her eyes, she edged along the safety, eyes tracking the distance to where Captain Aurus was standing, shouting orders she couldn't hear.

He'll know how to stop this—he has to!

As Kaimi slid forward another hand, someone grabbed the trailing end of her cloak and yanked. "What do you think you are doing?" Lieutenant Makane shouted even as he caught and twisted her arm behind her back.

Struggling within his hold, Kaimi managed to tilt her head enough to see the lieutenant holding her captive with one hand, while his other was affixed to the safety. His dark brown eyes, once patient with her questions, now burned with annoyance and anger. For a fierce moment, she wanted to let him drag her back to the safety of between decks, where she could hide from the energy coursing through her while the storm thundered above. Only the increasing pressure of impending disaster kept her from surrendering.

Her limbs ached, even as a new wave broke over the ship, breaking Makane's grip and swamping them both in sea-salted water. A sharp tang burst through her mouth, bitter yet not the choking vileness she expected. Forgetting the storm, she licked her lips.

Understanding coursed through her body, strange and powerful. She rippled with energy, could feel it building and growing, even as the waves grew. Her knees weakened until she was flat against the deck, looking up into the swirls of sky. For long moments, she knew nothing, except for the steady bursts of sensation accompanying each wave cascading over the side.

"Come on now," Makane said, pulling her up again.

"This isn't right. I can't stand it! The captain has to be able to stop . . ." She pulled one hand free and waved it out toward where the riotous waves broke over the side and poured across the canted decks. Without finishing, she dove against the rope, *knowing* the ship was going to fall hard across the ridge of a wave. As *Seadragon* shuddered, she held tight. Unprepared, Makane slipped. He cried out as he fell facedown into the swamping onrush and was battered backward against the side.

Kaimi screamed and grabbed for him. The water was faster, carrying the officer across the deck. Her vision blurred as she became the rush of water against wood, pressing her attack with perfect single-mindedness. She moved with sudden synchrony— targeted, structured—more precise than the new timepieces she had seen in the capital.

Like nothing of nature could be.

"This can't just be a storm," she shouted, leaping to her feet, resonating with horror. Captain Aurus had his back toward her. No first level magis, he wouldn't know of the limits around shapings. No one could cause a tempest like this from far away. They'd have to be in the eye of the storm. She peered about for the master. *Come on—where is he? He'll recognize it.*

A deep ache coursed through her chest and she turned toward the sea. A dark body-shaped patch floated on top of the waves, borne up and not dragged down. There was nothing in the dead form that reminded her of Tywyn; even so, she knew the master was dead. There would be no help from there. She had to grab the captain's attention. She stumbled over to where the first lieutenant was, now sitting up and violently retching.

Though her stomach lurched in sympathy, she pulled Makane close and shouted in his ear. "It's a trap. The Gida are out. They have to be. They can't be controlling this storm from far out. They've got to be right on top of us."

Kaimi could only imagine how she sounded— warning of their enemy without any background knowledge of the war or of fighting. She recognized the confusion on his face. *He thinks I'm mad.* She made ready to rush the captain if Makane tried to draw her away, but the first lieutenant's dark eyes had grown large and were studying her with rapt attention.

She followed his eyes downward, to where the seawater swirled across their feet. It circled their place on the deck in a gentle, even pool, despite the storm swirling around them, still battering *Seadragon*'s sides.

"Come on," Makane said, grabbing her arm. She yelped as he dragged her forward, crossing the entire deck faster than she had made it ten feet.

"Captain!" he shouted, voice swallowed instantly by the wind. "Captain!"

Captain Aurus's attention was on the massive double wheel of the ship. "Come on—pull it!" he was shouting. Six men were attempting to hold the course steady, their naked backs straining against and beneath the press of the weather. It wasn't until Kaimi and the first lieutenant were a hand's span away that the captain turned.

"Lieutenant," Aurus said, anger filling his words. "Get her below. What do you think you're doing? I'll have you before an inquiry for this."

Makane ignored the captain's threat, motioning toward Kaimi. She would have looked away but she could hardly move; the water weaving around her brought warm numbness despite the bitter chill of the rain.

"The Gida are nearby, she's certain of it. If they learn of our orders, far more will die."

The captain's disbelief was plain as he took in Kaimi's frayed and sodden appearance. He shook his head, raising his hand—no doubt to order her away. *If only the water would ease—surely he'd see them.* They had to be right in the center of the storm. She *knew* from her studies that drawings could not be cast from a distance without losing power. If they were in the center, so were the Gida.

She gasped as the ship rocked beneath them—fell to her knees as the sea calmed, bringing the ship almost to a halt. Rain continued to hammer down, but the water took it in, placating and soothing the turbulent streams. As a wave of exhaustion broke over Kaimi's head, she met the captain's eyes. Fear swelled within as she realized the enormity of what she had done.

The captain didn't hesitate. "Lookout!" he bellowed. The single word echoed all the way up the mainmast.

It was as if the wind itself waited for the response; quiet for a moment then rousing to a howl just as a panicked, "Enemy coming across the bow—four cables and closing," came back from the tops.

"To quarters!" the captain ordered, even as a rumble echoed across the water. Seamen screamed as balls of fire-powered metal tore through their unprotected ship. If she hadn't been on her knees already, Kaimi would have pitched forward. Instead, she scrabbled for purchase. Around her, men careened through the hatchways and ran toward their stations: the long can-

non lining each side of the lower two decks, and
guarding the four corners of the quarterdeck. This was
the reason for having fire-trained powers on the ship.
Even those with the weakest fire ability could launch
heated iron shot.

"We'll never make it 'round in this wind!" Makane
shouted, even as a second wave of fire broke over the
ship. A deep cracking rent the air, and the deck rose
slightly as part of the foremast came down, the wind
throwing it out to the sea before it could land among
the unprotected seamen. Fire burst from where the
enemy's cannon had struck, lively despite the rain.
Those seamen not manning cannon scurried about
with hoses, trying to put out the fires.

"Starboard to fire when ready," the captain commanded, ignoring everything beyond the enemy ship.
Seadragon's deck pitched as thunder sounded from the
cannons below, releasing their own torrents of fire.
The air sizzled though at this rough angle, no shots
connected.

Frozen by the chaotic din of the *Seadragon*'s sudden
entrance into battle, Kaimi couldn't take her eyes off
the smoke puffing out of their enemy's cannon, cannon she knew from the ongoing screams had found
targets. The Gidan ship was a match to their own,
right down to the two decks of cannon and the gilt
figurehead—in the Gidan's case, a woman with wind-
swept hair and bared breasts. The only signs it was
not of Shoteth origin were the green and yellow Gidan
flag waving from the ship's mainmast and the fact that
its cannon shutters were painted a crisp green instead
of blood red.

Then Kaimi noticed the rain, its sharp pinpricks im-
pinging on the water everywhere but around the other
ship. What few sails it had unfurled were caught in a
well-balanced wind.

That's impossible!

The image of Tywyn's body floating amidst the
whitecaps rose before her eyes. *That ship is responsible,* she thought, forgetting about the ships' similari-

ties. A metallic tang filled her mouth as she bit her tongue. More bodies would be joining his soon. Shuddering, she knew if they didn't do something—if *she* didn't do something—*Seadragon* would be the Gida's next victim.

Shutting her eyes, Kaimi reached for the torrents of water falling over *Seadragon,* trying to grasp control. The driving rain continued.

It's just like at the academy—nothing. Hot tears joined the rain on her cheeks.

No, I have to do this. I have to. Shifting her focus, Kaimi concentrated on the power in the tumultuous sea—on the salted water sluicing over the side. Deeply entranced, she found a well of calm despite the turbulent air.

Calm will do no good here, she thought angrily, willing the water to boil. The deck shook under her feet, pressure building and growing. Fire heated her cheeks as the shot of a strong Gidan magis took out the great wheel. Captain Aurus continued to call out orders. Not a word made it to her ears. All she could hear was the rushing of water as it fought her grasp. All she could see was the black emptiness behind her eyelids, though her insides churned and her breath strangled.

As enemy shots crashed through the ship sparking more screams, blood coursed over the deck to mix with the salt of the ocean. Anger flared through Kaimi's chest and exploded, barreling water upward through shackles of air, and the *Seadragon* along with it. Together, ship and water rose and rose, until it felt like she was standing on the edge of a precipice and the only way left to go was down.

She opened her eyes as the wind died and *Seadragon*'s bow tilted forward at the very edge of a breaking wave. With the sails in shreds, she could see forward too easily. Dull sails hung even with her sight, bereft of wind: the enemy's royals and topgallants.

Oh Waterlord. Bile rose in her throat as she realized they were hanging almost overtop the enemy.

If she released the giant wave, it might kill the Gida, but it could also tear *Seadragon* apart.

Vision frozen on the Gidan ship, Kaimi felt the silence. If she relaxed her hold, they'd be in the same position—and no doubt the Gida would not play games a second time. Her only choice was to get them before . . .

"Oh Waterlord—look!" It was Makane. The lieutenant ran to the edge of the quarterdeck and pointed. At the heart of the Gidan ship, one sailor scurried up the mainmast. Even as Kaimi felt her strength weakening, the seaman made it to the top and yanked down the Gidan flag. The scrap of cloth fluttered down to the deck, landing at the feet of a red-jacketed man whose face she could not make out clearly, though she took him for the ship's captain. The Gidan picked up his country's flag, folded it against his chest, and knelt with his head bowed.

Shouts of joy rose from *Seadragon*'s lower decks; she ignored them. Her legs refused to hold weight as she struggled to hold the unseen press of water back from the Gidan ship. Their surrender wouldn't matter if she let go. *We could all still die.*

"Take it easy." The captain took her shoulders, holding her steady even as he commanded her efforts. "Let it go a bit at a time. You can do it. You have been trained for it."

Kaimi felt reason starting to return. She *had* been trained for it. It didn't matter than everyone had given up on her—that she herself had given up hope of ever becoming a true magis. Whatever the cause—she had power now, and a thousand lives were hanging on her next action.

For a wild moment, she wanted to let go—to let the sea take them all.

Yes, the academy would welcome her now that she had proven her power. She was sure of it. But she didn't want to go back; she didn't want that life, those chains. She didn't know whether to laugh at the irony of it, or cry at her sudden loss of freedom. With power, she'd become the bargaining chip her father had always wanted to play.

She shivered under the taunting waves as they rushed over her mind offering freedom from entanglement. All she had to do was let go.

Shrugging out of the captain's hands, Kaimi stepped forward. In the midst of the ship's company, she was alone.

Up in the tops, a single man started to sing.

The tune was out of place on the unmoving deck, only sails furling or unfurling tended to bring out the sounds of the sea. As the tune picked up more voices, it seeped through her panic, calming her muscles. She recognized the song as one often sung by the topmen to the ship. Respect. Duty. Honor of work well done.

This time the song was for her.

Struggling under the weight of newfound power, tears welled in Kaimi's eyes. *They trust me.* A stranger among them, yet they trusted her to bring them through. A trust that she, like her mother before her, could not refuse.

Resonating with the offered support, Kaimi released her grip on the wave, sinking with it until only music remained.

It took several days for the *Seadragon* to make repairs, and to regain full steerage capacity. Kaimi missed most of the action, confined to her cabin by exhaustion and weakness. On the fourth day, she regained the deck in time to see the newly patched sails set. Captain Aurus called out orders as needed, chatting amicably with Makane between times. They both turned as she came onto the deck. Heat rising on her face, Kaimi looked away, catching view of the enemy ship to starboard.

At her back, the captain chuckled. "Be easy. I refused to let the seamen greet you with a barrel of ale. Said you weren't used to ship celebration."

When Kaimi turned, Captain Aurus had a small

smile on his face. He motioned her to join them. "I'm giving Makane command of the *Raiden*," he said. "He'll be taking the ship and prisoners back to Shoteth. If you want to return, you can have a place with him. He'll see you safe to any academy of your choice."

For a moment, she wanted to say yes. Wanted to go back and prove to everyone back at Lake Kelyar that she wasn't powerless. *But would they even believe me?* If she returned to the academy, she'd be able to show them nothing. Her power wouldn't score the lake at all. Even if she could, would she ever feel like she belonged? They had already shown that they cared more about power than partnership. She wanted no life like that.

"I have a sea-born power," she started, then hesitated.   Around the deck, members of the ship's crew worked busily, though she had a feeling it was more make-work while they strained to hear the conversation.

"I suspected as much. It's why you called the wave and didn't halt the rain," the captain said, nodding for her to continue.

"It seems a power useful to a life aboard ship. I'd need training, but the journey to Traeis *will* take a dozen more ten-days."

"So you want to continue to Traeis? You can—"

"There's a naval academy there, is there not?" Kaimi broke in, her voice growing loud. The sea picked up her nervousness, and the ship shuddered.

She met the captain's eyes with a deep-held breath. After a moment, he swept his hand outward to take in the full length of the ship. "There'd be a lot more to learn. As I've said before, it's not just about power. It's not an easy life, especially for a woman. You're far and few between on great ships—you'd face a lot of dissent, and not always from the Gida."

"But right here and now, I can make my own decision," Kaimi said. "I know it won't be perfect—but it would be my life, and a life of honor. I want to protect

Shoteth, but I want to do it my way. I've noticed you
take each person on the ship for their own. You accepted me as a governor's daughter. Will you accept
me among you?"

The captain shook his head. "That is for the Admiral at Traeis to decide—you *are* the governor's daughter after all. I wish it could be my decision, but you
must know the ramifications of your actions go far
beyond this small patch of ocean."

Kaimi sighed, knowing his words for truth. She
might have power, but her father had connections.

"Of course," the captain added, with a smile. "Considering our orders are to take over the Gidan settle-
ments off Cape Meridon, I can't imagine the Admiral
refusing your offer at such a precipitous time."

The Colonial Age

Filled with hope for a better life, some fleeing perse-
cution, many people undertook the long and dangerous journey across the Atlantic to make a fresh
start in the New World. They found a strange and
wondrous land, offering promise, potential, and peril,
including its own inhabitants. It was a time of first
encounters and lasting, profound change to the face
of humanity, even for those who'd chosen to stay, or
were left behind, in the Old World.

Blood and Soil

Ceri Young

Andreas comes to us while we are asleep to tell us there are men coming.

We are most often asleep now, but Andreas comes and tells us things anyway. He is hoping we can still hear him, hoping we will respond.

"They are building a road here," he said. "In this part of the forest. They will go through and cut down the trees and make a route that goes from here all the way to Chebucto. They will be able to bring troops back to fight the Indians. They will bring supplies. It will be a good thing for the town," he says to me. He does not say, "But maybe not a good thing for us," even though I hear it in his voice. He is worried. He is worried that it is happening again.

"You do not need to worry, though," he tells us. "I will be helping to build the road. I will help them build it so that it does not come too close to here. You will never even see the men. I will keep them away. This time."

Every time Andreas comes I try to move for him, to show him I hear and I understand. This time I try harder than ever, because I want to tell him that it is all right and that I am not worried. I am not afraid of the men and their axes, I want to say. But I still cannot move. I stay asleep. Andreas waits for a long time to see if anyone has heard him. He waits until the light is almost gone and he will have to go home in the dark. Then he sighs and says goodbye.

I would say goodbye, if I could.

After Andreas goes, I think more about the road and what it means. When we first came here, there were no roads. There were only footpaths between the houses. This suited us, for we had come to the new world to be alone. Now the town is growing. Roads mean travelers, and travelers mean less isolation. That is fine if the men do not come here looking for us. Andreas says we are safe. I believe my brother.

It was the men who made us leave Germany. Traditionally, the *Baumenvolk* have been called the luck of the forest. We travel to villages around and test the soil. We say which farmlands need to rest, what will grow best where.

One year, the crops failed. It was not our fault; there was a drought. But that did not matter. The men came to our village. They called us witches, accused us of waylaying travelers and cast a thrall over the men in our family. Then they set fire to our village. They drove us out. They killed my mother and father.

Then they began hunting those who escaped.

It was Andreas' idea to come here. He heard the offer of land in the new world. Andreas said, men will not bother us there. The new world is vast, he said. We will have our own land. It will be far away from everything, and they will leave us be. We will be safe.

I think this is why Andreas visits me so often. He is the reason I am here. He thinks it is his fault that I cannot wake up. He blames himself.

But Andreas is the reason I am alive. Back in the old country, he saved me from the men of our village. He woke me up, silenced me, ran with me into the forest to hide when they came with their torches. He helped me to find the members of our family who had run away. Later, Andreas saved us on the ocean, too.

*   *   *

On the ocean, you cannot touch the earth, not for weeks or months. That is death for our kind. Andreas is clever, though. He fashioned a special pair of wooden shoes for each of the women. They were deeper than the ones most people wear, and into these he put a quantity of soil from our homeland. They were awkward, but they would keep us alive.

The shoes would also keep our nature hidden from people who might accuse us of witchcraft. We had left behind the men who killed our family, yet we did not know who might share their prejudices. Until we reached the new world, our roots must remain a secret.

It was a cold, wet day when we set out. All around us, people were saying their goodbyes to loved ones. Our goodbyes were silent ones—to the land, and to our dead. We joined hands and prayed for their souls. I wished that my parents were there to send me off. I even imagined I saw them in the crowd, but that was foolish. If they had not been killed, we would not have had to leave.

When we launched, I felt as if my heart had been torn from me. I watched the land recede from the crowded deck. It was not long before I could see nothing but water all around me. It made me feel sick.

How can I express the horror of the journey that followed? I think we would never have left had we known what was ahead. We were all sick, with the rolling of the sea and with the poor rations we were given. The food was rotten, the water stank. The hold where we slept was nothing but bare floors and bunks. We were crowded together with others on the ship. We took the farthest bunks we could get against the wall, placing the men between us and the rest of the crew while we slept, for a little privacy, to stay hidden.

Our feet hurt in the shoes, and the soil in them grew dry and crumbly. Even after I had eaten, I would still be hungry. No, that would be true anyway, for there was never enough to eat. But it was as if I had another hunger, a void that food could not fill, that could only be filled by walking on fresh soil. Then the fever hit.

On our ship there was a man who played minister to the sick. He was not a minister, but he knew many sermons, and he would read to the sick and pray with them. We did not like him. He was nosy and proud, always telling people what to do. He listened to gossip and passed secrets, causing fights among people who were already angry and tired from hardship.

When Dorothea fell sick, he insisted on coming and praying with her. Since the man caused argument when he did not get his way, we felt we could not say no. But Andreas and I both watched closely while he sat with our sister.

Dorothea was delirious by then, not knowing what she said or to whom. So when the man came and took her hand, she took him for a relative. "My feet are hurting," she said. "You must take off these shoes."

Andreas gently refused, but the man did not listen, saying that the sick must be humored. He reached for Dorothea's feet and had the shoe off before Andreas could grab his hand. Feeling the earth torn from her, Dorothea gasped, and began to struggle. Andreas tried to put the shoe back on, but not before the man saw her feet. Below the knees, the skin becomes brown and bark-like. The feet taper to points, and the soles of the feet, pale and white, reach out searching for the soil. I rushed to put the shoe back on before my sister's thrashing attracted any more attention. Andreas dealt with the man.

He knew exactly what we were. He did not seem afraid, but looked from my sister to me. A smile played about his lips. I knew he was thinking of who he might tell this new bit of gossip. Andreas spoke to him, saying that there were reasons our nature must be kept secret, and entreating the man to come somewhere with him where they might talk privately.

When Andreas came back, he was alone. The man, he said, had gone onto the deck. He never came back. I do not like to think about it. He was not a nice man, but he did not deserve to die. But if he had not, my family would be dead.

The seas were rough that night. He may have fallen overboard.

Hardships were all but forgotten when we sighted land.

From the harbor, Malagash was exactly what we had been promised. The land was lush with forest and field. It was so beautiful. When we finally docked, I wanted to kick off my shoes and run to touch the fresh earth, but Uncle Jacob grabbed my arm and held me back before I had even left the boat. I turned to him, angry at being stopped, but he pointed at the shore.

There were people all along the docks who had come down to meet us. They wanted to see the new settlers.

"We do not know who to trust," my uncle said. "You must hide a little while longer."

I came very near to pushing him into the harbor.

It was hours before we had been allowed off the boat, hours more before we were given our plot of land. Hours of walking and fidgeting and wanting to kick the shoes off despite the warnings. All of the women were the same, and we stayed together talking, keeping our minds from what we most wanted.

Finally, finally, our family had a small shelter where we could be alone. Finally, all of the women together took off their shoes, and together touched the land for the first time. When I sank my roots deep into the soil, I felt as if I had come to life again. The land was good, the earth rich, and it did not taste so very different from our homeland soil.

We could not have known how different it would be.

The first year was difficult. We were told that we would be given fifty acres of land each, and more for bringing a family. But when we arrived, it was to find a town surrounded by a palisade wall. There were Indians in the area, we were told, and they were violent. The British military had set up blockhouses in order to protect the town and the roads leading to it, but small groups and lone travelers were often attacked. People very rarely went outside the town walls, and when they did it was in groups, and with guns.

This was a blow. We faced danger from outside the town, but perhaps more danger from inside it. We could not know who we could trust with our secret. We women had to keep our shoes on during the day as we went about our work. Even at home we needed to be very careful. People visited the house often, stopping in unannounced. We had to keep ourselves carefully hidden.

It was the British government who came to our rescue. Malagash was set up to provide food for the growing town of Chebucto, and if we stayed within the walls we would not have enough food for ourselves, let alone another town. To encourage us to move onto the land, they set up more blockhouses, and gave us the materials to build protected houses. The raids, they said, were not as bad as they had been made out to be. If all of our family lived and worked the land together, they said it would be safe.

So we built a house as far from the town as we dared, surrounded by a large wall to keep out intruders. Always at night, someone would be up, watching for attack. The militia, and the soldiers from the blockhouse, visited often. Still, off on our own, we could walk around without our shoes. The women, who had grown weak on the voyage, who were kept weak the year we stayed in town, grew strong again. Our farm prospered as well, for we knew how to work the land, what to plant and where. For the most part, we had the freedom and isolation that we sought.

That was before the illness came. That was before the men came to build their road.

*　　　*　　　*

I wake late at night, days after Andreas has visited. It is not fair. I wish I could tell him that we mostly wake at night now, and perhaps he would stay and talk to us. Yet, even if I could tell him, the woods at night are dangerous for him, and he might not be able to find his way home in the dark.

It is almost worse when I am awake. I can move, but I cannot move. If I leave this place, Andreas will not know where I have gone, and I will not be able to tell him. I would lose my sisters and cousins who are asleep around me. I would be truly lost then.

I hope sometimes that I will stay awake. I imagine that I have finally learned to live with the land, and that it will not reclaim me and root me to the spot, as it has done. But always, no matter how hard I hope and pretend, I feel the need growing in me to send down my roots. And I fall asleep again.

Tonight I am not the only one who awakes. Shortly after I begin moving around the grove, Dorothea begins to stir. I can hear her branches moving in the wind. I go to stand next to her, to hold her hand as she opens her eyes. They are hard to pick out among the bark that is her face. I cannot believe that this thing, now more tree than woman, is my sister. I cannot believe that the land has done this to us.

Dorothea is younger than I am. She too has heard the worry in Andreas' voice, and it worries her. "If they bring the road here, with their axes, they may kill us," Dorothea says. "Andreas is afraid of this."

"Andreas will change where the road goes," I explain to her. "He will make sure we are safe. He always does."

"Andreas," she says angrily, "is the reason we are here. Andreas is the one who brought us *safe* out of our homeland to die here."

Some of us are like this—blaming Andreas and the other men for bringing us here. They brood while they sleep, and they grow bitter and angry. Others of us live in hope that one day we will walk free again. But it is hard to keep up hope the longer we are here.

Sometimes I feel as they do, that we should never have come, and that Andreas is to blame. Other times I remember our home burning, remember that we had nowhere else to go, and I know Andreas did what he thought was best. Whatever the other women say now, we all agreed to come and saw no alternative.

I try to defend Andreas to Dorothea, but tonight the words sound hollow even to me. When Dorothea feels herself rooting again she goes back to her place even angrier than before.

How could we have known? How could we have guessed, a world away?

It was the shouting that brought me from the house out into the courtyard. There were many people there, shouting at one another. Two men were holding Maria pinned by the arms. She was not struggling. Two others were helping Uncle Jacob to his feet. He had a cut on his forehead that was weeping blood. His axe was on the ground.

"How could you attack your own father?" One of the men was demanding.

Maria's reply sounded dazed. "He was going to hit me with the axe," she said.

"He was chopping *kindling*," Hans said. Then, to no one in particular, "She ran up to him and struck him, and knocked the axe from his hand. She attacked him."

"The wood," Maria said. "You hurt the wood." She was looking at the chopping block. Then she shook her head, and seemed to come to herself. She looked up at her father. "What is it I've done?"

Maria was shut up in the woodshed until something could be done with her. She seemed to have no recollection of attacking her father, only that she had heard him chopping wood, and felt a pain, and was sure that he would hurt her.

I felt worry knot my stomach then, for I knew that I had felt the pain too. Not as if I were being attacked, but as a curious buzzing, a pulling at my roots that told me that someone was chopping wood in the courtyard. I had thought I was coming to understand the land. Now I suspected it was something else.

Two days later, Dorothea came to get me, screaming that something was wrong. Maria stood, rooted to the ground in the way that we do when we rest. She would not wake when we called to her. When she was eventually able to move, she told us it was as if she had sunk her roots deep into the ground, so deep she would never be able to move again. As if she had become part of the land.

Maria's skin began to change. Her arms and legs became more and more bark-like, scaling over by inches every day. She woke less and less often, and I watched her skin with growing fear. We tried every medicine and plant we knew, but nothing helped.

Then, one by one, the other women started to succumb to it, too. We became violent whenever wood was being cut—axes had to be kept out of sight, the kindling split behind one of our houses. Even then, the sound of chopping would sometimes bring us running. Sometimes the men were scratched and bruised. Hans suffered a broken arm, Jacob a broken leg.

It was Andreas who found out what was causing the madness. He went to visit Malagash one day, and there was a minister there, one who had spent time among the savages. He was laughing about their superstitions, the ways that they spoke of the land as if it was a living thing.

"Do you know why they call this place 'Malagash'?" he asked my brother. "It is a word that means 'evil that is in the land.' They think we are crazy to farm here. They think we anger the spirit that is in the soil!" The man laughed at the idea, but Andreas took his leave and rushed home, to tell us what he had learned.

I wish his knowledge had helped. Yet what can one do when there is evil in the soil? I cannot stop touching it, even when I knew it would make me sick. We talked of moving, but we had nowhere to go. Where would we be safe?

I was one of the last to become sick, but in a way that was worse, knowing all the while what was coming for me. I prayed every night that it would pass me by, that I might be spared. And every time I took a step, and every night when I rooted and slept, I feared. Every man in my family watched me as I walked. I knew that they were thinking I would be next. I thought of running away, but where would I run? All along the way I would touch the ground.

Something had to be done. We were growing more and more tree-like, more rooted to the spot, less able to be around wood that was cut. And everywhere there was cut wood: the kindling, our houses, our tables, the wall around our houses.

There was a meeting of everyone in the family and it was decided. Those that were so sick as to be asleep most of the time were taken into the forest, and left there. Some of the younger women objected, but most of us knew we had to go.

Those of us who were awake picked a spot deep in the woods, a clearing where we could put down roots and be left alone. It was far from our camp, but not so far that we could not be visited and taken care of. One by one, we were taken there and rooted, standing with our silent sisters.

At first, they visited often, speaking to us of things that were happening, telling us that they missed us. Eventually, all of the women from my family were brought to the grove. Then, one by one, our uncles and cousins stopped visiting. All but Andreas.

This is not as lonely as it seems. So deep in the forest, no one passes, not even the savages. There is no cut wood to call to us in pain the moment we touch the soil. We may sleep here, and sink our roots deep. And we are not lonely because we are not alone. When we awake, we are always surrounded by those we love, by those who understand and suffer with us.

When I feel myself falling asleep again, I comfort myself with those thoughts. We are in less pain here than we would be elsewhere. And though the women with the longest roots pine for the homeland, at home we would surely be dead. That cannot be better.

Andreas comes back. I can tell he is nervous, but he says nothing about the road. He talks and talks about life in town and our family. The spring has been good for the livestock—we have three new foals. My uncles have planted new fields, they expect many crops this winter, maybe enough that they will not need the government's rations. The governor at Chebucto has written, praising our industry at working the land. Andreas stays for a long time, talking to us, talking to himself. I can tell there is something he is not saying.

He gets up to leave. I hear him turn.

"The road is coming here," he says. "Not to your grove, but through this part of the forest. I could not stop it. They will be here soon now, a few weeks at most. I am sorry. If you must leave, if you still can, go to the south. I will look for you there. I will find you."

It is useless to tell us to leave. We cannot even move most days. I think I wake less and less often now. *You lied to me,* I think. *You lied and you said I would be safe.* I am so angry, so angry I want to grab him and shake him. *How can you do this? How can you leave us here?* I manage to move an arm, a violent rustling, but I cannot do more. I hear him pause, but he does not turn back.

My cousin Maria wakes shortly after Andreas leaves and comes to stand by me.

"We have been forgotten." She says in a voice that is a hiss. "Andreas is the only one who ever comes to visit us. Why do you think? The other men have forgotten. They are ashamed of us and they have exiled us here and forgotten us. Even Andreas has turned his back on us now. I am going, but I am going to the west of here. There is more forest there, more places

for us to hide and be safe. Andreas is useless to us
now. He could not save us from this disease, and now
he cannot even save us from men.

It is only days later that I know the road is coming.
It is far off, but I can feel the prickling, the sense of
the world being changed, the pain of the trees being
cut. I can hear the timbers falling.

The men are coming. I hope they do not come
any closer.

Yet they do come closer. And closer.

Over the next few weeks, more of my family leave.
None of them go south. They all head west. I am torn,
now. If I wake, I do not know which way I will go.
Will I run to the south so Andreas can find me? Will
I run to the west, and try to find my sisters? Perhaps
if Andreas finds me, then we can go and look for
those who have left. If I can tell him where they have
gone. If I ever wake again.

They come so close the glow of their firelight signals
a warning, like the torches the men carried when they
came to burn our village. I can feel the trees they
have cut. It is as if my roots are raw skin, chafed away.
I am dead inside. As they get closer I think, those
trees could be my sisters. They could be me. Very
soon now, it *will* be me.

Andreas comes walking, arguing with one of the
men. They are talking about where the road will go
tomorrow. The man says it will go here, and I am
afraid. Andreas disagrees. He says that this stand of
trees is unlucky, that it is different from the others
and that it would be bad to cut the trees down. It is
clearly a fairy fort, he tells the man. Bad things will
happen to people who cut these trees.

Many of the men in Malagash are superstitious.
They would listen to Andreas about the bad luck. This
one does not. I hear Andreas grow increasingly desperate. The man says to him that he can leave if he

does not wish to cut these trees. He can leave and not get the bad luck. I can hear that Andreas is torn. He and the other man go away again.

Andreas comes at night, just for a moment.

"I hoped to find more of you gone," he says. "Run if you can. They will come here. They will kill you." He looks to us for a response—anything at all. Not one of us moves. Not one of us speaks. Andreas sighs heavily. "There is one more thing I can do. I will try to stop them. But it is best if you are not here. Please run."

If I do not wake tonight, tomorrow I will likely die, and my sisters with me.

I stay alert all night, trying to move, trying to wake myself up. Around me, I know the others are doing the same. We are afraid. Most of us manage to move a little, but not enough to get anywhere. Our roots go too deep.

Tomorrow the men will come, and we will die.

In the morning, there is a hue and cry in the men's camp. Someone is dead. I can taste his blood in the soil.

Andreas has killed the man who would have brought the road here. I can hear the voices calling. Now, they will kill Andreas. I hear the men chanting for his blood.

They will kill my brother. For trying to save us. Because they would not listen. Then they will kill us. Then they will kill me.

These men. Just like the ones who came before, who drove me from my home. Now I must run again.

I am moving before I realize it. The trees spring to life all around me. From the corner of my eye I can see some of my kin are also awake, and they move with me.

I see the men before me. Some are holding guns and knives. Others are holding Andreas. These are the men I attack first, my arms sweeping down in blows. Some of the men see us and raise their mus-

kets. Others grab axes. They fall down. They do not
get up again.

*You will not drive us away again. You will not kill
my family again.*

When it is over, Andreas is the only one alive in the
camp. He sits on the ground, dazed, staring at nothing.
The other women stand around, unsure of what has
happened, unsure of what to do.

We are covered in blood. The soil beneath us is wet
through with it. We drink it into our roots.

I approach Andreas, reaching out an arm to touch
his shoulder. He recoils and looks up at me. I see his
eyes, wide and wild. He is afraid. This time he is not
afraid of the men, or the road. He is afraid of me. He
says nothing, only stares.

I say nothing. There is nothing to say. All this time,
he thought to make us safe from the men. In the end,
it was the men who needed protecting from us.

I turn to my sisters, and together we walk away into
the deeper forest, moving easily now, heading west,
leaving Andreas behind.

We are finally awake.

Fletcher's Ghost

Liz Holliday

Manila, 1762

"*Te amo,* Maria," Danny said. It was nearly all the Spanish he knew.

Maria stared at him out of the half-dark. The cold night air, the stink of the docks, the clamor of the nearby tavern all fell away from him as he thought at her: say it back, say it back.

"Don't say such things, Danny," she said at last.

"Please," he said. "Come away with me. We can—"

"What would I, a Catholic, do in England?" she asked.

"It won't matter. We won't let it matter." He reached out to touch her.

Someone grabbed him from behind and yanked him back. He flailed to keep his balance but slammed into the side of the tavern.

"Hands off, Inglez."

Danny stared up. The Spaniard was enormous and there were two more behind him. Lantern light glinted on the knife in his hand.

"Don't—" Danny started.

A strange moaning noise came from somewhere above them. The Spaniard looked up. Danny followed the line of his gaze and saw a figure silhouetted on

145

the roof of the warehouse opposite. It was smaller than a man, larger than most apes.

The Spaniard moved towards Danny.

The moaning noise came again. The creature leaped down, pushed off the wall of the warehouse with one foot, and landed in a crouch between Danny and the Spaniard.

Danny stared into its face. The creature was surely human, though with dark eyes huger than any man's, skin as white as the moon, and fingers that ended in hooked talons.

"Madre de—" one of the sailors whispered.

Out of the corner of his eye, Danny saw Maria cross herself.

"Maria, get behind me," Danny whispered, hoping she would understand him. She didn't move.

The first Spaniard moved forward. The creature whirled round. Light flashed on the Spaniard's knife. The creature lunged forward. A terrible rattling hiss came from its throat.

The Spaniard brought his blade up to meet the creature, but he was a fraction slow. The creature slashed at his arm with its wicked talons. Someone screamed. The blade flew out of the Spaniard's hand and the creature caught it out of the air.

For a moment the Spanish sailors held their ground. Their leader nursed his injured arm. Blood, black in the dim light, dripped onto the ground.

The creature feinted towards him with the knife.

The sailors broke and ran.

The creature turned.

"Maria, get behind me," Danny repeated. He stared at the creature. He wondered what it would do if they tried to get past it. "If you hurt her, I will kill you," he said.

He thought of his father, laughing at him when he'd said those words. His fist coming down on Danny's seven-year-old face. I'm not seven now, he thought.

The creature took a step forward. Now Danny saw

that its arm was smeared with blood. Its own or the Spaniard's? He could not tell.

The creature said something unintelligible. Its voice sounded rough, as if it hadn't spoken in a long time. It tried again. "I have help you. You help me."

"You can speak," Danny said.

"Englis'. Yes." The creature glared at him out of orange eyes. "Help me."

Danny stared at it, assessing. He did not think there was any real chance he could get past it against its will.

"Let her go and we'll see," he said. The creature nodded slowly. "Go," Danny said.

Maria hesitated. Then she slid past the creature and was gone into the darkness.

"Now," Danny said. "What do you want?"

"I have hear others say—you are fletcher? Fletcher is arrow maker, yes?"

The question was so unexpected that Danny laughed aloud. "Me? I'm no arrow-maker, man. My grandfather, now, he was. And his grandfather before him."

"And he have taught you?"

"No. Yes. Well, that's to say I watched him, sometimes. He made arrows for competitions. For his lordship, d'you see?"

If the creature understood, it gave no sign of it.

"Then you help me?" The creature held out its hand.

"No," Danny said. "I can't help you."

"But you must. Must make arrows. If not you, who?"

"I don't know," Danny said, his patience exhausted. "Someone will, I expect."

In daylight, Maria was even more beautiful. Danny watched as she stowed bundles of clothes onto the cart. He was afraid her family were going to join the Spanish rebels in Bacalor. He wished they would just leave, though the thought of her going threatened to

Liz Holliday

tear his heart in two. Anything would be better than
her getting caught up in the fighting.

"Let me help you," he said, as she struggled to
tighten a rope across a ragged bit of sacking.

"If you would help me, go," she said. "My father
will be angry if he sees you."

"Then I'll beg him for your hand," Danny said.

"And I will say no, as I said no before," said a
voice from behind Danny.

Danny turned. Senor Ramirez was a bull of a man,
and his face was red with fury.

"Sir, I implore you to reconsider," Danny said.
"Our two countries are at war, it's true. But must war
between nations be echoed in war between those who
might otherwise be friends—"

"*Entrar la casa*, Maria," the older man said. "And
you, *cabron*. You leave, now." He clicked his fingers.
One of Maria's brothers stopped what he was doing
and started across the yard. A knotted rope-end swung
from his hand.

Danny felt his face burning, but he turned and left.
He had only got a few yards past their gate when he
heard a faint hissing sound.

Darkness moved against deeper darkness in the
shadowy mouth of an alley. A heap of rags resolved
itself into a figure. Danny found himself staring at the
creature he had met the night before.

It came at him. The brilliant sunshine turned its
pallid skin fishbelly gray, but its orange eyes were
hazel. Its injured arm dangled uselessly. It was swollen, with streaks of yellow forming around the wound.

"Help me?" it said.

Danny pulled a coin from his pocket. He ran his
nail over its edge to make sure it was only a copper.
As a ship's carpenter's mate he was tolerably well
paid, but there were limits.

He tossed the coin at the creature's feet. "Take that,
and my thanks for your trouble, and be off with you,"
he said.

"But I not wants penny," the creature said. Danny

walked away. "I wants arrow. Must have arrow." The creature's voice rose to a wail behind him.

"I'll do what I like," Danny's father said, but the woman he was threatening was Maria.

Danny tried to push her behind him but there was someone else there.

"You touch our women, you die," said the Spaniard.

He held up his knife. It was as long as Danny's forearm and wickedly sharp.

"I won't," Danny said. "I promise you, sir, I won't."

But suddenly the knife was wreathed in blood and Danny couldn't breathe.

Couldn't breathe, and the Spaniard was laughing, filling up Danny's world with his voice, his face.

Danny's eyes flicked open.

The creature was kneeling across his chest, crushing him. It stared down out of orange eyes.

Danny looked around. The men he was sharing the room with were still sleeping, or seemed to be. In the bunk above him, fat old Tom Winters turned in his sleep, making the underside of the mattress bulge alarmingly.

The creature nursed its injured arm, now horribly swollen, in its good hand.

"You helps me," it said. "Make arrow."

"I can't!" Danny said, and flinched at how loud his voice was.

"But you must," insisted the creature. "I have help you."

Much more of this and the others would wake, Danny was sure. Heaven knew what would happen then.

"All right," he said at last. "I'll help you. But not here."

"I have place. Good place. I show you," the creature said.

He clambered off the bed. Danny followed him to the window. It was a short drop to the ground below.

The creature was surprisingly nimble, considering its bad arm.

Danny followed it through the quiet streets. A glance at the moon told him it was past three in the morning. He could only hope they weren't caught out so long after curfew.

But luck was with them and soon they came to a burnt-out warehouse. Danny followed the creature inside. The smell of charred wood overlaid the older, ingrained scent of the fruit that had been stored there. It wasn't unpleasant.

The creature had made a camp in one corner: a few rags piled on a straw pallet for a bed, a surprisingly neat stack of cooking things, and a circle of stones around a firepit where embers still glowed orange-red in the darkness.

"You live here?" Danny asked. It was a far better home than he had expected.

"Yes yes," the creature said. "Sometimes here. Sometime in the forest, in a proper hut up above the ground. But I knew to find arrow maker I must be here, in the whitefolk-city. Look. I show."

He went to a corner in darkest shadows and moved aside some rags. Beneath it there was a heavily carved box. He tried to open the lid but winced against the pain.

"I cannot," he said at last. "You helps—"

"I know," Danny said. "I help you."

He went over to the creature.

"Is my box," the creature said. "All my important things. Treasure, yes?" Danny nodded. "You not take," the creature said, as if this possibility had only just occurred to it."

Danny flipped the lid open. There were several bundles inside, each one wrapped in oiled sacking.

The creature reached in and touched one. "See?" it said. "I have collect all what you need to make arrow. I try before, but I spoil, so I need to find someone. Fletcher, they say. Fletcher makes arrow."

"Yes but I—" Danny had intended to say—but I really don't know how to make arrows even if I did watch Grandpa a time or two. Yet the desperation in the creature's eyes and voice stopped him. He looked around for anything to put off the inevitable. The creature cradled its wounded arm against its chest. "Let me see that," Danny said, more roughly than he intended.

"Is nothing. Not hurting," the creature said, but it held out its arm.

The wound was hot and swollen, the edges of the wound black with red and yellow streaks coming off it.

"Doesn't hurt, my arse," Danny muttered. "Here, let me help you—"

"Yes yes! Make arrow!"

"No—let me see what I can do for your arm. Then we'll talk about the other thing."

The wound was going to need lancing and cauterizing, he thought. He'd helped the ship's doctor a time or two when they'd skirmished with the Spanish. He'd poured rum down a man's throat then held him down while the doctor sawed his leg off then tarred the bloody stump.

The memory bought bitter bile to his throat. This wouldn't be that bad. He could do it. Though he had no rum and only his little pocket knife . . .

He squatted down, pulled the knife out and stuck it into the coals to heat.

"What you do?" asked the creature. "You not need hot knife for arrow?" It looked at its arm. It was beginning to understand, to panic. Danny could see it tensing.

"No," Danny said. "Don't think about it." He put a snap into his voice. "Sit down here. Talk to me—" He cast around for something that would hold the creature. "Tell me why you need arrows."

The creature sat down. It never took its huge eyes off the blade in the embers. "It a story that begins long ago. Long before the white people come here, yes? Before the dark brown people and the yellow people. Only people here the color of nuts then. And in those days was magic."

"Okay," Danny said, suddenly feeling at ease. Clearly the creature was just some poor simpleton. He would clean up its arm, make something resembling an arrow for it to soothe its obsession and send it on its way.

"Long ago, then, one day before I was born, my father was out hunting with his dogs but he had caught nothing and so as the sun went down he started home. There is a lake a few miles from Talubin—big lake, very beautiful. But this day my father he heard a big noise. So he get down and creep close to see what it is. He think maybe it is birds and he can catch some, yes?" Danny nodded, wondering how long the story would go on and how long the blade would take to heat. "My father, he was a great hunter. He crept close and what you think he see?"

"Birds?" Danny asked. "Animals?"

"No!" said the creature triumphantly. "Hundreds of ladies, all naked, bathing in the lake. Their clothes were left all around on the banks, like white flowers."

"I'll have none of your filth," Danny said, though thoughts of Maria came to him unbidden.

"Is not filth. For they were not girls like you think. And their clothes were not dresses, they were wings. They were star-maidens, come down to earth to bathe in the lake."

"I see," said Danny. "And I suppose he knew because his dogs told him?"

"No, he know because even while he watch some more star-maidens fall like fire from the sky—"

Danny laughed. He couldn't help it. The story was so ridiculous and the creature so earnest.

"You make fun. I not tell no more." The creature turned away and glared at the fire.

"I'm sorry," Danny said. He really didn't think the knife would be hot enough yet, and it would be worse than useless if it wasn't. "Tell the end of the story. I won't laugh anymore."

The creature turned back. Danny wondered how long it had been since it had anyone to tell its ridiculous tale to.

"Well then. The star-maidens were very beautiful. My father had a bad thought. He send one dog to fetch a pair of the wings. None of the star-maidens saw. As night fell, they came out of the lake and they sang and they danced to the rising moon. And then they put on their wings again and flew up into the indigo sky. Can you imagine that?"

"No, I can't," Danny said truthfully.

"But one of them, she not have wings—"

"Because your father stole them?"

"Yes," the creature said. "But he not bad man, not really. How not to be entranced by such a woman . . . but you know this. I have seen you looking."

"It's not the same," Danny said. "Maria is—"

"Ah, '*te amo,* Maria,'" said the creature. "She is beautiful too, but she is different from you. Perhaps— maybe not more different than my mother was from my father?"

"Your mother?" Danny said. The creature stared at him out of those huge orange eyes that burned like coals and for a moment Danny found himself believing it was the child of a star maiden . . .

The creature nodded. "My father persuaded the star maiden to go home with him. To be his wife, because his first wife was long dead in the earth. And so she became and shared his bed and did all the things a wife must do. And she said she was happy, but her face turned every night to the stars, to her sisters."

"And you came along?"

"Oh yes. I was the first, but there was another. My twin, you would say, though he was not a child of earth. There was nothing of my father in him, for he was born of the placenta that followed me out of my mother when I was born."

"How lovely," Danny said.

"You said not make fun," the creature said.

"Yes," Danny said. "I should keep my promise."

"You must, for I need you to make arrow," the creature said. "But I finish story. One day when we were between childhood and manhood, my brother found something in the garden hidden under a big stone: a package wrapped in a sack, but lighter than down. It was my mother's wings. That night, we took them to her and she was so happy! Her face shone like starlight. I remember it so well, after all these years still."

"What happened?" Danny demanded.

"She put the wings on and even though they were old and had been in the ground they bore her up. But we cried. Me and my brother. We loved our papa, but we did not want our mother to leave us."

Danny nodded, though he could not imagine loving his father, or ever wanting to stay with him. If he'd been able to get his mother away from him . . .

But the creature was going on, " 'Hush,' mama said. 'Hush, you shall come with me, then, where there is no crying, in the great heavens with the stars.' And she took us out into the garden and she got papa's biggest spear, and she thrust it into the ground—"

"The point into the ground?" Danny asked. It was all nonsense, of course, and yet he found himself wanting to believe it. Wanting to believe in star-maidens who stayed with men who loved them.

"No no. She pushed the other end of the spear into the earth and then she told us to run up the spear and balance on the point and then to jump . . ."

"I can't quite see that," Danny said.

"It is because you are a man of earth," the creature said. "I could not see it either. But my brother, he ran lightly up to the spear and jumped on it—his foot on the biting sharp point of it and yet he was not hurt—and sprang into the air. Smaller he grows. Smaller. Into the great heavens with the star-folk. 'And now you,' my mother said. And I tried. How I tried. But there was nothing to stand on, and I was afraid of the pain. And so at last she gave up and said farewell to me. And the story is told that she said I would leave these islands and travel far, and that I would have many children and from them the people who are white-skinned would be born—the people like you."

"That's ridiculous," Danny said.

"Is it?" said the creature. "My people, they likes this story. Yet I never did go anywhere. How could I, when perhaps-maybe my mother would come here again? But I tried many times to make a spear I could leap into the sky from. But I cannot. And then I see bows and arrows. I get bow. But I break all arrows. Lose them in forest. Now I have just some sticks and feathers. You make arrow and fire it from bow. I catch it and ride up to heaven to my mother and brother. Yes?"

"I suppose," Danny said. "But first I'm going to deal with your arm. I'm not having you dying of that wound. I won't have it on my conscience, hear me?"

"I hear," said the creature. It looked fearfully at the fire.

Danny took his belt off. "Bite down on this," he said. "It will help. And try not to make too much noise. I don't want the soldiers coming to see what's happening."

The creature stretched its arm out. Danny put his knee on the creature's hand to keep it fixed in place.

"Hurts!" said the creature.

"No, it doesn't," Danny said. He waited while the creature put the leather strap into its mouth and bit down.

"Get ready!" he warned. He pulled the knife out of the embers. It glowed in the darkness. Quick as he could he plunged it into the infected wound. Blood and pus sprayed everywhere, and there was the stink of cooking flesh.

The creature moaned. Tears glistened on its white cheeks.

"It's done," Danny said. "It's over."

Slowly, the creature turned its face to him. "Now you make arrow," it said.

Danny held the feather against the shaft of the arrow he was making, waiting for the glue to dry. The creature watched him as it had watched every move he had made since it revealed his treasures to him—four wooden sticks of the right size and length for arrow shafts, the wing feathers of some hapless bird for fletching, and two coils of hemp string for the bow.

The bow itself was a revelation—not a pretty thing, but made of good English yew without affectation. Danny demanded to know where the creature had acquired it.

The creature had refused to look at him, and in the end he had given up asking.

The creature shambled over to him. Its arm looked much better now; the swelling was down, and there was no pus in it.

"Arrows are made?" it asked.

"Two of them," Danny said. He had no idea if he had done a good enough job. He had only commonsense and his half-memories of his grandfather's workshop to guide him.

"Is enough," the creature said. "You not have time to make more today and I want to go to my mother tonight!"

Danny followed the creature past a jumble of small wooden houses that crammed together near the edge of the city. The creature seemed not to need a lantern and Danny was glad of it. If they were caught out after curfew . . . if they were caught leaving the town . . . Traitor, he thought. They'd call me a traitor.

I shouldn't be here, he thought. And yet the creature led and he followed.

They came, at last, to a quiet place where palm trees gave way to sharp-bladed grass and then white sand. The sea beyond was inky, and above it the star-studded sky stretched away.

The creature waved its hand expansively.

"My mother," it said. "She is there."

"Which one?" Danny asked. He couldn't resist it.

"I not know," the creature snapped. "Now you shoot arrow!"

Danny took the bow. It had been a long time since he had handled one, but the old memory, the muscle-memory, came back to him.

The creature stood in front of him. "You shoot up," it said. "Up."

For an instant, Danny entertained the idea of shooting the creature. He could be free of it. But it trusted him, and who was to say whether it had a soul—whether shooting it would be the same as killing a man?

So Danny aimed high, and on the creature's mark he fired the first arrow. The shaft sailed over the creature's head. It made a half-movement, as if it wanted to jump but something restrained it.

The arrow was lost in the darkness.

"Again," the creature said.

Danny breathed out and found stillness.

He loosed the arrow.

It flew up. The creature leapt for it.

Impossibly, the creature grabbed the arrow in both hands. For a moment there was a hint of white light, the merest flicker around the creature's fingers.

In that instant it seemed as if the arrow might lift the creature up.

"No!" Danny murmured. If it were possible, everything else was wrong, everything he knew. And yet part of him wanted the creature to go, to fly up, to be all that it could be.

And then the creature and the arrow fell back to earth. The shaft of the arrow split in three pieces along its length.

The world settled back into its old familiar patterns around Danny.

The creature sobbed quietly. Light glittered on the tears that coated its cheeks.

"Almost, it work," it said. "I go to my mother . . . you make other arrow. I go to my mother."

"No," Danny said. "Enough."

"You make arrow, I get your Maria for you," the creature said.

"No," Danny said. But the thought intrigued him and he said almost immediately. "What do you mean, you'll get Maria for me?"

"So she will come with you. Follow you. Be good girl, do what she told."

"Anything?"

"Anything," the creature said, nodding rapidly. "She be good girl."

"All right," Danny said. "You bring her here at sunset and I will have your arrow for you."

It will be all right, Danny thought as he slit fletches from a pinion feather. I'm not going to hurt her. I'm just going to . . . but he couldn't think of what he might do, if he could do anything.

The dying sun splashed crimson across the sky as Danny went down to the beach.

For a moment he thought they were not there. Then he saw them, where they stood in the shadow of three big palm trees: the creature and behind him, Maria.

He went towards them. The creature smiled, stretching thin lips across yellowish teeth. But Maria . . . Maria never moved, never smiled. Never said his name.

"See?" said the creature. "I have brought her for you. And now she is good girl. Will do whats you tell her."

Danny went to her. She stared at him impassively.

"Maria?" he asked. There was no response. He reached out and touched her on the cheek with the side of his thumb, as he had dreamed of doing so often but had never dared. "*Te amo, Maria,*" he said.

She should have protested, should have teased him. Something. Anything. But she said nothing.

"What's the matter with her?" Danny demanded. "What have you done to her?"

"I haves give her to you, as I promise," said the creature. "She is yours now. Will do as you say." The creature's eyes shone. It was proud of itself, Danny realized. "Or I say," it added. It turned to Maria. "Tell to Danny you loves him, Maria."

"*Te amo,* Danny," Maria said immediately.

He had dreamed of this, of winning those words. But her voice was flat. It was nothing, meant nothing.

"How have you done this to her?" he shouted.

"Shh, shh. They hear. Soldiers hear. Very bad, they hear."

"Yes," Danny agreed, lowering his voice. "But tell me."

"Is a gift from my mother. To keeps me safe. She loves me, my mother."

"But then, why didn't you do it to me? Or to the Spaniards that attacked you?"

"Is hard, hard. And the giving, it was long ago. The gift fades so I use it little." The creature smiled again. Danny wished it wouldn't. He had felt sorry for it and it had done this. "But you," it said. "You make other arrow. I go to my mother. I not need gift."

"And maybe I won't give you the arrow," Danny said.

"But I have got Maria for you," the creature said. "She do anything. You wants kiss? She kiss. Look."

The creature shambled over to her. It thrust its face towards her.

Danny shoved the creature away. Maria might have been made of stone for all the response she gave. She was so close to him now. He could smell her, the lemons she used to scent her soap, the underlying musk of her.

He could hear her breathing.

He kissed her, briefly, on the mouth. When she didn't resist, he did it again more urgently.

Still nothing. And yet he wanted her so badly. He let his hands move across her still body. She didn't move.

In his dreams, she'd been a willing partner. She'd whispered his name and held him close.

This thing he was holding was not Maria.

Danny pulled away. He turned to the creature.

"What have you done to her," he screamed. "What have you done to me?"

"Dones to her what you asked," the creature. "I don't do nothings to you."

"Yes, you have," Danny shouted. He slapped the creature hard across the side of its head. It shrieked and turned away.

He grabbed it and hit it again and again with his fist. "Why?" he said. He was out of breath. "Why?"

"Because it what you want. What you say."

"You must have known I didn't want *that*," Danny said. "No man could want that."

"I not know," the creature said. "I not. She do what she told, like good girl. That's what my papa say. Mother be good girl do what she told because—"

"What? But you said your mother was pleased to be with your father—"

"Mouth say she happy. Face say other thing," the creature said. "But she good girl, do what papa say."

"Or he'd make her," Danny said. Most men would. His own mother was wise and funny when his father was not there, but when he was, she minded her manners. "She was scared of him."

"Yes," the creature said. "I scared. Brother too. That why we not want her go. But she go, and brother go, and then just papa and me. And he so angry. He hits me. Like you hits me. Then with belt—"

"Why didn't you use your gift to stop him, then?"

"I did. But he just sit there. I have to feed him, clean him. I not likes. So in end, I . . . tell him to do a thing and then he no need feeding and cleaning."

"You told him to kill himself," Danny said.

The creature looked away.

Danny grabbed the back of its head and forced it round. "You killed your father, you wicked creature."

"I not sorry. Not for that. He trapped my mother. He did. He did."

"And you helped her to go and in return you got stuck with him," Danny said. It must have been terrible, but murder was murder and a mortal sin however you looked at it. "It's no wonder you don't know right from wrong."

"Oh I know I do wrong. Not first wrong thing I did." The creature twisted out of Danny's grasp.

"You did worse?" Danny demanded, advancing on the creature. He made a wild guess. "Did you kill your mother too? Is this all some mad tale to account for—"

"No no," the creature said. "Not kill her. Worse. You not make me tell. You not."

"All right," Danny said. "I won't make you tell me but you have to release Maria from your gift. Can you do that?"

"Oh yes," said the creature. "I can. But I not. You shoot last arrow and I release her."

"Oh, really," Danny said. "What's to stop you going back on your word?"

"No no, I not. I not be here. I be in sky with mother. I not understand why you want Maria free, but why I not do it? I be so happy I do anything."

"It's what you do when it doesn't work that worries me," Danny said. But he couldn't think of any other way of making the creature release her.

So, once again they stood in the darkness. Danny once again aimed over the creature's head. And once again he thought of shooting for its heart. If he had been sure killing it would release Maria he would have done it. He thought he would. But he couldn't be sure and couldn't risk trapping her forever in that hell.

"Now!" said the creature.

Danny loosed the arrow. It flew up. The creature caught it.

Light blazed around the creature. For an instant, it hung in the air.

"Well I'll be—" Danny said.

The creature crashed back to earth.

"No," it screamed. "Not again, not again."

Convulsive sobs racked its body. Danny was moved to pity despite everything that had happened.

He sat down next to it.

"Hush now," he said, as if the creature were a little child. "Hush. There will be other arrows, other chances."

"No," said the creature. "No more. I can't. Is useless. She not wants me anyway—"

"But you were so close," Danny said. "I didn't believe any of it, you know. Nothing. But you were almost flying. And you shone like starlight." What am I saying? he wondered. Why am I encouraging this filthy little beast? But yet he patted its shoulder, soothing it as he might a feral dog.

"You not know. She hate me. She hate me, not want me. She take good child because she know I bad."

"But you said you were too heavy to run up the spear," Danny said. "How does that make you bad?"

"I say that. You believe? You stupid, then."

"Most gracious of you to say so," Danny said.

"No, you listen. She put spear. Brother go. She smile, smile, yes? But I go and she look at me. Hard look. Sometimes you look like that, but she look harder. Because she know. And I start to run for spear. *But she looking at me* and I cannot run. Because she know . . ."

"What? That you did something?"

"Yes. I not want her to go. And I know she want go, because who want to stay with papa?" the creature said.

Danny nodded. He'd left home as soon as he could but he worried about his mother constantly. "What did you do?" he asked quietly.

"I found her wings."

"Yes. You said."

"No, not then. I found them long before. Papa puts

them in box under loose floorboard. It squeak. I think maybe if I fix it, he pleased. But I find box under, and in it her wings. All white and soft as baby hair." For a long moment the creature did not speak. It stared at the ground and its bony fingers moved restlessly across its thighs. "I not want mama to go. You understand? Or I want go too. But there is one pair of wings and I did not know she had plan to take us. So I took the wings and I hid them in the garden. And every day I think of them, and the days are long, and weeks and months, and then a year and two, and I hurt inside from thinking. You understand?"

"Oh, I do," Danny said, and meant it.

"And then my brother find the wings and there is nothing I can do. And all bad thoughts come true, because she goes and he goes and there is just me and papa and papa's belt . . . you see?"

"I do," Danny said. "But I do not think she meant to leave you. Why would she? She loved you."

"But I bad," the creature wailed. "I not mean to be. But I bad and I hurt her and I want—"

It's a child, Danny thought. It's a child, trapped in that unthinking moment of bad decision. It's no wonder it did that to Maria . . .

"Did you tell her you were sorry?" Danny asked.

"I not. Not then. I too scared. She leaving. I want to say, I sorry. I love you mama. Not leave me, please not leave me."

"Then tell her now," Danny said. "She's up there, a star. Surely they hear everything?" He had no idea what he was saying. He only knew he had to drive the creature to the point where it would release Maria, and he dared not mention that in case the creature retreated into grief and mania again.

The creature stood up. It raised its face to heaven. "I sorry, mama. I stole your wings. I bad, I bad. But I was scared you leave. I was scared I be left. I sorry."

The air shivered.

The light came down from heaven, a blaze of glory that shimmered and coalesced until a woman stood

there. She was so beautiful that Danny could hardly
bear to look at her. She stretched out her wings and
they seemed to envelop the sky.

"Oh my child," she said, and her voice was like the
shattering of crystal. "What has become of you?"

"I sorry, mama. I sorry I hid your wings."

"Oh child," said the star-woman. Her voice was full
of disappointment, and the sound of it was more than
Danny could bear. "Is that your guilt? Have you even
now not learned the wrong you did me?"

"I sorry," the creature said. "I not want you to
leave me with papa."

For a loathsome instant, Danny was back at home.
His mother was pushing a bundle of food and a few
coppers into his hands and telling him to go, go before
his father woke. And he had gone and left her because
it was all he could do. "I can't," he'd said. "You
must," his mother had answered. "Make something of
yourself. Find yourself a good wife and treat her well,
that's all I ask. Trust me, Danny, it's all a mother
wants for her child."

Trust, he thought, and knew what wrong the star-
woman could not forgive.

He took a step towards the creature. The star-
woman turned her awful, glorious gaze upon him. He
looked away. Looked at the ground. But took another step.

"Listen," he said to the creature. "You did a bad
thing to your mother. But what was the worse thing?"

"I not know. I only know I sorry and I right. She
not love me, she hate me."

"She's your mother. She loves you. I promise you."

"Yes," said the creature, but it didn't sound as if it
believed him.

"Didn't she protect you from your father?" It was
a guess, but there had been so many times at home . . .
he knew he was right.

The creature made a sound that was half sob and
half word. It took a long, shuddery breath. "Yes," it
said at last.

"Of course she did," Danny said. "Because she loved you. So why would you think she would leave you?"

"Don't know," said the creature. It shrugged and turned away.

"Don't you think it's a bit insulting to think she would leave you? Perhaps that's why she's angry."

"Yes but I scared," said the creature. "I not . . . brother is . . . brother is like her. Beautiful one. Her beautiful boy. Me, I like father. So I think she protect me because sorry for me, but why she want ugly one with her?"

"You should have trusted me," said the star-woman. Her voice was like breaking ice.

Danny felt his bowels loosen just at the sound of her. But he had to continue, had to free Maria.

He looked up at her, although he thought his eyes would burn away.

"He thought he wasn't good enough for you. He was a little boy scared of losing his mama."

"Who are you to speak thus to me?" said the star-woman, and Danny was sure he would die.

But there was Maria.

"I am . . ." he paused. He was sure the star-woman would know a lie if she heard one. And so he said something that he knew was true, even though it had only been true for a few moments. "I am your son's friend."

The star-woman regarded him. "It is good that he has a friend," she said at last. "And perhaps there is truth in your words." She turned to the creature. "Why didn't you trust me, my son?"

"I was just so scared, mama. I'm sorry."

"Then so am I," she said. "You should come now. It is not earth that weighed you down, but your guilt and my anger. And the things of earth no longer become you. Be free of them."

She motioned with her hand, a movement Danny could never later quite recall.

Light blazed around the creature. He stood tall. His

features, his bones, everything changed. Bright wings
burst forth from his shoulders.

Another light fell from the sky. A young man, so
like the being who had been the creature that there
was no telling them apart.

"My brother," each one said at the same moment.

"And now we are almost finished," said the star-
woman. She turned to Danny. "But a true friend de-
serves a true gift, and you have a good heart. What
would you have?"

Danny thought of the gift she had given her son,
and the damage it had caused, and knew he must
choose carefully. He could ask for Maria—the real
Maria, not the witless creature she had become—to
love him truly. He thought the star-woman would
grant it, that she had that power. But it was not something a man of good heart would do. His mother
would be appalled.

"I want Maria to be free of whatever your son did
to her," he said. "If she's to love me, I'll have to earn
that love and make a place where we can be together
in this world."

"That is not in my gift," the star-woman said.
Danny stared at her, appalled. But she turned to the
being that had been the creature. "My son," she said.

"It is done," he said. "I'm so sorry for the hurt I
caused you and her, Danny."

"It's nothing," Danny answered out of habit.

"No, it's not. If we've learned anything this night it
must be the value of acknowledging our failures,
wouldn't you say?"

Danny nodded. Then he surprised himself by laughing. "Your English has improved."

"The body I was wearing had mostly forgotten how
to think. But that part of my life is finished with now,
and I thank you."

"As do I," said the star-woman. "But you have not
chosen a gift of me, Danny Fletcher."

"I would not know what to choose," he admitted.

"Then let me choose for you." Perhaps she saw him

flinch. "I'll give you no double-edged swords, Danny Fletcher. Just the promise that if you choose wisely— and I know you can—you will find what you seek and earn what you deserve. But are you sure you do not want her love?"

"I want her love," Danny said. The star-woman raised her hand, so he went on quickly, "but I want to earn it."

"Then I was right. You have chosen wisely. But do not forget that other woman you owe so much. You should seek her too."

"I will," Danny said.

"Then farewell, Danny Fletcher," said the star-woman.

"Farewell," said her sons. "Farewell."

There was a blaze of light so fierce that Danny threw his arm up in front of his face and still it blinded him.

When he could see again, he looked around. Maria was standing by the palm trees.

She was smiling.

Danny went to her.

Immigrant

Sandra Tayler

Goibniu ran his gnarled brown fingers lovingly over the wooden gears. The gears were motionless now, but soon they would run. His yellow eyes traced the path from the huge mill wheel, across the gears, and into the spinning machine which would make the thread. The cotton mill was almost complete.

Startled by the sound of human footsteps, Goibniu instinctively ducked into hiding. It was Samuel leaving the mill to go to dinner. Goibniu scrambled to follow his friend. He didn't want to be left here alone. Being alone always made him aware of the emptiness of this land. It was so different from back home. England was full of monoliths and groves and magical boundaries, as the Fae creatures lay claim to territories. America had none of these things. Goibniu had never cared much for the other Fae, but now he missed them.

The door of the mill was already shut when Goibniu reached it, but it didn't matter. He never used the door anyway. There was a loose board next to the door that was perfect for his two-foot-tall frame. He blinked in the bright sunlight. Samuel was already half way to the house. Goibniu looked around for other humans. He was always wary of humans, but particularly since that man on the steamboat had shouted "Demon!" and summoned a priest. Samuel said it was because Americans had never seen Fae. Goibniu just knew that being seen caused a world of trouble.

There were no humans, but Goibniu's gaze was drawn across the field to the edge of the wood. There stood a fox. It was not only a fox, but also Fox, imbued with a greater spirit, the essence of Fox. Goibniu swallowed. A second spirit lurked by the stream. He could sense it, but not see it. These spirits were neither human nor Fae. They were larger than anything he had encountered before. He could feel the power they commanded. And they watched him constantly. Goibniu ducked his head and dashed after Samuel.

Waterman coalesced near the stream bank, his yellow spines blending perfectly with the reeds. The man exited the wooden structure which straddled the waterway. Today Waterman was not interested in men. Today he was watching for the new creature that had come to live at the man-house. Its arrival affected this place like ripples on a pond. He had come to see the source of the ripples. It emerged only a moment later. It was small and brown, shaped like a man. It scanned the world with yellow eyes and pointed ears. Waterman watched as the small gnarled shape ducked its head then dashed after the man. It reminded him of the twisted tree roots which so often found their way into his stream.

Fox trotted up. "It is not a spirit." Fox flicked her ears to indicate certainty. "It is bound to that form. It is not an animal. It thinks as a man does. Yet it has power, so it is not a man."

Waterman ruffled the spines on his back before dissolving his corporeal form. He could think more clearly when he dwelt in the flow of the water. "He is like me, bound to a place. His place is that body." Waterman was sad for the strange spirit, bound to so small a place.

Fox pawed the ground. "Fear rolls off it in waves."

Waterman murmured assent. He too felt the strange

spirit's fear. So much fear for such a small being. "He is out of place. Lost. That is why he fears."

Fox grinned bloodthirstily "Then we should drive it back where it came from. It has no place here."

"You are quick to judge."

Fox sat up in surprise. "You would let it stay?"

Waterman ruffled the water. Then he ruffled it again. "He does no harm," he answered at last. "We must watch and wait."

Fox scratched her foot against the ground in protest, but did not argue.

Goibniu whisked through the house door with Samuel and scaled a beam to his perch in the rafters. The smell of food wafted up from the table below. Goibniu's stomach rumbled. He eyed the pantry near the table. The risk of being seen was too high. He'd get food later. While he waited, Goibniu listened to the humans. Samuel's voice was the sound of home, so different from the flat American accents of the others. Lulled by the cadences of conversation, Goibniu closed his eyes. A loud laugh startled him awake. Samuel was laughing. Goibniu had not heard such laughter from Samuel in years. Samuel had been a young boy when he last laughed so freely. Goibniu peeked to find the cause of his friend's joy.

Samuel sat at the table across from the daughter of the house, leaning toward her. She smiled broadly at him; completely focused on the joke they shared. All the pieces fell into place. The times that Samuel had stopped work on the mill and come to dinner early. The fact that Samuel did not talk to Goibniu as much. Samuel was in love with the girl.

Goibniu scuttled along the beam to get a better look at the girl. She was not pretty. Girls in England were much prettier, and Samuel had left them behind.

"So you will come to the picnic tomorrow?" The girl reached over and touched Samuel's hand.

"Of course. I wouldn't miss it." Samuel smiled again.

Goibniu straightened as if shocked. Samuel was not going to work on the mill tomorrow. That girl was going to steal him away. Anger surged through Goibniu's body. He stomped his feet. Then he scurried across the beam and kicked dust down on the girl's head. It floated softly through the air and she did not even notice. He wanted to jump on her head and scratch her eyes out. To prevent himself from making so stupid an error, Goibniu ran to his nest and curled into a tight ball. Tears leaked from his eyes. The mill would stand empty tomorrow. Samuel would not be there to design new gears, or make them, or set them into place.

Goibniu remembered vividly his one look at a working mill. Samuel was apprenticed to a mill overseer, and had regaled Goibniu with tales of intricate machinery. He had to see it for himself. He'd waited for the goblin, whose territory the mill was, to be asleep. He'd crept through a crack in the wall. The thrum of the machines vibrated his feet. The whirling spindles dazzled his eyes. His hands itched to touch and learn the workings of the machines. A few minutes were all that Goibniu dared to stay. He stretched them as long as he could, then crept away before the goblin woke. The memory of the whirling, thrumming machines haunted him. He had to find a way to have such machines for his own. But so weak a Fae as he could never hold such an amazing territory. Then Samuel had begun to talk of America.

Dinner was over and the humans had gone to bed before Goibniu trusted himself not to do anything rash. His joints creaked as he uncoiled. One extra day was not the end of his dream. But what if this girl had another picnic? What if Samuel got married and forgot about Goibniu? Samuel's father had done that.

"Goibniu!" Samuel's whispered voice drew Goibniu from his nest. He peered down into the room below. Samuel was in night clothes, holding a bowl, and searching the room for the Fae. The smell of bread and honey in milk wafted from the bowl. Samuel had not forgotten him. Goibniu's spirits soared and his stomach rumbled. Lured by his favorite treat, he scuttled down a beam. Samuel put the bowl down on the floor. Goibniu ate voraciously.

Samuel waited until Goibniu had slowed down before he spoke. "I won't be working on the mill tomorrow."

Goibniu froze with a bite half to his mouth. He looked up at Samuel reproachfully.

"It is just for one day," Samuel placated. "Hannah and her friends are having a picnic."

Goibniu wasn't hungry anymore. He dropped the bread back into the bowl.

Samuel watched the action. "Are you all right?"

The wood floor was smooth under Goibniu's hand. He felt the softness of it. "You will work on the mill after tomorrow?"

"Of course I will!" Samuel laughed. "Why would I travel this far, arrange finances, and board here with a blacksmith just to give it up now?"

Goibniu fidgeted. "You like the girl."

Samuel sobered. "Hannah?" He looked toward the stairs that led to her room. "Yes. I like her very much."

Heaving a big sigh, Goibniu turned to leave.

"Wait, what's wrong?" Samuel's voice called him back.

Goibniu turned to look into Samuel's concerned eyes. "You will marry her, leave the mill, and forget me."

"Oh, is that all?" Samuel's face lightened. "I'm not my father. Grandfather didn't forget you, did he?"

Grudgingly, Goibniu shook his head.

"I won't either. Besides, I can't possibly afford to get married until the mill is a huge success. I owe more money on that thing than you would believe."

Tension leaked out of Goibniu's shoulders as he studied Samuel's face. He could always tell when truth was being spoken. The mill would be finished. He would have his glorious machines. Goibniu smiled.

Samuel smiled as well. "I think we may be able to test the machine soon. Not tomorrow, that's the picnic, but the day after maybe."

Hungry again, the brown Fae finished off the last of the bread. Samuel sat next to him, lost in thought. Goibniu was using his finger to get the last bits of the honey when Samuel spoke again.

"Do you like her? Hannah, I mean."

Goibniu sat back. "She is American."

Brow crinkled, Samuel replied "Not all Americans are like that man on the boat. Besides, he had good reason to suspect you were a demon after you 'fixed' the steam engine."

Goibniu hunched over. It wasn't his fault that he'd never seen a steam engine before. He knew how it worked now. It had been as fascinating as the mill machines. But the man and his priest had made sure Goibniu could not stay.

Samuel leaned toward his small friend "Hannah is different. I've been telling her about Fae and I think she almost believes me. Won't you please meet her, speak with her?"

Jaw clenched, the Fae shook his head. "No," he whispered hoarsely. Then he scurried away to his nest.

Waterman was sleeping when a change in the water rhythm woke him. He floated up the stream to find the disturbance. It came from the man-place straddling the waterway. Attached to the man-place was a wheel. Its paddles chopped the water endlessly. This close to the wheel, there were no rhythms to ride. He needed to get upstream. He needed the song of the rocks and the banks, not the endless slap of wood on water. Waterman coalesced and lifted his head high to see. No men were in sight. He pulled himself onto the bank and began the land traverse around the wheel. Every step was heavy. He tired quickly.

The water-spirit was half through with his traverse when Fox came running up. She put her ears back to laugh at his predicament.

Waterman did not stop his slow march. "What do you want, Fox?"

"I felt the rumble through the ground and came to see what it was."

"Rumble?" Waterman put his hand to the ground, but earth did not speak to him.

"The building thumps like war drums."

Waterman continued his walk. He needed the water. Fortunately the distance was short. He splashed back into the stream and sighed with pleasure. The song of rocks and banks filled him.

Fox flicked her ears. "Are you finished watching and waiting now?"

Waterman looked down the stream at the endlessly turning wheel. Beyond the wheel there were eddies and curves of the stream that were part of himself. He could not feel them. His stream had been cut in two. Waterman turned sad eyes to Fox. "Yes, I am finished waiting now."

Fox smiled.

Goibniu danced impatiently. "Now?"

Samuel sighed. "No, Goibniu. I have to fit these last three spindles into their shafts before we can turn the machine on."

Goibniu ran to watch the wheel shaft turn. On the other side of the wall the wheel itself slid through the water smoothly. Samuel had set it into motion an hour ago in preparation for the coming machinery test. Goibniu caressed the lever that would connect the mill gears with the wheel gears. He hopped from foot to foot while Samuel fit the spindles onto their shafts. Then Samuel took hold of the lever. Goibniu watched, breathless, as Samuel pulled the lever and the gears engaged.

Creakily, the whole system came to life. The spindles began whirling. Wooden gears clattered against one another, making an ever-louder racket. The machine went faster and faster. Goibniu's heart beat faster too. *This* was what he had come so far to have.

The clank and clatter of the working mill sung in his bones. Here was a whole building that *worked*. It filled with the noise of things being made. The other mill had human workers who had scurried about like ants feeding the machine wool and pulling off skeins of thread. There would be workers here too. Dozens of workers. And the mill was his. No one could take it from him. Goibniu leaped and danced for joy. He did not even mind that tears rolled down his cheeks. Samuel wept too, while grinning from ear to ear. Goibniu pressed his face to a beam and reveled in the thrum of the machines. For the first time he was completely happy in this new land.

CRACK! For a frozen instant neither Goibniu or Samuel could make sense of the sound. Then Goibniu knew. It was the sickening sound of wood smashing. Gears all over the mill slowed to a clanking and clattering halt.

"No." breathed Samuel. He began searching for the break. Goibniu turned as if drawn by a magnet toward the waterwheel. In the silence Goibniu could feel the terrible nearness of at least two spirits. They were just outside, beyond the wall. Goibniu shimmied along the wheel shaft and squeezed outside through the opening in the wall. He had to see.

A whole section of the wheel was smashed. It sat motionless in the water. Movement caught the corner of his eye. He turned and saw a monster. It had the bulging eyes and wide mouth of a frog, but arms and legs like a man. Except no man had claws or razor spines all over his back. As Goibniu watched, the yellow monster submerged in the water and dissolved into nothing.

Pieces of the wheel bobbed, caught in eddies of the stream. Goibniu stared at them. The wheel was broken. The only sound to be heard was the cheerful burbling of the stream. Behind him the mill sat silent, dead. His chest ached. His lungs cried out for air and he gasped his first breath since sighting the smashed wheel. A second shuddering breath followed the first.

The third breath was steadier, but the fourth breath was a sob. Goibniu slid to the ground and clutched a fragment of wood.

"Good heavens!" Samuel had come around the side of the mill. He stepped down the stream bank and into the water to get a better look. Water swirled around his knees as he examined the damage. "What on earth did this?"

Samuel was not asking him, but Goibniu knew the answer. For the first time since his arrival here, there were no spirits nearby. Their sudden absence proclaimed guilt. They had done this. They had killed his beautiful mill. Samuel would surely fix the wheel, but the spirits could break it again. The board clutched in Goibniu's hands snapped. He unwound his fingers from the pieces and let them fall to the ground. He stood and stalked toward his nest. There were herbs he'd brought from the old country that he would need. He had just enough for one powerful spell.

"Waterman! Wake up!" Summoned from his timeless float in the rhythm of the stream, Waterman opened his senses. It was night now. Fox crouched on the stream bank looking toward the man-house. Beyond Fox the strange spirit worked on something. Fierce anger radiated from the stranger like rays from a dozen suns. Waterman coalesced so that he could see.

The stranger had constructed a man-shape out of grasses. He was dancing around the man-shape and chanting. The world was filled with magic flowing freely, but each movement of the dance and each word chanted pulled on the flows. Waterman closed his eyes to observe more clearly. The stranger was drawing them in and weaving them around the man-shape. Raw anger was woven there too. Waterman had never seen flows treated so before. It was a powerful making. Occasionally the stranger paused to glare at Fox, but he did not see Waterman camouflaged in the reeds.

Fox shifted, ready to flee. "What is it doing?"

Waterman signed for silence. He opened his eyes to watch the dance. Then closed them to watch the flows. The stranger was tiring. As the spirits watched, he took an ember and thrust it into the man-shape. Flames licked over the form. Wisps of the smoke blew toward them and burned Waterman's eyes. He blinked. His nostrils flared at the smell of burned dried plants. The plant smells were unfamiliar. They had come from far away. As the man-shape burned, it slumped and the magic weave shifted. The stranger began to push the burning pile toward the stream.

Waterman gasped. His eyes widened. Fox retreated from the flames, but Waterman dared not flee. When the flames hit the water, the accumulated magic would disperse in a cloud. It would poison the entire area, forcing spirits away.

Waterman surged up the bank. He seized the flaming man-shape in his large hands. The stranger, eyes wide, cried defiance, but he was too small to prevent Waterman from taking the bundle. One, two, three, strides away from the stream. Waterman's hands burned, his body steamed. He could carry it no further, so he hurled it with all his strength. The bundle scattered into flaming pieces as it struck the ground.

Waterman turned back to the water. His hands still burned though they no longer touched fire. He needed his stream. Something struck his back. It was the stranger, kicking, shrieking, and pummeling. Waterman twisted violently to shake him off, then dove into the soothing stream.

Impact with the ground drove all the breath from Goibniu's body. The ruins of his manikin lay in smoldering piles already growing dim. Still gasping, he struggled to his feet. A furry body struck him from the side, knocking him down again. The world was confusion of snarls, teeth, and red fur. Goibniu tried to strike back, but Fox was far too fast. Pain and terror overwhelmed all else. Goibniu tried to run. He stumbled. Pain lanced through his legs. He could not walk. He curled into a ball around his pain. Fox continued to savage him.

"STOP!" A voice resonated. The attack ceased. Goibniu still huddled in a world filled with pain. Slowly the pain receded and focused to specific places on his body. His arms, legs, and back all throbbed with each beat of his heart. The shuffling step of a large foot crushing grass landed close to Goibniu's ear. He looked up. Standing over him was the yellow monster. The one that had smashed the mill wheel. Death could not possibly cause more pain than he felt right now. Goibniu closed his eyes.

"He is wounded. He will die without help." The resonant voice came from the yellow monster.

"Let it die." This smaller sharper voice came from Fox.

"He was angry because I damaged the wheel. A vixen will defend her cubs; she does not deserve to die for that."

"A wheel can not be a cub. It will put the wheel back. The wheel hurts you, Waterman."

The monster, Waterman, was silent. Goibniu opened his eyes again. The Waterman had stepped back. It sat with arms skewed to prevent its blistered hands from touching anything. Fox stood nearby, ears flat against her head.

Waterman tilted his head. "He may build the wheel again, but we still must help where we have injured. He must be taken to the men at the man-house." Hope flared in Goibniu's heart. They would take him to Samuel.

Fox shifted from foot to foot. "You take it then."

Waterman turned a blistered palm toward Fox. "I am too slow. The men would see me."

"You ask too much." Fox snarled.

The Waterman turned his second palm to Fox, pleading.

"Oh, fine!" Fox barked.

Goibniu watched as Fox trotted closer, then gently grabbed and lifted him. Goibniu's feet dragged along the ground. He was too large for Fox to simply carry. Each of Fox's trotting steps caused pain. Goibniu stifled his gasps. He did not want his reluctant rescuer to abandon the task. He tried to watch the progress of the ungainly journey, but his vision kept fuzzing. Then the smooth boards of the porch were underneath him. He heard Fox scratching at the door and a human footstep.

Goibniu opened his eyes to greet his friend, but it was not Samuel. It was the girl. Her eyes were wide as her gaze met his. Her hands were clutching a broom. In a moment she would strike him with it. Goibniu tried to push himself up on his hands, to flee. But his arms had no strength. He could not even crawl and Fox had gone.

"Please! Don't hurt me!" Goibniu flung up a hand.

For a long moment the girl did not move. She carefully knelt next to him and reached a tentative finger to trace his brow. Goibniu flinched at the cool touch.

"I did not believe Samuel." She breathed. Her eyes brimmed over with wonder, not fear. Goibniu felt tears on his own cheeks as well. She would not hurt him. He lay back on the smooth boards, letting his mind be carried away in the waves of pain while the girl ran for Samuel.

Healing wounds itched. Goibniu snaked his fingers under the edge of a bandage and scratched. The girl, Hannah, would scold him for it when she changed his bandages later, but just now Goibniu didn't care. He picked up his walking stick and continued the trek to the stream. He was still not well enough to walk so far, but thanks were long overdue.

Waterman sensed his approach and coalesced midstream. Goibniu lowered himself to sit on a rock before he spoke.

"You saved me from Fox. Thank you."

Waterman gave a slow nod. "Fox is impulsive. I am sorry she hurt you. I am sorry my spines hurt you. I am glad you are healing."

Goibniu studied his feet, then looked over at Waterman. "I hurt you, too."

Waterman lifted his hands out of the water and turned the palms toward Goibniu. The flesh was peeling to reveal healthy new skin underneath. "I too am healing."

The walking stick scraped along the ground as Goibniu's hands fiddled with it. He studied the strange yellow face. The bulgy eyes had friendly crinkles at the corners. Goibniu's face was just beginning to smile in response, when he sensed another spirit hurrying near. It was Fox bounding toward them at top speed. She skidded to a halt across the stream from Goibniu.

"What does it want?" Fox growled.

Waterman half turned to Fox. "He came to give thanks. This is . . ."

"Goibniu," the Fae supplied.

Fox crouched low, ready to spring. "And when it rebuilds the wheel? What will you do then?"

Waterman did not answer. Fox shifted in satisfaction as the moment stretched.

"I have a plan about that." Goibniu offered tentatively. The plan was half of the reason he had come. He'd thought long and hard about the problem of the wheel. He needed his mill and Waterman needed the stream. The two spirits turned to him. Fox still crouched with teeth bared, but Waterman was interested. Goibniu knew he could not expect more. "When I traveled here, I rode on a steamboat. It had a machine that used fire and water to run machines. It would only need a few buckets from your stream and it ran better than the wheel."

Waterman dipped lower in the water to taste it. "And the men will build this?"

Goibniu looked toward the mill where Samuel was working. Samuel had been bewildered by Goibniu's shift from make-it-work-now to let's-take-longer-to-build-it-right. Slowly though, Samuel began to see that Goibniu was right. The steam-powered mill would be better over the long haul.

Looking back to the spirits, Goibniu simply answered "Yes."

Waterman smiled.

Fox sat up from her crouch and flicked her ears. "It still doesn't belong here, Waterman." She trotted away.

Goibniu shifted on his rock. He was suddenly fatigued and dreading the walk back to the house. A splash from Waterman drew his attention.

Waterman met Goibniu's eyes intently. "You arrived here like a pebble flung into a calm pond. When a pebble hits water, it causes ripples. The ripples bounce off each other and the water is no longer calm. But then the pebble rests on the bottom and the ripples get smaller and smaller."

Goibniu was pinned by the intense stare. He tried to make sense of the words.

Waterman continued "Fox is right. You do not belong here." Then Waterman smiled, his eyes crinkling. "You are just beginning to belong."

Waterman dissolved back into the water and Goibniu was left sitting next to a burbling stream. Goibniu smiled, his fatigue gone. He looked down the stream toward the mill. It was farther than the house, but if he walked down there he could see the construction of the steam engine. Then perhaps Samuel would give him a ride back to the house. Goibniu leaned on his stick and hummed as he hobbled. This was a good place. He was going to be happy here.

THE AGE OF PIONEERS

Once the foothold on the New World was firmly established, there was only one way to expand—West. The rich land was opened to wave after wave of pioneers, who brought with them the technology, religion, and warfare of the Old World. Native populations could only withdraw before their advance. It was a time when old collided with new on a wild landscape that challenged any to survive.

A Small Sacrifice

Kristen Bonn

The Earth quivered under my hands, straining away
from my sure and steady touch. Never before had
I placed such a demand on her. Hill after hill folded
under my hands, and when the land had been
stretched to her limits, I anchored the mass with a
narrow, plaited sinew.

I had worked since before the dawn. Now, in the
heat of the day, my arms ached from the unaccus-
tomed exertion. Another rivulet caressed the curve of
my ribs before melding into my sweat-soaked tunic.

I pulled the final Earth-cord from my belt and knotted it through the last bone anchor. The cord was
pulled so tightly I could hear a low thrum as a breeze
scampered by my feet. I whispered a prayer of hope
and gratitude as I sat back on my heels.

Tendrils of hair clung to my cheeks. I made a half-
hearted swipe at them with the back of my wrist. The
most strenuous task was done, though, I thought as I
surveyed the rope work strung around me. Now there
was only one thing left to do to save my people. I
needed to return to camp and let the Elders know the
circle was finished. We would be ready to move to
our new, permanent home.

I shoved that thought aside as I staggered to my
feet. Right now what I needed was water. Exhaustion
propelled me to my horse and I pressed my face into

her neck, inhaling the thick scent of sun-warmed horse, dust, and grass. The thought of water was the only thing that gave me the strength to mount up. As I rode home, I could see the darkening sky in the west and realized the breeze that had tickled my feet had been cool. Not a good sign.

Umpahtah met me as I rode into camp and helped me dismount. I was grateful he let me steady myself against him for a moment.

"It's done?"

I nodded my head against his chest.

"Your grandmother has been asking for you." He pushed a water skin into my hands. "Go be with her. I'll let the Elders know it is time."

As I approached the shelter, I saw her lying on the buffalo skin. I knew she was an old woman. People had started calling her Bird-Woman, more for her appearance than any affinity with feathered creatures, but her spirit was indomitable and lent her frail body the weight and presence of a much younger woman.

Now, though, she looked as if a strong gust would pick her up and carry her over the Soul Bridge. Reluctant to disturb her, I sat outside. I took a deep pull from my water skin and watched her sleep. Her breathing was erratic, as if her spirit was struggling to leave for the next world. *She shouldn't be so close to dying.* It was my fault that she laid here at all.

Just yesterday, I'd sat here under the same cottonwood tree.

I was avoiding the Elders' summons. That was about to come to an end, though, I thought to myself as I watched Umpahtah walk up the rise to meet me. I felt a twinge of irritation. I wasn't a child who needed to be escorted to camp. I just didn't want to go right then. *And isn't that a childish thing to think?* asked the voice in my head.

"When did you become the Elder's runner?" Guilt gave the words more bite than I intended.

Umpahtah shrugged and sat next to me. "They

didn't send me. I just thought you'd like to know what is happening." He leaned back against the trunk.

Far enough away from camp to keep most people away, this hill had become my refuge. To the south, I could see our camp and the nearby river, a silver snake undulating in the grass under the prairie skies. Flanking the camp were the great mountains; snow-capped white rising to meet brilliant blue. Here, more than any other place, we were sustained by Mother Earth as we followed the Great Cycle.

"You saw Firewind return?"

"I did." I plucked a tall blade of grass and started peeling it into strings. "Why?"

Umpahtah regarded me for a moment, then looked back toward camp. "His brother was killed by the White Man's warriors."

My hands stilled. "Red Deer was everything to him."

"That's why he is demanding the Elders ride against the settlement immediately. Not that they will agree to that." He drew up a knee and laced his fingers around it. "He also says he knows why you and your grandmother can't fold the land anymore."

"What?" I jumped to my feet, gesturing at the scene before us. "Folding is what brought us to this valley again."

Umpahtah held up his hands to placate me. "Peace, Cricket. I know you can still fold the land, but the whole tribe knows it's taken a greater toll on you both lately."

I looked down at the twisted blade of grass in my hands. It was true. The land had a different weight to it as we followed the Great Cycle deeper south. But that didn't mean we'd lost our ability.

I dropped the grass and dusted off my hands. Looked like I needed to meet with the Elders after all.

"Come on, I'll fold us back to save time." I started to kneel on the ground.

He pulled out a braid of sinew and hair. "Don't you need your Earth-cord?"

"Where did you get that?"

Umpahtah flushed under my glare. "I picked one out of your tent before I came, in case you needed to hurry back."

I snatched the cord from his hand and coiled it into my pouch. "I only need Earth-cords when I anchor the land for the tribe to travel. I can walk across the folds on my own."

His crestfallen look made me snort. "I won't make you walk the whole way back by yourself. If you hold my hand, you can walk the folds, too."

I knelt back to the ground. This was a simple fold. Camp was close and I could see exactly where I wanted to go. Breathing a prayer of gratitude for Mother Earth's willingness, I released the power in my hands and felt for the anchor I had set in camp. *There.* The land softened in response, ready to be gathered up.

I pulled.

I screamed.

Pain lanced through my breast. The ground cried out, unable to form to my hand. The anchor slipped from my grasp and I fell to the earth.

Umpahtah was next to me in an instant. "What happened?"

"I don't know." My voice sounded far away to my ears. "Something in camp blocked the land from folding."

He placed a steadying hand on my shoulder. "Can you bring us just outside camp? Or do you need me to help you back?"

I blinked away a haze of tears. "Let me try again. There is a stand of poplar trees near camp that I should be able to use as an anchor." Power flowed back into my hands and I reached for the roots, tugging gently at first, wary of a painful repeat. I pulled the land with great care, feeling the folds push up in front of me.

"Give me your hand," I told him. "It will feel like

you are walking on river rapids, but you cannot fall. I'll release the earth once we get there."

He stepped onto the folds, flashing me a grin as he found his balance. It was different when we moved the whole tribe. The Earth-cords helped the land lie flat, creating a pathway so people, supplies, and animals could move smoothly across the folds.

The Elders gathered at the edge of camp. There, surrounding the camp, were great lengths of some kind of metal. They lay on the ground, heavy and inert, as big as a warrior's arm. I pressed my hand to one of them, half expecting another painful jolt. Instead, I was filled with a sense of otherness, of wrongness. This metal did not belong to the Earth. I had felt iron before—its brittle, unyielding surface—but this was *different*. Something had been added to the iron, creating a substance that would not flex and flow with Mother Earth.

"Cricket." I looked up at my grandmother. "Walk with me."

I wiped my hand on my tunic and followed.

It was Firewind who had brought the metal into camp. The White Man had great lengths of it, stretching across the land. Huge smoke-belching creations ran along these tracks, moving people and supplies.

"Our survival depends on following Mother Earth's bounty. We can't fold past it, Cricket." Grandmother looked through me, perhaps seeing the land as it used to be. "Before we are cut off, the Elders have decided we must retreat."

An icy pit formed in my stomach. "What do you mean, *retreat*? As we have moved, the White Man has followed. Where would we go that we could be safe?"

"We mean to tie off this valley, Cricket." She took my hands in hers. "You and I will create a ring surrounding this valley while the tribe waits outside. Once the ring is stable, the tribe can move back onto the land. Then we will sever the cords that keep us tied to this world."

"This is madness talking! Not travel the Great Cycle?" I tried to pull my hands free, but her grip was strong. "Grandmother, we could all be killed trying to retreat this way." I decided to try a different tactic. "What did Firewind say about this decision?"

"Child, what do you think he said?" She expelled a long breath and released my hands. "He called the Elders cowards, not fit to follow in their forefather's footsteps."

"What did they say?"

"Firewind is free to stay with the tribe if he chooses. However, if he chooses to seek vengeance for his brother, he will need to leave."

"He will leave, you know."

Grandmother shrugged. "The Elders expected he would sooner or later anyway. Come, Cricket, I need help readying the Earth-cords."

I stood fast. "What if I want to go with Firewind? What if I don't want to be trapped here?" My heart beat like a captured bird at the daring of my words.

Her shoulders slumped. "You must do as you see fit, Granddaughter." She entered her tent without a backward glance.

This would be an overwhelming task without my help. She didn't have the strength and stamina to create this circle. Perhaps I could get Firewind to talk to her again, convince her to stop.

Crossing camp, I found him outside his tent, securing the last of his belongings. Every movement was anger. Maybe he wouldn't be willing to help. Still, I had to try to save her.

"Firewind, I need you to convince my grandmother that there is some other way."

"The Elders made it very clear, Cricket. I no longer belong to this tribe." He tightened the strap on his pack so fiercely I thought it would break.

"Please, Firewind. I am scared for her."

He rounded on me, but bit back his retort. Instead he gave me an unfathomable look and pushed past me, headed toward her tent.

Grandmother had laid her Earth-cords out and was checking them for damage. A pang of guilt went through me when I saw them. Her cords were so old; the sinews were brittle and fraying. They had only a few trips left before they were completely worn. How could she think she could do this? Her cords wouldn't hold.

When she saw Firewind approach, she straightened. Disapproval pulled at her mouth.

"Your granddaughter seems to believe that I can make you change your mind." He looked at me and shook his head. "This is crazy, Cricket. She is the one who cast me out."

Grandmother's voice carried quietly over his outburst. "You were offered the choice, Firewind. No one cast you out."

"You lie!" All motion around us died away. "Ever since you decided I was not good enough to be chief and marry Cricket, you have sought out any way to remove me from the tribe."

Chief? When had Firewind ever said anything to me about wanting the responsibility of leadership?

"A wise man understands when the risks are too great, Firewind. You ask the Elders to sacrifice the entire tribe for your own personal gain." She turned back to inspect her cords.

"My personal gain." Firewind reminded me of the cougar he had once cornered on a ledge. Trapped and snarling, she had paced back and forth a long time before finally launching herself into the battle to her death. "You think this is about my personal gain?" He continued to advance toward my grandmother. My step back from him became my biggest mistake.

"You have denied my leadership. You have denied me my rightful bride. You have denied me my brother's vengeance. You even think to deny me my home and tribe." He sprang, and she crumpled to the ground with a sickening thud. "There is no gain in this for me, old woman."

Stunned, I looked into his eyes. In them I saw only

madness. Into the stillness he whispered, "Make your
escape now, Cricket, before she takes everything away
from you, too." And then he was gone, mounting up
on the run.

The camp burst into life again. Umpahtah was at
Grandmother's side, checking her injuries. "Her ribs
are broken, Cricket. We'll have to carry her to
shelter."

"Cricket." Her voice was thin with pain.

Umpahtah laid a hand on her arm. "It's all right,
Grandmother. She will follow us to the shelter. Don't
talk now." He eased her onto a makeshift travois and
helped carry her away.

Shock numbed my mind. The man I thought I could
count on was gone. The camp was in shambles, both
from his outburst and from the travel preparations.
My grandmother had been attacked and lay injured,
and possibly dying. *How had it gone so wrong?*

Her Earth-cords lay in a tangled heap at my feet. I
crouched down to pick one up. So old. So tired.

Could I anchor myself to one place? When I closed
my eyes, I could see this valley, spreading itself wide
from the mountains. Fish and wildlife were plentiful
here, as well as many of the herbs and berries we
depended on. Perhaps Mother Earth could sustain us
here and we would no longer need to follow the
Great Cycle.

I gathered Grandmother's Earth-cords then. They
could not be used for this task. But my cords—young,
strong, unblemished by years of travel—could create
our new home.

Now I looked up into the tree and took another
drink. The undersides of the cottonwood leaves were
turned up, flashing silver, a sure sign of the approaching storm.

"Cricket?"

I scrambled to her side, all tiredness forgotten. "Do
you need anything?"

She shook her head slightly. "Is the circle complete?"

"I finished setting the pathway just a little while ago. Umpahtah is telling the Elders we can move across now."

"And it's holding?"

"For now, yes." I exhaled sharply. "But I don't know how long the anchors will hold. Everyone needs to cross soon so we can tie off the circle."

Grandmother watched the leaves overhead. "There's a big storm coming, isn't there? Will you watch it with me?"

I smiled. From early childhood, I loved the feel of a storm. Grandmother was the only one who would sit out and watch them with me. I took her hand, her papery skin cool against mine. "Of course."

She brushed back a tendril of hair from my cheek. "Perhaps the rain will clean you up a bit then, hmm?" She started to chuckle, then winced in pain.

"Do you need the healer?"

"No, Cricket. I just need to rest." A cold gust of wind blew through the shelter. "You should rest too. You still need to tie off the circle."

"Don't worry about me." I tucked the skin around her to protect her against the cold. "I'll be fine. I'll see you inside the circle." Kissing her forehead, I rose and left.

Umpahtah waited outside for me. The wind was getting stronger and the cords on the path created an eerie sound. Midnight clouds, streaked white with hail, obscured the distant mountains. I prayed we could get the tribe moved to safety before the storm hit.

"Cricket, come walk with me." Umpahtah took my arm and led me past the path. "You told me walking on the folds was like walking on rapids?"

I nodded.

"Well, there is a section of the circle that doesn't feel like that."

Even as we approached, I could feel a difference. Alarmed, I ran to the Earth-cord. "It's starting to fray." The earth under my feet shifted uncomfortably. "Run back and get one of Grandmother's Earth-cords. I'll use it to strengthen mine."

He hesitated. "Go!" I shouted.

A fat raindrop struck the dust next to the cord. One glance at the darkening sky convinced me I didn't want to be caught outside. I bent to the cord again. It couldn't have frayed this fast. *Unless it was tampered with.* Sure enough, there was a knife cut near the anchor.

"I know you're there, Firewind," I called as I stood.

"I see the Elders' messenger boy has been busy playing guard." Firewind rose from behind a grassy hillock.

Wary of his approach, I tried to step back, but a gust of wind pushed my forward. "What are you doing here?"

"I was thinking about the benefits of your retreat. I'd just need to split a cord and create my own pathway. Then I could come and go as I please and the White Man will never find me." Madness crept into his eyes again. "I could kill them, one by one, and your world would be my refuge." He took another step and crushed my Earth-cord into the ground.

The cord sang out in fear and the land roiled under me. Firewind couldn't tell, but I knew the cord was close to breaking. If it snapped, I had no idea what would happen. *Where was Umpahtah?*

Thunder rolled in the distance and the cold wind rippled my tunic. I had to do something to free the Earth-cord. I rushed forward, intent on knocking him off balance, but he had been ready for me. He spun me around and laid his knife at my throat. Panic darkened my vision. How could I be so stupid? If the cord wasn't repaired soon, the earth would break free and create a rift, dragging all my people into the depths.

Another raindrop splashed on my face, bringing me back to my senses. I had to get away from this madman. "What do you want from me?"

His chuckle rumbled across my back. "What I've

always wanted. Power to make the decisions and not take orders from a bunch of dried up old men."

"None of this will bring Red Deer back."

His knife tightened against my throat. I could feel its bite against my skin and a thin stream of warm blood mingled with the cold rain trickling down my neck. "Don't say anything you might regret later, Cricket."

"You can't kill me, Firewind. I'm the one who controls the land."

He seemed to consider that for a moment. Perhaps I could still reason with him. His next words killed any hope.

"I am quite sure that I can manage without you now. After all, you've set the anchors and cords. All I need to do is split a cord and step through." To demonstrate, he pushed his toe into the cut cord, and stepped into the gap.

In that moment, the earth buckled. With one foot precariously placed in the sinew, Firewind struggled for balance. Seizing the opportunity, I slipped down to the ground to save the cord. It was raining in earnest now and the wind whipped my hair into my face.

Something whistled past my head.

Firewind landed hard on me. I fought to get out from under him. I heard my name and the weight of Firewind rolled off me. I sat up and fingered the blood staining my shirt.

Umpahtah crouched down, bow in hand. "Are you hurt?"

Realization dawned. The blood on my tunic was not mine. Firewind lay behind me, an arrow through his throat.

"No, I'm fine." I reached over and yanked the offending foot from the cord. "How did you get a clear shot?"

"Your grandmother pulled a fold out from under you both. When you went down . . ." He shrugged, leaving the statement unfinished.

"My grandmother?" Through the rain I could see a small figure huddled on the ground. I lashed out with my fists at Umpahtah. "Why did you bring her out here?"

I ran to her side. She was pale, so pale. Wet strands of hair straggled across her face. "Grandmother, what were you thinking?"

"Take the cord." She struggled for breath. "Replace the one Firewind split."

I glanced down at the cord in my hand. It was one of mine. "Where did you get this?"

"I thought Firewind would tamper with the circle." She paused for a moment to catch her breath. "When Umpahtah came back, I had him take me to the pathway and replaced one of yours with one of mine." She closed her eyes as another spasm of pain passed through. "Your Earth-cords must form the circle, Cricket. Mine will never hold."

"Umpahtah, take her back to camp. Take her to the healer." I ran back to the cord. Glancing back, I saw my grandmother cradled in his arms.

Lightning streaked above me. I had to make the repair and get to safety. I knotted my new cord through each anchor and then whispered a prayer that the anchors were still secure before I removed the damaged one. The land sent up another quiver of protest, but held fast.

Rain slashed across the sky. The muddy quagmire sucked at my feet. I half-ran, half-slid to the circle entrance. The sky lit up around me. I could see hastily erected shelters near the camp center. I hoped everyone was there; there would be no second chances. At the pathway, I reached my Earth-cord first. This was the cord I would use to tie off the circle. Then I'd just release my Grandmother's cord and we would be separated from the world around us. I struggled with the knot, my hands icy cold. The ground slid from under me as the pressure on the folded earth released.

I needed to tie off the circle before the land broke free. I knotted the Earth-cord through the near anchor, pulling it as tight as I could. Then with a prayer for forgiveness, I rammed my hands into Mother Earth.

She wailed at my demands. The land under me slipped and bucked, but I held strong. Slowly, I pulled the land toward me, reaching for the final anchor in the circle. Hailstones stung my body as Father Sky had joined in the protest. My muscles burned with pain and exhaustion.

Finally, the anchor was within reach. Numb fingers tied a clumsy knot. I fell back on my heels, swiping at the strands of hair plastered to my face. Now my grandmother's worn cord was the only thing connecting the circle to the world outside. The land beneath me twisted, yearning for freedom. Mother Earth would not be restrained much longer.

I crawled through the mud back to the anchor at the entrance to the pathway. The rain ripped fibers from the worn braid and the wind screamed though its length. I started to undo the knot. The ground twisted beneath the anchor.

I froze, hands on the knot, realizing my mistake.

If I released this anchor first, I would have no way to control the folds. With the pressure and strain they were under, the energy would slam into the circle, ripping through my Earth-cords. The land would be rent asunder.

It would have to be the anchor point on the circle to be released first. Then I could step backwards, slowly playing out the folds like a fishing line. The circle would be safely separated from the world.

And I would be outside the circle.

Tears mingled with rain on my face. I would be cut off from everything I held dear. But I had no choice. The survival of my people depended on me.

Lightning cut the sky and I saw a misshapen figure coming toward me, huddled downward against the rain and hail. Another flash revealed the figure. Umpahtah carried my grandmother toward me.

"What are you doing here?" I yelled to make myself heard over the storm.

"She insisted. Said it was her job to finish." He set

her down next to the anchor and she crouched over the knot.

"Has madness taken both of you?" I pushed Umpahtah out of my way and knelt by Grandmother, covering her hands with mine. "You have to stop, Grandmother. Please, let him take you back to shelter."

She looked at me, her face drawn in pain. A sad smile played about her lips. "You said you would watch the storm with me, Cricket." She shook her head and cupped my cheek in her palm. "I'm not sure that being out in the rain has cleaned you up though."

I touched my face. Matted hair and mud met my fingertips. My laughter turned to sobs. There, kneeling in a river of mud, I clung to my grandmother.

"Shh. Hush now, Cricket." Her gnarled hand stroked my head.

I pulled back, longing for the sight of her face. "You knew, didn't you?" I whispered. Her eyes, bright with unshed tears, gave silent assent.

She glanced over my shoulder. "Umpahtah, take my granddaughter home, please."

Strong hands gripped me. "She's right, Cricket. We must go." In response to his words, the ground lifted sharply, causing us to stagger.

One more tearful kiss and then Umpahtah and I withdrew, away from the immediate danger of the circle's edge. Rain continued to pound against us.

Lightning sporadically illuminated the scene. I watched Grandmother untie the anchor and wrap the Earth-cord around her waist. I could feel the land shift, straining for a new balance point. Each step she took seemed to move us further downward, as if we were being lowered over the edge of an invisible cliff.

The sky exploded to my right. A bolt of lightning struck the cottonwood tree, shattering its heart. Grandmother stumbled and fell. I ran to help her, but landed hard in the mud, tackled by Umpahtah. The land swayed crazily back and forth, suspended only by the single cord, wrapped around a dying woman.

"You can't go to her, Cricket." His weight pressed

me into the ground, his voice harsh in my ear. "Let her last memory be that of you standing proud, honoring her warrior spirit."

He was right. I only made her task harder by clinging to her. I nodded my understanding and staggered to my feet, unbalanced by the land. In the next flash, I saw she too had regained her footing but was bent double in pain. I ached to run to her, to take her burden. Instead, I stood tall, keeping watch, as she stepped out of my life.

Once at the end of the cord, she touched her hand to her heart, then raised her arm in farewell.

She knelt to untie the last anchor.

The land fell away from my feet in a dizzying blur. I shrieked and grasped for Umpahtah. Pain exploded behind my ear, and I fell, unconscious.

"Cricket?" A voice carried across the darkness, full of concern.

I cracked open one eye. I was in the healer's tent, warm and dry. Umpahtah sat by my side, holding a steaming cup of liquid. "Willow tree bark," he said, following my glance. "For your head."

I pushed myself upright. "Did it work?"

"Yes. The Earth-cords are lost somewhere in the folds. Our world is now separate from the White Man's world."

"I need to see it."

He nodded and set down the cup. He steadied me as we walked to the burnt-out husk of the cottonwood tree. The storm was long past. White clouds scudded across the clear blue sky. The river meandered along through the grasses. Everything looked the same. Everyone was safely here. Except one.

Umpahtah pulled me close. "She was right, you know. The metal tracks would have made it impossible to survive if we had stayed."

Tears slipped unheeded down my cheeks as I looked out at the valley that had become our forever home. "I know, Umpahtah. I know."

Pony Up

Linda A. B. Davis

Henry had only stumbled a little bit on the tricky words when he read the advertisement posted by the front door of the general store out loud. "Wanted: Young, skinny, wiry fellows, not over 18. Must be expert riders, willing to risk death daily. Orphans preferred. Wages $25 a week."

Now, after deciding he fit the requirements, he stood in front of the hiring man who studied him and Mazie with unreadable eyes and a tight mouth. Henry swallowed hard and bounced lightly on his heels, hoping he'd be up to snuff. He wasn't worried about Mazie, his stout, painted Pegasus pony. She was on the small side, but she was strong of body and heart and would thrive in the dangerous employ of the Pony Express.

The hiring man finally spoke. "Are you sure she's of Pegasus stock? Her wings aren't in yet."

"Sure is," Henry replied. He couldn't help but puff his chest out a bit. "Check the glow on her brand. It's official Cheyenne Pegasus."

"How did a boy your age get a real Pegasus?" The hiring man lowered his brows in suspicion. "She's not stolen, is she?"

Henry gasped. "No, sir. My grandmother's a Cheyenne medicine woman. She gave Mazie to me."

"Well," the hiring man said. "You look about right.

You'll have to take a land route until her wings come in. See the station manager for your assignment. You can water the horse out back."

Henry couldn't help but smile as he led Mazie through the small group of young men and their horses, some Pegasi. Spirits were high here in the warming March sun, the boys almost giddy with the anticipation of adventure. Henry wondered if they'd still be smiling when the rigors of the trail hit. Death would be more real then, not just a word meant to challenge their sense of immortality.

Henry ran his hand down Mazie's muzzle as she drank, feeling the strong bone beneath and the coarse hair atop. She was his love, her heart being big and her strength beyond. The only thing he'd change about her if he could would be to give her wings. She'd be a real Pegasus then, and he'd be a real man.

The station manager reminded Henry of a turnip, round and rather ruddy. He swaggered over as Henry threw Mazie's reins over the post.

"Kind of a runt you've got there, boy. My name's Landy." He sucked some air through a spot between his crooked, yellow teeth.

"She's fast as she needs to be," Henry replied. He pulled himself up as tall as he could. "The hiring man said to see you for an assignment."

Landy waved his hand the way of the station. "Come on, then. Let me check my schedule."

The Kearney, Nebraska, station was small and dark, dust dancing with abandon within the few streams of sunlight that dared to peek in. The wooden shack housed a few cots and a table with two rickety chairs.

Landy shuffled through the papers on the table. He spoke as he searched. "You'll leave at dawn with an experienced rider to learn the route. Then you and that runt of yours are on your own. I hope she's better than she looks. You, too."

"What? The poster said young and skinny."

Landy laughed. "It also said wiry. That means lean and mean."

"Well," Henry protested. "I can be mean."

"Like a pup, I bet," Landy said with a smile. "Be here at dawn, ready to go."

Henry cleared his throat. "Sir?"

"Hmmmm?"

"I don't have anywhere to be tonight."

"Orphan, huh?" Landy sucked more air as he thought. "Stay here tonight then. You'll get paid after your ride, and then you can make arrangements in town."

Henry nodded. "Many thanks."

Dobytown, the nickname for Kearney, was noisy that night. Party music from different adobe-type buildings mingled in the streets to create a nonsensical rhythm. Women of disrepute laughed loudly as lonely men dragged them through the streets. Henry even heard shouting several times, mostly followed by gunshots.

He was grateful to be here, though. This was the start of a new life, a place where he could finally belong. It wouldn't matter here that he was of both white and Cheyenne blood. He would fit in as long as he did the job.

Henry figured he had nothing to lose by trying. His father had always said, "You can't win if you don't play." He'd said it right up to when a sore loser shot him at the poker table. Stanley Orr lost big that day, but it didn't make the theory any less sound.

"We can do this, Mazie," Henry whispered, the sound almost lost in the cold, gentle breeze. "You and me. We can be heroes. They'll write about us in those dime novels."

Mazie whinnied softly and shook her head, her glossy mane hair brushing Henry's cheeks. He laid his head against her neck, feeling the warmth of her body join his own. He could see the moon behind him in the reflection of her eye, and he wondered how close she'd be able to fly to that moon once she got her wings.

Henry stretched out on the cot he'd moved outside. The noise of the town was distracting at first, but then not so much as he relaxed. He huddled under the two worn and ratty blankets, hoping there wouldn't be any bugs looking for a new home.

Henry awoke in the grayness of dawn to hear harsh voices nearby. He kept his eyes closed as he determined the voices were coming from around the corner of the station.

"I'm not riding with a boy. I need real backup. Butterfield will win the contract for his stagecoaches if we lose this one."

Henry recognized Landy's voice in reply. "What am I supposed to do, Tom? We've already sent the others away to come back later. The package will be here any minute."

"You didn't know what was in it before now?"

"I just got the telegraph. Lincoln's trying to tell the nation that things won't change before the South goes and starts a war. That address needs to get to California soon."

Landy spoke again after a short pause. "The boy's got a Pegasus. That's got to mean something."

"I reckon," Tom said. "But if we get ambushed, that mustang will need wings. And I saw her just now. No wings."

"They're all you've got," Landy said.

Tom snorted. "Might as well be nothing."

Henry was sitting upright rubbing his face when Landy came barreling around the corner. He saw that Henry was awake.

"Guess you heard that, huh?"

Henry nodded. "We're lots better than nothing."

"We'll see," Landy said. He tossed Henry a biscuit, two hard pieces of bread separated by a slice of cured ham. It would fill his stomach nicely, tasty or not, though probably not, judging by the hardness of the bread.

"There's a pile of hay and grass around the corner

for your horse. Feed her and be ready to leave in thirty minutes." Landy glanced back as he turned to leave. "And take that cot back inside."

Henry spent his time preparing for the ride. He checked the load in his six-shooter and saddled Mazie. A Pegasus rider rode up in front of the horse's body to allow room for the wings when spread. It took some getting used to, but Henry had taken to it quickly. He always saddled for wings even though Mazie didn't have them yet. It was a crapshoot as to when they would sprout, and he wanted to be ready.

When he and Mazie reported to the front of the station, Henry stopped short. The Pegasus standing there was magnificent. He was a pure black mustang, almost 17 hands high, tall for his breed. His blackness was almost blue, the color so dark and rich.

Henry closed his mouth as realized he was gawking at the wings. He couldn't see their span since they were down and layered against the body, but they lay like a second skin. Their coal color held an almost ghostly glow that swirled freely within its own splendor.

Henry assumed the man placing the *mochila* over the animal's saddle was the unseen but reluctant Tom. He moved with confidence as he arranged the blanket-like carrier to his satisfaction. There were four pockets, or *cantinas,* padlocked at each corner of the small leather blanket. Tom's weight would keep the carrier in place as he rode.

He turned and tossed Henry an identical *mochila.* Henry stood holding it, unsure of what to do with it.

"It's a decoy, boy," Tom said. "Put it on your horse like I've got mine."

Henry did so, adjusting the blanket so the weight would be even. He then turned and approached the blond stranger to hold out his hand.

"We haven't been introduced. My name's Henry Sun Cloud Orr. This here's Mazie," he said as he nodded her way.

Tom paused, his head cocked slightly as he moved

forward to take Henry's hand. His clear blue eyes met Henry's light brown ones with interest.

"Tom Sneads," he replied. "And this is Shame. Your first ride?"

"Yep. But this is supposed to be a land route for a regular horse."

"It is. This route's rider broke his arm yesterday. Me and Shame are just filling in."

"We're ready for anything," Henry said.

Tom smiled. "That's good, 'cause it could get ugly. You know what we've got to carry?"

"I do," Henry said. "We'll get it to the next station." He gulped, hoping it would be true. He didn't want to be the one to muck up the most important delivery in the history of the Pony Express.

"Let's ride," Tom said as he mounted Shame and trotted to the road. Henry followed as they aimed their steeds to the west of town. They pushed the horses hard but not full out, both of them kicking up dirt and leaving a trail.

Land routes existed because Pegasi were still horses and therefore better runners than fliers. The Express only designated a route as an air route when there were mountains, canyons, water, or snow blocking the way.

Henry saw some canyons in the distance, but they mostly passed through prairies which had their own beauty. He especially loved the purple coneflowers that carpeted the plains in the spring and summer. He remembered spending many happy days gathering these plants with his grandmother for her remedies. The Cheyenne used them to fight mostly fevers and infections but also any snakebites that came along. The flowers weren't in bloom yet, but Henry wondered if Brown Deer might be in this very field come harvest time.

He hadn't been allowed to see Brown Deer since his mother had died two years ago. Stanley Orr told Henry that the Cheyenne didn't want him because he was a half-breed. He said that Brown Deer's respected position was the only reason the tribe had tolerated him as long as they did. Henry wasn't sure what to believe, but he had no way to find out. He did know that, even if so, the Cheyenne wouldn't be the only narrow-minded folk who thought that about him.

"Boy! Look!" Henry startled from his reverie as he whipped his head around to face Tom and Shame. The sun was now hot and high, with the previously damp air now being dry. He noticed Tom's sweat seeping through the seam of his leather hat.

Tom jerked his head to face behind them, and Henry turned to see what had his attention. He saw a billowing, growing cloud of dust.

"Oh, no," Henry said quietly. They were being followed fast, and from the size of the dust cloud, it was probably by five or six men. They were too far away for Henry to see them individually, but he knew they were there, hidden somewhere within the oncoming haze.

"What do we do?" Henry hollered.

"We ride!" Tom settled forward, tapped Shame with his spurs, and leaned into the motion.

They rode full out for the next few minutes. Henry knew who it was behind them, and he was sure Tom knew it, too. It had to be the Butterfield men.

John Butterfield's Overland Mail Company was in competition for the U.S. mail contract for their stagecoaches. Their desperation today wasn't so much about having influence on the direction of the nation, but about money. They were certain to win the million-dollar contract if the Pony Express lost Lincoln's Inaugural Address. Butterfield was only months away from being put out of business by normal competition, and this contract meant his survival.

"They're not getting this package." Henry's face hardened as he considered the stake. He slapped Mazie lightly with the reins to urge her on. "Yeee haaa!"

He could barely see Tom through the fine, dry dust

he was now choking on. Tom kept looking back, apparently anxious to have Henry and Mazie catch up with them. Henry had to admit that Tom and Shame were quite able to go faster, or even fly, but they hung back, probably not wanting to leave Henry and Mazie to this band's mercy.

Henry heard a gunshot from behind him. The bunch was getting close enough to shoot at them? Well, that meant one thing for sure. They were close enough to shoot back at.

Henry pulled out his Colt, aimed behind him as best he could, fired twice and then twice again. He heard a howl of pain, but he didn't take the time to see who fell back.

He then heard the whine of more bullets as they whizzed past his head, but Henry startled as he realized they were going in the opposite direction. He looked up to see Tom shooting past him through the dust. Henry hoped Tom could see him better than he could see Tom.

"I've got an idea, Mazie," Henry said. When Tom looked back again, Henry motioned to him.

Tom slowed down enough to let Henry pull alongside of them. Henry waved his hand forward, motioning for him and Shame to go on.

"Let's split up," he said loudly. "You go ahead with the package, and I'll draw some of them off of you by heading to the canyons yonder." He pointed to the north. "That way you can fly."

Henry tried to push the thought of the outlaws catching him alone to the hindquarters of his brain. There was no telling what they would do to him. He'd probably want a gunshot to the head by the time these men were finished.

Henry was grateful to know Mazie would be safe, no matter what. It was rotten bad luck to hurt a Pegasus. Everyone knew it would provoke the wrath of thousands of warrior ghost Cheyenne, the keepers of the Pegasi. He'd heard horrible stories around the card tables about the bloody vengeance they wrought on anyone that foolish. Henry counted on the thieves having heard the same stories.

His fear for Mazie was that she'd be forced to do their bidding. Her soul would be sullied by what was certain to be plebeian activities. The best Mazie could hope for under their possession would be to become part of a stagecoach team. While that was fine for a normal horse, it was degrading to a creature born of such noble breath. Oh, yes, the white man called these creatures Pegasi because of their own, ancient myth, but this particular bloodstock had royal Cheyenne origins to which outsiders weren't privy.

Right now, as they were being determinedly dogged, separating themselves from Tom and Shame in order to split the bandits' power was the only option Henry saw. He waved forward again to Tom.

Tom grimaced and shook his head. "I can't go ahead! You've got the real package, not me. There's no time to switch."

Henry's stomach rolled heavily. He had the real package? Why would the Express give him the real package? Yes, the thieves would expect the older and stronger rider to have the mail, but how stupid was that to actually put it with him, a greenhorn without even a winged horse?

He looked back to the individual riders now. He saw five of them, and they'd be on top of him and Tom in a matter of minutes. What should he do?

He yelled to Tom again, trying not to suck in the surrounding and suffocating dust. "You fly! They don't know you don't have the real package." He knew that at least two men would follow Tom and Shame on the ground, hoping to keep up until they landed. That would leave three chasing him, and maybe he could lose them in the canyons.

Tom shook his head sideways as he responded. "You don't know where the next station is."

"I'll find it. Five more miles west, right?"

"Yep! Good luck, kid! You've got heart."

Shame unfolded his wings as he ran and raised them off of his body. He spread them skyward to create a glorious width-span. Henry almost lost his focus on the chase at hand as he marveled at the sight of feathered midnight. When Shame put his wings into motion, they literally blocked the sight of the landscape past them. Henry watched for a few seconds more as the beast lifted from the ground and soared. What a beauty.

Henry shook his head to reclaim himself, and then he jerked the reins to his right, northward. Mazie left the trail easily and headed to the canyons. They were only a mile or two away, but Henry still wasn't sure they were going to make it.

He glanced back to see that three riders had followed Tom and two had stuck with him. Henry had the odds with him, and he hoped it would be enough. The duo seemed to be closing the gap though as he could now hear their shouts.

"Jones, go to his right. I've got his left."

Henry rode as if his life depended on it, knowing he couldn't allow them to hem him in. They might only take the package, or they might kill him out of meanness.

The sound of the pounding hooves joined the rhythm of the blood rushing through his ears. He was relieved to now be breathing air instead of Tom's dust, but his chest was still burning. He wondered how Mazie was holding up under the increased stress. Mustangs were a hearty lot, but she'd never been put to the test like this before.

"Are you okay, girl? Can you make it? We've only got a little farther to go before we hit the canyons."

Henry felt the slam into his right shoulder before he heard the shot. Only by instinct did he manage to not pitch forward from the impact. He'd never been shot before, and Henry let out a loud grunt before he gained control of his voice again. He didn't want to scare Mazie, so he rode for a few seconds in silence.

Then the pain hit. It was all he could do to not

succumb to the delicious temptation of blacking out. Things in front of him started to swirl, and he felt dizzy. His body leaned at a slight tilt, and Henry knew he was in serious danger of falling off. He quickly considered the consequences, and made a decision. He spoke, as much to himself as to Mazie. It helped him clear his thoughts.

"Mazie, I'm going to jump off in a minute. I want you to keep going. You'll have a better chance to get away without my weight. You can find your way back to the station after you lose the bandits. The package will be late, but the Express will send it out again."

Henry swallowed down a surge of pain as he readied for his fall to the ground while Mazie was running at top speed. This was going to hurt. Just as he started to let go, he heard a voice.

No. You can't jump. The mochila *won't stay on the saddle without your weight to hold it down.*

"What?" He must be losing more blood than he thought. That was Brown Deer's voice coming from inside his head, but it was Mazie at the same time.

Stay in the saddle. We're going to fly.

"You need wings to fly."

Hold tight. It won't take but a minute.

Henry considered this with what reason he had left. "You let me get shot before you did this?"

Until now you were only a rider. The Breed requires a sacrifice before we can truly bond. Once you show a commitment to someone or something else, we will fly for you.

"Let's get gone then before I pass out."

As they spoke, Henry felt the heat coming off of Mazie's body. He didn't know if Mazie felt the same kind of burn as the one blazing in his shoulder, but Henry worried for her, the heat so intense. There was also a thick, charring smell, like a fire raging through brush. Henry thought he might be sick, but he tried to quell the nausea, not wanting to defile his Pegasus friend in her moment of glory.

In the corner of his vision, he could see a bright

golden glow coming from Mazie's brand. He also thought he heard a humming noise, but he might have only imagined it. Henry knew his senses weren't reliable right now.

Mazie's white and cinnamon wings, painted as well, literally emerged from under her hide to lie on top. It was as if they had been hibernating, just waiting for the right moment to exist. Through his fog, Henry could hear more shouts behind him.

"She's going to fly!"

"Shoot before they're gone. But don't shoot the horse!"

Henry heard more shots ring out as Mazie began her liftoff. Another bullet grazed his right arm, the one attached to the injured shoulder. A stinging pain erupted just above his elbow, but it was manageable. He tried not to drop his gun.

Henry only had two shots left, but he might as well use them. Gritting his teeth, he was able to lift his arm enough to empty his gun in the general direction of somewhere behind him. He heard a loud curse in response, and Henry smiled with satisfaction.

He and Mazie were now high enough to be out of shooting range. Henry carefully holstered his empty gun and leaned forward for stability, letting Mazie do the work. She circled back around to the trail they'd left, and headed westward again. Henry looked behind and under him to see the men and their horses standing still, watching. He hoped they were figuring out what they were going to tell Butterfield.

Rest, Henry. It won't take long in the air.

"Are you really Brown Deer?"

The voice chuckled. *No. I'm still Mazie. Brown Deer lent me her voice so that you would be comfortable.*

"Does she still live?" Henry asked, afraid to hope. He'd just gotten used to not having his father around. He wasn't sure he could withstand another loss quite so soon.

She does, Henry. She awaits your visit. Rest now. I'll get us to town.

Henry knew she would, so he closed his eyes and concentrated on the sound of Mazie's new wings pushing against the air. It was a soothing whooshing sound, and the only distraction was the occasional bird or two.

He rather liked this flying thing, Henry decided. He would definitely do more of it, but next time, he'd try not to get shot. It would be easier all around.

Gold at the End of the Railroad

Elizabeth Ann Scarborough

*There is little documentation of the critical role played
by immigrant supernaturals when their various peoples
came to the shores of America looking for a better life,
but here is one account, told by an eloquent Irish friend
of my family, about how the Irish and the Chinese, and
hence the entire transcontinental railroad, were assisted
by otherworldly beings from their native lands.*

A nd what is it you think you're doing here?" Patrick Finnegan asked the new man on the job. The
short fellow with the red muttonchop whiskers didn't
look as if he could drive a nail, much less a railroad
spike. But that wasn't the cause of Finnegan's distrust
of him. "I thought we left your kind with your blarney
and your tricks back in Ireland to bedevil the
landlords."

"Now, Paddy, don't you go bein' that way," the
little man said in a brogue even thicker than Patrick's
own. "I'm from the Auld Sod. I'm here to help you."

"Auld Sod my arse. Sod off, you," Finnegan said.
"The bosses are already on our backs without the likes
of you stirring up trouble. They don't want to pay us
fair wage for our labor and are threatening to bring
in Celestials to replace us. They'd leave us stranded
out here without wage, food, or water if I know
bosses, and I think by now I do."

"Of course they would, Paddy lad. Of course they would. That's why I've come to see to you and the boys. You'll be needin' my help."

"And what is it you can do that won't make things worse? You with your worthless magic and promises of fairy gold!"

" 'Tis the likes of me who make the worthy among the Irish rich, and did you not come here to America to get rich?"

"I came here to America to keep from bloody starving. Not that I had much choice. The landlords packed the ships with us and piled us higher than a long winter's stack of turf. Where were you to help us when me old mammy died and then me sisters and their children? Leprechauns help no one. Everyone knows that. You lead us on with false hope and then run off leaving us with hands full of dust and potatoes too diseased to feed to any livestock unlucky enough to still be alive."

The little man clucked his tongue reprovingly, "Now, now, Paddy, I know it's been hard. We've not had it easy ourselves. We've had to stay hidden these many years while their lordships were in charge—too Irish, you see, promotes nationalism, you know. That being the case, it should be clear to you that I am here now to help you and your crew get what you have coming to you and give you the edge you'll need when the Celestials arrive with their dragons." He hissed like a teakettle. "Nasty things, dragons. We've none of their row in Ireland and who do you think it is saw to that?"

"You can't take credit!" Finnegan says. "Sure everyone knows it was me own name saint, Patrick, drove the snakes from Ireland and everyone knows as well that your dragons are nothing but great bloody serpents."

The little man took a pipe from his waistcoat, and a very fine waistcoat it was to be out here in the middle of nowhere among the great unwashed company of railroad men. Finnegan's own hair was as red as the little man's own but you'd never know it for the grease, the dirt, the sweat, and the soot clinging to it. That fine waistcoat wouldn't stay fine for long if the little man made even a pretense of doing the least of the jobs Finnegan and his boys had been working.

Which brought him to the business at hand. "Now then, are ye going to work or are ye going to blather about serpents and such all day?"

Someone yelled at him. "Finnegan!"

He turned his head and hollered back, "What is it you want?"

"Who the divvil are ye talking to, man? We need you here to sing us that bloody song again so we can line the bloody track again. The bleedin' thing goes wanderin' off the very moment we try to lay some new."

Finnegan glanced behind him before he rejoined his crew, and was not at all surprised, given the nature of his recent visitor, to find that he was quite alone in front of the tent and not a soul in sight under the height of the normal man. Paddy's lads, starved as boys in the famine and aboard ship, were not large fellows but none of them was as small as all that. Good scrappers they were, and most of them good in a fight, but they were not large and there was nothing out of the ordinary about their strength.

"If we were to have a supernatural about the camp, why could it not have been the giant Finn McCool?" Finnegan muttered. "We could have used him on the crew."

He joined his boys while the bosses looked on critically. "They've just been standing here, Finnegan. We're not paying your men to twiddle their thumbs while they stand around waiting for you to show up. I hear the Celestials organize themselves and never take a moment's rest until the day is done."

"Right you are, Mr. Throckmorton," Finnegan said, setting his face in a chagrined expression and tipping his cap. "Sorry I am about that, Mr. Throckmorton, but it was a bit of a personnel problem I was after dealin' with, sir."

Inserting himself between Maloney and O'Hara, he growled out the side of his mouth, "And may the first engine to run on this track roll right over you, Mr. Throckmorton, sir."

Then he commenced with the truly foreign part of the job, something his background as the descendant of generations of Irish harpers and shanachies had ill prepared him to do. He started the track-lining song he'd learned from the black fellas he'd met when he finally got his first job in America after making his way from New York to Georgia. The "No Irish Need Apply" signs were out in force then. There were men from home a fellow could approach about jobs and places to live and such, but there was a price to pay for such influence as they wielded. Heartsick from the losses of home and kin he'd suffered in coming to America, he was in no fit frame of mind to put on a yoke for a fellow Irishman when he'd escaped that of the landlords at such great cost. He thought if he got away from where there were so many of his countrymen in the great cities, he might have a better chance at proving himself for the clever and able fellow he was.

That was how he'd come to work on the railroad for the first time. A displaced Paddy, while less familiar to the drawling employers in the South, was of the right complexion to be put in charge of the blacks, at least for appearance's sake. The truth was, Paddy saw from the beginning that he had more in common with the blacks than the bosses. For their part, they treated the young fellow with the amusing voice with surprising kindness, rough lot though they were. They'd taught him the track-lining song, even the dirty verses that made the men work harder and got the work done quicker.

Now he began it, mimicking the drawling bawl of

the work crews, and trying to get his lads to sing with him.

"Woke up this mornin' "—he sang and then all of them threw themselves against the handles of the flat gandy shovels they had inserted beneath the errant tracks and grunted, "Huh!"

"Looked like rain' "

"Huh!"

"Pick and shovel' "

"Huh!"

"This track again!"

"Huh."

You started off with the more socially acceptable verses and then as the men got tireder added in the dirty ones to make the work more interesting. The problem was, although he and his black coworkers had shared many of the same kind of sad stories of separation and privation, the black men he'd learned the song from were great big fellas, strong from all kinds of work, and his lot ran more to the stringy and wiry, quick on their feet but without the same stamina for the heavy labor.

Still, once he got the way of it and learned the railroads were taking on crews for the great railway to the west, he'd taken his skills along the tracks, and when there was an opening for a man or one could be made, sent for one of his own to come join the work party. That was how it was done and it was the right thing to do. Once you had enough of your own together, you could set terms more to your liking. This far along in the job, and so far out west away from the big eastern cities, there'd be little enough the bosses could do, they'd thought.

But then someone in California got the bright idea of bringing in shiploads of Chinese from the west. They were small too, but they were strong and there were millions of them and they never got sick from the dysentery that had his men weak from the runs or too cramped to swing a hammer much of the time.

The little bastards never seemed to get tired either, just sipped their tea now and then and they were good to go. They also worked for even lower wages than the Irish crews.

But he'd have bet a month's pay, and in fact was doing just that, that even the Celestials couldn't get the hang of the work song for track lining, each "huh!" grunted by five men moving the track only a wee little bit. Oh, his boys could sing the song but they couldn't make it move the bloody track the way the black fellas he used to work with could.

This was the sort of thing that made him and the boys look bad and the bosses think them ineffectual. So it came as no surprise when the powers that be made good on their threat and the Celestials walked down through the pass and into the camp. There they set up their own tents where they cooked their strange-smelling food and smoked their strange-smelling pipes and talked their lingo faster than a Dubliner. It had always been a question of when, not if, they would arrive, to Paddy's mind, but that did not cause him to walk over and welcome them.

The next day they were swarming all over the cliffs, lowering each other in baskets and exploding the hell out of the hills making way for the tracks while his boys were still trying to line the ones they'd already laid.

When Finnegan went to turn in that night, he was seriously disturbed by what he'd seen. Sure if this kept up, he and his boys would be sent home without their pay and then where would they be?

He found his cot occupied by the leprechaun, who was enjoying a peaceful smoke. "Ah, Patrick me boy, and what did you think of your Oriental brothers now they've come to show you how it's done?"

"The little divvils surely know how to work," he said. "And they're good with the explosives and have no fear of heights."

"You're not sure how to beat them, are you, lad? Well, I tell you, their secret is that dragon of theirs.

Keeps 'em safe from falling and makes them explosions for 'em any time they ask at all. They just point to the spot, clear out, and the dragon does it for them."

"Is that what you call it?" Finnegan asked. "I'd have sworn it was dynamite."

"That's on accounta you only have mortal eyes, me boy. You can see me because you're of the kind of folk that see my kind of folk. But you can't see the dragon cause she's Chinese. But I've seen her and a fine slinky lady she is too. All red and gold and breathin' fire. Very focused she is, to be sure, on helpin' her kinfolk."

Finnegan wasn't about to stand around jawing with the little man all night. He knew his rights. Quicker than he thought he could possibly move, he leaped on his bunk and pinned the little man to it by his coattails. "Enough of your row, praisin' Chinamen and their fire-breathin' dragons. I've got you now. Give up your pot of gold and we'll leave this miserable job to them and go to San Francisco and live like kings."

The leprechaun merely chuckled. "It's not that easy, Paddy boy. Not that easy by half. I left me old pot of gold in Ireland. All the gold I can give ye is at the end of this railroad, and well enough ye know it's not got an end as yet. That's up to you and your lads. Now let me up."

"Do you take me for a fool? I know better than that! You owe me that gold or at least three wishes."

"One wish."

"Two then."

"One and a half. Me final offer. You can't stay here and hang onto me forever and work tomorrow as well, so what'll it be, Paddy?"

"Very well. One and a half it is then." He was thinking fast and hard what his wish and a half should be. They'd need to be attached wishes, as it were, and he'd not be selfish, being as how the gold was not for the immediate taking anyway. "Here's the thing. We need to keep this job and if you say it's this dragon makin' the Celestials look so good and only you can see the dragon, how about you get it to go away?"

"Be reasonable, lad! She's a dragon! She breathes fire and flies through the air like a bloody great bird! How am I to make her go away, and me just a poor wee man without his pot of gold or so much as a rainbow to ride on to get there if I had it?"

"Hah!" Paddy said. "Try usin' your blarney on her instead of me. That seems to be the strong suit of your kind. I'd think you'd do it for free so as to keep the Celestials from outshinin' the Irish."

"There's your half a wish then," the little man said, easily extricating himself from Paddy's grip by vanishing again.

The next day, by midday, the Chinese had cleared a mile and started laying the gravel bed for the track while Finnegan and his boys were still trying to line up what they'd laid two days before.

He thought they'd never quit and then, suddenly, a storm blew up and the men in baskets bounced against the cliffs until they had to be hauled up again. Meanwhile, their explosive sets fizzled ineffectually and the Celestials took a tea break and jabbered among themselves, frowning. If they were Irishmen, or even English, he was sure they'd be scratching their heads and asking, "What the divvil?"

He knew it was the leprechaun's doing, but had the little man not reckoned that when the Celestials had to stop for the storm, so were his boys delayed by it, so where was the good in that strategy? Finnegan said as much that night when he found the little man once more puffing away on his pipe while lying on Finnegan's own cot.

"Have a bit of patience," the leprechaun said, stroking his beard with the hand not holding the pipe. "These things take time, but you leave it to me. They're fiery passionate creatures, dragons, and the Chinese ones are crayturs of the wind—"

"Well, then, someone as full of hot wind as yourself should be very attractive to the beast," Finnegan said.

The leprechaun winked one green eye. "I see you take my point, lad. I'm slowed up a bit that she speaks no Irish and I speak no Chinese but then, the language of love is universal and I've no doubt that by tomorrow she'll be eatin' out of me hand."

"Mind she doesn't singe it clean off," Finnegan said. "Now get off me cot and go back to yer courtship."

He thought no more about the leprechaun in the rigors of the day. The wind blew in great moaning circular gusts, whipping the gravel against them, blowing the dust into their faces so that they had to wear kerchiefs over their noses and mouths to breathe.

They laid another few feet of track and then came the time to line it and they pushed their shovels under the steel in the prescribed method and positioned themselves for the heave when the bit came around in the song for them to do it.

"Bein' as how the weather is so inclement today, lads, I think we'll start with the dirty verses this time," Finnegan told his crew.

"Ah my Colleen-huh!"

"Love you well-huh!"

"I can make your-huh!"

"Belly swell—huh!"

They sang some even more risqué than that. By the third verse the track still lay about where it had and was only a bit wetter from the drizzling rain that had begun soaking through the men's clothing.

Then on the final "huh!" the leprechaun popped into view a ways down the finished track, running for all he was worth toward them. Behind him a trail of dust hoisted by the wind wound after him.

"Save me, Finnegan!" the leprechaun cried. "She's after me! She'll be after makin' me the faither o' her eggs, a job for which I am unsuited altogether!" He was in a right lather to be sure and he raced straight for them, lined up behind their upright shovel handles.

"I thought you said you could handle her," Fin-

negan said, pushing the little man off him as he tried
to cling to his shirttails.

The leprechaun danced back up onto his shovel
handle and along it like a tightrope walker. Looking
behind him with great trepidation, he hopped from
one foot to the other; dancing a regular jig he was.

Watching the comical fellow, a tune popped unbidden into Finnegan's head.

"Saints preserve us, Finnegan, how are you doing
that?" Maloney asked him, pointing to the shovel
blade, which scooted the rail up and down with the
wild bouncing of the handle.

Finnegan looked down and saw what was happening
and quick as a wink began shoveling gravel under the
shifted rail to hold it in place.

"What are ye doin'?" the leprechaun cried. "While
you play with the rocks the great beast will have me!"
He leaped to the next shovel handle and performed
the same dance. Maloney joined Finnegan in scooping
gravel into the depression left by the shifted rail.

The leprechaun moved on to the next and the next
but then there were no more shovel handles and he
was away like the wind, down the opening the Celestials had carved into the mountain until Finnegan
could see him no longer. The rain whipped after him
and disappeared. A rainbow stretched over the tracks,
the end beyond the pass in the mountain blown by
the Celestials.

"What was that all about then?" Maloney asked.

Without missing a beat, Finnegan winked as if he
were telling a tall tale and said, "Sure and wasn't it
the little people come to Amerikay to show us the
proper Irish way of linin' the track. We've been doin'
it all wrong, you see, trying to use foreign music and
all that. Here, you lot, clap for me while I show you
how it's done."

And as if he were showing his mettle to the prettiest
girl in all of County Cork, he leapt onto the handle
of the set shovel the way he'd seen the little man do

it and jigged his way up it while the boys clapped except for Maloney, who quickly shoveled the gravel under the track to hold it in place.

The boys thought this was a fine game, and each was eager to demonstrate his agility and fine footwork to outdo the others, who clapped, whistled, and shoveled the gravel in to hold the track in its new position. One man on the end of a shovel handle could move the track easier than five men grunting and pushing and singing those slow songs that belonged to men of a different race and place.

The crew ahead of them kept laying the track and they kept lining all that day.

The boss came over to see what it was Finnegan's crew were doing. At first he was skeptical but he couldn't argue with the results they were getting, and by the end of the day he declared that he was more impressed than he ever had been with their work and that there would be a bonus in it for them if they could do as well when it came time to lay the last ten miles of track.

Their method of gandy dancing spread to all the Irish crews working on the railroad, but none were as quick or light-footed as Finnegan's team, who had been inspired, whether they knew it or not, by the leprechaun, who had in turn been inspired by the Celestial dragon. When the railroad ended with the golden spike, Finnegan and his men received their golden bonuses. Not long after, hordes of other men took the great trains West to join the rush to the California gold fields and beyond, but Finnegan and his lads, having worked their way there to be Paddy on the spot, as it were, had already laid claim to some of the richest digs.

Patrick Finnegan never did say how he came to be so lucky in his prospecting, and there were some who claimed there was something almost supernatural about his knowing where to pan and where to dig. Finnegan himself said he had simply become a good man with a shovel while working on the railroad and it was that and the luck of the Irish that led him to dig in the right places.

But Finnegan told this story on to my granddad, no mean storyteller himself, about how the leprechaun for once provided his people with something far more practical than fairy gold. Patrick swore to Grandpa that every word was true and my Grandpa said he saw the very shovel on which the leprechaun danced. Whether or not the part about the dragon is as true, I'm not sure, since according to Finnegan only the leprechaun and the Chinese Celestial workers could see it, but he added, "Sure if the half of it's true then why not the entire article altogether?" And that's good enough for me.

THE PRE-MODERN AGE

Most historians agree that the modern era was born in the dark days of the Second World War. Before it began, yet after the heyday of steam power, was an age that played witness to countless wonders of technology and miracles of science. The world changed on an almost daily basis, and people found themselves dizzy trying to keep up. It was an age, truly, of wonder—wondering at humanity's seeming triumph over the forces of nature. How, then, could the mythical, mystical, or metaphysical hope to compete?

The Stone Orrery

Jennifer Crow

A brief, sleepless summer had settled over Saint Petersburg, and Nadya stood outside the gate of the Voronezhsky Palace, trying to glimpse something that shouldn't exist. Every so often, when the breeze lifted the leaves, sunlight caught a glint of curving metal. When it did, her breath hitched in her throat. If she could find a way in, the metal beast might save her and her mother.

She leaned against the decaying gate, straining her thin arms. Though she'd seen fifteen winters, she was small for her age, and at first the gate did no more than groan. But at last the hinges gave way, flecks of rust pattering around her. The gate hung crooked in the wall, leaving a gap barely wider than her head. Sideways, she pushed through, fingers digging into the crumbling mortar of the wall.

Within, the garden had run riot. Ghosts of paths led deeper, toward the charred ruin of the palace, but vines and wild grass nearly obscured the flagstones. Nadya drew in a breath. The air was heavy with the scent of something sharp and green, like sun-warmed sap, and beneath it the mossy, earthy smell of decaying vegetation.

"Now," she whispered. The sound of her voice gave her courage—that, and the thought of the warm, sweet pastry she could buy with a few of the kopeks the professor had promised her. All she needed was to produce an antique wonder for him. "This must be something marvelous."

The way to the metal beast led through the darkest part of the wilderness. She pushed into the vines, biting back a cry as thorns dug into her cheek. Afraid for her eyes, she held up her hands and pushed through, letting the spines scratch her palms.

It felt as though the garden didn't want her to go on; twigs snagged at her hair, vines twined around her ankles. As soon as she fought free of one captor, another seized her. But at last she pushed through the last barrier into a little courtyard, and disappointment bit deep into her heart.

The metal beast was as wonderful as she'd hoped, but was as tall as she was and far wider than her outstretched arms. Much too heavy, she knew, to carry back to the professor. Curving sweeps of tarnished brass, inscribed with leaves and birds, held spheres of smooth glass. *No, stone,* she thought as she brushed her fingers across the smooth surface. Cold even in the sunlight, they were the most beautiful things she'd ever seen—green, purple, gold, even a flecked blue. Though that one, she saw, was broken.

She touched a shard that still jutted from the setting. A little loose, like the tooth of an old monster, it came free in her hand. She cupped it in her palm and studied it. No chisel mark marred the smooth curve of it; someone had carved out two half-spheres and joined them together somehow. She tucked it in the pocket of her dress and resumed her exploration.

Nadya thought she detected a faint line around the green ball, but it was a translucent gray stone sphere that held her attention. Something moved in its depths.

She bent closer, sure it must be a trick of her eyes, a shadow seen through the stone. But when she laid her hand against it, the shadow moved, coiled.

Nadya took the sphere in her hands and tugged. With a faint ping the ball came loose and she dropped it. When it hit the flagstones, it broke open along the seam, the two halves falling apart to release a column of smoke. The shadowy pillar took on a woman's form, though Nadya could still see the trees behind her.

A ghost, she thought, and backed away until the vines embraced her with their rough arms. She tried to turn, but they held her fast. The shadow woman approached, her face pale as cream against her dark dress and darker hair. Her fingers, which faded to mist at the tips, brushed Nadya's face. They left chill tracks on her skin.

"I'm sorry," Nadya babbled. "I didn't know. Please forgive me."

"Do not fear." The woman smiled, as cold and sharp as the winter wind. "I have longed for a visitor."

Nadya cowered against the vines. A thorn dug into her neck, and blood trickled down her back.

"Release her," the woman said. Her voice snapped, and the vines pulled back.

Nadya took a step, legs trembling. "How did you—"

"This is my garden. They must obey. As must you, since you carry a bit of it with you." She stretched out her hand. Nadya's fingers drifted to her pocket, where the cold shard of the sphere lay.

"I need it."

"Why?"

So Nadya explained about the professor's research, and his quest for objects from the past. The woman watched her with unblinking eyes, a lion's eyes, gold and honey and blood. At last Nadya held out the shard in reluctant hands. "He won't believe me if I don't show him."

"And then there will be no money for you."

"No medicine for my mother. No rent." *And no pastry,* she thought, but she didn't say it aloud. Still, the way the woman's tongue touched her pale upper lip, it seemed she understood the unspoken. Or perhaps she'd heard Nadya's belly; it rumbled again.

"Take it, then. But promise me this in exchange:

bring the professor to me." Her shadow fingers
brushed the broken stone, and Nadya tucked it
away. "Soon."

"I will," Nadya promised. She turned, and the vines
and branches rustled out of her way, leaving a pathway open all the way to the broken gate.

Beyond the palace garden sunlight flooded the quiet
street. A black carriage passed, its curtains drawn despite the heat, the doors lacquered in a red and gold
design. Nadya stayed well clear; now, in the reign of
the third Alexander, Yelagin Island no longer held the
brightest flames of Saint Petersburg society, yet her
threadbare dress and smudged apron still made her
stand out.

Back in the city proper, she trudged through the
bustle of the markets. Wood and canvas stalls crowded
the sidewalks, offering secondhand clothes and books,
overripe fruit and stale bread. Even that was beyond
her means, at least until she found the professor.

Yet he wasn't in his office at the university, nor
would the doorkeeper take a message for her. Nadya
fingered the stone shard in her pocket and shrugged,
unwilling to let the withered doorkeeper see her
disappointment.

The trip home took longer—the tenement lay on
the fringes of the city, near the Winter Market. Her
steps dragged as she ducked down an alley to a courtyard strewn with garbage. Ignoring the perpetual
stench of boiled cabbage and urine, she climbed three
flights of stairs to the narrow room she and her mother
rented. An enterprising landlord had partitioned off a
larger room, with thin boards for walls and a door
that never quite closed.

Nadya waited for a moment until she heard her
mother cough, then entered. "How are you, Mama?"

Her mother coughed again, a wet gasping that
caused Nadya's own heart to seize in her chest. "Well
enough," she said at last. "Did you have any success?"

"A bit." She pulled out the remnant of the blue

stone sphere and handed it to her mother. "I found this in a garden. One of the abandoned palaces."

"You must take care. Ghosts don't like visitors."

Nadya thought of the smoke-tinged woman and shivered. "I don't suppose they do. But look at it. The professor will give us lots of money."

"Buckets. We'll be able to move to the front of the building with the clerks and army officers. And eat pastry until we burst."

"Don't tease, Mama."

"Oh, you're too young to lose hope. Look at this little miracle you've brought home—I feel better just seeing it." She handed it back and tried to stifle another cough.

"It sounds worse. We must take you to the doctor when I'm paid."

"It costs too much. And the medicine doesn't help." She waved delicate fingers at a stoppered glass bottle that held a smear of greenish-brown fluid.

"It will if you take it as you should." Nadya opened it, releasing the smell of peppermint and pine and alcohol, so sharp it burned her eyes.

"Not now. It makes the coughing worse." Her mother lay back on the pillow, her pale blue eyes distant. "Tell me more of the garden."

So Nadya told her, and her mother listened with the faintest smile playing at the corners of her mouth. And she didn't cough, not once, until Nadya finished.

"Tomorrow, all will be well." When Nadya sat on the edge of the cot, her mother took her hand in a papery, fragile grasp. "You'll see. Sweet buns and wine for all. Do you remember the story of Vassilisa the Bold? Only think how bold *you* have been today."

Nadya sat beside her until her breathing changed and she knew her mother had drifted to sleep. Then she gently freed her fingers and spread her own blanket on the floor.

The next morning, on her way to the university, she lingered for a moment in front of Filippov's window.

On shelves decorated with paper cut in the shape of snowflakes, silver trays as wide as her arm held cakes and pastries. Colored icing trickled over the edges, and cream oozed out of the thin, flaky layers.

Nadya licked her lips. A man in an apron, sweeping the floor before the first customers of the day, paused in mid-motion to glare at her. With one last glance, she hurried on.

Professor Barshansky was in his office, and looked as though he'd spent the night there, what with his rumpled suit and unshaven face. When she stood in the doorway, he was so engrossed in the papers on his desk that he didn't acknowledge her at once. Finally she cleared her throat, and he sat back, annoyance creasing his face. "Yes?"

"Nadya Aleksandrovna, sir. You told me to come to you if I found any artifacts."

"Ah. And you've found something." He cleared away the papers. "Show me, please."

She worked the shard of stone from her pocket and laid it on the desk. When she started to explain, he cut her off with a quick gesture and an "harumph." He turned the stone over in his thick fingers, his wild eyebrows knit in a frown as he studied it. At last he said, "Worthless."

"But it's carved. Someone made it."

"Yes, well, it's lovely work. I've never seen anything like it before. But there's no context."

"Context?"

"Who made it, where it was found . . ."

"Oh!" She allowed herself a little smile, then. "It's part of a machine."

"A machine?"

"Like the new mills by the river, only much, much nicer." She described it, and the professor's expression shifted between incredulity and hope. At last he said, "Well, I think you must take me to this marvelous machine."

Nadya had hoped the professor would hail a hansom, or at least pay the fare for one of the horse-drawn trolleys, but it seemed he meant to walk all the way to Yelagin Island. As they went, the city woke up around them. Shopkeepers set out their wares and called to passersby, governesses led their charges on promenades, a few late revelers staggered home looking the worse for wear. The air held a hundred scents, animal and vegetable and mineral.

Nadya stopped at the broken gate of the Voronezhsky Palace. "In here. If you look to the right, you can just see it through the leaves."

It took a little while for the professor to wedge himself in the gateway at the right angle. "Fool girl," he muttered. "Might as well look for the wind in a field."

And then his muttered curses stopped, and she knew he'd seen it. He pushed against the gate, and it groaned as it widened. Nadya followed.

"This place wasn't abandoned very long ago," he said, wrestling with the vines. "Such wildness in the garden is most unnatural."

Nadya thought of the vicious thorns and their mistress and hung back. "I'll wait here."

"Nonsense," the professor said. "Come along. You can show me exactly where you found that piece of stone."

She pointed him in the right direction and trailed after. Soon the courtyard opened before them, the machine like a metal tree. The professor gasped and then paced around it in silence.

"An orrery," he said at last.

"What, sir?"

"A machine to measure the movement of the planets in the heavens. There's the sun at the center. Tiger's eye for the stone."

He pointed them out in turn—green malachite for Venus, the broken lapis lazuli orb for earth, with its alabaster moon. There were others, but Nadya lost count. She hoped the professor's fascination with the machine meant money for her and her mother. "So it's very old?"

"It predates 1846, at least."

"How can you tell?"

He straightened, hands clasped behind his back. "William Herschel's planet is represented, but not Leverrier's. And anyone who had the skill to create a masterpiece like this would surely have known of his find. So this is forty years old at least, probably more." He spoke with his chin in the air, as though addressing the heavens.

"Of course," he continued, "it will take a good deal of work to return this to the university."

"Your pardon?"

"I must take it back for further study." He picked up the two halves of the translucent gray sphere and fitted them together.

"I don't think she'd like that, sir."

"She?"

"The woman who was here. She came out of that ball you're holding."

The professor regarded it for a moment and burst out laughing. "A woman—out of . . . ridiculous, my dear." He slotted the globe carefully into place. "Saturn. Once, it must have had a ring around it. No, you need not embellish the story. It is quite spectacular enough as it is. I suspect this may be the work of Igor Salitsev, the noted artisan."

"His son Nikolai, actually."

Nadya started. She hadn't heard the woman's approach, though she had to have passed through the surrounding undergrowth. The professor smiled, as though it was perfectly natural for someone to slip unheard through a riot of overgrown shrubbery. "Really, such a thing is impossible to say without further study."

"I watched him make it. He let his father have the credit." The woman trailed her finger over the nearest orb. Though she'd gained an aura of substance since being freed, Nadya noted that she still lacked solidity.

"Ridiculous," the professor said again. "You aren't that old. Though if you have some provenance for it,

I'd dearly love to see it. And of course, you must tell me if you own it. The university—"

"Will not be taking my orrery. Though I might allow you—and you alone—to study it further."

The professor cast a glance at Nadya, as though she might mediate between him and the woman. Nadya was about to shrug, but she decided to speak up. Better that than lose her commission for finding the orrery. "Is there no way to solve this to the satisfaction of you both?"

"The orrery cannot leave my garden, or else I will be trapped forever. But the professor is welcome to study it, if he will also make repairs—and bring it in line with current knowledge."

"That would be butchery!"

"Is it any less cruel that I must stay here between then and now? Look at me!" Her hands brushed his face and he jerked back with a gasp. "I sent the girl for you so that we might help each other—the orrery for my freedom. Think on it—we will speak again." She turned her back, took two steps and vanished into the leaves, as completely as if she'd never existed.

Nadya released a shuddering breath. "I'm sorry," she told the professor. "I thought she wanted to see you."

He blinked and shook himself. "Not at all. Such a curious thing is a great pleasure. And I am sure I will find a way to bring her around to my point of view."

Nadya wasn't sure whether the 'curious thing' was the orrery or the woman. "She is very like a ghost."

Professor Barshansky scooped up half of the translucent gray sphere and polished it with the hem of his coat. "Smoky quartz. You don't often see a piece of such size and quality." He tucked it close to his body, holding it in place with one arm, and led the way back to the street.

Nadya followed him even after he passed the street that led to her tenement. They had almost reached Filippov's before she summoned the courage to speak. "Sir?"

He grunted in response, neither turning nor slowing.

"Sir, you promised to pay me for the artifacts I found."

"Ah." He stopped and patted his pockets without looking at her. "I seem to have left the money in my office. Come by tomorrow and I'll pay you then."

"But—"

He continued on his way, leaving her on Filippov's doorstep. Nadya spared a brief glance at the trays of tea cakes, hand pressed to her aching belly, and then she hurried home.

She waited with her hand on the door latch. The eternal gloom of the hallway settled around her. No sound came from within; Nadya feared that, while she wasted the morning with the professor, her mother had come to that final crisis alone.

At last a rattling breath and spasm of coughing dispelled that fear. *But no money for medicine,* she thought as she pushed the door open.

"How did it go?" Her mother half-sat on the cot, propped up by old blankets rolled into makeshift pillows.

"Not well. I think he means to cheat me." She bit the inside of her mouth. Tears would serve no purpose.

"Perhaps you're too hasty." Her mother listened as Nadya poured out her tale of the morning. "Go see him tomorrow, as he said. Allow him the chance to make it right. Remember, in the tales fortune favors those who don't despair."

Nadya nodded and stared at her hands clasped over her knees. Like the woman in the stone sphere, she felt herself fading bit by bit. *Soon,* she thought. *Soon I'll be no more than smoke, haunting this place.*

When she went back to the professor's office the following day, it was empty. The door stood open, and the air smelled of stale tobacco and old paper. After a moment, she eased the door closed and poked through the drawers of his desk. Surely he wouldn't begrudge a kopek or two—he'd as much as promised. But she found only the half-sphere, which she settled in the crook of her arm.

A book on the desk caught her gaze; it was open to a portrait of a dark-haired woman with a lion's eyes. 'Princess Elena Vorozhenskaya in a portrait painted in 1825,' read the caption.

She pushed away the book and sat. Her feet ticked against the floor like the beating of a heart. A cough brought her out of her seat; a stout man with a wide red face glared at her. "Who are you? What are you doing here?" He sounded as though he spoke around a mouthful of gravel.

"I'm waiting for the professor."

He looked her over. "You're not a student."

"I'm . . . assisting in his research."

The man spotted the half-sphere and clamped his fingers around her wrist. "You brought him that?" She nodded. His eyes narrowed. "If you find any more like it, you might bring it to me. He's a cheap wretch."

Nadya pulled her arm free; for all his heft, he had soft, plump hands. "Do you know where he is?"

"That old fool left here about an hour ago, heading west." He didn't touch her again, but bullied her out the door with his fat belly, and slammed it closed behind her.

West, she thought. That meant Yelagin Island, and the orrery. She thought of the woman waiting in the shadows and shivered. But though she wanted nothing more to do with the lost garden or the orrery, her empty stomach twisted in a knot. She had to follow.

Nadya took a roundabout route from the university to the island, avoiding the food shops. Further along, she still smelled roasting shashlik, rich borscht, and kasha boiled with honey, but the ripe stench of bodies living and dead overlaid the more pleasant odors, and her appetite dwindled.

When at last she reached the island, afternoon shadows had lengthened, giving the gates and roofs an odd elongated cast. Dust stung her eyes and the air vibrated with the hum of hordes of flies.

The gate of the abandoned palace still hung off-kilter from its hinges. Yet the husk of the palace showed signs of life. Here and there lamps glowed, gold against the charring of the fire. New vines crept up the walls, tendrils winding into every doorway and window.

Nadya pushed aside a looming branch. "Professor Barshansky?"

"Help." A pale hand stained with blood emerged from the foliage. At first she hesitated to take it. "Please," he said, and leaves rustled as he struggled to free himself.

She gasped when she saw his face, and stepped back. He'd fallen among the thorns, and they'd torn his skin mercilessly. When Nadya appeared, they snaked in her direction, but snapped back as soon as they touched her. "How is this . . ." she wondered aloud.

She leaned closer, and bit by bit the vines released the professor. He had paid a price for his trespass, though, and blood streaked his face. Worst of all were his eyes, for the spines had dug in, and his wounded, sightless gaze focused somewhere to the side of where she stood. She took his hand and winced at the sticky blood on her fingers. Gently she freed him until he could crawl into the more open space of the courtyard. "You shouldn't have come alone."

"It must be mine. If someone else found it—"

"No one will find the machine," she soothed. "But now we must go back to the university and your friends."

"Not without the orrery." But when he tried to touch it, some force held him back, so his seeking hands scrabbled at the air. "I hired a cart—"

"It's gone."

"So you reconsidered." When the professor took a step forward at the sound of the woman's voice,

Nadya held him back. "Please let him come to me. Poor man, I can help."

Nadya let go of Professor Barshansky's hand. His blind eyes focused on a point somewhere over the woman's head until she reached out with shadowy fingers and brushed first his cheekbone, then the line of his jaw. "The thorns are cruel."

"The orrery," he whispered. "Such beauty—it should not be hidden away."

"Some things are not meant for mortal eyes. I also have paid a steep price." Her fingers slid down to his and his hand clenched, but he couldn't quite grasp the princess.

Nadya took the half-sphere from her pocket. "He stole this, highness. And he hired a cart to take the rest."

Princess Elena stepped back. "But he can help me. He must! You said yourself, professor, one of the planets is missing." She pushed the arm of the machine closest to her. It groaned and stirred and ground to life. The air shivered. "The energies Salitsev built into it remember a different time—a time when there were only seven planets."

"So it's linked to the past—like you?"

"I am not linked. I am trapped." The princess pushed at an arm as it swung past, and the pace of the orrery's turning picked up—and kept increasing, though no one exerted force on it any longer. As it sped in circles, Nadya found she could not look at it straight on—the air quivered, and the trees and house on the far side rippled. For a moment, the shattered hulk of the palace regained its windows, the pristine white of its bricks. She gasped.

"The girl sees. Tell him."

Nadya described what she saw. "It's impossible. Yet . . ."

"Have a care," the woman said. "If you move beyond the boundaries of my time, there is no telling where you might end up."

"Adrift in time?" Professor Barshansky's voice was thoughtful.

"And no way back."

"Why do you wish to leave here?" Nadya asked. "To never age or die . . ."

"Once, my garden rang with the voices of friends and family, guests and servants. Now . . . the silence in which I live is not to be envied."

Nadya thought of the crowded tenements, the stench, the cries seeping through the walls. Her mother's wracking cough. "There are worse things."

"Enough chatter," the professor said. "How can I see this miracle? How can I see at all?"

"One step," the princess said. "No more than two, and I will take your hand, bring you to my time. But you must promise—*promise*—to help me. I cannot bear to stay here alone any longer."

The professor dabbed at the smudges of blood on his cheeks. "And I would have to stay until the orrery was repaired to your specifications?"

"I would like to think that is not a hardship. You will not hunger or grow sick."

"And then the orrery is mine? Your word?" He smiled, one gold tooth winking.

Nadya gritted her teeth.

"So be it." The woman reached out. "Take a step."

"He means to cheat you," Nadya said. But the princess gave no sign that she'd heard.

As Professor Barshansky lifted his foot, Nadya seized his arm. "Wait."

He stretched until his hand reached into the distortion and a shiver passed over him.

Nadya turned to the princess. "He promised me money. He said he'd pay me if I found such things as this for him."

"I'll pay once I have my sight—or the machine." He wiped at his bleeding eyes.

"Pay her." The shimmer in the air dimmed.

"Not yet. Not now."

"Pay her." The machine creaked, slowed.

"Fine." He took his leather wallet from his jacket and held it out. "I know how much is there," he told Nadya. "Even blind, I could count it. No thieving."

"Now," the woman said.

"Go find that cart," he told Nadya. "We shall need it for the machine." He drew in a shuddering breath and stepped forward. The world shivered around him. "I . . . I can see again." He looked at his hands, kissed his fingertips. Then he looked up and caught sight of the palace. "It is true."

"Come."

Princess Elena beckoned to him, but he shook his head. Still smiling, he took a step back. "I apologize for disappointing you, dear lady, but I have other plans. I—"

Nadya came up behind him and gave him a shove. He vanished.

The machine screeched and stopped, so abruptly it might never have moved. Nadya's hands crept out and swept the emptiness in front of her.

"What have you done? Now there is no one to help me. My hope—my freedom . . ." The princess began to wail, a sound like all the grief in the world.

Nadya clutched the professor's wallet. Coins clinked faintly, cushioned by a thick sheaf of bills. "He meant to take it, highness. He would have left you here alone."

"I cannot bear it. But wait! You could stay. What is there for you out there?" Princess Elena gestured, and the vines inched into the courtyard, their leaves a feather-brush on Nadya's legs.

She flinched. "I must care for my mother."

"She is dying?"

"I can't leave her."

"No, you mustn't. But is there no way you can help me as well? I have waited so long."

Nadya pondered the princess' question. "There is another man at the university, a colleague of Professor Barshansky's. He, too, is interested in the sphere."

"And he could help?"

"Perhaps." She stared past the woman, to the crumbling brick of the palace. "I can try."

The princess smiled again like the lonely end of winter. "I would be grateful."

"I am glad to help." She pocketed the professor's wallet and gave the machine a push. As the arms spun, faster and faster, the palace of the past appeared once more in all its beauty. Everywhere time passed, everywhere death was inevitable—except in the garden. "May I ask a favor?"

"Name it." Princess Elena stood with a vine draped over her shoulder. The leaves caressed her cheek.

"My mother—may I bring her here?"

"To stay?" The princess clapped her hands. "A guest! Delightful. And the fresh air will do her good. Yes. Fresh air—and a little time with me. You could both use a little time, I think." She gestured, and the vines snaked back, leaving the way open. "Come soon."

"I will." Nadya waved and hurried to the gate. She might still catch Professor Barshansky's rival in his office. But first she meant to stop at the apothecary's for another bottle of medicine, and perhaps Filippov's for a cream puff. *Two cream puffs,* she corrected, as she crossed from the garden into the sharp light of noon. At the gate she looked back and caught a glimpse of gleaming metal, and a shadow that might have been the lonely ghost of a princess.

Sphinx!

Tony Pi

7th of Floréal, Year 117 of the Graalon Revolution

I was fussing over the final bone articulation of an *Archaeosphinx hierax* skeleton when the sound of echoing footfalls broke my concentration. I set down the hollow carpometacarpus fossil in my hand and turned to see who had disturbed my work.

A mustached young man stood at the archway, bathed in the ruddy light of the foxfires-in-amber that illuminated the exhibition hall. His short frock coat and the sword at his side marked him as a sergeant from the Prefecture of Police. Though he obviously came to speak to me, he seemed momentarily struck dumb by the mounted giant falcon-headed sphinx skeleton I had been assembling.

"Dawn is an odd hour for a museum visit, Sergeant," I said. "How may I be of assistance?"

The policeman doffed his cap and smoothed down his mop of straw-like hair. "You are Professor Tremaine Voss? Chief Curator of Aigyptian Magic?"

"I am."

He breathed a sigh of relief. "Sergeant Carmouche at your service, Professor. Your housekeeper directed me here. Chief Inspector Lebret urgently requires your expertise. Please come with me."

The name "Lebret" sounded familiar, though I

couldn't place it. "All I want is to go home and sleep, Sergeant," I told Carmouche. "Could the Inspector wait?"

"I'm afraid not, Professor," he replied. "If you do not help Inspector Lebret now, in an hour's time a sphinx will be loose in the city."

Sphinx!

My weariness fled when he mentioned the word. "A *living* sphinx? But they're extinct!"

"If you say, Professor. The Inspector will explain."

The hieracosphinx reconstruction could wait. I grabbed my walking stick. "We mustn't tarry then, Carmouche. Lead on!"

Carmouche drove us through the streets of Ys in the horseless carriage, heading northwest. I was impressed by the machine's speed, less so by the foul alchemical smells issuing from its alembic engine.

"When did sphinxes become extinct, Professor?" the sergeant asked.

"The *archoleons* prospered ten thousand years ago. It was an age when griffins terrorized the skies, merlions ruled the waves, and androsphinxes challenged one another with riddles of blood," I said. "But the basilisk plague ended their reign, turning their flesh to sand and their bones to stone. Their fossils are all we have left to prove they once lived."

Indeed, it had been the prospect of working with newly unearthed *Archaeosphinx* fossils that lured me to Le Musée d'Ys a year ago, though it meant relinquishing my archaeological chair at the University of Carlyon and moving to the Continent.

"Then sphinxes couldn't possibly exist today?" Carmouche asked.

A shrewd director from Chimère Studios had asked me the exact question six months ago, during a consult on a silent film.

"There are a few mad theories to the contrary," I admitted. "Lost worlds. Beasts frozen in glacial ice. Hidden empires at the center of the earth. Excellent fodder for the flickers, but generally dismissed in academic circles."

"What about Aigypt?" Carmouche asked.

Everyone always asked about Aigypt. "Some scholars believe a few sphinxes may have survived there, worshipped as living gods," I said. "The pharaohs had sphinx colossi built to venerate them, and archaeological evidence from the ruined city of Criopolis does seem to support the theory. Ancient Aigyptian might even be the language of the sphinxes. However, any sphinxes in Aigypt likely perished long ago. Some might even be mummified." Now *there* would be a find for the museum!

"I'd pay to see sphinxes on the silver screen," Carmouche said.

"So would most of Graalon," I said, thinking of the country's two new vogues: palaeontology and that marvel of modern alchemy, film. The director from Chimère certainly saw the potential.

The Seawall, a magnificent feat of Ysien engineering, loomed before us. The great dike had kept the forbidding waters of the Atlantean Ocean from flooding Ys for countless centuries. Carmouche stopped the horseless by the foot of the north Seawall stairs. "Inspector Lebret awaits us up top, where the view to the sphinx is best. Do you need a hand up the stairs, Professor?"

I gave him a light thump with the head of my walking stick. "You may think me a fossil, young man, but I spent my youth traipsing the world in search of lost ruins. I have the constitution of an ox."

As we climbed, I remembered where I had heard the name Lebret before. "Heavens! Is Lebret the hero of the Tarasque affair?" I asked Carmouche.

"The same," the young sergeant replied.

Five years ago, a string of murders held the city of Ys in the grip of fear. For months, the killer taunted the police with letters signed *Tarasque*. Lebret was the genius who finally solved the villain's identity, shooting him dead during a deadly rooftop struggle. "Chimère made a film about him, didn't they? *Le Mort de Tarasque?*"

Carmouche chuckled. "Yes, but you shouldn't mention the film to the Inspector, Professor. He was aghast that Chimère would make a film about the murders. Said it glorified crime."

Wind whipped the scent of the ocean to the top of the Seawall where the grim and hawkish Inspector stood stone still, peering through a spyglass at the sea. A gaunt man in his forties, perhaps ten years my junior, Lebret bore only a slight resemblance to the actor who portrayed him on the silver screen.

With the naked eye, I traced the source of his focus. A ship had run aground on a rocky isle in the shallower part of the bay, far from the deep waters of the western harbor. A scattering of small rowboats skimmed across the waves, heading towards the waking city.

Carmouche cleared his throat. "Inspector, I've fetched Professor Voss as you instructed."

Lebret lowered his spyglass and turned to me, pumping my hand once. "Professor. Forgive my brusqueness, but we have little time before that thing escapes into the city." He pressed the spyglass into my hand. "Tell me, what do we face?"

I raised the spyglass and sought the islet. I knew sphinxes were long extinct, but what if this one happened to be real? A living specimen could change everything we thought we knew about the fearsome creatures that once ruled the planet.

The spyglass revealed that a steamer had indeed run afoul of the rocks, but it was the great umber creature aboard that made me gasp aloud. Easily twice as tall as a man, the man-faced lion beat its dusty wings as it padded across the deck, its mouth and claws stained dark.

"Is that blood?" I asked.

Lebret nodded. "It has killed several men aboard. Why hasn't it flown?"

I examined the beast closely. For all its majesty,

something seemed false about it, and it took a minute's scrutiny to determine what. The wind did not ruffle the feathers on its wings. My heart sank. It wasn't a live sphinx, after all.

"It may look like an androsphinx, but it isn't real," I told the Inspector. "My guess? It's a creature of clay."

"A golem?" asked Lebret.

"You need an expert in Exodian golemcraft, Inspector, not me," I said.

"We haven't the time, Professor Voss. That monster may seem trapped on the Mermaid Rocks, but the formation is a tidal island. In an hour, low tide will reveal the land bridge currently submerged, allowing it to reach shore. Do you know anything about golemcraft?"

"The basics, of course, but—"

"It may be enough. A knife is not a sword, but cuts flesh nonetheless," Lebret said. "How do we destroy it?"

"Immersion in water would weaken and ruin its shape, but it intuitively understands that," I said. "Forget bullets. You need at least a keg of cannondust to blow it apart."

Lebret sighed. "I doubt we can ask it to hold still long enough for that."

Carmouche interrupted us. "Inspector, we found the man who hired the *Black Plume*. Our men pulled him and his wife out of the water. Sir, it's Alain and Katarin *Bertho*." He indicated a drenched couple further down the Seawall who had climbed up a rope ladder on the ocean-side. It had been lowered earlier by the police to bring up evacuees from the rowboats.

I recognized the renowned Chimère director who had consulted me on Aigypt and his starlet wife straight away. I was a great admirer of Katarin Bertho née Villé, seeing all of her flickers at the *ciné*. In a medium without words, her face alone carried the story. To look at them now, they were but shadows of the prideful man I had met and the haunting beauty who graced the silver screen.

Alain Bertho was my age, looking grizzled from days at sea. The much younger Madame Bertho stared back at the dot of island, a look of terror marring her perfect face.

"I know him!" I said to Lebret.

"As do I," Lebret said, frowning. Then I remembered Bertho had directed *Le Mort de Tarasque*.

"He and a man named Fabius came to see me a few months ago, asking about the Aigyptian Cult of the Sphinx for a new flicker," I said.

"The *Black Plume*'s last port of call was Criopolis," Lebret said. "Could they have run afoul of an Aigyptian curse?"

"I sincerely hope not," I said, remembering my own harrowing encounters with ancient Aigyptian tomb spirits. Archaeology was a deadlier profession than many would think.

"They better have an explanation," Lebret said. "Listen while I speak to the Berthos, and ask questions I might not think of. We must find a way to destroy the sphinx, and soon."

We approached the Berthos. "*Monsieur et Madame,* I am Lebret," the Inspector said. "I believe you know Professor Voss?"

"Yes, of course," Bertho said, though he barely registered my presence. Despite his recent ordeal, he seemed fixated on the Inspector. "How can I not know the Great Lebret? It is an honor to meet the Hero of Ys at last!"

"I am not worthy of such an epithet, Monsieur," Lebret said, pinching his brow.

"Please, Inspector, there are men still trapped on the ship," Katarin pleaded. Her voice sounded nothing like I imagined when I watched her flickers, but dulcet nonetheless. "Find Deniel; he can stop it."

"We will do all we can, Madame." The Inspector took off his cape and draped it around Katarin's shivering shoulders.

"Katarin, I told you, Deniel Fabius is dead," Bertho

said. "He let the sphinx go rogue and died for it! Inspector, you must retrieve the film and equipment still on board. My masterpiece—"

"Monsieur!" Lebret roared. "Men are dead, a monster threatens my city, and you *dare* to ask for inconsequential things? You are here to answer my questions, not make demands. Understood?"

"We'll help, won't we, Alain?" Katarin said to her husband.

Bertho growled but nodded.

"Good. First question: who is Deniel Fabius?" Lebret asked.

"Our golemist," Bertho said.

"And our friend," Katarin added.

"We were filming *Sphinx,* a great and tragic love story between a woman of our times and an androsphinx, the last of his kind," Bertho explained. "I wanted to shoot on location in the desert and Criopolis with real actors and a life-sized sphinx, not with the homunculi stand-ins that Mandragora Studios use. Their alchemists could never duplicate the nuances real actors bring to the roles. We had achieved previous successes with Fabius' golems in earlier films. Enkidu in *Gilgamesh contre Enkidu.* The Gargoyle in *Les Carillons d'Ys.* The companions of Ankou in *Le Mort de Tarasque.*"

Lebret winced at the mention of Tarasque, but I finally understood how they did the monsters in the Chimère flickers. In the film, Ankou, the personification of Death in Graalon mythology, had been accompanied by two very realistic skeletons to collect the souls of the dead. I had wondered how they made them seem so authentic. In contrast, the creatures in the films from Hespereia always seemed clumsy, lacking the subtle detail so convincing to the audience.

"Was there any trouble with the sphinx during the shoot?" I asked.

"None at all," Katarin said. "It followed Deniel's instructions perfectly."

"You mean my direction, my love," Bertho said.

Katarin ignored him. "When we finished the film, Deniel returned the sphinx to the ship's hold, removed the magic parchment from its mouth, and destroyed it. There was no reason for it to have animated!"

Inspector Lebret looked at me for confirmation.

I nodded. That much I knew. "An Exodian incantation is written on calfskin parchment and placed in the golem's mouth. Without it, the golem is nothing but clay."

"Then how did it come to kill so many?" Lebret asked.

"Perhaps it was sabotage," Bertho said. "I wouldn't put it past the Hespereians."

"Let us consider the evidence first," Lebret said. "Take us through the series of events that caused the tramp steamer to stray from its course, Bertho."

"This morning before dawn, Fabius came to our door, desperate to speak to me in private," Bertho said. "As Katarin was asleep, I went on deck with him so as not to wake her. He seemed nervous, as though he had done something terrible. But before he could tell me the truth, the sphinx escaped its hold and attacked us. I scrambled for cover, but Fabius stood his ground, commanding the golem to stop. It wouldn't listen. Fabius took a claw to the chest and tumbled over the rail into the sea."

Katarin paled.

"And then?" Lebret asked.

"The sphinx went mad, destroying whatever it could reach. It caught a sailor and ripped him apart with teeth and claws. The captain sounded the alarm, and I rushed back to our cabin to wake Katarin. When we made it onto deck, it had already destroyed the pilothouse and killed the captain. It was utter chaos. Those who could escape the sphinx leapt into the water. Those who couldn't . . ." Bertho closed his eyes. "I don't know how many live."

I furrowed my brow. "Mister Bertho, did you or your crew take anything from the ruins? A jar, an

amulet, perhaps a ring? Or, goddesses forbid, mummified remains?"

"Not to my knowledge, Professor. I took your warnings seriously," said Bertho, indignant. "Then again, I
did not search the crew's belongings. Given Fabius'
odd behavior, though, I would not put it past him to
have done that very thing."

"Deniel wouldn't think of stealing an Aigyptian ar-
tifact!" Katarin protested.

I agreed with Madame Bertho. During my consulta-
tion session, Deniel Fabius' questions never touched
on artifacts or the Criopolis site. He was far more
interested in my analysis of sphinx morphology, about
how they looked and how they moved. That and several other things about Alain Bertho's account did not
ring true to my ears.

"Inspector, might I have a word with you in private?" I asked Lebret.

"Of course. Excuse us, *Madame et Monsieur*."

We walked farther down the Seawall.

"Bertho's hiding something," the Inspector said.

"I believe he is," I agreed. "There are contradic-
tions in his story. Magic might not seem to be gov-
erned by rules, but it is. Some laws are inviolate. Take
the laws of golemcraft, for example. A golem cannot
be given a voice. A golem cannot animate without
its parchment of power. A golem can never disobey
its creator."

"And yet Bertho claims it came to life without the
parchment, and that it disobeyed and killed Fabius,"
Lebret said, mulling over the paradoxes. "A riddle
indeed."

Riddle? Lebret's comment sparked a train of
thought I should have considered earlier. "Inspector,
may I borrow your spyglass again?"

"Certainly."

I sought out the sphinx once more, focusing on its
wings and the articulation of its joints. They were per-

fect. Too perfect. A creature that size, made of clay, would sag under its own weight. The clay could only keep its shape if it had a proper frame.

Goddesses, the Sphinx used teeth and claws to rend those men apart. Clay couldn't possibly be strong enough to do that. Bone, perhaps. Stone.

"I think Fabius used the fossilized skeleton of a sphinx for the golem's frame," I said to Lebret. "There's no other way for a creature of clay to hold its shape. If he did, then we're in a world of trouble."

"How so?"

"Among the sphinxes, only the androsphinx and his female counterpart, the gynosphinx, have the power of speech," I explained. "Speech also gives them their riddle magic. The *Aigyptian Book of Mysteries* tells us that riddles are the key to a sphinx's magic, controlling even its life and death. A sphinx lives so long as its riddle of blood remains unsolved. Riddle games between sphinxes are not for leisure, but duels to the death."

Lebret shrugged. "We aren't dealing with a living sphinx."

"True," I admitted. "However, a disputed passage in the book seems to imply that a new riddle of blood could return the spirit of a sphinx to its bones."

"You believe the sphinx skeleton somehow found a riddle of blood?" asked Lebret.

"I don't claim to understand how, but it isn't beyond the power of Aigyptian magic. What if the death of Deniel Fabius hadn't happened as Alain Bertho claimed?" I said. "After all, the clay golem would not have animated without its parchment. Neither would it have disobeyed its maker."

Lebret stroked his chin. "Bertho killed Fabius and tried to cover it up."

"Exactly. Suppose Bertho killed Fabius and tossed his body overboard. The mysterious disappearance of Fabius would indeed constitute a riddle of blood. His traumatic death, combined with his connection to the golem, must have awakened the spirit of the sphinx."

"When is an accidental death not accidental? When it's murder," said Lebret. "Then we only need to solve the riddle of blood to put the spirit to rest?"

"That's the theory."

He raised his spyglass and regarded the isle. "It still moves."

I sighed. "It must hear the answer to its riddle."

"So we make Bertho confess," Lebret said, his voice troubled. "I'll take him in the rowboat."

"Unless it only understands Ancient Aigyptian," I said. "According to the *Book of Mysteries,* a human may challenge a sphinx with the proper incantation. By the rules of the riddle game, the sphinx must give its riddle of blood and wait nine breaths for the answer. If the challenger failed to give the right answer or any answer at all, his life was forfeit." If I had a choice I would rather avoid facing the sphinx, but I knew my civic duty. "It seems you need me after all, Inspector."

"Then we better make damn sure Bertho tells us the whole truth," said Lebret.

We returned to the couple and confronted Alain Bertho.

"Fabius used a real sphinx skeleton, didn't he?" I asked. "Where did he get it?"

Bertho shrugged. "I don't see why it matters, but we acquired the specimen from a trader in Aithiop."

"Fossil thief, you mean," I said.

"That's not all we suspect," the Inspector said. "Did you kill Deniel Fabius, Monsieur Bertho?"

Bertho was taken aback. "No! Why would I wish my friend harm? Tell them, Katarin!"

A look of fright seized Katarin's face, and she backed away from her husband. "You knew?" she whispered.

"What does your husband know, Madame Bertho?" Lebret asked quietly.

Tears welled at the corner of her eyes. "I—Deniel and I . . ."

Alain Bertho reached for his wife's hand. "Katarin."

Katarin pulled away from him and clung to Lebret, sobbing. "Yes, Deniel and I had an affair, Inspector. Alain must have found out. Why, Alain? I already ended it because I couldn't bear to leave you!"

Bertho trembled. "Goddesses, I didn't believe him. . . ."

Lebret took that as his confession. "Alain Bertho, you are under arrest for the murder of Deniel Fabius. Carmouche!"

Sergeant Carmouche stepped forward. "Yes, Inspector?"

"The cannons at the terminus of the land bridge. Are they ready?"

"Yes, but we may have to trust our luck, sir."

"I'd rather rely on intellect, Sergeant. Prepare a boat to take the four of us to the Mermaid Rocks. You, me, the Professor, and Bertho."

Carmouche's mouth dropped open. "Sir?"

"Now, Sergeant. The tide waits for no man."

"Yessir!" Carmouche rushed to the rope ladder and shouted to the people below.

"You're taking me back to that *thing?*" asked Bertho, trembling.

"Confession is good for the soul, Monsieur Bertho, especially when it saves a city," Lebret said. "Do this and it may even save you from the gallows." He waved an officer to us. "Madame, go with Sergeant Royer. He will see you safely home."

"Take me away from him," Katarin said, and turned her back to her husband.

"Katarin!" Bertho cried, but she would hear him no more.

"Are you ready, Professor?" Lebret asked.

"Always," I said, twisting the silver lion's-head that capped my walking stick.

Carmouche and Lebret rowed as Bertho and I watched each other wearily in the rowboat. We were halfway to the Mermaid Rocks when I realized our mistake.

"We must turn back," I told Lebret. "It will try to kill all of us."

Bertho snorted. "That's stating the obvious."

"I know you are afraid, Professor, but you must have courage," said Lebret. "The city depends on you. You are the only one who knows the truth *and* its language."

I shook my head. "Fear isn't the problem. I mean it will try to silence the truth. The spirit knows Bertho is the key to its blood riddle, so if the truth dies with him, it cannot be banished back to the Land of the Dead."

"But now you all know," Bertho said. "You're *all* marked for death!"

I nodded. "Exactly. When it realizes that, it will hunt down anyone and everyone it believes could destroy it."

"How could it tell who does and who doesn't?" Carmouche asked.

"It won't," Inspector Lebret said. "It will massacre all of Ys to bury the truth."

"That's why we have to turn back and telegraph what we can to Aigyptologists in other cities, in case we fail here," I insisted.

"We don't have time," Carmouche said. "The land bridge!"

The natural causeway was emerging from the ebbing tides. At our speed, we would not reach the island before the way to shore opened for the sphinx.

"To the bridge, then!" Lebret shouted, and rowed doubly hard.

I kicked off my shoes, balled up my socks, and rolled up my trouser legs.

We made it to the land bridge before the waves lost their battle to drown it.

The sphinx saw its opportunity and leapt off the *Black Plume* onto the rocks, racing for the strip of land to its freedom and feast.

Lebret stepped out of the boat onto the causeway and helped me out of the boat. Cold water washed over my bare feet.

"You're mad, Lebret! There's no way we can stop *that*!" Bertho cried.

"We can try. Carmouche, stay in the boat with Bertho. If the Professor and I fail, it means Bertho did not tell us the whole truth," Lebret said. "In that case, force it out of him however you can and shout it to the sphinx."

"But I don't speak Aigyptian, Inspector!" Bertho said.

"Luck with cannonballs or luck with words, either way we need Lady Fortune's smile," Lebret said. "One last thing: my confession."

"Sir?"

Lebret drew his sword. "I too have a riddle of blood. It may not be fodder for the sphinx, but nevertheless, I feel it is time for the truth." He took a deep breath. "When I finally caught Tarasque, he surrendered to me, almost eager to have his day in court. I knew in my heart I could not allow the monster to live. If he ever escaped, he would kill again. I had to protect my city, even at the cost of my soul. There was no heroic struggle as you portrayed in your film, Bertho. I killed the monster in cold blood, and lied about the manner of his death."

I did not fully understand why Lebret chose to confess now. "You did a great service, ridding the city of Tarasque. No one would fault you for such a deed," I told Lebret.

"No one but Lady Justice and myself," Lebret replied.

"It's coming," Bertho cried.

The clay sphinx tested the waters washing over the land bridge and decided the causeway was safe enough to tread. It raced towards us.

Lebret readied his sword. "Professor. Stand seven paces behind me and shout your challenge when I give the word."

I took my place but protested. "The phrase is too long—"

"I will buy you time," Lebret said. He pushed the rowboat back into the water against Carmouche's protests.

Goddesses, he intended to sacrifice himself. I now understood his confession. He wanted atonement.

Carmouche realized Lebret's intent at the same time I did. "No, Inspector, let me!" Carmouche said.

"No, Carmouche, you have a bright future ahead of you," Lebret shouted. *"Now,* Professor!"

The sphinx was upon us.

I cried out the words of the challenge in ancient Aigyptian as the beast clawed at Lebret, knocking his blade aside like it was straw. *"Great Sphinx! By the Sacred Sun—"*

Weaponless, Lebret pounded the creature with his bare fists, to no avail. The man-faced sphinx grinned, revealing lion-like teeth of stone.

"—of Two Horizons, calm and hear—"

The sphinx sunk its fossil teeth into Lebret's right arm. Lebret cried out in pain.

"—my Answer to your Riddle of Blood!" I shouted.

Hearing the challenge, the Sphinx froze, Lebret still in its jaws. It did not give its riddle as I expected. Why?

Precious seconds passed before I realized it couldn't speak. It was clay and bone, and golems had no voice.

Counting wasted time, I had four breaths left to live. I started giving my solution to its riddle of blood in halting Ancient Aigyptian, revealing how Alain Bertho killed Deniel Fabius.

At the end of my answer, the jaws of the sphinx went slack, releasing Lebret. With its riddle of blood solved, the spirit had been banished from its bones. Small waves lapped at the silent, now unmoving clay figure.

"Inspector!" Carmouche cried and jumped out of the boat, wading through the water towards us.

I reached Lebret first, kneeling to examine his

wounds. The sphinx had greatly devastated his arm, and he was bleeding badly. I tore off my shirt and tied it high on his arm to stanch the flow of blood as best I could.

"Thank you, Professor," Lebret said, his voice weak. "You saved Ys."

"Carmouche will carry you back, Inspector," I comforted him. "You'll pull through this."

"Perhaps," Lebret said. "I was right. Confession is good for the soul."

He smiled and closed his eyes.

Carmouche lifted the Inspector into his arms and hurried towards shore, leaving me alone with the clay sphinx. The beast would have to be disassembled, of course, either by innocent hands or by the rain and the waves. I made a note to telegraph the Lyonesse Museum and recommend that they reconsider their plans for an exhibition of androsphinx fossils.

I glanced at Alain Bertho, head buried in hands in the rowboat, and wondered what he regretted most: losing his wife, his masterpiece, or his freedom?

As for Lebret? Once again he did what he must to save the city, proving he truly deserved the epithet *Hero of Ys*. I only hoped he lived and learned to accept it.

A Bird in the Hand

Queenie Tirone

I knew I had their undivided attention the moment I dropped the swanky red feather on the table. It shimmered with its own glow in the dark room, lighting the joint up. The man known as Mr. Xang glanced down at it now, inspecting it with his gaze. He didn't dare touch it. He didn't even dare make any suggestions of what he was thinking.

He looked up at me now, his emerald slanted eyes shrinking into deeper slits,

"You have one chance to live, Mage," he said coldly, as the guards who stood on either side of him folded their arms, "Tell me about the Fenghuang."

I had felt the breath in my lungs heave as soon as the feather was away from my hand. I tried to reach for it again, but Mr. Xang pulled it closer to him and watched me. He knew I was in pain. He could probably sense the spell that was slowly killing me too.

He was an elf after all. Their kind is magic personified.

"Please," I pleaded, knowing full well I wouldn't finish the conversation without that feather. And Mr. Xang knew it, too. He slid the feather towards me.

"If it makes you useful, you may have it."

I took the feather and held it to my chest. It began to work almost instantly, "We have a mutual enemy, Mr. Xang. He has something I want, and I know for

259

a fact he has something you want. And there isn't much time. Let me explain . . ."

So, the day it happened, this dame walks through my door. Her hair was like firecrackers it was so red, and her eyes, perfectly cut sapphires that grabbed you by the collar and demanded your attention. It made me wonder why a high-class fairy like her would hire a bum like me.

I hadn't had a job in months. In fact, when she came sauntering through the door, I was napping. She must have used magic to get in, because the door was ten times her size. Fairies only stand about five inches tall at most. I had the art of napping down to a science. My feet were propped up on my desk, keeping me perfectly balanced as I leaned back in my chair. I'm sure she was pleased to watch me like that. I could picture her taking five minutes to watch my napping. Maybe she even heard my gentle snores and giggled. Dames like to laugh at schmoes like me.

She fluttered above me and touched me gently on the shoulder with a few taps from her feet. Though I appreciated the effort to not startle me, it happened anyway. I fell backwards and even lost one of my shoes in the process. At least my loafer didn't knock her in the face or anything. That would have been a great first impression.

So I clean myself up, brushing my hair back and dusting off my pant legs. She's watching me the whole time with an amused expression. I'm glad one of us was happy. She sat down in the seat across from my desk (in a chair that's way too big for her) as I picked my chair off the floor. My mouth tasted like gunpowder. As I smacked my tongue to the roof of my mouth, I saw the empty bottle of Jack Daniels and sighed.

"So, can I help you miss?" I say to the gal, but my voice sounds raspy. Like I've been sucking on a rusty pipe all night.

She loses the humor to her face, and places a picture in front of me. I take out my magnifying glass to get

a better look. It's an old fairy woman, her eyes alight
and the same color of blue as the dame's. Her hair is
a silvery white color, and her wings look like they've
seen better days. Other than that, she doesn't look a
day over twenty.

I look up from the picture as the doll starts telling
me her sob story. It's hard to listen to it when I'm
losing myself in her voice. Fairies always have such
gorgeous voices. They sound like sirens pulling you
out to sea. But I still got the basic jist. Her grandmother had gone missing. She wanted me to find her.

You see, I do all sorts of jobs. I've solved murder
cases, thefts and arsons, even caught some crooks who
worked for the Orcish Mob. Never mess with an orc
mobster. They may not count too well, but they always
remember a face. But back to the dame. She's ex-
plaining how sick her grandmother is, and how she
doesn't usually go out much anymore, so her being
gone for three days is unusual. I'm trying not to fall
asleep listening to her soothing voice, so I start to take
notes to remind myself of what she said. When she's
finished talking, I fold the piece of paper and slip it
into my pocket.

"I'll see what I can do."

You'd think it would be easy to find an older fairy
lady in the 1920s, but it's not. They're rare, sure, rarer
than elves, orcs, and dwarves, but when a fairy disappears it doesn't send off smoke signals or anything.
So I had my work cut out for me.

I started at the fairy grandmother's home. The thing
that's most annoying about fairies' houses is how small
they are. Not only did this one live in a tiny doll
house, the house was located inside her landlord's
home. So I had to charm an old bat-of-a-woman until
she finally let me in. People can be picky about strange
guys invading a gal's house.

And I'm a strange-looking guy. The blue in my hair
doesn't make me the most subtle-looking human on
the planet. Hence why I love my fedoras. When we

got inside, it took me a few hours before I found anything useful. And I had to look through this stuff with a magnifying glass and tweezers. Amongst a pile of miniature notes, I found a business card the size of my thumb that struck my eye. It had a picture of a vibrant firebird in the right corner, and the name *Zax the Magic Man* in bright red letters.

Zax . . . I'd heard that name before. And when it finally dawned on me, I read the back of the card. It said, "Specializing in rare magics that can cure any illness."

Bingo.

I'm sure Zax had some lead to where the fairy went.

I never liked snake oil salesmen. They're slimy at best, and usually work under shady means. While magic is welcomed and encouraged, it is also kept under strict wraps. But some people make their own rules about who uses what magic and when. Some things don't change, even if we think we are more civilized now than back in medieval times.

Anyhow, I called the address on the card. Not many go deep into the downtown core unless they are up to mischief. When I got to the door I was greeted by the sounds of a loud hacking cough, the guy sounded like he had choked on his lung.

Suddenly, a slot in the door no bigger than half a face slid open. Through the cutout, I saw two large red-rimmed eyes. The man's forehead was dripping with sweat, and I watched as he smoothed back the stray strands of hair that barely covered the bald spot on his head.

He looked like a winner already.

"Hello," the gruff voice said, peering at me through the cutout. His eyes scanned me up and down, then began scanning the road around me. "You're alone, right?"

"Yeah," I nodded, "You Zax?"

"Yeah, what's it to ya? You looking for goods?"

For *goods*. I hate when they make magic sound like dope.

"Sure. The kind you advertised on your card." I passed it to him through the grate, and he eyeballed it before handing it back to me. "What kind of goods you got?"

"Well, I got some nice naga scales from India. Still fresh. Um, some pixie dust from Ireland, And some tuatha juice from Scotland. Oh, and of course, I got phoenix tears from China. You looking to buy, pal?"

As he listed off the different magical beast bits, I felt my skin crawl under my shirt. I was hoping he didn't kill any of those creatures to get those parts, but I wouldn't be sure until I got to check him out.

"You know, I think I could use some of those tears you got," I replied. I could hear him make a satisfied grunt behind the door.

"Excellent choice, my dear sir! I assume you will want to check out the goods?"

"Of course," I said, sounding as eager as I could.

He took a few more looks around then slid shut the slot in the door.

"Well, come on then," Zax said. He waved me in, then slammed the door shut behind me. I watched as he turned each deadbolt. I felt like we were being sealed into a vault.

This guy sure did his homework.

He had a vast collection of magical creatures, as well as rare mystical gems, plants, and other materials. This Joe had the sword of King Arthur! How he got his hands on it I can't even begin to imagine! Jeez Louise!

But what really caught my interest was the way he took care of these goods. Excalibur was left point down into the dirty floor, leaning against a table with scattered magical gems sitting in broken bottles of dust and oils. The busted oil jar was dripping onto the sword itself! No telling what that oil was, or how it could change the properties of Excalibur.

But when I saw his treatment of the magical creatures, my heart sank into my stomach. He kept pixies in vials just big enough for them to lie down in. A chimera was curled in the corner of its steel and glass cell. It looked hungry, and one of its heads lifted to look at me as I passed it. It pleaded with me with its lion eyes and nearly broke my heart. I also found a naga chained and sealed in a cage no bigger than she was. Her shining snake tail barely fit in the cage at all and was pushed up against the side of the glass. When she saw me, she pressed both her hands to the window of her prison, and we exchanged glances. Despite the fact we were different species, we shared a common bond. We both looked tired, old, and like we were down on our luck.

I tapped the glass and heard the vibrations in it. Magic. A binding spell. I could let all these beasties free if all that was holding them were binding spells. Binding spells were my specialty. But this guy was good. I could hear there was something more. He had magics overlaying the binding spells, and didn't seem to care about the rule that mixing different colors of magic is dangerous. He had red magic binding spells over black control spells, and those overlapped white drowsiness spells.

"Jeez . . ." I murmured out loud, but Zax was busying himself elsewhere.

"Hey, mister, you may want to see this."

I followed the sound of Zax's voice into a smaller room. It was curtained off with magical beads, and as I pulled the beads back I felt the spells woven into it.

The spells were to keep the phoenix calm.

It was a gorgeous bird. Eyes like molten lava, feathers the color of the sun itself. Sadly, I could tell its flame was being suppressed. Normally, it would have more than small sparks of fire coming off its body. The poor thing looked pained.

I also noticed a fairy grandmother petting the

phoenix's head. The same fairy grandmother I was looking for.

"Isn't she a beauty? I milk the tears from the bird myself. It's real easy to do once you know the trick. Wanna see?"

I wanted to say no. I wanted to stab him with Excalibur back there. I wanted this guy *dead* for hurting all these beautiful beasties. But I had to see. I also had to know who he was supplying this stuff to. Then I'd bust his balls.

He took the fairy off the phoenix's head. This startled both the bird and the fairy, who knew something horrible was about to happen.

With a malicious grin, I watched him pull a wing off the fairy.

I felt horrible for just seeing this, but I had to keep my cover. It wasn't time to nab him just yet. But the noise . . .

The phoenix gave a harrowing cry that brought tears to my eyes. I'm not one to be moved by a bird's tears, but her sorrow was so deep and intense . . .

Zax didn't feel it, though. He was used to the noise she made. He placed the wounded fairy back on the firebird's head, and took a jar off the table beside him. He filled it to the brim with the phoenix's tears. She wailed the whole time.

I bit back the lump in my throat and tried to keep my cool, "Nice job. Is that fairy a friend of hers?"

Zax smirked proudly as he handed me the jar, "Yeah, they like each other. The fairy was a customer of mine, but when she saw all these creatures, well, she didn't want to leave them. Fairies have magical properties that can fetch a nice price on the market, so I let her stay. Or more appropriately, she has to stay now. She likes the bird so I keep them together. And if I beat on the fairy, it makes the bird cry, and that's what I need to get the tears."

What a monster this guy was.

"She's a bit of an old fairy, don't you think? Maybe

you should let her go. You can't sell something that old."

Zax frowned, "Nobody needs to know that. I just sell her dust. It's like pixie dust but does different things. By the way, the tears are worth 500 clams."

A man could live quite comfortably on 500 clams. He could buy himself a nice car to go with a big house. One of those new cars with the shiny chrome rims and smooth black paint job. Normal Joes like me don't even dream of owning one of those cars. On a good day, I have a few nickels in my pocket to buy me dinner.

So why was he living amongst this junk?

"I'll have to get some from my boss then," I replied, and watched the fairy take one of the tears from the phoenix and rub it on her wound. Zax turned his back on us, and reached for one of the vials that held a pixie. He dumped the poor thing in his hand and shook her violently until dust sprinkled onto his dirty table. He then forced her back into the vial and began snorting the dust.

Bloody dope fiend. Not only was he a dealer, he was a user too.

"Who do you work for, then?" Zax said, rubbing his nose on his shirtsleeve, "Let me guess, Fat Tony? He sure likes his exotic magics. Though he usually isn't interested in healing magics . . ."

"Yeah, Fat Tony!" I said, relieved he gave me a name to drop, "One of his cronies got himself a nasty wound. Cut his hand clear off."

"Jeez . . ." Zax said, and rubbed his stubbly chin, "You know, he uses trolls to do his dirty work?"

Trolls! Panic started to stir in my guts. If Zax knew enough about Fat Tony, then he also knew by now I didn't. Because trolls can heal themselves, and there's only one way to take down a troll . . . And phoenix tears won't heal those wounds.

He was ready for me too, the rat. Before I could cast a protection spell he threw some purple dust in my face. It exploded right in front of me, and the next thing I knew I was out like a light.

*   *   *

I came to several hours later to discover that my hands
had been cuffed behind my back—with damn anti-
magic bracelets, no less. I tried to squirm and slip my
hands out but it was useless. When I looked up, there
was the phoenix and her fairy friend. The fairy looked
down at me with a sad smile, and waved hi.

I nodded and grunted.

She floated down to sit on my shoulder, but I was
busy watching Zax. He was cooking something up for
me, I could tell. Blue smoke clouds exploded in front
of him, and he was chuckling under his breath.

The fairy moved. I felt her wings tickling my earlobe
as she whispered, "You came to rescue us, didn't
you?"

I nodded and whispered back, "But I didn't plan to
find her." I looked up at the firebird above us, who
was also watching me.

Those eyes, so intense. I almost lost myself in her
pained stare.

"Maybe I can help you . . ." She whispered, and
flew up towards the firebird. But before I could ask
what she was planning to do, Zax came back. He had
a nasty grin on his face.

"You just don't get it, do you, Greg Meridian," Zax
said, as he flipped through my wallet. "Ah, here's your
magical dick license. Nice. Thought you could bust
me, huh?"

He tossed my wallet at my shackled feet. I glared
up at him.

"You messed with the wrong guy, dick. You have
no idea how powerful I am." He knelt down in front
of me and took my chin in his oily hands. I spat in
his face. He snarled and wiped the spittle away, but
let out a dark smirk in return.

"You think you're a hero, don't you? Like you can
save these poor creatures from the big bad Zax. Well,
I got news for you pal, magic is only good for one
thing . . ."

He reached behind him and grabbed a bubbling vial,

filled to the brim with liquid pain. I knew that spell he concocted. It was Enervate. I was screwed.

". . . power." It was like watching the warden come to deliver you to the electric chair. I didn't see it, but I felt something land in my hand. It was soft and warm, like a picnic blanket left baking in the sun all day. I squeezed it hard as Zax forced my mouth open.

And that was that.

I'm dying of Enervate and the only thing that's keeping me going is this feather.

Mr. Xang rested his chin on his folded hands as he was listening to my tale. I hoped it made the impression I was after. Having these guys as allies would sure help, even if they were criminals.

"How did you know to come to us?" he asked.

I watched an elf woman in a green cheongsam enter the room. She had a tray of tea that she placed on Mr. Xang's desk. She poured him a cup of tea, then left without a single syllable uttered. I watched him sip his tea before I replied.

"I didn't. I had a hunch. You see, I know a little bit about most magical creatures. I have to in my line of work. What I know about phoenixes is that they are life spirits, and they come from many places, including China. In China, they are revered as symbols of the empress. And this firebird, she looked special. I noticed she wore a necklace with a royal crest on it. Nothing I've seen in the Western world as far as crests go. So I let my hunch find you. My guess is you've been looking for it for a while."

Mr. Xang put the tea cup down and grinned. It was the first sign of genuine emotion I saw on that hard face, "You are good, Mr. Meridian. I respect a human with good eyes."

"Thank you." I was hoping with a comment like that, maybe we were becoming friends. Or at the very least, Mr. Xang wasn't going to kill me.

"I will let you work with us," He said, and I wanted to roll my eyes at him. Yeah, let *me* work with you, now that I've done most of the work for you. Typical mob bosses. "Mai Ling, you will go with Mr. Meridian to this Mr. Zax."

That's when she stepped out of the shadows, moving like a leopard on the prowl. She had her hair in an elegant bun, her midnight black locks pinned to her head with a snazzy dragon hair dressing. Her cheongsam was crimson and flowing, with fiery phoenix feathers decked in gold along the sleeves and neckline.

"She is the ambassador of the Empress," Mr. Xang said, putting my curiosity to rest. "She is the guardian of the Fenghuang."

She bowed a greeting to me. I would have bowed back, but my body was still very weak. The feather only did so much.

"Lead me to her," Mai Ling said, and I felt the skin shudder down my back. Her voice rang of raw power. It washed over me in waves, and gave me a little more of my lost strength back.

We were shuffled into a beautiful Morris Cowley Bullnose, a boiler that was made just this year. The driver opened the doors for us, letting the lady slide in first. Now this was high class.

When we got there, I warned her about his powers. She flicked her long lashes at me, making my pulse race, "Follow behind me. I don't want anything else to happen to you."

I chuckled. What a doll! But I'm no wussy man. And she was an ambassador! I was responsible for what could happen to her.

"Don't worry about me, Miss Ling," I said, trying not to wince even though I was in terrible pain, "I can't let anything happen to you. If I survive this mess, I'd be walking into another with your death on my head."

She smiled at me in a way that made my head swim. Dames. One of my greatest weaknesses. I bet she thought I was being cute.

I pulled out my old bean-shooter and waved the

dame behind me. I don't know what I was thinking.
How was I going to get back in with all those bolts
and magical seals he had on the door?

But that's when the broad behind me showed her
stuff. She walked right up to the door, and placed her
hand on the rusty steel frame. She slid it up and down,
touching as much of the surface as she could. When
she found what she was looking for she said, "Dust
out!"

So I did as she told me. I backed off a few paces
until I felt I was a safe distance away. I knew elves
have magic of their own, but I didn't know a thing
about what it could do. Everywhere Mai Ling touched
was glinting a hot white color. She stepped away herself, and joined me on the other side of the street.

"Ready?" She said with a grin. That's when I noticed she had two pointed canines.

BOOM! The door blew right off its hinges, and all
Mai had to do was snap her fingers.

Of course, this brought the weasel out of hiding.
The fella was yelling and screaming, waving his arms
around. He looked like a puppet.

Mai Ling took one look at Zax, and that's when
she got sore. That pointed smile changed into full-on
snarling jaws of sharp teeth. She changed from a
pretty little china doll, into . . . well . . . a dragon.

I had never seen one in person. Seen plenty of pic-
tures and explanations of them, though, so I knew
they could fly, spit fire, and wield some of the most
powerful magics going. But I didn't know they could
shape change into dazzling babes.

She sure scared the bejesus out of old Zax. He trembled at her appearance, and I don't blame him. She
wasn't even sore with me and I was intimidated by
her sheer raw power. Her scales glistened with it. Her
eyes burned like shooting stars.

She opened her massive mouth and a flaming explosion spat back at Zax. I took my fedora off and covered my face with it, but it didn't stop the smell of

charred flesh from burning my nostrils. Something to remember: always have dragons on your side.

When I moved my hat to put it back on my head, she was a beautiful gal again, smoothing out the wrinkles in her china doll dress. She adjusted the hair pin and turned to look at me, her eyes sparkling but soft.

"That . . . will be our little secret," she said. Like a stunned bunny, I nodded and let her saunter into the building. She started to dispel all the magic keeping the animals locked up. Many of the creatures thanked her as they escaped. When we got to the beaded curtain, she snarled and dispelled that too. The beads melted into raindrops of color at her feet, and I made sure to carefully step over the goo puddles, so not to get any on my new loafers.

But when we got the bird, it was too late. The fairy was weeping, trying to scoop up the ash in her little hands.

There goes my chance at lifting this spell.

I sighed and leaned against a clean wall feeling beaten. The feather was keeping me going, but its power was waning. I'd be dead in a few hours.

"I'm sorry, kid," I said to the fairy grandmother. I know it's silly to call an old lady kid, but I wasn't thinking straight.

Mai Ling began collecting the dust reverently. She put it into a sack she pulled off the floor. The fairy started to hassle her, but Mai gave her a kind look. It was enough to show the fairy she was here to help.

"Greg . . . you brought a dragon here?" the fairy said. Things were looking kind of blurry right now, but I managed a nod.

"Yeah . . . she . . ."

I fell to my knees, and I heard a crack as I did so. Someone called my name but I couldn't tell whose voice it was. I swear, before I passed out, I saw flames explode in the sack Mai was holding.

Ashes to ashes . . .

*   *   *

I woke on a rickety old bed, with a spring poking at my spine. But other than being uncomfortable, I was fine. Better than fine, in fact, I felt sharp. Even my lungs were feeling strong, like before I started smoking.

I sat up and Mai Ling greeted me with a smile and gently coaxed me back down. "You need your rest," she said, smiling, but I didn't get a peek at those fangs this time.

"What happened?" I asked, looking around. The fairy was on the end of my foot, smiling so wide it filled her whole face. I was also pleasantly surprised to find the phoenix perched on the night table beside me. And boy did she look swanky. All her beautiful feathers had come back, with rippling fire under the wings. And somehow, she looked younger. Like a thousand years younger.

She smiled at me and bowed, opening her wings.

"She is thanking you, Mr. Meridian," Mai said, still smirking at me, "You risked your life to save her, so she gave me some of her tears to heal you."

I chuckled and nodded my thanks to the bird. This time when I met her lava gaze, I saw only joy inside that stare. And it made my day.

"Doll, you can call me Greg," I said to Mai. "You've earned it."

The beautiful grin on her face only grew wider as she looked down at me. She even brushed my shaggy blue streak away from my eyes, "OK Greg, I think you also owe me a night on the town. I would like to go to the Green Papaya."

Was she asking me out? Not that I was complaining. Then again, she was a dragon, and used to getting her way. And was I going to turn down a dragon? You got to be kidding me.

"I'd be honored, babe," I said, knowing full well my grin was splattered like red paint across my face, "But I need to take Miss Fairy home first."

She nodded, "I have to bring the Fenghuang back

to Mr. Xang. He will take care of her until we can return to China."

That was one dame I'd never forget. And sometimes, I still miss her. But it's not like I have the dough to get my sorry self to China anytime soon. And besides, she may have had a good time with me, but she was way out of my league.

But still, I'll never forget her, or that case. And when I really miss her, I pull out the phoenix feather and feel its heat.

THE AGE AHEAD

What lies ahead? We can only speculate. Science and technology have opened up new vistas of wonder, but the simple tenets of faith in the unknowable and belief that there are always mysteries behind every answer may be enough to allow the magical and fantastical to continue on . . . into the future.

Mars Bound

K. J. Gould

No one knew what would happen to an elf who left earth.

Sheela was about to find out.

Remembering the argument with her father was not the most auspicious way to start her 40-million-mile journey, but it was what Sheela thought of as the countdown approached zero.

"It will end badly," he had intoned.

"Is that a prophecy or a curse?" Sheela had snapped back, stung by his refusal to share her joy at being chosen for the mission.

"Neither," he'd replied, "but it always ends badly when elves involve themselves in the affairs of men."

Sheela shrugged off the memory. Really, what else had she expected him to say? His faction had been against elves revealing their presence to humans in the first place, years before Sheela had been born. She'd thought he had come to terms with it, watching her grow up with human friends and human interests. If his old separatist attitudes still lurked beneath the surface, there was nothing she could do about it. Besides, she'd made up with him before she'd left.

"Please understand, Father," she'd pleaded. "I *must* go."

He had hesitated only a moment before nodding. How could he not understand? The human space program, especially Mars, was all she'd talked about as a child. Of course, he'd teased her about it, making a great show of checking her ears to see if the tips were pointed. "Are you *sure* you're an elf?" he'd ask, while she giggled at his silliness.

She'd tried to lighten his mood by promising to come straight home when she got back, and tell him all about her Martian adventure . . . yes, *every single detail,* no matter how small. "It'll probably take weeks," she'd added with a mischievous grin.

He'd laughed, then, gathered her into a hug, and tickled the tips of her ears. "Just checking," he'd murmured, before he turned away—but not fast enough that she'd missed the fear haunting his liquid-silver eyes.

Left unsaid was the reason for his fear: Elves were creatures of magic, and the source of that magic was earth. No elf had ever left earth, nor wanted to. Some of the older Loremasters thought that she would die, and she suspected that her father was among that number. Sheela threw in her lot with those who thought that she would merely become mortal, like humans. She had always thought the older elves were too dependent on magic anyway. They didn't know how to live without it, and therefore didn't believe it was possible. But she did—growing up with human friends had taught her that she didn't need magic to do most of the things she'd wanted to do.

Even so, during the training, she'd been surprised to discover how often she called on magic without thinking. She was just as bad as the older elves when it came to small things. Need a tool on the other side of the room? *Reach* for it, and the magic would place it in your hand. Have to catch something when both hands were busy? Tell the magic to do it. She'd learned to control those impulses in the year since she'd been accepted for the training. Mostly.

The rumble of the engines turned into a roar. Earth clutched at her, no more willing to let her go than her father had been. The g-forces pressing her into the couch masked the draining away of the magic . . .

at first. By the time the shuttle reached the *Christa McAuliffe,* waiting in orbit, there was a curiously debilitating void in her senses where magic used to be. She cast about for an analogy . . . maybe like an old sailor, staggering about on land as his muscles betrayed him by making the constant, unconscious adjustments so necessary on the rolling deck of a ship. *No,* she rejected the comparison, *not quite.* Magic was more than an impersonal force of nature, like the sea. It had a presence. Less than a consciousness, but . . . an awareness that responded to the wielder.

Loremasters disagreed about that, too. Some of them thought that magic itself was aware, others thought that the "presence" was just the remnant of elves who had dissolved into the magic. To Sheela, it didn't matter anyway. Magic was what it was.

By the time the crew had gone through their preflight checks, Sheela had almost gotten used to the absence of magic. She couldn't get over how bland everybody looked, though. She'd never really been conscious of the fact that she saw people with magic as well as with her eyes. It was just another of the elements that made up how a person looked, like the color of their hair or their height. Now she realized that the magic gathered around elves and some humans had always made them seem more *there* to her, more solid, more real. Her best friend in the crew, Cameron Saunders, in particular, had been among those 'solid' humans. It was disturbing to see him looking like everybody else.

The entire crew gathered in the Hab One wardroom for the send-off 'cast. When they finished here, the attitude thrusters would fire to orient them for Mars, then the big fusion engines would shove them out of Earth's orbit, accelerating halfway to Mars, then decelerating the rest of the way. At least then they'd have gravity, even if it was only one-third of earth-normal, and her stomach would settle down. She hoped.

Sheela wormed her way through the crowd to Cam. It wasn't easy. Cam was the poster boy for tall, dark, and handsome and most of the female crew members vied for his attention. But she used her elbows, and the purchase offered by her Velcro booties, to good effect, and made it in time to talk to him before the 'cast started. Keeping an eye on Mission Commander Levitt, she leaned toward him and asked, "Do you feel different?"

"Well, of course," he answered. "We're weightless."

"No, I mean . . ." she hesitated. She'd tried to talk with Cam about magic during the training. He'd insisted he couldn't see it, couldn't feel it, and didn't want to talk about it, so she'd dropped it. But she wondered if its absence had affected him. "There's no magic here," she said finally. "I was wondering if you'd noticed any difference."

"Hmm. Well, I *do* feel a bit odd, but that's just the weightlessness." He looked at her and added, "But, you know, *you* look a little strange. And . . ." He paused for a thoughtful moment, "it's interesting that . . ." Levitt gave the "quiet" sign, and Cam stopped, then whispered, "later," out of the side of his mouth.

Levitt made his little speech about this colony effort being a new chapter in human—and elven, he added belatedly, nodding at Sheela—history, threw in some "next frontier" stuff, and finished up with thanks for all the nations who had contributed funds and personnel. Pretty boilerplate, in Sheela's estimation. Well, there probably weren't many people watching anyway, so what did it matter? This was the *Christa*'s third trip to Mars. The public's attention was all wrapped up in the colony ship being built in orbit.

She waved with the others when Mission Commander Levitt said goodbye, then headed for her bunk, along with the rest of the non-flight crew, to get strapped in for maneuvers. She and Cam were both assigned to Hab Two quarters, so they had a chance to talk on the way.

"What's interesting?" Sheela asked, without preamble, as they floated into the Hab One core.

"Huh? Oh, well . . . hard to explain." He handed her through the hatch to the tube that connected the

cores of the two habs. Cam pulled himself through the
hatch, and they shoved off together to float down the
tube before he continued. "Have to back up a bit, I
guess. I was remembering what you'd said about why
you couldn't do magic tricks, and . . . well, you know
I'm handy with machines."

"Handy" was understating it by a couple of orders
of magnitude, in Sheela's opinion. She didn't think
there'd been a machine built that he couldn't fix. It
was a good quality for the mission's primary equipment maintenance engineer to have. She nodded for
him to continue.

"Well, the thing is," Cam shrugged, "I never really
had to work at it. I've just always seemed to know
what was going on with a piece of equipment. I mean,
I had to look, but still, I had an idea of *where* to look.
Just now, though, going through the pre-flight, there
was a glitch in one of the compressors, and you know,
I didn't have a clue." He shook his head, "Not a
clue." He shrugged again. "Anyway, it was a weird
thing. I thought it might relate."

"Maybe. I've told you that magic hangs around you,
even if you say you can't sense it." He made a face
at her, and she laughed. "I know, I know, you don't
believe me, but I think that the 'knowledge' of what's
going on with a machine is how magic communicates
with you. And it *does* relate to what I said about
magic tricks. After all, you *need* to know what's going
on with a machine."

Early in the training, about the third or fourth time
somebody asked her to do a "trick," she'd tried to
explain that magic didn't work like that. Magic responded to need, and intent, and purpose. She'd had
a hard time coming up with an analogy that humans
might understand. "It's like, oh . . . like asking a horse
to jump a fence when there isn't any fence. Or asking
a sheepdog to round up the flock when there aren't
any sheep. It can't figure out what you need it to do,
because there's nothing that *needs* doing."

That had satisfied them, so she'd left it at that. Even

though it was really only part of it. There were some
mages who could fool magic into doing tricks, but it
was frowned on. Sheela more than frowned on it—
she detested anyone who would do such a thing. It
was a betrayal of the relationship between magic and
mages. Magic sought the company of those who could
sense it, use it, direct it. It *wanted* that connection.
Even more, it wanted to be *useful*. To take advantage
of that to trick it into doing something purposeless,
was just . . . wrong.

"Hey," Cam touched her arm, "guess we better get
strapped down."

Sheela started out of her reverie at his touch and
looked around. Somehow, they'd made it to Hab
Two's core without her noticing. She grinned at him
as he pushed off toward his quarters. "Sorry. Day-
dreaming. See you later, and we'll talk more." She
grabbed a handhold and launched herself in the opposite direction, toward her own quarters.

The crew had been assigned quarters within the two
habs without regard to mission function, but Sheela
suspected that the crew would sort themselves out into
the "lab coats" and the "hard hats" before they
passed the moon's orbit. That's what they'd done during the mission training, anyway. Not that the hard
hats were really "grunts," though they called themselves that, too. They all had advanced degrees and a
record of accomplishments to prove their abilities. It
was just that, with a primary mission of building a
settlement capable of supporting 3,000 humans in two
years, there would indeed be a lot of grunting going
on.

Sheela's problem was, she didn't know which group
she belonged to. Although she had PhDs in several of
the life sciences—elves took a long time to mature,
and she was nearly twice as old as most of her fellow
crew members—her primary assignment was agron-
omy. She was basically the gardener, in charge of setting up and running the greenhouse. Of course, first
they had to *build* the greenhouse. So that put her in

the hard hat category. But she was also secondary for medical services, which was more like lab coat territory. Well, she'd just stick with Cam. That decided, she suited up, SOP during maneuvers, tapped the com button on the side of the helmet to open—also SOP— and set the bunk into its acceleration couch configuration.

It didn't take long to settle into shipboard routine. Most of the crew members had no real flight duties. Their time was spent training for their backup positions and training their own backups. Thus it was that Sheela spent far less time with Cam than she'd have liked, and *far* more time than she'd have liked with Violet Mandel—"Shrieking Violet," in the privacy of Sheela's mind. Vi had been needling her since the training started, more than a year ago now. Nothing overt, that she could be called on. Just constant little digs. Maybe she just hated elves. Some humans did. But Violet was also a backup for Medical Services, so they trained together most of the time. Sheela was quite fond of Avasa Dalal, the primary doctor, and another one of those magic-attracting solid humans. But, since most of her time with Ava included Vi, that wasn't as pleasant as it could have been. Nor did it help that Vi was better than she was. Sheela still had to fight that momentary impulse to use magic. It slowed down her reaction time, a bad thing in situations where speed counted.

They'd only been out a week when the first radiation warning came. Six hours in the close quarters of the core with Vi and six other people—none of whom were Cam; he'd been up in Hab One when the alarm sounded—hadn't helped Sheela's temper. When the all-clear sounded, Sheela went to her quarters with a damp towel and wiped down, then she headed for the wardroom for a bite. She heard Vi's grating voice before she got there.

"I bet she used magic to get on the mission," Vi was saying. She was sitting at one of the tables, with her back to the entry, talking to Ava. "You know, messed with their minds," Vi added, making a flicking "woo-woo" gesture with one hand. Ava looked up and saw Sheela standing there, and made a shushing sound, nodding her head at the door. Vi turned around, and then smirked at Sheela's glare, unrepentant.

Enough!

The last, thin thread of her control snapped at Vi's sneering dismissal of Sheela's years of studying human sciences and the past year of struggling *not* to use magic. Two long strides brought her to Vi's side. She grabbed Vi's shirt and hauled her to her feet. "I didn't need magic to earn a place on this mission, and I *certainly* don't need magic to deal with *you*," she ground out, her other hand closing into a fist. But her intention to throw the punch that would wipe that smirk off Vi's face got lost in the sudden realization that it was true. She *didn't* need magic. Of course, she'd joined the mission on the assumption that she could live without magic, but she'd never really *believed* it until this moment.

Sheela carefully unwound her fingers from Vi's shirt, noting with a small satisfaction that the smirk was gone anyway. "Ah, you're not worth it." She turned around to leave, and found Cam standing in the doorway, grinning at her. "What?" she demanded.

" 'Bout time," was all he said.

Sheela suited up and cycled into the unpressurized bay to check the pods containing her seeds one more time before she had to strap in for the orbital insertion maneuvers. Most of the bay's floor space was taken up by the ship-to-surface shuttle that would ferry the crew assigned to Hab Two down to the surface, while Hab One was flown down to join the other two Habs left from previous missions. Pods of supplies that couldn't be sent in advance—including, most important to her, the seedstocks for the greenhouse—lined the walls, held in place by thick cables. As she came around the nose of the shuttle, movement over by the launch tube caught her attention. Cam's bright red suit was inside it, up to the waist. No doubt Cam was making his own last minute checks.

There was no air to carry the sound of the snapping cable; it was the jerk of the pod directly above the launch tube breaking loose that drew Sheela's eye. It dropped slowly in the low gravity, but it massed enough to crush Cam. In a panic, she thrust out her hand and *reached* for it before overriding the impulse and tapping the com button on her helmet.

"Cam!"

She heard a "clunk" over the com as her shout startled him, then he clumsily backed out of the tube and looked around. She pointed up at the pod, nearly upon him now, and shouted, *"Move!"* He looked up, and reacted instantly, diving to the side to get out of its way.

He almost made it.

The hard case of the boot had protected his foot, but his leg was pulped from mid-calf down to the ankle.

It took three of them to get the pod off his leg and carry him up to the tiny med bay in Hab One. Sheela stood beside Cam, holding his hand in anguished silence, as Ava examined him, and gave him the grim news.

"I'm sorry, Cam. I can't save it."

Cam, white-faced with pain, just nodded. Sheela suspected he'd figured that out already. "Now?" he asked.

Ava tapped her finger against her chin. "No. I don't have time before we start insertion maneuvers. I'll wait till we're in orbit. You can ride out the maneuvers right here."

She turned to Sheela, "And you can't. I'm sorry, but you'd better go get strapped in now."

Sheela made her way to her bunk, and suited up for maneuvers in a stupor. Cam's injury was her fault. If she hadn't wasted time trying to stop the pod with magic, he might have had time to get out of the way. If she had been able to use magic, she'd have been able to stop the pod. Or at the very least, heal his leg.

Her dream—of being the first elf on Mars, of proving that elves could live without magic—that selfish, prideful dream, had both crippled Cam, and made it permanent. She lay in her bunk, paying no attention to the maneuvers and the accompanying com chatter. She was too busy trying to find a bottom to her despair.

Her fog continued while the crew prepped Hab One for its descent to the surface; while she cleaned and locked down her quarters on Hab Two; while she suited up and took her place on the shuttle. She passed Cam's empty seat on the way to her own. He would be going down on the Hab, instead, missing his right leg from the knee down, and strapped into a med bay bed. Ava had offered to let her assist in the amputation, but . . . Vi was the better scrub nurse. Whatever her personal feelings for the woman, Sheela knew that. And she wanted Cam to have the best.

As the shuttle approached Mars, Sheela's mental fog lifted as she slowly became aware of . . . something. An insane, alien muttering, disturbing the silence in that space where magic used to be. A moment more, and she was sure: *magic*. It wasn't like any magic she'd ever known. This magic was wild, chaotic, unstructured—and it had its own purpose. It *wanted* her with a need so strong it nearly paralyzed her.

It clearly was aware of her and of her ability to sense it.

Well, that answers that question. I doubt that any elves have dissolved into this magic, she thought, in an absurd tangent.

The magic *reached* for her, jolting the shuttle.

"Wind shear!" a voice shouted in her ear. Another voice disputed it.

"Not. Wind." she forced out. "Magic." That was all the attention she could afford her crewmates. She *reached* back to the magic, sending a soothing tendril of calmness toward it.

When it felt her touch, the magic redoubled its frantic efforts to *reach* to her. *Oops.* She felt the magic's overwhelming need to be with her. To be *not alone* anymore.

Time slowed. She became hyperaware of everything around her, even as she maintained her focus on mastering the magic, soothing it with her presence without letting it slip from her control. The shuttle rocked and bucked in the magic's need, throwing her against the restraints. Metal shrieked with strain. Slowly, slowly, she felt the magic begin to respond. The rocking lessened. Metal-shriek turned to relieved groan as the strain eased . . .

Then the magic, in some misunderstanding she couldn't spare the thought to sort out, altered some vital component of the engines. Sheela was enveloped in sudden quiet, broken by the gasps of the other crew members coming through the com. She didn't know enough about the engines to direct the magic to fix whatever it had done.

"Do something!" someone shouted. Sheela felt the magic cringe away from the fear in that voice. The shuttle slued and dropped, tilted nearly vertical.

No! Sheela fought to control her own fear; struggled to bind the magic to *her* purpose. But it was too strong, its need too great, to be controlled that way. Maybe more elves, working in concert, could do it. Here, now, there was only Sheela. And only one way to make *her* purpose the magic's own.

Sheela felt tears prick at her eyes.

Please understand, Father. I must go.

Before she could change her mind, Sheela sent her *self* into the magic. She felt a rushing out of her awareness that was also an infilling of something else, something more . . . then suddenly, she *was* the magic. But somehow, she was still Sheela, too. She hadn't expected that. Maybe it wouldn't last for long. No matter, she had time enough to do what she needed to do. Sheela/Magic cradled the dead weight of the shuttle, and gently lowered it to the Martian surface.

There. Whatever else happened, her crewmates

could handle it now. And she would help, if she could, in her own way.

Time passed.

Sheela/Magic kept the little nodes of Other-consciousness within her awareness. They were scant company; she could not truly communicate with them. Still, she tried to make her presence felt. Sometimes, she *touched* the slightly brighter nodes that were Cam and Ava. Sometimes, she even felt a response. Sometimes she sensed Cam's fledgling attempts to *reach* for something with magic, and *reached* back, to place it in his hand. And if Cam's stump healed overnight, and if the plants grew a little healthier than expected, and if the oxygen generators worked a little better, and if sandstorms never seemed to come close enough to the domes to damage them . . . well, perhaps the others might believe that it wasn't *just* good luck.

Time passed.

And then, a great brilliance flared in Sheela/Magic's awareness, as the first group of colonists was ferried down. She restrained herself, mindful of the near-disaster of *Christa*'s shuttle's descent. The colonists would be even more at risk than her crewmates had been—they wouldn't be wearing suits. Three hundred lives, with only a thin metal shell protecting them from the near-vacuum of the Martian atmosphere. Sheela/Magic waited, long, endless moments while the colony ship's shuttle descended; while it touched down and rolled to a stop; while the gangway was extended and pressurized.

Finally.

The shuttle's hatch opened. A great gaggle of humans came through, heading for the processing desk. Following them came the source of the brilliance that had dazzled her, a group of about fifty elves. One of them, a kind-faced, silver-eyed elf, stepped to one side to let the others pass him by. A slow smile spread over his features as he cocked his head.

Sheela/Magic *reached* to tickle the tips of her father's ears.

Angels and Moths

Costi Gurgu

It's night, it's quiet, but above all, it's freezing. I lie tightly curled in my bed. My stomach grumbles and my teeth chatter. The cold bedsheet seems damp. I feel someone touching my back; I recognize her touch. She draws me into her arms to warm me. It's a familiar feeling, but it's impossible. Tears spring to my eyes as the person at my back begins whispering a lullaby and rocking me in her silky arms.

"Dana?" My voice quavers.

The lullaby stops. It is again quiet and freezing. I turn over. It's her!

"What are you doing here?" I blurt. The question seems absurd, but my wife smiles. "You're dead," I tell her quietly.

The smile vanishes and she nestles against my chest, shivering. I take her in my arms, remembering the cry, then the sound of crushed bones. I remember the outside intervention outfit lying on the morgue's metal table, soiled, torn, its visor smashed. I remember the mutilated body pulled with difficulty from the ragged outfit, her face the only thing still whole, but scratched by dozens of frozen shards, the mouth twisted in horror, the staring eyes frosted. It had been a stupid accident, something that should not have happened. But there was Dana, lying on the morgue's table . . .

"You're dead," I repeat. Teardrops tremble on my cheeks as my hands slowly touch her hair.

"Hush," the woman whispers, and places a cold finger on my lips.

Somebody else slinks into the bed, on my other side. I try to turn and see who it is, but suddenly the room fills with bodies and I can't move. I'm suffocating under the growing weight. Panic darkens my sight, and I tremble. My mouth gapes, searching for air. I try to cry for help, but I have no strength left; I choke. I'm losing . . .

I wake with a start and breathe greedily. It's night, the silence dark and heavy. It's not cold—it's actually very, very hot. Breathing easier now, I fall back on the pillow. It's wet. I haven't had a nightmare in months, and never one so vivid—and never one I remember after I wake up! I'd thought I was over the loss of Dana, yet I'll probably never be. I'll only get used to the pain, never forget it.

I'm completely awake now. Sighing, I stretch toward the night table and switch on the lamp. In the light, I notice something on my pajama sleeve. I look closely, see small, black letters. And not only on the sleeves, but also on the shirt, on the bottoms—I jump out of bed, my heart thundering in my chest. The sheets! Scribbled all over them are small lines of letters, with what seems to be the same three words repeated line after line, column after column.

It's another nightmare! I'd laugh, but fear strangles me. The walls, the night tables, the curtains, the lamps—the three words venture into the tightest corner, the smallest cranny. The whole room is covered with the same lines, although they seem written by different hands. No two look alike, yet all are the same message: *I forgive you;* sometimes, *We forgive you.*

I withdraw, panting—I need to wake up!

Closing the bedroom door behind me, I look around, terrified, but the living room is clean. I rip my pajamas off, open the bedroom door and throw them inside, then I close it again. I crouch naked in a corner, pressing my back against the cold wall. I pull my knees up to my chin, rest my forehead on them, and close my eyes. I remain still, trying to control my breathing.

I don't know how long I slept, but I'm startled awake by the sound of the alarm. It wasn't a dream—I am naked in my living room. I have a splitting headache. I rise from the floor, groaning over stiff limbs. I decide to check the bedroom, but a knock on the apartment door stops me as I'm heading that way. I hesitate with my hand on the doorknob. The knock comes again, louder. I postpone the bedroom check, glance at the clock, and notice that it's an hour before the time I usually wake up. The next knock sounds more insistent. I snatch a toss cushion from the couch to cover my nakedness and open the door.

The military aide barely looks at me. "You're urgently needed in Command," he reports.

I dress and follow him wordlessly.

The maddening sound of the alarm ushers us into the Command Room. The red lights flooding the walls remind us of the state of war we've just entered. The officer in charge sees me and waves me toward him.

"Cambry, I'm in communication with the President. He's discussing the situation with the Council; in a few minutes we'll have his orders."

"What happened?" I ask, confused.

"An hour ago we received an S.O.S. from the landing team. The message lasted only eleven seconds and we didn't have the chance to reply. Everything ended much too quickly."

"What ended—"

"Listen, Richard," he interrupts.

The S.O.S. recording fills the Command Room: *"Odyssey, we're under attack . . . no warning . . . they're inside the shuttle . . . they're too fast—God, no—"* In the background I hear screams, something that sounds like flapping wings, strange rattles. Then silence. Not only the message, but the whole attack seemed to have lasted no longer than eleven seconds.

The landing team, the *ambassadors* as they've been called in the past few days, have been murdered within seconds inside their own shuttle, which had also become the office of the human diplomatic mission to the Flutzan world. All four elite military officers, eliminated effortlessly.

"Half an hour after the assassination, we received a written message," the commander says.

I look a question at him.

"A message from the Flutzi," he adds, handing me a freshly printed piece of paper.

I read: *The Flutzan Empire requests a meeting with a man without faith. Send him down immediately to discuss terms with us and retrieve the bodies.*

Everybody is watching me. I don't know how I'm supposed to react.

"I sent for you, Richard, because you're the only available atheist in the sector who also has military training. The President is reading your file as we speak," the officer explains.

Only at this moment do I realize what's happening. Fate has a strange way of arranging my life. After Dana's senseless death, I thought I could get revenge by giving up God. And to make it official, I even changed my status in my papers, from Christian to atheist. Fate likes irony.

"The President has authorized the mission," the commander is saying in a serious tone, as if he's bestowing an honor. "Launch Pad Three. You have five minutes to equip yourself. Richard Cambry, it's been an honor to know you," he adds.

I nod silent assent, salute him, and exit the Command Room. The alarm has stopped. It's quiet again, with only red lights revolving on the walls and still-sleepy people running to their emergency positions revealing the situation.

*   *   *

The pod roars as it descends toward the location of the shuttle, which has turned from a diplomatic base into a grave for its four occupants. I have exactly twenty-seven minutes until contact—less than half an hour to prepare myself for what will probably be my last minutes of life. If I was still religious, I'd pray, but now I have to stick to my position. I might have said good-bye to my family, but Dana was my only family. *I forgive you* was written all over my bedroom immediately after she'd held me, sharing her warmth. It's absurd. I've never believed in an afterlife, or any of that other paranormal shit, but something happened last night.

I recall the scene right before my departure. My psychiatrist, Dr. Henderson, was waiting for me in the corridor leading to the launch pad. Nobody knew about my mission besides Command and the President—or at least nobody should have known. Still, Henderson was there, waiting for me—*me*.

"He told me to assure you that you're forgiven," were his first words. The doctor is a respectable and prominent personality, so I didn't think for a second that he'd been behind the incident in my bedroom last night. The coincidence was frightening.

"Who told you, Doc?" I asked, trying to sound calm.

"He told me to let you know that the angels need you," Henderson continued.

"Who told you all this?"

"Help the angels fly, he told me."

I didn't have time for this; the pod was ready and the chronometer was measuring my last minutes on *Odyssey*. I decided to let it go, attribute it to coincidence.

Twenty-two minutes. I scratch my arm and discover with a start that there's something written in red paste directly on my skin: *Don't be afraid.*

I swallow, my mouth suddenly dryly. Instantly, I'm sweating. I look at my other arm and indeed, the message continues there: *You're not alone.*

But I am alone! The pod is small, with no place for someone to hide. I should be alone! Suddenly the control screen steams over and somebody, or something, writes in capital letters, *I'll help you.*

It's so very hot in here.

Fourteen minutes until my meeting with the mysterious Flutzi. That's it, I'll think of something else. *Odyssey*—humankind's first generation-ship and probably the only one for a long time, considering the enormous cost—has reached its destination after 317 years of traveling. Humankind's first journey to another star system has ended successfully. First contact with an intelligent alien species, which is theoretically very advanced, and three days of successful communication. Until something angers the Flutzi enough for the radical measure of murder, apparently without worrying about consequences. Less than a week after first contact, humankind is on the verge of war with the first and only intelligent species it has met in the universe.

And I, Richard Cambry, will be the weight to shift the scales toward war or toward peace. I haven't the slightest idea whom I'm supposed to meet, what the agenda is, or what my diplomatic powers and limitations are. Total ignorance. And on top of it all, somebody forgives me right before the final conflict!

I step inside the shuttle. The decompression room is empty. I straighten my clothes, draw a deep breath, and open the door. A single step takes me over the metallic threshold; I stop, a huge knot in my throat. The four corpses are sprawled around the common room, each human envoy lying where he or she fell. Deep wounds are plowed through their flesh, the blood clotted in dark crusts. The floor is painted dark red. I turn my face to the wall, vomit boiling in my throat. I succeed in controlling my fright and nausea, and again face the slaughter.

I hurriedly cross the room and exit into the central corridor. On both sides are the crew's rooms, and at the other end lies the cockpit. Its door is open and in the light flooding from it into the dim corridor, I see a silhouette. A strange shape. Waiting for me.

"Oh, Lord," I whisper, then I stop, surprised. It's been two years since I last invoked God. Even before Dana's death I did it rarely; there was no need to.

I walk the distance slowly and enter the cockpit. A visceral fear squeezes my stomach, but I'm telling myself this is only a natural reaction to the unknown, the xenophobia hidden in every one of us. At first sight, the Flutz resembles a giant butterfly, almost the size of a grown man. The resemblance to an Earth butterfly starts right with its face, which has a tightly coiled proboscis and huge eyes with dozens of facets. It has two pairs of legs and one pair of arms, and its wings are gathered on its back like a ship's sail. I can see only their white exterior surfaces, crisscrossed by nerves.

I don't feel the repulsion that a bug would induce in me, but only the fear generated by the insect-like appearance of its black and spiky members, as well as the fear in realizing that an intelligence so alien probably has nothing in common with the human mind and therefore with our values and references. How could we ever hope to really understand each other?

On the control-board is a receptacle that resembles a broken eggshell, filled with a viscous, yellowish liquid. The Flutz pushes it toward me. *It wants to poison me,* is my first thought, then I change my mind: *no, it wants to drug me.* The paranoia that began with Dana's death has grown exponentially after last night's nightmare. Thoughts roll frantically through my head as I try to keep my fear, cultural shock, and confusion on a short leash.

Paralyzed by indecision, I don't make a move. The alien pushes the receptacle toward me again. I don't have another solution—I need to move forward. I lift the receptacle and smell its contents. Vaguely honey-like. More fragranced, though. I watch the Flutz's black, multifaceted eyes as I taste it. Pollen, nectar—

that's it, nectar! Delicious! Still staring at the Flutz, I swallow it all.

I feel its heat spreading through my body, then rising to my brain. The sensation is terrifying! Panic strangles me—something is crawling through my head and I have no way to stop it, I can't put my hands under my skin, or plunge them through my skull to rummage after the intruder. I clutch the control-board to avoid making a stupid move.

Suddenly, a crackling noise like static invades my brain. A crunching sound, like bone grinding on bone, but amplified and overlapping the background of static noise, starts forming words directly in my mind.

The effect won't last long. We need to hurry.

I try to calm down, ignoring the noise and watching the Flutz curiously. It doesn't speak; it doesn't have a mouth with which to speak.

I know you can understand me. I asked only one to come. One with no faith.

"Holy crap!"

The word "holy" suggests a religious belief . . .

I suddenly realize that it's telepathic. I swallow dryly and interrupt. "It's only an expression, with no religious connotations in this case. It's used to express fright or surprise."

I'm sorry if I scared you. Which one of you is the faithless messenger?

I look around. There's nobody else here besides the Flutz and me. So I volunteer, "I'm the messenger. My name is Richard Cambry."

I'm Ximb, emissary of his Highness Wide-winged Dead Head. You must come with me.

Exiting the shuttle, I notice again the blood-colored words that have been drawn on my arms: *You're not alone.* A cold sweat prickles my back and I trip, but regain my balance before falling on the Flutzan emissary and generating an incident even before we start the discussions. So, in truth, I'm not alone!

We descend to a green glade filled with flowers of all colors, where two Flutzi are waiting. They are evi-

dently from a different class than the emissary—taller
and more imposing, with their giant, thickset bodies
covered in golden fur and their wings smaller and
gathered on their backs. They have only one pair of
legs, golden and viciously spiked like sawblades, and
two pairs of arms ending in bony, double-edged
blades. Warriors. The pair follow a few steps behind
us.

As we reach the glade's edge, I notice we are actually on a mountaintop; at my feet lies a magical valley.
As far as I can see, everything is a green paradise
painted with the vivid colors of vast fields of flowers.
On the far side of the valley stretches what I guess is
the Flutzi's urban equivalent, although it has nothing
in common with human cities. All the buildings seem
made from textiles, stretched between giant trees and
overlapping in fluffy curves—cocoons, grown on several levels. In the center of the city I can distinguish
a structure made of radial canvases combining on different planes at varied angles, and completely transparent, perfectly rounded cupolas.

The imperial city and residence. The Flutz's thoughts
rattle through my brain.

"It's beautiful." I can't hide my admiration.

Beautiful, yet fragile, Ximb amends.

I breathe deeply and turn from the scenery. "So
what happened?"

*From my discussions with the human envoys I con-
cluded that our civilizations are based on fundamen-
tally different concepts. Our world . . .* It pauses and
turns toward me, then resumes. *Our world is domi-
nated by spirituality, by the miraculous, by magic.*

"Magic is nothing but a science so evolved that nobody can explain it rationally; therefore it's considered
supernatural or even divine."

It lets me finish, then goes on calmly, as if ex-
plaining to a rather dim student. *Wrong. Humans fail
to see the truth, but magic has nothing to do with science. Magic is divine in origin. It belongs to a different
plane of existence and it is not for everybody. You are*

*born with magic qualities or not. And if not, you have
no way to acquire it, no matter how much you try or
what you study.*

After a few moments of silence, it resumes. *Tell me:
why did you choose not to believe?*

"I believe in reason, I believe in science, I believe
in evolution. I believe in a universe in which we don't
need gods, or miracles."

That's good.

"Is it?" I ask, confused.

*You have decided not to believe not because you're
convinced that there is nothing divine, but because you
don't need the divine presence in your life. You can
live without it.*

I can't answer that. I don't agree with the Flutz, but
I didn't come to the planet to discuss philosophy. I
cannot forget that a few steps away from us are the
human emissaries' corpses.

*We need to enter the second stage of our meeting. I
ask that you continue doing everything I say. Don't get
scared and obey me completely.*

I look at it suspiciously, but I wait to see what it
asks of me. The two warriors lay at my feet a weaving
of flowers and leaves, like some of kind of carpet. It
has a strange pattern and the colors tend to fluctuate
inside it.

You can both step on it, its thoughts whisper to me.

I obey and try to ignore a fearful shiver at the idea
that there is somebody else next to me, someone I
cannot see, someone visible to the Flutz. I feel the
verdant mat lifting me above the ground.

*I'll start a magic ritual that will allow you access to
another plane of existence—that miraculous plane
which you decided long ago to bury, to ignore, and in
the end, forget. Don't get scared, no matter what you
see or feel, and never leave the flowers' protection. Not
even for a second.*

The flower mat carries me to the center of the glade.
The two warriors are nowhere to be seen. I try to

watch Ximb with scientific curiosity. It stands before
me and for the first time opens its wings. I'm
breathless—they're bigger than they seem when gathered together on its back. And on their upper surface,
they're strongly colored with patterns of red, white,
black, and yellow—predominantly red with a black
pattern, the white and yellow only accents on the
black areas. It starts flapping its wings in a definite
rhythm, joining that with movement of its arms. The
geometric pattern on the wings continues along the
undersides of its arms and over its chest. It rises grace-
fully into the air in a sort of aerial dance, darting
about like an animal pursued by predators.

From the flower mat rises the heavy scent of
crushed petals. I feel a little dizzy. The dance quick-
ens, although I have the impression that in fact my
perception has altered. I notice, somewhat alarmed,
that the flowers' scents numb my senses and distort
my perception of the surrounding reality.

Ximb's dance is much too fast now to be followed.
It seems to open unseen doors in the air, passages
through which slink shaking and horrible hairy shapes
with torn wings and fiery tongues. It's hot, difficult to
breathe. My eyes sting. The static crackle in my brain
has a hallucinating cadence. I feel something flowing
down my cheeks. I raise my hands to wipe my eyes,
and blink in pain. Everything is foggy.

The noise has stopped, as has the Flutz's aerial bal-
let. I regain my breath and notice that my hands are
smudged with blood from my cheeks. Blood that came
out of my eyes, I realize with an uncharacteristic calm.

Now you will see the truth.

I keep my feet inside the floating floral carpet as it
takes me back to the glade's edge. The whole depression has filled with a motley crowd. I swallow hard at
the sight. The paradise is gone; in its place is a gigantic
war camp, populated by thousands and thousands of
fantastic creatures that move among the tents, the
hastily built barracks, the stallions and beasts of bur-

den, the huge fires where chunks of meat cook, burning black circles in the luxuriant vegetation of the Flutzan world.

Do you recognize them? Ximb's rattle surprises me. "How could I?"

Richard, even if you don't believe, you must have heard stories containing at least some of them.

And then I begin recognizing them. The revelation crushes me. Indeed, there is the Olympian gods' camp, on a rocky summit. In a corner of the valley, elves' detachments are arranged in perfect order, their guards keeping back dwarves and nasty gnomes. Dragons circle in the sky. A few steps lower than where we are, an ogre gang fights over a Flutz corpse with a few trolls with blue skin and red fur.

There are a thousand times more on the other side of the mountain and in the surrounding valleys and hills, Ximb's thoughts whisper.

"This is an illusion," I answer, dizzy.

Oh, no, I can assure you, all these are as real as you and I. If you step outside the protection of the flowers, now that you have witnessed their preparations, you'll be noticed, smelled, sensed by all these divinities and creatures, and you'll have to face them.

"But it's not possible! They're only stories—"

I stop mumbling when I see again the bloody writing covering my right arm. There's a new line: *Stories that have forgiven you for the blasphemy of not believing in them.* I inhale deeply and avoid the Flutz's eyes.

The Flutz continues, unruffled. *Now, look to your left, beyond the city.*

I perceive a crowd similar to the one around me, but I can't distinguish the details. "What should I see there?"

The Flutz sorcerer makes a discreet sign and my eyes shed tears again, then suddenly I can zoom in on distant targets. I study the expanse of fields on the other side of the city, where a swarm of bodies moves, mandibles clacking—beasts born from the most despicable nightmares.

For now, I have limited yours to this side of the city. The wizardry still works because it is alien to the earth deities. But not for long. The others, though, the ones that you saw on the far side, they're our gods and creatures. They started gathering there last night. And we can't hold them there.

"I don't understand."

Richard, even if you decide not to believe in gods or fairy tales, all of these will continue to exist in the shadows deep in your soul. You take them with you everywhere you go. And now you have brought your entire mythological existence to this side of the universe. Even if you have banished them from your consciousness, you have still worn them permanently in your being and now they're here, in our world, ready to take it by force.

The Flutz pauses to let these ideas sink in.

Our world is too small and crowded for such an invasion. What you see beyond the city is our divine army preparing to confront the invaders.

"That's insane," I protest, terrified by the implications.

It will be a bloodbath, a slaughter of cataclysmic proportions that we, the Flutzi, cannot watch from the sidelines. It will be our apocalypse, to use one of your terms. The Flutzan world will cease to exist after this confrontation. Our civilization will fall into ruin; we cannot know if there will be any survivors left to rise and start all over again. It is the End of the World War. I know in detail all the prophecies, and I recognize the signs now.

I remain silent, overwhelmed by all these revelations. The scientist in me keeps saying that everything I've heard and seen is impossible. And yet, on a different level, a deeper one, I begin to believe.

We killed your envoy hoping that once the only humans among us were dead, everything they brought

*with them would vanish as well. We were wrong, and
we are sorry for the crime we committed. But the truth
is that we're desperate. And you, Richard, you're our
last chance.*

"What could I do?"

*There's only one solution left—you need to make the
final step in the evolution of the human species. Give
up for good and forever everything that is divine and
magic in you, uproot faith, abandon creation, and they
will all disappear into nothingness.*

"Is such a thing possible?" I ask without thinking.

*I'll give you a magic potion that you must distribute
to all humans. Tomorrow morning, when you awaken,
everything will be forgotten.*

I look again at the valley that bustles with creatures
from fairy tales, legends, and myths. Human culture
and civilization, in the flesh. Deicide or apocalypse?
What right do we, humans, have to destroy a world?
But how to choose? How can we choose?

"All right," I agree to gain some time. "Give me
the potion."

Ximb leads me back to the shuttle. The two warriors
join us. This time I see the forest around teeming with
fantastic beings, for whom I do not exist as long as I
don't leave the flowers' protection.

A few steps from the entrance I stop, surprised. On
the metallic hood, above the cockpit, a character waits,
leaning on his sword. I know him as the archangel
Michael. His eyes, searching the surroundings, pass
over me—I am as invisible to him as I am to all the
others. And yet, he suddenly seems startled; somehow,
he can sense me. Like a blind man, he gazes blankly
at the general area where I'm standing.

What happened? the Flutz sorcerer asks me
anxiously.

I swallow and try to answer, but I can't take my
eyes or thoughts off the angel. I've seen a lot of movies and cartoons containing dragons, elves, and
dwarves. But how many times in life does one have
the chance to see a real live angel? And even more,

the archangel Michael himself! *"Help the angels fly,"* I remember Dr. Henderson telling me before my departure. Now, I understand.

Don't look. Close your eyes and go! Ximb commands me.

But I can't move. The angel deposits his gigantic sword on the shuttle's metal hull, and kneels. His white and shining wings stretch to the right and to the left; he puts his hands together in prayer and lowers his eyes. He remains in that position, mutely imploring me, the man, the mortal, the sinner Richard. I feel tears flowing down my cheeks.

The Flutzan emperor's emissary makes a sign. The two moth-warriors jump onto the hull next to Michael. They cut down God's messenger with their arm-blades as if he's only a wax doll. I try to scream, but everything happens too fast.

Richard! I perceive the sinister rattle of the sorcerer's thoughts.

In the heat of the moment I can't control my feelings and I look at it with hate, then I breathe deeply and calm down. Ximb is not doing anything but protecting its world. My decision has nothing to do with it or its deeds. The choice is still between deicide and the Flutzi apocalypse.

"I'll go back to the planet and let them taste their own medicine. They've infected me with a virus that would have created an epidemic on board *Odyssey*. They're very advanced; we won't have too many chances against them. So my advice is, leave orbit as soon as possible and never come back to their world."

The Chief of Security is quiet for almost a minute, then replies, "The President agrees with your solution. He wants you to know that the people of *Odyssey* are profoundly grateful. You will live forever in our conscience, as the first hero of our colony. God bless you."

The transmission ends. The shuttle is silent again.

"I expected an ending like this." A woman's voice.

Startled, he turns to the cockpit's entrance, then smiles. "Eve, I told you to stay on the ship. Now you've condemned yourself to exile."

"Story of my life." She grins and sits in the copilot's chair. Then she looks at the corpse lying behind the chairs. "He didn't make the right decision?"

"I don't know what decision he would eventually have made," Adam replies, casting a disgusted look at Richard Cambry's body. "He vacillated between us and them until the very last moment. Even after we all forgave his sins, even after Michael sacrificed himself in front of him, he still had his doubts. People are weak."

EDITORS

Julie E. Czerneda is an award-winning, best-selling author and editor, with a dozen novels (the most recent being *Riders of the Storm* from DAW) and fourteen SF/F anthologies in print, the most recent of those being *Misspelled* from DAW Books. World-building plays a crucial role in her writing, and she always looks for original, thoroughly conceived settings in what she prefers to read, so it was with great delight that she agreed to work with Rob St. Martin on this project. Not to mention she got the chance to learn more cool history!

Rob St. Martin earned his BA in History at Concordia University because "history is cool"—with the full understanding that to most people, that statement made no sense. Regardless, he found the past filled with amazing stories and incredible characters, and wanted, in some small way, to bring that to others. While at university he co-edited (and later, became editor-in-chief) for a series of anthologies of short stories written by his friends. His short stoires, reviews, and articles have appeared in magazines, e-zines, a one-shot comic about William the Conqueror, and *Misspelled,* edited by Julie E. Czerneda. His longer works include the *Truthseekers* YA series and the *Squirrelman* trilogy.

About the Authors

Kristen Bonn lives in Keizer, Oregon, with her two preteen boys, two teenage girls, eight ever-present cats, and one incredibly supportive and creative husband. She attempts to divide her time fairly between her family and her two jobs, one as an elementary school library assistant and the other as the executive director of the local youth symphony, neither of which relate much to her degree in interior design. She fills her spare time as a voracious reader, a decent quilter, and a developing handbell player. Trapped indoors during Oregon's dreary, wet winters and pollen-filled springs, writing became a perfect outlet for Kristen to transport herself to other worlds filled with blue skies and abundant tissues. "A Small Sacrifice" is her first published story.

Though born and raised on an Ontario tobacco farm, **Brad Carson** has spent most of his time in cities working in theater, where he learned the craft of writing dialogue and the value of strong coffee. Currently he can be seen—or not seen as that is the nature of the job—as a background performer in movies and television. He has planted trees, managed bookstores, painted buildings, wheel-barrowed gravel for swimming pools, and served as a security guard. These days he lives in Toronto with his life mate, Arlene Stinchcombe, and a wayfaring cat named Mooch. The former is his collaborator on a high fantasy series called *Knights of the Penta-*

cle, and the latter just likes to be scratched behind the ears. "Here There Be Monsters" is his first professional sale in the fantasy genre.

Jennifer Crow began studying Russian in high school, and quickly fell in love with the history and culture of that country. When she visited what was then the Soviet Union as a student ambassador, Saint Petersburg was her favorite stop on the tour, so it was only a matter of time before the city made an appearance in one of her stories. Jennifer's work has appeared in a number of print and electronic venues, and several of her poems have received honorable mentions in past editions of the *Year's Best Fantasy and Horror* anthology. She lives beside a waterfall near Buffalo, New York.

Linda A. B. Davis was originally schooled in journalism but has decided that writing science fiction and fantasy is a lot more fun. She enjoys creating worlds and characters that she would like to see become real. Her work has appeared in various Web and print magazines as well as local newspapers. Her other anthology story, "Winds of Change," appeared in *Something Magic This Way Comes*, edited by Sarah A. Hoyt. Linda lives in northwestern Florida with her husband, Steve, and their teenage daughter, Erica. They are all graciously tolerated by three dogs, a cat, and a rabbit. The rabbit rules.

Urania Fung, a daughter of Chinese immigrants, was born in Kansas and raised in Texas. Her father's love of Asian myths and fantasies made it easy for her to spend her childhood immersed in videos and books of the genre. Inspired by the author Jin Yong, she began writing stories in eighth grade. She has been a finalist in the San Gabriel Writers' League's Writing Smarter contest and the Writers' League of Texas Novel Manuscript Competition. She is co-editor of *Mascot Mania: Spirit of Texas High Schools.* She has an M.A. in English, and she has taught English in China and in Texas.

Although **K. J. Gould** has had several nonfiction articles and essays published, she has always considered
writing fiction to be a private pleasure. Doing it in public makes her nervous. On the other hand, getting paid
for writing fiction revives dreams of authorhood that
she has nurtured since she discovered that actual people
got paid actual money for writing the stories and books
she so loved to read. While she awaits the Famous Author Fairy's tap of the wand, she lives in southeastern
Michigan with her husband, an ever-changing number
of four-footed "kids," and a large backyard, where she
indulges her inner child's need to play in the dirt.

Costi Gurgu is a Romanian writer born in the city of
Constanta on the Black Sea. He currently lives in Toronto
with his wife, Vali. He is a graphic designer and an illus-
trator and has been the art director of *Playboy* magazine,
Madame Figaro magazine, and *Tabu* magazine. His more
than forty stories have appeared in different Romanian
magazines and anthologies and have won numerous
awards. He has a story collection, a novel, and has edited
three KULT anthologies. "Angels and Moths" is his first
North American sale. He had a turtle, Cleo, which apparently suffered from seasickness and flysickness and
couldn't cross the ocean to its new home. He is sure
Cleo will roam the Carpathians for many centuries.

Over the past 25 years, **Nina Kiriki Hoffman** has sold
many novels and more than 250 short stories. Her
works have been finalists for the Nebula, World Fantasy,
Mythopoeic, Sturgeon, and Endeavour awards. Her first
novel, *The Thread That Binds the Bones,* won a Stoker
Award. *Spirits That Walk in Shadow,* a young adult
novel, came out in 2006, and her novel *Fall of Light*
will be published in 2009. Nina does production for
F&SF, teaches short story writing, and works with teen
writers. She lives in Oregon.

Liz Holliday is a British writer who lives in London
with the obligatory cat. The equally obligatory list of

past occupations includes theater director, bookshop owner, senior playleader, and teacher. She's now given up all that to write full time. Her original fiction has appeared in anthologies and magazines in the U.K., U.S., Europe, and on the net. One of them was short-listed for the Crime Writers' Association (UK) short story dagger and later adapted for the U.S. TV show "The Hunger." She has also written ten TV novelizations, piles of sf/f-related journalism, educational material, Web content, and games—which is what you end up with when you have a grasshopper brain.

Natalie Walker Millman is a former English literature and history teacher who now enjoys the perils and benefits of working in her home office. She has traveled extensively, and is a long-time student of martial arts. Raised on a diet of myths and legends, she's been an avid devourer of science fiction and fantasy since she learned to read. She lives with her family in Toranto.

Jana Paniccia lives in Toronto, although she tries to get out of the city as much as possible, preferably to visit more places she's never been before. Thanks to *Ages of Wonder*, she already has her eyes set on the next horizon: sailing on a tall ship. One day! Her short stories have appeared in a number of antholgoies, morst recently *Children of Magic* and *Fantasy Gone Wrong*. She also co-edited the DAW anthology *Under Cover of Darkness* with Julie E. Czerneda, released in 2007.

Tony Pi is something of a sphinx himself. Is he an award-winning writer or a well-traveled linguist? A winner of the Writers of the Future Contest in 2006, Tony's poetry and fiction have seen print in *On Spec, Abyss & Apex, Tales of the Unanticipated*, and elsewhere. He enjoys fantasy with a twist of mystery, served on a bed of history. From the Louvre to the Royal Ontario Museum in hometown Toronto, museums have been his constant muse. Then again, when you least expect it, Doctor Pi descends upon a Canadian university and challenges students with fiendish riddles in linguistics. Or he may quiz you on the words you use and how you pronounce them, to uncover the secret of how dialects change over time and spread over geography. One or the other, both or more? Tony simply smiles like Schrödinger's Sphinx, basking in the paradox.

Elizabeth Ann Scarborough grew up hearing tales from the Wild West told by her Grandpa Scarborough, a former working cowboy, and his brother, her Great Uncle Hap, who learned to use a bullwhip and later, while working as a carpenter for MGM, imparted this knowledge to actress Maureen O'Hara who needed to use the whip for a role in a western. Scarborough became better acquainted with tales of leprechauns and Irish history both in Ireland and America while visiting Anne McCaffrey at her home in County Wicklow. At last count she's written 36 novels, 22 solo and 14 with Anne McCaffrey, including the 1989 Nebula winner *Healer's War*. Some of the many short stories she's written were collected in an anthology called *Scarborough Fair*. When she's not writing she's designing and making jewelry and doing the bidding of her co-resident felines. For more information on any of the above, visit her website www.eascarborough.com.

Karina Sumner-Smith is a Toronto-based author, Nebula Award nominee, and Clarion graduate. Her short fiction has been published in a number of anthologies, including *Children of Magic* and *Mythspring*, and magazines such as *Strange Horizons, Lady Churchill's Rosebud Wristlet*, and *Fantasy*. Karina also works in Canada's oldest science fiction bookstore and co-owns a small jewelry design company.

Caitlin Sweet has been an ESL instructor, a trombone teacher, an administrative assistant, and a doula. Her first novel, *A Telling of Stars*, was published by Penguin Canada in 2003. It was nominated for an Aurora Award, a Crawford Award, a Locus Best First Novel

Award, and long-listed for the Sunburst Award. Her second novel, *The Silences of Home*, was published in 2005 and nominated for an Aurora Award. The editors of SFSite placed it at number four in their Best SF and Fantasy Books of 2005 list. She has been working on her third novel for far too long. Caitlin lives in Toronto with her family.

Sandra Tayler spends the majority of her days juggling meals, dishes, transportation, and laundry for the four children she shares with her pet cartoonist (and husband) Howard. She manages his business in the slices of time she finds sandwiched among the kids' sandwiches, yet still finds gaps large enough to accommodate a compulsion to write. Her writings include essays, a blog, short stories, and her husband's paychecks. Tens of thousands of schlockmercenary.com readers would be amused to see her hand the cartoonist a check which she wrote, he endorses, and then she cashes (and spends). "Immigrant" is Sandra's first published story. It is enthusiastically and vaingloriously beating its chest in front of the rest of her work, which can be found at sandra.tayler.com.

Queenie Tirone is her real name. Honestly. And no, her mother was not a hippie, though she wishes that were true. She feels ripped off she doesn't live in a castle. She's a young Canadian writer who loves fiction in all its forms, but her main interest lies in fantasy and horror. Some of Queenie's hobbies include spoken word, video games, and working part time as assistant editor of Burning Effigy Press. Dreams and nightmares are her passions.

Born a Malaysian with a hint of Dutch bloodline, **Ika Vanderkoeck**'s passion for writing began when she was twelve after an accidental encounter with a fantasy novel left her mind reeling with ideas. A prank call to a local production house got her into the media industry when she was very young, where she worked as a host for a children's program. She became a scriptwriter when she was seventeen, before continuing her studies at a local university. Ika currently works in a local media conglomerate and is in the process of finishing her first fantasy novel. She also loves listening to Celtic and pirate shanties when writing, a hobby which has developed into an interest in the medieval era, the Celtic culture, and the golden age of piracy.

Ceri Young's work has appeared previously in *On Spec* magazine. She originally hails from Halifax, Nova Scotia, where she can trace her family roots all the way back to the first German settlers at Lunenburg in 1753. She holds a Bachelor of Arts from Mount St. Vincent University (Halifax), and a Bachelor of Journalism from the University of King's College (also, Halifax); in both places she learned how to ask the right questions, and write down the answers. Her love of history, mythology, and folk belief is self-taught. She enjoys finding new and obscure mythologies and combining them to create new stories. Ceri currently lives with her husband in Montreal, Quebec, where she works as a writer and editor.